REBECCA THORNE

THIS GILDED ABYSS

Copyright @ 2023 Rebecca Thorne

For permissions, contact: *rebeccathornewrites@gmail.com*

Cover Illustration by Eilene Cherie (EileneCW)
https://www.artstation.com/eilenecherie

Cover Lettering and Luminosity Blueprint by Amphi
https://amphi.studio/

ISBN 979-8-9866924-6-3 (*print edition*)
ISBN 979-8-9866924-5-6 (*ebook*)

1 2 3 4 5 6 7 8 9 10

www.rebeccathorne.net

For anyone who fought for
your life in Rapture.

Glad to know I'm not the only
one scarred by that game.

the Luminosity

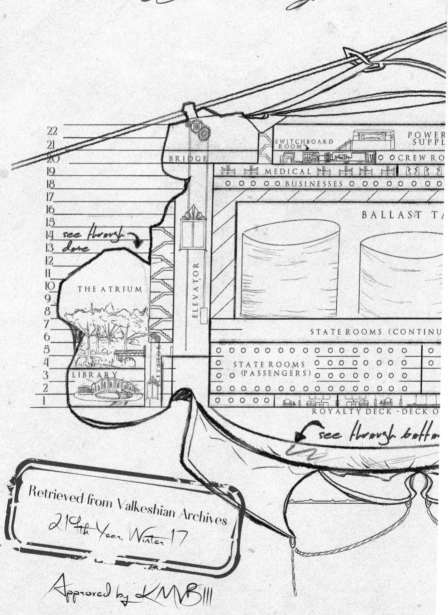

22
21
20 — BRIDGE
19
18
17
16
15
14 — see through
13 — dome
12
11
10 — THE ATRIUM
9
8
7
6
5
4
3 — LIBRARY
2
1

SWITCHBOARD ROOM

POWER SUPPL...

CREW RO...

MEDICAL

BUSINESSES

BALLAST TA...

ELEVATOR

STATE ROOMS (CONTINU...

STATE ROOMS (PASSENGERS)

ROYALTY DECK - DECK O...

see through bott...

WER
PPLIES

SOLDIERS QUARTERS

W ROOMS O

GAMBLING HALL

STEWARD ROOMS

T TANKS

TINUED)

PROMENADE

CK ONE

ottom

see through dome

DINING ROOM

WELCOME ABOARD

SHIP ENTRANCE

22
21
20
19
18
17
16
15
14
13
12
11
10
9
8
7
6
5
4
3
2
1

ELEVATOR

Railway of the Luminosity

Fall

Valkeshia

Property of Subarch
Kessandra Marie
Verdermere Bittean III

Author's Note

Please note the content warnings, and read at your own risk. This book is **not** cozy.

But it does have lesbians.

And to my mother, who asked me not to write spice into my books... you may want to skip chapter 23.

(What can I say? It sells.)

Content Warnings:

Extreme violence, gore, blood, vomiting, near-death experiences, character death, dismemberment, decapitation, drowning, explicit sex, sudden spread of disease, loss of physical autonomy, PTSD, anxiety, manipulation, gun violence, hallucinations, war, thalassophobia.

1

SERGEANT NIX MARR KNEW SHE WAS SCREWED WHEN she stepped into the locker room amidst murmurs of visiting royalty.

The Valkesh Army's spirescraper—tall, circular buildings that stretched into the sky like stalagmites—was built in the shadow of the royal's Grand Palace. But despite their proximity, despite all the *honors* and *gratitude* the Valkeshian government proffered its military, the royals continued to enjoy existence elsewhere.

All but one, at least.

And that one happened to be a pain in Nix's ass.

"—come to watch us train." Garith, a kid on her squad, had their head buried in their locker. They only wore briefs and a tank top, their olive-toned legs on full display, but their excitement was unfazed by their physical state of dress.

No one had noticed Nix enter, which meant her squad

1

would be working on situational awareness next. She crossed her arms, her camera tucked under one elbow. "Who's watching us train?" Her voice was sharp, and all twelve soldiers snapped to attention.

It would have been satisfying if cold dread hadn't tightened her chest.

Garith resurfaced from their locker, clearing their throat. "Ah, s-sergeant. Didn't see you there."

"I noticed," Nix replied. "Who's visiting?"

"Subarch Kessandra," an older ensign, Leon, said. He was close to making sergeant himself—and was arguably the nearest thing Nix had to a friend. He flashed a wry smile and gestured at the camera. "Find anything good this morning?"

She barely heard him. A sudden roaring in her ears drowned him out, and a flash of an unbidden memory: Quian, laughing a little, shoving her shoulder as they lounged in a utilitarian recreation room. *"Kessandra is just a person, Nix. I think you should go for it."*

She shouldn't have listened.

"Sergeant?" Leon asked cautiously. They all had moments like this, brief instances where they'd zone out, where their hearts would pound a bit harder. But normally, Nix had better control. *Normally,* she could detach, shake off the panic, and handle the here and now.

She drew a trembling breath, scrambling for calm. "Found a cardinal in the snow. Images might be blurry, but a few should turn out."

The camera in her hand—an Autographic Prime LZ,

which cost enough of her salary that most days she felt guilty looking at it—was folded into a compact box, easy enough to tuck away in a locker during drills. A brass clasp at the top ensured the lens stayed compressed until needed. She fiddled with it as she stepped to her locker.

Her squad watched mutely. Once she set the camera on a shelf and peeled off her jacket to prepare for their drills, noise picked back up. Unfortunately, so did the conversation.

"I just can't believe *the* Kessandra is coming here. She's the best royal." Garith sounded starstruck. They finally tugged on their trousers, hopping on one foot to pull them over their boots.

Nix watched the debacle out of the corner of her eyes. Could have just taken the boots off first, but whatever.

"That's because Kessandra is the only royal who'd bother to visit." Beside Garith, Claire patted deodorant under her armpits, her voice heavy with sarcasm. "*Everyone else* is required to commit their firstborn for the army, but not them. Eighteen subarchs, forty-three tertiarchs, and of course, Our Esteemed Primarch—and she's the first to join. That automatically makes me like her."

"You'd better watch your tone about the rest," Leon said, warning in his voice.

Claire clamped her mouth shut, eyes sweeping to Nix.

"He's right," Nix said begrudgingly. She was already wearing her uniform, and tossed her sergeant's jacket into her locker. As always, she tucked her camera behind it— none of these kids would mess with her stuff, but she

Rebecca Thorne

didn't want to open the invitation. Other squads used these lockers too. "Plus, she only served for three years — she's been discharged for four. Hardly a glowing career."

She pushed the words through gritted teeth, but couldn't help the sarcasm.

"That's because she moved into PR." Claire gestured at the sepia-toned photograph mounted near the training room's entrance. It was Kessandra posing with a serviceman's pistol, offering an encouraging smile to the camera. Underneath, a placard had been mounted with heavy golden bolts: *Don't be afraid to draw blood, soldier!*

Nix stared at the poster longer than necessary, unease churning in her gut. She wanted to be the vindictive, anger-bound person who'd kill Kess, given the chance. She curated fantasies of it: a knife to the throat, maybe. Carving out her fancy ichoron eyeball. Or possibly just shoving her off a spirescraper's balcony and watching her fall, fall, fall.

But they were just fantasies. In truth, the anguish of Kess's betrayal hurt more than any blade.

Garith glanced her way, oblivious to her thoughts. "Come on, Sergeant. You have to admit even those three years were impressive. Five deployments to the front lines—"

Sure, deployments spent in cushy intelligence meetings while the Triolans massacred my friends, Nix thought darkly.

"—before she *requested* an assignment to the ichoron mines. The only voluntary assignment in the army, and she took it willingly!" Garith stole the jar of deodorant

4

from Claire, patting some under their armpits. Claire gasped indignantly, and they flicked some in her face. The white powder did little to hide the freckles on her ivory skin. She spluttered, coughing, and it dissolved into a scuffle.

Deodorant dusted the floor, obscuring marble-like swirls of rose-gold that normally gleamed under the locker room's incandescent light. None of them could afford ichoron accouterments themselves, but this close to the Grand Palace, the spirescrapers were practically painted in it. The entire building was absurdly ornate: crafted with towering ceilings and sky bridges and rose-gold windows. Frivolous displays of wealth, considering most of the soldiers here were from the lower shortscrapers—the slums.

Nix heaved a sigh at the mess. They'd have to clean that up later, but for now, there were more important matters. She clapped her hands to regain attention.

"None of you better accept that assignment."

A few of her squad rolled their eyes—they'd heard that before.

Ichoron was the rarest substance in the world: a viscous liquid extracted from tunnels deep below the ocean floor. When properly refined, it enhanced anything it touched. Plated on buildings and ships, ichoron protected from assaults of nature and man. A single drop inside a bottle of wine could get a heavyset man drunk for days—while a bandage soaked in it could heal him after a nasty battle.

Ichoron was the rose-gold prize of their war with the Triolans. It propelled Valkesh's entire economy, and they paid for it in blood.

Some people understood that better than others.

Beside Nix, Leon slicked his dark hair with some gel, lips pressed into a thin line.

"What?" Nix asked.

"I've considered that deployment. To the ichoron mines." He cast a cautious glance her way, anxiously rubbing his arms. His sandy brown skin was marred with scars, same as Nix's—parting gifts from the Triolans on the front lines.

Nix tensed, slamming her locker shut. It stopped the scuffle between Garith and Claire, earning everyone's attention.

"I'll say it again, since clearly you haven't been listening. Stay away from the mines—all of you." The words alone called more unwanted memories: restrictive dive suits, craggy underwater tunnels, darkness so absolute it felt like a crushing weight. Despite her best efforts, the horrors lingered, a shadow lurking over her shoulder.

Always.

"There are safer ways to find glory, and easier ways to make money. Do you understand?" Nix glared at them each in turn, her squad, her kids, *hers* to protect. But she hadn't been able to save Quian. Not from the mines. Not from Kessandra.

It felt like Quian's ghost lingered in the corner of the

locker room. She remembered him standing there so vividly, how he used to grunt as he yanked on his boots, how he'd twirl his practice sarrant and accidentally smack people as they dressed. She'd been an ensign too, then.

It felt so long ago.

Leon frowned. "The mines can't be that bad. You survived, didn't you?"

Her squad only knew about her first deployment—the easy one. Not the second, where everything went wrong.

They'd never basked in the grandeur of the *Luminosity*, the luxurious airtight ship that descended into Valkesh's unforgiving ocean. They'd never befriended soldiers on the isolated upper decks, spent the three-day journey to Fall forming lifelong bonds. They'd never marched beneath the domed utopian city, where rose-gold ornamentation and rich people gave way to damp, icy tunnels and a military base so far underground they called it "the Crypt."

They'd never watched those lifelong bonds fall away one by one. Even if they survived in body, only a few survived in spirit.

Her squad couldn't know. Even Leon, her closest friend, had no idea what the mines were really like.

Nix scowled. "Don't start waving me around as a reason to get yourself killed. The primarch *has* to promote that deployment. The call of danger, the patriotism of retrieving ichoron, the payments your family earns afterwards—it's a media campaign, one carefully constructed to entice new recruits." Her eyes cut to the poster again, to Kessandra's smiling face. "But there's a reason no one returns to the mines."

The words hung between them, lethal as a bullet.

"That's why Kessandra is a hero," Garith dared to say. "She saved seventeen soldiers from the mine collapse."

Nix's chest was tight again. She wrenched her long hair into a ponytail, tied it off almost aggressively. It was deep brown and wavy, braided to her scalp on the right side. A strange hairstyle for the military, where most preferred to keep their hair short. Less to grab in a fight, after all.

Nix *wanted* them to grab her hair. Get in close.

Meet her blade.

"I heard she pulled soldiers out one by one." Claire said, dusting the white powder off her shirt. She shot Garith a warning look as they reached for more deodorant.

Zarl, Claire's sometimes-boyfriend, puffed his chest. "My cousin is stationed in the royal tower. He said the primarch was livid that no one caught the tunnel weakening before the collapse—he ordered it closed immediately." He cast a glance at Claire, as if that information might impress her.

Nix, meanwhile, barely suppressed a shudder. Rocks shifting, mutely raining around them. Dust blurring the water, limiting already terrible visibility. The shove of a current too powerful to fight. And a dark shape lurking in her peripheral, looming over her as she struggled to swim up, get out of the mines—

"Nix?" Leon said quietly.

The conversation had dissolved into chatter about Kessandra, about the mines, and about simpler things like their upcoming leave and what the cafeteria might serve tonight. She hadn't even noticed them lacing their boots, preparing for drills like normal.

They were acting like Kessandra *wasn't* lurking on the edges, poisoning everything.

"I'm fine." But her tone was distant, pained. Leon was taller than her—most people were—and she tilted her head to meet his gaze. Desperation clawed at her soul. "You aren't really considering the mines, are you?"

He hesitated. "We can talk about it later."

Nix swallowed past the sand in her mouth.

Leon tossed her a small bronze lock. It was a luxury not many bothered to spend money on, but he'd bought one last year and shared whenever she didn't have time to drop off her camera before drills.

Nix caught the lock, but didn't meet Leon's gaze. "Line up. Western mat."

"But Subarch Kessandra is here." Garith still couldn't seem to get over that. "Aren't we putting on a show for her?"

Nix narrowed her eyes. "We're training so you survive our next skirmish with the Triolans. Unless you want your corpse preserved in the ice at Sveltal Point?"

Garith shivered. "No, Sergeant."

"Western mats. Move it."

They hustled out the door to the adjoining training

room. Leon only cast her a careful glance before following, leaving Nix alone in the locker room. Silence lingered in their wake, and she lifted the shirt off her camera, running a finger along its square shape.

It was the exact camera Quian always talked about buying. He used an antique of a thing, back when they'd spent their days in the Marr casten — something four times as big that took pictures half as nice. *It's an heirloom*, he used to say proudly. *The things this camera has seen, Nix. You couldn't even believe it. But someday, I'll get something smaller.*

He died, and Nix bought his fucking camera. And every time she used it, she thought of him. After all, photography was his hobby, not hers. She never really cared to wait for a photo to develop, not before...

Well. Before.

Mutely, Nix covered the camera with her jacket, then clamped the bronze lock over the locker's door.

Her eyes slid to the poster of their beloved subarch, and a surge of anger swallowed her. Because Kess wasn't visiting them: the army, some random squad. Subarch Kessandra Marie Vendermere Biltean III wouldn't waste her precious time watching a group of ensigns spar.

No, Kess was visiting *Nix*.

She'd sworn to leave Nix alone — and she couldn't even follow through on *that* promise, could she?

Well. Nix wasn't some starry eyed twenty-one-year-old anymore, swept up in the glamor of a romance with a royal. Whatever they'd found together on the *Luminosity*, cultivated in the darkness of the mines—it died down there.

Nix's breaths were steady now. Cold determination settled over her shoulders.

This time, Kess would be the one to lose.

2

THE TERTIARY TRAINING ROOM WAS MASSIVE, WITH A ceiling four stories high and enough floor space for an entire platoon. Seven other squadrons were already dueling on the mats. The clack of wooden sarrants— coupled with grunts and shouts of hand-to-hand combat— violently contrasted to the gently falling snow beyond the floor-to-ceiling windows. On the balcony, another squadron—the fifty-fourth, probably—practiced poor-weather rappelling down the vertical edge of the spirescraper.

After all, army recruits couldn't be afraid of heights. Not when the Triolans prowled the skies on islands of metal and steel, always hunting for a way over the protective mountain range that circled the city of Valkeshia.

Nix compartmentalized all of it, then discarded their surroundings just as fast. Because only one thing mattered: the woman chatting with their commander, ignoring her squad entirely.

Kessandra.

She was really here. Nix had hoped it was a baseless rumor, but of course, she couldn't be that lucky. A thought intruded: *Who's going to die this time?*

On cue, Leon joined her, eyes cutting to the subarch. "You said you're fine, but you don't seem fine."

A flash of fear had Nix imagining Leon grasping his throat, gasping for breath, writhing in dark mines deep under the ocean floor. She imagined Garith pinned under falling rock, bleeding alone; imagined Zarl or Claire turning toward a dead-end, panic rising as they spun in a maze of tunnels while their air supply slowly ticked to empty.

She imagined Kessandra swimming below the entrance to the mines—a pool far deeper than it looked, centered in a metal room that carried an unnatural chill—choosing who surfaced for precious air, and who didn't. That wasn't how it happened, but sometimes, late at night, it was hard to tell the difference.

"I slept poorly last night," Nix replied.

Last night. Every night.

Leon frowned at her, but he seemed to realize she wanted a topic change. And naturally, his eyes were glued to Kessandra. Everyone's were; even without a formal announcement, there was no doubt who she was.

"Huh. The pictures don't do her justice." His tone was curious, prodding.

The subarch was clad in a ceremonial army uniform: black slacks, a white dress jacket studded with rose-gold orders, ichoron-woven epaulettes, and an aglet over her left shoulder. Considering she was Nix's age—twenty-five—and barely had three years of military experience before her forced retirement, all those medals made her look fucking absurd.

Well, that wasn't true. Kessandra was stunning in that uniform. She held her shoulders back and her chin high. Her white military beret perched on obsidian hair, which was twisted into a low, no-nonsense bun. Even her deep mahogany skin was dusted with powder to hide her freckles, giving her an almost ethereal appearance. The primarch couldn't have chosen a better royal to be the embattled military heroine.

"That's one opinion." It sounded petty, but Nix couldn't help it.

Leon smirked as they walked to the western mats. "Oh, come on, Sergeant. Isn't she just your type? Tall. Poised. Accomplished. Remember Nadine?"

Nix heaved a long-suffering sigh. "Everyone remembers Nadine."

"She beats Nadine." Leon jerked a thumb at the subarch.

The worst part was, he was right.

"Then why don't *you* date her?"

"Come on. Word still gets around about her time in the service." Leon grinned. "She swings one way, and it's nothing I could entertain. But I'd still love to live vicariously through you."

Nix grimaced. She suddenly felt very underdressed, even in typical military attire. Her own skin was as pale as a seashell and it showed every old scar, every healing scrape. Maybe she should have worn her sergeant's jacket to this training session after all.

Her words were curt. "Thank you for your input, ensign."

Leon raised his hands in defeat. He took his place shoulder-to-shoulder with the other ensigns, waiting for Nix's signal. She contemplated them, then glanced over her shoulder at Kessandra and their commander. It was surprising the commander was bothering with them at all —he rarely addressed Nix, and her squad was one of hundreds.

But they'd never had company like this before.

Sure enough, Kessandra gestured at Nix's squad. The commander nodded, and they walked over.

Nix swallowed a groan. Even the commander wouldn't fight Kessandra's authority. In the army, he outranked her... but she was a royal, so that wasn't quite true. It created a silent conundrum, one the officers were glad to leave behind when the primarch concluded Kessandra's active service.

She had a nice, dignified life in the palace. What the hell was going on?

Nix didn't have to wait long. The commander nodded

at their crisp salute, clasping his hands behind his back. Everyone straightened under his critical stare.

Kessandra's hair was pinned in a swoop over her right ear, and she'd positioned herself to hide the ichoron eye — clever, intentional—which meant people only earned glimpses as she admired the training room, the other squads, anything but Nix's team. She came all this way, only to wait for the perfect opening.

How typical.

"Sixty-first," the commander said. "This is Subarch Kessandra Marie Vendermere Biltean III. You should know of her: pristine military service, top ranks in training and beyond, five tours to the front lines and one to the ichoron mines… and of course, saving the lives of seventeen fine soldiers during the Hectron Tunnel collapse."

Now Nix shifted her gaze, accusatory, to Kessandra.

The subarch was still ignoring her.

"My Esteemed Subarch." The commander gestured at them. "They're yours."

Finally, Kessandra faced the squad. Her ichoron eye — the same rose-gold as the floors, the walls, the medals on her uniform—could now be fully seen, and a few ensigns stiffened. Nix didn't blame them; it was jarring outside of the carefully curated, sepia-toned photographs.

An ichoron eyeball may seem like a prize. It allowed perfect vision in the dark, offered the sight of an eagle during the daytime. But it was one of the rarest implants, simply because of the physical cost: there was nothing organic about Kess's right eye anymore. Easier to have ichoron teeth that were as sharp as an animal's, or tubes in the ears to improve hearing.

But Kessandra never did things the easy way.

"First," the subarch said, and her warm words washed over them like music, "I would like to extend our immense gratitude for your service in holding off the Triolan invasion. The primarch, his family, and the entirety of Valkesh know what you've sacrificed for our safety and comfort."

She had the voice of a politician, someone born basking in the spotlight. Her tone was perfect, the exact amount of friendly inflection to sway the troops. *I'm one of you*, it said. *Trust me. Follow me. Die for me.*

Nausea churned in Nix's stomach, and she felt hot all over. Kessandra had strolled in here like she was choosing a chicken for dinner. Which one of her ensigns would Valkesh's favorite subarch dress and devour?

"I've earned the honor of a special assignment and need one fantastic soldier at my side." Kessandra smiled. "I've heard wonderful things about the sixty-first."

Fuck you, Nix thought. If Kess needed the best, she could choose one of the special operations squadrons. The sixty-first were infantry. Barely a step above the recruits in boot camp. Loathing simmered in Nix's chest.

"I'm here to test your combat abilities. Impress me, and you'll earn a place at my side."

Now Nix snorted.

Kess fell silent, finally deigning to look Nix's way. Her

carefully blank expression was more unnerving than if she'd glared or offered a wry smile.

The commander narrowed his eyes. He was an imposing man with skin like stained leather and the personality to match. "Sergeant! You will offer the subarch respect—"

Kess held up her hand, silencing him.

Despite Nix's thudding heart, despite sweat trailing down her back, she squared her shoulders and held Kessandra's gaze. Daring her to contest the mocking noise. Daring her to lie in front of all these people.

The subarch stepped forward until her face was inches from Nix's. Unlike other royals, Kessandra didn't bother with perfumes, but her scent was still enough to make Nix's head spin. Shampoo fragranced with orange, cut with starch from the immaculate uniform, and an ever-so-subtle hint of cloves and cardamom—Kess's favorite blend of tea.

Nix hated that she knew that.

Kessandra's lips tilted upwards, and the air electrified around them.

"What's your name, soldier?"

She knew Nix's damned name. Nix almost pretended that they were intimately familiar again, just for the outrage... and to remind Kess of all those dark nights they'd stolen away, of the hot, passionate kisses Nix had peppered along her skin. But Nix wasn't that person anymore. As far as her squad knew, she'd only deployed to the Crypt once—a year before the Hectron Tunnel Collapse.

As far as they knew, she'd never met Kessandra until now.

So, as much as Nix wanted to spoil Kess's secrets, she had her own to keep. Her words were measured, icy. "Sergeant Nix Marr."

"Nix." Kessandra tasted her name, and it sent a chill up Nix's spine. "It sounds like you've volunteered to be my first opponent. Are you prepared to spar?"

Nix was startled into a hollow laugh. Her voice held an edge of steel; if she had her way, she'd slice Kess to ribbons with it. "No offense, but you may want to pick someone else. Warm up a bit first."

The commander pinched the bridge of his nose.

Kessandra tilted her head, and her organic eye—a deep, smoky green—glittered with amusement. "Then you feel I won't be a match for you?"

It finally felt like she had the upper hand, and Nix couldn't contain her smirk. She'd pay for this later, once the commander got her alone—but now, in this moment, Kess was *hers*. "I think you've spent too much time in your ichoron tower, Subarch."

Garith squeaked at Nix's bold words. Claire covered her mouth.

Kessandra merely chuckled. She stepped back, shrugging out of her dress jacket, removing her beret. Underneath, she wore a sleeveless black shirt like the rest of them. Her dress slacks weren't as flexible as their training trousers, but she didn't seem to care. Her bare arms were toned, her body in perfect fighting condition. Late at night, sick with loss, Nix imagined that Kess had succumbed to grief, stopped taking care of herself... but of course, the subarch would never allow that luxury.

Kess set her folded jacket and beret on a bench, then gestured to a nearby mat. "Shall we test that theory?"

Nix had wanted nothing more in four years than to slap Kessandra to the mats for what she'd done. Her tone was almost vicious. "It'd be my pleasure."

"The pleasure is mine, Sergeant." Kessandra's words held the same lingering threat.

As they chose their wooden sarrants for the spar, Nix stole a glance at her squad. Leon's jaw was unhinged, and Zarl smirked in anticipation. The rest seemed conflicted on who to cheer for: their sergeant, who protected them over years and deployments, or the royal they all adored from afar.

Except Kessandra never stood a chance.

The subarch may be excellent with a serviceman's pistol, but Nix ruled the bloody land of close-quarter combat—and the sarrant was an extension of her own body. The meter-long sword-spear was a Valkeshian promise of death; even the wooden practice ones could break bones and bruise flesh. Over all their tours to the front lines, the sixty-first hadn't lost a soul, which was largely thanks to Nix's skill on the battlefield.

She'd be damned if Kessandra broke her streak.

Of course, the subarch had trained with the sarrant

too, and it showed. Kess's fingers curled around the center of the extended hilt, holding it horizontal, her feet sliding into a picture-perfect stance of defense.

Nix barely refrained from rolling her eyes. Always defense, with Kessandra.

"Subarch, are you ready?" the commander asked.

Kessandra nodded curtly.

He didn't bother checking that Nix was also prepared. He simply raised a hand and shouted: "First to pin, three second duration. For honor; for victory! Fight!"

Kessandra didn't move. This was one of her tells: she relied on that eye of hers too much. Used it to analyze the slightest movement, as if *seeing better* meant she became some kind of battle expert. Her ichoron eye glowed as she watched Nix pace the edges of the mat, clearly waiting for her to make the first move.

Kess didn't have to wait long; Nix was feeling fairly murderous.

She twirled her sarrant, and while Kess's eyes traced the movement, Nix lunged. A fast jab to the chest had the subarch backpedaling, and Nix spun, wood whistling through the air. She skated her grip down the shaft, using the distance between her hands to apply more power. The "blade" slammed into Kess's bicep with enough force to make the weapon shudder in Nix's grasp.

A real sarrant would have made Kess an amputee.

As it was, she sucked in a ragged breath, but responded instantly. Her sarrant swung upwards to parry. The *clunk* of wood on wood echoed, and Kess sliced low, fast as a viper. Nix leapt backwards, but the tip grazed her stomach, scraping the skin underneath her tank top.

Through the sudden pain, Nix was dimly aware of her squad cheering her on. Silence was frowned upon in the training room since it wasn't realistic on the battlefield. If sound became a distraction, a soldier wasn't focusing enough.

So, when Kessandra spoke, her quiet words were lost in the din—a wry remark for Nix's ears alone: "Huh. Guess I haven't spent too much time in my tower."

Her lilting tone had Nix's heart racing. Her lips curled in disgust. "Whatever happened to leaving me alone?" She lunged again, driving the pommel in an arc towards Kess's skull.

The subarch deflected the hit, but the pommel glanced off the woman's shoulder. Kess grunted, gripping the spot as she danced backwards. Satisfaction spread through Nix like wildfire: that would bruise.

"I figured you missed me." With a devastating smile, Kess darted low, slipping around Nix to drive the sarrant into her back.

Nix twisted into a low kick and swept Kessandra's feet out from under her. "Naturally. The nation's favorite subarch. Must be terrible to know one subject doesn't adore you."

The royal grunted, rolling away just as Nix's blunted blade drove into the mat—a few seconds delay, and Nix would have stabbed Kess's chest. Kessandra leapt to her feet in one fluid motion, then swung her sarrant in a wide arc. But her hands were placed too close together, and the move didn't have enough force.

Nix met the blow, using the thin divot at the base of her blade to lock their weapons in place—just for a moment, just for a breath.

"I see," Kess replied. "And here I was hoping to ask for your help."

There it was. Nix had been waiting for the truth behind this visit.

The shouts of the sixty-first were far away now, like the two of them had stepped into another world. Here, it was the beating of her heart, Kessandra's heaving chest, and the scrape of their weapons straining against each other.

Nix leaned in close enough to feel the subarch's breath on her cheek. "I helped you once—and my best friend didn't come home."

"History repeats." Kess twisted her weapon to wrench the sarrant out of Nix's hands. Fuck. The weapon clattered to the mat, and the shouting got louder. Simultaneously, Kess's voice dropped, barely audible. "There's been a murder. A massacre."

"Yeah, four years ago. Trust me; I'll never forget." Nix grabbed the staff of Kess's sarrant, her fingernails cutting into Kessandra's hands—and in a brutal move, Nix kicked her chest and wrenched the weapon away.

The subarch's grip broke easily, and she crashed back to the mat.

Nix advanced, spinning Kess's sarrant so the point

faced downward. Irritation boiled in her chest. This woman had the audacity to come back to the army, pretend she belonged, challenge Nix to a fight and then remind her of the mines?

Absolutely not.

But Kess just twisted on the ground, propped on her elbows, staring at Nix. Her perfect bun had come loose, a few braided strands of dark hair framing her face. "I'm not talking about the Hectron Tunnel, Nix. This happened two weeks ago."

Nix tensed, her sarrant pausing over Kess's throat.

"One—" the commander called.

Kess took advantage of her hesitation, clamping her legs around Nix's ankle. With a violent twist, she slammed her into the mat. The second sarrant spun away from them, and Kess wound up straddling Nix's hips, pinning her hands. She leaned over Nix, sweat gleaming at her temples, lips set in a tight line. "The primarch is sending me back to Fall. To the mines."

What?

Nix went still, combat forgotten amidst those words. Distantly, she was aware of the commander counting down again, aware of her squadron groaning in dismay, but all she could see was Kess's green eye—and her glowing rose-gold one.

Kessandra had sworn she'd never return to the mines. Nix, too. It was the only thing they agreed on.

"Match," the commander shouted. "Victor: Her

Esteemed Subarch. Congratulations, Subarch! An excellent fight."

Nix had lost.

Kessandra climbed to her feet, then offered a hand.

Nix slapped it away, gritting her teeth. She pushed upright, rubbing the raw scrape on her stomach, and paused by Kess's ear. "Sounds like your funeral, Nines. Just make sure I get an invite."

The nickname lingered between them, an old reminder. It started as a sarcastic acknowledgement of Kessandra's impeccable appearance: how she always "dressed to the nines," even when there were bigger issues at stake. Over their deployment, it shifted to something fond, affectionate.

Now Nix sharpened the word into a knife's edge.

But before she could stomp back into line, Kessandra took her arm. Her gaze was chilling. "Quian was unfortunate, but he isn't the only one who perished. Something is happening—and I don't have long to discover the truth."

Didn't have long until what?

But then her other words sank in. Adrenaline was already thrumming post-fight, and Nix had clenched her fist before she realized it. Only her commander's piercing gaze quelled her dark impulse.

Instead, Nix hissed, "Quian was *'unfortunate'*?" The words carved into her chest, spilling blood. A whole childhood gone in a minute, crushed under the weight of the ocean. "Say that again."

A wooden sarrant could kill, if wielded properly.

For a brief flash, Kess's expression was unreadable. A thousand words spread between them, words Nix needed to hear, words the subarch refused to voice. Nix waited—waited for the apology she'd expected, waited for the truth she deserved, but Kessandra simply drew a breath and said, "As with deployment to the mines, this is a voluntary assignment. I beg you to reconsider."

"Go fuck yourself." The threat was snarled, low enough no one else heard.

Kessandra's smooth mask slipped back into place. Foreboding sent an icy chill through Nix's veins, but Kess merely gestured back to the line of waiting soldiers. "I see. Thank you for your time, Sergeant."

Awkward silence lingered as Nix trudged back to her spot, like she was taking her place in front of a firing squad.

This wasn't over.

Kessandra smiled prettily. "Who'd like to spar next?"

3

VOLUNTARY ASSIGNMENT, HER ASS.

Kessandra didn't make a decision that day, although she fought eleven more vicious spars. Leon got in a few good hits. Zarl fought her last and was the only one to pin an exhausted Kessandra on the sweat-slicked mats. It wasn't a *win*, per say, but smug satisfaction coursed through Nix's veins regardless—and then guilt flared, because she could never let Kessandra take Zarl, or Leon, or anyone in her squad.

Not again.

But Nix didn't want to board the *Luminosity* either. She'd learned a long time ago that Kessandra's pretty smile was like a sunset over the ocean, painting shark-infested waters in hues of crimson and gold.

If Kessandra took Zarl, that would mean she truly *was* after the best fighter in today's matches. If she left empty-handed, Kess had ulterior motives, and they centered around Nix. She held her breath as they wrapped up the training session—but Kessandra simply saluted them, said cheerfully, "Thank you for your time," and left.

She was limping, Nix noted smugly, although she forced her gait into something natural enough that no one else would realize. Lumos forbid a royal show weakness.

The moment she was gone, the commander rounded on her, looming like the Ever-Storm over the Deates Sea. His expression twisted in fury. "Sergeant Marr. A word."

Shit. He didn't usually use that tone. She stiffened, saluting crisply. "Commander."

Her squad stumbled back to the locker room, but a few cast sympathetic glances her way. The other squads were clearing out as well, so there was her silver lining: at least she'd be too busy speaking with the commander to deal with the chaos of multiple squads changing for dinner.

He led her to the corner of the training room, near the balcony, and for a moment she wondered if he was pissed enough to shove her over the railing. But he just clasped his hands behind his back and set his jaw. "If the primarch heard how you spoke to his grand-niece today, he would have you arrested. Dishonorably discharged. You were raised in the Marr casten; the shortscraper life is *luxury* compared to that fate."

Nix nodded.

The commander's expression softened. "I've read your file, Sergeant. I know you deployed with her."

Panic flared. Nix didn't reply—because he wasn't

supposed to be talking about this. Neither of them were. If anyone overheard…

But they were alone. And after what she'd said to Kessandra in front of her squad, no one would question a disciplinary discussion between a sergeant and her commander. Clever, actually. She could see the curiosity in his eyes, but he was a professional, a lifelong soldier.

And so was she.

"Two successful tours in the ichoron mines… and you still somehow have your head. With that kind of record, you should be on a fast-track to commander."

"What's your point, Commander?"

He massaged his brow. "My point, Marr, is that someone *very* high up doesn't like you. Which means that you and the subarch may have more in common than you think."

"The subarch seized her honorable discharge, blacklisted me from any meaningful promotion, and retreated to her cushy palace life for four years. She basically told me to go fuck myself." Nix was overstepping, but she didn't care. A "file" hardly told the whole story. She liked her commanding officer, but this was beyond his expertise. "So, forgive me if I don't exactly believe that statement. Commander."

The title was tacked onto the end, and only because his lips had pressed in warning. It seemed to pacify him somewhat, made him inhale slowly and contemplate his next words.

"Your squad has the best return rate I've seen in two

decades—not a single soul lost over a dozen tours. So, this shouldn't be hard to understand." The commander smoothed his dress jacket, his tone firm. "Subarch Kessandra is one of us. She fought on the front lines, toured the mines, and prioritized our soldiers over her own life. I'll be frank, Sergeant: I don't believe she's visiting Fall of her own volition. And I'd hate to risk her safety over your stubbornness."

Kess was in danger.

That should have bothered Nix more. Instead, she felt like laughing, because *obviously*, Kess was in danger. She was a politician, as cunning as she was ruthless. Even if her enemies wouldn't dare attack outright, they were perpetually lurking on the edges of her life.

But that was nothing new to Kessandra. She wouldn't bother tracking Nix down for a vague threat—especially under the ridiculous guise of needing a "bodyguard." No, if she wanted Nix's help, there was another reason.

Which meant Kess had manipulated the commander like everyone else. After all, Subarch Kessandra Marie Vendermere Biltean III *always* got what she wanted.

It delighted Nix that Kessandra would lose, just this once. "With respect, Commander, her safety isn't my concern. I have a squad to manage." Nix crossed her arms, daring him to challenge her decision. "Was there anything else?"

Kess's words of a "voluntary assignment" hung over both their heads.

The commander sighed. "Only to consign your

punishment: cleaning duty for four weeks. I want this training room sparkling. Mops are in the closet. Put your back into it, soldier." He waited for her responding salute before turning on his heel. His dress boots clicked smartly against the polished marble floor, and in moments, the training room's main door closed behind him.

Nix was alone.

She drew a shaking breath, glancing out the rose-gold windows to her left. It was nearly black outside now — Valkeshia was nestled beyond the Sveltal Mountain Range, far enough north that winters were brutal and dark. But the incandescent lights of the training room illuminated the spirescraper's balcony, and the snow gently piling on it.

Beyond, barely visible through the snow, the shadowed tower of the Grand Palace loomed. It was connected to the army spirescraper and a few others on lower levels via glass bridges, but the upper levels — the royals' — were isolated by design. Even within their levels, every royal had their own suite and private terrace that overlooked the city.

Must be nice.

Nix tried to ignore the acid bite of anxiety as she trudged to the closet for the cleaning supplies. Out the windows, a cardinal flitted past, a smear of red against the pristine snow.

THE WEEK PULLED PAST, and Nix found herself grateful for the extra duties. She moved from sparring, workouts, and target practice into scrubbing every surface of the Tertiary Training Room, pushing herself so hard that she collapsed into her bunk each night and was asleep in seconds.

Kess didn't come back. It made Nix feel like every breath might be her last.

When their day of leave finally arrived, Nix leapt at the chance to flee the army spirescraper and head somewhere safer: home.

The royals lived in the center of Valkeshia with richer citizens spread around them, but the outer ring of the city contained the shortscrapers: low, blocky buildings of concrete and steel divided into neighborhoods, or castens.

Only the rich had surnames. Down here, a person was labeled where they grew up. Nix belonged to the Marr casten. Made up of four buildings around twenty stories tall, the casten's only noteworthy claim was that three decades ago, its fifth building had collapsed in a fire. The Marr children swore ghosts of the fifth haunted their hallways.

Nix knew they weren't lying.

Of course, she didn't make it out of the army's

spirescraper before Leon caught up to her. "Ah, Sergeant! Hang on a second."

She paused in the plush hallway. The walls were black, accented with geometric trim painted rose-gold to mimic ichoron. Warm yellow chandeliers illuminated the hallway with incandescent bulbs, and a cheerful *ding* chimed every time a soldier summoned one of the elevators.

Leon panted a bit, catching his breath. She crossed her arms, quirking one eyebrow while he gathered his wits.

"Going to visit your dad? Or is it a photography day?" He gestured at her camera, secured in a custom leather case on her belt, and the sarrant strapped to her back. They were her two most prized possessions, and she never left the army's spirescraper without them.

She shrugged. "Been a while since I went home. Might be both."

"You could come drinking with the rest of us." His lips curled into a smile. "Lanskin's been asking about you."

"A bartender always asks about their regulars when they stop coming." Nix patted the camera. "Found a healthier hobby. You might want to consider the same, Leo." The nickname came easy, considering their history.

Leon laughed. "Sergeant, if I could afford one of those cameras, I wouldn't be deploying to the mines."

That stopped Nix cold. Her eyes flashed. "Say again, ensign?"

"Ah, that's actually what I wanted to tell you." Leon grimaced, fishing papers out of his jacket pocket. The yellow parchment was sealed with the primarch's stamp, type casted in the formal font of the army, signed with a flourish by a commander far too experienced to give them the time of day otherwise.

Nix skimmed the words, but they all blurred together. And she didn't need to read to comprehend. She'd seen these papers... twice. Her heart pounded, and her mouth was suddenly very, very dry.

"I can't put it off anymore," Leon said, squirming under her silence. "I know you have opinions, but they'll never consider me for promotion without a bold statement. And all the highest-ranking officers did their time in the Crypt."

Nix's words were sharp. "And countless more died there."

Leon looked a lot like Quian. Leon's sandy skin may be a few shades darker, his dark hair curlier, but their easygoing smiles and level-headed personalities were the same.

Nausea washed over Nix in a violent wave. Soon Leon would be in that bulky dive suit, lowering himself into the innocuous pool in the center of the Crypt—the black water swallowing him whole—him flicking on a meager light that would barely illuminate his fingertips, much less the craggy surroundings...

It was suddenly very hard to breathe.

"You can't go." Her words came out more aggressive than intended.

He blinked, taking a step back. She held the papers like she was going to rip them in half, and his eyes flicked to them. While he raised his hands in a pacifying gesture, his tone dropped—calm and steadying. "I'm so sorry, Nix. You've done an incredible job training us. Every single person on our squad knows we'd be dead without you—but we can't be ensigns forever."

They couldn't. That was true. Realistically, she was lucky to keep her soldiers as long as she had. But in the past, her ensigns had left for special forces, outpost assignments, or honorable discharges—they didn't go to the mines.

A dark thought flitted through her mind, and she blurted it before she could stop herself: "Did Kessandra put you up to this?"

A few soldiers nearby glanced her way, eyebrows raised at the casual name. Leon noticed, laughed, waving them off. "She's talking about our friend from the Koplin casten. Not Her Esteemed Subarch. Sorry for the confusion."

The soldiers shrugged and boarded an elevator, yet again leaving them alone in the hallway. Nix had to brace herself against the wall—she hoped it looked like she was casually leaning, not like her world was crashing around her.

"Sorry," she whispered.

"Nix." Leon stepped closer, gripping her arm in a comforting manner. "We've been friends for, what, three years? Trust me when I say I'm taking your warnings seriously. *Trust* me when I say this wasn't my first choice, or even my fifth."

Nix's mouth was dry. "It's the payments."

"I told you my sister is having a baby. We just found out her pregnancy is... complicated." He winced, his jaw tight. "Those payments will make sure the baby survives. That *she* survives. She's my little sister, Nix; I have to help."

Not Kessandra, then. That should have made Nix feel better, but it didn't. Not really. She carefully folded the papers, handed them back. "When do you leave?"

He tucked the papers almost reverently into his jacket. "The *Luminosity* docks in three days. I have to board before it departs again for Fall."

And under Fall, the long tunnel to the Crypt. To the pool. To the mines.

Nix suppressed her shudder, but only barely. She took a few breaths, couldn't manage to force a smile. But her voice was steady. "You're a great friend, Leon. Take care of yourself down there."

He smiled. "I will."

She walked past him, then paused at the elevator. "If you see glowing red eyes—get the hell out of the tunnels."

And she boarded the elevator, pressing the button to the bottom floor. As the doors slid shut, the horror on Leon's face stuck in her mind.

4

NIX WOULD BE THE FIRST TO ADMIT IT: THE CITY OF Valkeshia was stressful as hell to navigate.

She knew why. When Valkesh splintered from the Republic of Triol generations ago, they were trapped in a tight geographical area. The mountain range that protected them from invasion also hindered their expansion, which meant the primarchs of old needed to build *up*, not out. The result was a convoluted mess of aerial walkways and hidden staircases through hundreds of towers that stretched towards the graying, winter sky like rosy fingers.

In the center ring, the royals' playground, the towers were expensive, expansive, and expertly designed. Huge walkways, floor-to-ceiling windows, plant-filled atriums sixty stories off the ground. But as Nix descended, the scenery changed. Lavish geometrical décor gave way to utilitarian options: stained concrete instead of plush carpet, flickering bulbs, small windows boarded up to protect against the cold.

It was home... but after so many years away, Nix wasn't sure where she belonged. She was comfortable in the concrete safety of the Marr casten's short, squat buildings, navigating metal staircases with ease. No door here was locked, because everyone was family. Food was shared. Company was plentiful. Trust built here was thicker than even viscous ichoron.

And yet, from the moment she entered their shortscraper, Nix expected to see him.

Quian.

Her eyes roamed the dark corners where they used to play hide-and-seek with ghosts they couldn't quite prove existed in the light of day. She passed the spot where Quian dared to ask a girl out, waving away Nix's jeers while the girl blushed prettily. (She was more interested in women than men, so Quian shoved Nix in her path next—and Nix couldn't deny they had a good time.)

And then, the outcropping. It was intended to be a walkway to the shortscraper that collapsed, but all that remained was a charred husk of rebar and concrete. They used to slip past the tarp, press their backs against their building, feet dangling over the edge, and whisper about the future.

It was a long time ago.

Now Nix ventured onto the outcropping, eyes glazing over the wreckage no one dared to touch, and tugged out her camera. The clasp slid open, and the bellows lens popped out. Her pounding heart calmed as she played with the camera's settings, adjusting the aperture and shutter speed.

There was something relaxing about photography, something Nix couldn't capture anywhere else. It narrowed the world to an ichoron lens, a tiny viewfinder —it made everything terrible seem distant and manageable. Even with Quian's ghost lingering behind her, even the tragic visual of the building before her, Nix felt like she could breathe again.

She framed the shot. Snapped the picture. A satisfying *click* echoed over the rubble.

How it'd turn out was anyone's guess, but Nix didn't care. It was about the process for her, the manual effort of capturing something others overlooked.

It said: *I see you. I remember. And I will never forget.*

The lump in her throat was getting hard to swallow past, now. She coughed, cautiously folded the camera again, and tucked it into the leather case at her thigh. Safe and secure until next time.

"You have to get over this," she whispered. It was true, but saying the words out loud didn't stop the way her eyes trailed down to the numbers they'd etched on the building.

Seventeenth. Fifty-eighth. Their original squadrons, back when they were young and idealistic and stupid. Quian had carved his, declared he'd kill more Triolans than Nix. She'd laughed, stole the knife, etched her own. A promise.

Both of them killed Triolans.

They weren't bragging about it afterwards.

Nix scrubbed her face. She cast one final glance at the rubble far, far below, then stepped back into the empty stairwell and descended to the final floor.

She'd barely opened the stairwell door, a metal, utilitarian thing, before she heard the commotion.

It was weird that she hadn't run into anyone yet. Normally just entering the Marr casten meant she was swarmed with children measuring her biceps, teenagers asking to borrow her sarrant, adults asking how the war was progressing. But this time, she'd made it to their floor without issue.

Now, the hairs on her neck prickled as she saw why. There was a crowd of people mingling in front of her father's apartment.

Uh oh.

They didn't seem concerned, which was something. Fear lanced through her chest, but the energy here was excited, maybe curious—not sympathetic or fearful. And the second the door slammed closed behind her, they all turned.

"Nix! Nix is back." Wyatt was the only firstborn present here, a seventeen-year-old who would join the military next year. He waved with vigor, flagging her down.

As if she wasn't already staring.

The rest of the crowd parted easily. These were people she'd known since birth: army retirees and other citizens who'd learned trades like smithing, veterinary work, community relief. The rest were the ever-fortunate younger-born—people with the choice to enlist, rather than the order. Elderly and children made up the rest, but they seemed equally pleased she'd returned. Chatter of welcome engulfed her, and for a moment, she was *home*.

And then the whispers of royalty began again, just like they had in the locker room last week.

"A *subarch* is visiting your father."

"Said she had good news—"

"—believe it? The army's subarch, right here on the 12th floor."

Nix stiffened, a hot blade of dread lancing through her chest. Her ichoron-plated sarrant—earned only after her promotion, a true nod to her abilities as a soldier—felt heavy in its sheath between her shoulder blades. "Subarch Kessandra is here?"

What were the odds that she'd visit the Marr casten on the *exact* day Nix had leave and planned the same?

The second that thought crossed her mind, Nix almost laughed, the sound cold and cruel. Knowing Kess, those weren't odds at all. They were a calculated gamble, and the subarch's wagers always, always paid.

One of the army retirees puffed his chest. "The only royal who'd make it this far. The only one who would bother."

One of us, the commander had said. Nix really had to respect just how thorough Kessandra's curated image was —her following was apparently larger than Nix ever imagined. It felt like a poison seeping through her community. Misguided pride.

"Then I guess I'm needed inside," Nix said, offering a placating smile to the starstruck crowd. They let her through with ease, but their curiosity was a palpable thing. Nix batted it aside, shoved open her front door, and delved into the apartment.

Kessandra was perched on the grungy couch, a chipped teacup in hand, smiling like she was in a banquet hall. Nix's father was sitting in his typical armchair, but even he'd leaned forward, pulled his shoulders back in respect. And to her surprise, Melana, Quian's mother, was standing in the kitchen, steeping a bag of cheap tea.

Everyone glanced her way when Nix slammed the door shut. The crowd remained in the hallway, undoubtedly pressed against the block walls, straining to hear the conversation within. And seeing how close Kessandra sat to her father, it wouldn't be a pleasant chat.

Her protective instinct flared. Nix unsheathed her sarrant, sweeping it in a threatening motion. The apartment wasn't large, but she fought within the Triolan's floating islands, all tight metal hallways and aggressive enemies. This wouldn't be different.

"I'm shocked you came down here. The shortscrapers are dangerous. Accidents happen all the time."

The corner of Kessandra's lips quirked upwards. A custom pistol was holstered at her thigh, black metal accented with rose-gold. Most likely, the barrel was ichoron—she used to favor those. They fired with more force, and the bullet of an ichoron pistol could travel farther than a rifle's shot.

If this did dissolve into a fight, Kessandra was at an advantage. But if Nix moved quickly, she might get a slice in before —

"Nix," her father said, his voice stronger than she'd heard in years. "Leave your sarrant at the door. We have a guest."

"I'll keep it."

"*Dyanix.*"

Her mother used Nix's full name all the time — but after she died, the name died with her. Now it stopped Nix cold. Kessandra demurely dropped her gaze to her teacup, taking a delicate sip as if this were a regular occurrence. Her pistol was left untouched.

Nix's father's gaze was hard, even as his hands trembled in his lap. They'd started shaking after *his* Fall deployment — and never stopped, not in thirty years. The only thing that soothed him now was ichoron-spiked medicine, purchased with the stipend Leon so desperately sought.

Nix had ventured into the mines twice for a reason, after all.

Her father was still scowling.

"Fine." Nix left her sarrant by the front door and walked stiffly into the living room. After a moment's consideration at the empty space on the couch, she decided to stay standing. Faster access to a defensive stance if Kessandra tried anything.

And then—Kessandra smiled at her.

Not like she had on the sparring mat, enthralled with the challenge Nix presented, or afterwards, filled with icy promise. No, this was an old smile. The quiet, *I see you, and I love what I see* smile, where her lips just barely tilted upwards and her eyes scrunched in happiness, in connection. The smile that had Nix falling well before they'd reached Fall.

Nix's stomach flipped, and a surge of loathing followed hot on its heels. Why was she still so attracted to this woman? After everything, a small part of her was excited to see Kessandra perched in her father's living room.

It wasn't that Kessandra was beautiful, or that she was royalty. It was *her*: her wit, her charm, her poise. It was the way she fell apart under Nix's touch, the way she made Nix feel like the most important person alive. Nix had never been more treasured than in Kessandra's arms.

How *quickly* the subarch had given up that treasure when things got tough. It had been so easy for Kess to walk out of Nix's life. Meanwhile, Nix spent years picking up the shattered pieces of her heart.

Quian died—and Kessandra left.

Nix remained with nothing but haunted memories.

Melana was still in the kitchen, watching the whole affair. Before, the woman had been boisterous, charming, a little mischievous. Best friends with Nix's mother, once upon a time. After two deaths—first Nix's mother, wrought with illness, then Quian—Melana was a shell of her former self.

Maybe they both were.

It was easy to ignore that dazzling smile.

"Why are you here, Kessandra?" Nix didn't bother using her full name.

Her father and Melana didn't know everything that happened in Nix's second tour of the mines, but they knew about her royal fling. They knew it turned sour. And yet, her father still replied, "She has a title, Nix. One you are required by law to use."

Kessandra waved it away. "It's perfectly fine. This is a casual visit amongst friends."

Nix glowered, spoke through gritted teeth. "*Kess.*"

Before her father could scold her again, Kessandra spoke primly. "I'm here with a proposition. One I believe you may want to consider."

Of course she was. Nix massaged her brow, drawing breaths to calm her thudding heart. "The answer is no. Whatever it is, whatever you're offering, we're perfectly fine on our own."

"Considering the price of ichoron is rising steadily and your stipend hasn't, I sincerely doubt that."

The words were spoken carefully, but they might as well have been a lightning bolt from the Ever-Storm. Her father averted his gaze, suddenly silent. His trembling hands tightened into a fist, and his taupe skin suddenly seemed more sickly gray than healthy brown.

"What do you mean?" Nix wasn't sure who she was addressing.

Kessandra traced the rim of the teacup with her finger.

Her manicured nail scraped lightly against the porcelain's chip, then continued its circle undeterred. "It's no secret I want you on the *Luminosity* with me when it disembarks, but I'm not opposed to negotiating. Thus my visit—I thought I'd see if Captain Vectoran needs anything specific."

The use of his old title seemed to reinvigorate him. He'd left the military when Nix was born, but his career had been distinguished before then. Nix's mother's had, too—they were both captains when they met. Now, his eyes cut to the dual ichoron-edged sarrants mounted over one of their tiny windows, crossed in an X. He straightened, lifting his chin.

"I appreciate the offer, Subarch Kessandra—"

"He's fine," Nix interrupted, clenching her fists a little too hard. "We're *fine*."

"Nix."

Melana's voice cut through the apartment.

She'd always been like a mother to Nix. Now Nix flinched at her tone and turned slowly. Melana was still steeping that same teabag—she didn't seem inclined to drink it. Her lips, touched with burgundy lipstick to accent her striking bronze complexion, were pinched. "A word, dear."

Kessandra averted her gaze, yet again playing the demure visitor. As Nix moved into the kitchen like a child's wind-up toy, Kessandra asked, "Your assignment was overseeing the greenhouses near the mountains, correct? How was the food production there?"

"We managed, but with the population now—" her father started, and their voices faded into the mutter of conversation.

In the kitchen, Nix stood with her back to the living room, blocking Melana from Kessandra's view. After all, with that ichoron eyeball, Kessandra could read lips—a skill Nix hadn't believed was real until Kess proved it on three separate occasions. Now, Nix just had to pray the subarch hadn't added ichoron tubes to enhance her hearing.

"She's lying, right? You're doing okay," Nix whispered.

Melana's dark eyes drifted to the living room. She subtly shook her head. "Ichoron is getting more expensive. We've dropped his medicine to every other day, but... it's taking a toll."

"But my stipends were supposed to—" Nix cut off, her body rigid. Whining was a child's game. She shifted to what was important. "Why didn't you tell me sooner?"

"It isn't your problem, dear. The last thing you need is to worry about your father. The casten is pooling resources; we'll do what we can. If nothing else, we can sell their old sarrants for extra coin." She clenched the mug in her hands, her gaze piercing. "You do *not* have to accept the subarch's offer, Nix."

She did, though. Even those sarrants wouldn't float them long.

And Kessandra knew it, even before Nix did.

In the army tower, the idea of venturing into the mines

had left Nix breathy, terrified. But now everything slid into place with startling clarity: a gemstone that finally caught the light. *Fight or flight mode*, her old sergeant used to shout. *You'd better choose fight*, he'd snapped.

At least Leon wouldn't be venturing into the mines without backup.

"I appreciate your help. The casten's help." Nix's voice was strong and steady. "But I'll make sure you have everything you need."

Melana's energy shifted, and her lips pressed together angrily. Her eyes flicked to one of the photographs on display: sepia-toned, nearly washed with glares from poor exposure. In it, Melana and Nix's mother were arm-in-arm, laughing. Quian took the photo, but he spent so long setting up the shot that their mothers had dissolved into laughter at the absurdity of holding their pose.

Nix remembered laughing with them, loitering behind Quian. She remembered his excited gasp as he snapped the photo at just the right moment, and how he'd enlisted the help of a photographer in the Koplin casten to develop it.

Melana considered the photo now, and a new fire seemed to ignite. She scowled. "Don't let her use you. The royals promise the entire ocean, then drown you in its depths. If you accept this, your father will never be able to forgive himself."

But Nix had already made up her mind.

"At least he'll be alive to have the choice." Nix pressed a kiss to her cheek. Melana was warm, soft, familiar. Like home. Despite her obvious anguish, she didn't interrupt as Nix strode with purpose into the living room.

Kessandra and her father stopped their small talk immediately. Nix loomed over Kess's position on the couch.

"Subarch Kessandra. A word, if you please."

"Nix—" her father said.

Nix raised a hand to cut him off, then gestured at the front door. Her eyes never left Kess's, and that ichoron eye pierced her soul. "Alone, if it pleases Her Esteemed Subarch."

Prim and proper; they both knew what that meant.

Kessandra gently placed her teacup on the scuffed table in front of the couch. "It was a pleasure speaking with you, Captain."

This time, her father didn't reply—not a word.

5

NIX OPENED THE FRONT DOOR, SHEATHED HER sarrant between her shoulder blades, and guided Kessandra past the chattering crowd of shortscraper citizens. A hush fell over them as they gaped, but no one intervened when Kessandra strolled past as if she owned the building.

She probably did, actually.

It was both admirable and irritating how Kess took charge. She walked with purpose away from the apartment, the crowds, as if this entire venture was *her* idea from the start. Nix trailed behind her, her eyes tracing Kess's fitted white jacket and black slacks. It wasn't quite the military uniform, but it was a close enough mockup that no one would guess her roots.

How clever.

At the end of the hallway, Kessandra stepped confidently into the stairwell, then turned to face Nix—as if a major walkway through the shortscraper would be a *suitable* place to chat. She raised a questioning eyebrow.

Nix rolled her eyes and gestured with two fingers. "Not here. Follow me and keep quiet."

"Nix—"

"Kessandra, I am not in the mood."

The subarch clenched her jaw but dutifully followed. They went down, down, down, straight to the ground floor. The spirescrapers on the upper level of Valkeshia were connected with arching bridges and outdoor plazas, but the only way to traverse between shortscraper castens was through tight alleyways. The snow barely reached this deep into the city, but it was still frigid. The street level was packed with loud, grungy people shuffling through the grime like debris in the ocean.

For once, Nix hoped Kessandra was paying attention. For once, she hoped the royal *saw* what life was like here.

Unfortunately, the shortscrapers also saw them... and Kessandra couldn't be anything less than a beacon of wealth, considering her posture, confidence, and attire.

"Take off that jacket," Nix hissed. Nothing would fix Kessandra's posture or confidence, but they could address one thing, at least. "You look like a spirescraper citizen. Prime target."

"I'd like to see a thief try." Kessandra sniffed, fingers brushing against the pistol at her thigh.

Nix stopped short, and Kess had to dance backwards to keep from plowing into her. "You're pretty far from your ichoron tower." Her voice was low, heated, barely audible. "If you thought fighting in a Triolan island was bad, you'd be wise to remember they weren't nearly as hungry. Or as desperate. I doubt you can fire your pistol that fast."

It was pleasing, watching Kessandra's lips purse, watching her careful façade crack—even just a bit. She glanced at the people nearby, drew a short breath through her nose, and slipped out of her jacket. She shivered in her shirt, a soft cream piece that still looked far too luxurious. But there wasn't much to do about that—at least folded over her arm, the jacket looked cheaper.

Sort of.

"Keep your head down. Don't show anyone that eye." Nix's voice left no room for negotiation.

Kessandra rolled her eyes—the rose-gold ichoron eyeball followed the motion seamlessly.

Together, they merged into the crowds. A few street carts were grilling unidentified meat, flavored in a rich, savory sauce local to the shortscrapers. The scent made Nix's mouth water, but now wasn't the time for a meal— and anything purchased down here would probably make Kessandra sick.

Of course, the cold wasn't helping there. The press of hot bodies was a stark contrast against the icy air, and it didn't take long before Kessandra was shuddering. Nix should feel bad about that, but she didn't have the energy for anything but smug satisfaction. This was probably the first time in four years that Kess had experienced discomfort.

"So, how have you been—" Kessandra tried to say at one point.

Nix held up a hand, cutting her off. "We're not doing this right now." Or ever.

They lapsed into silence again.

Despite Kessandra's casual clothes, it didn't take long for people to squint at her manicured appearance: smooth skin, rose-gold clips in her braids, the way she walked with a confidence born of influence. A few onlookers drifted closer. Nix physically muscled one of them away. His eyes cut to her ichoron sarrant, a marked identifier of a ranking officer in the army, and he slunk back into the crowd.

Kess gripped her jacket a bit tighter, keeping her eyes on the ground. But Nix didn't miss the way she rested one hand on her pistol, just in case.

Nix delved off the beaten path, towing the subarch through a series of progressively emptier alleyways until they arrived at a sliver of cliffside on the edge of Valkeshia. A rusted railing was anchored between the thick walls of two shortscrapers, sparse protection to keep anyone from plunging into the writhing ocean far below.

Here, sandwiched in solid stone with the gleaming ichoron city at their backs, they were finally alone.

Which meant Nix wasted no time shoving Kessandra roughly against the wall. "What the *fuck*, Kess?"

Kessandra grunted at the force of the shove, then raised one perfectly shaped eyebrow. "You'll have to be more specific."

Her casual tone was grating. Nix slammed a hand beside Kess's head, bending in close. Kessandra was taller, just by a bit, but now their noses were nearly touching. Nix's fingers scraped against the rough stone, seconds from throttling the woman. "Don't play stupid. Bribing my father with life-saving medicine to get me back to Fall? This is a new low, even for you."

"I'm hardly bribing." If Kessandra was perturbed by their proximity, she didn't show it. Her ichoron eyeball gleamed in the alley's dim light. "Tours to the Crypt always pay. What I'm offering is an advance—one your father can clearly use."

"You couldn't just *give* him the money? Out of the goodness of your heart, or some shit?"

She pressed her lips together. "There are... other factors at play."

"There always are." Nix growled, shoving herself away from the wall—away from Kess's endless schemes.

Beyond the rusted railing, the ocean churned, tumultuous as always. The Ever-Storm that raged above it never ceased, which meant the surface was impassable by sea or air. It was the only reason the Triolans hadn't flanked Valkeshia from the west.

But it also meant that the only way to Fall—and the Crypt—was underwater, where the violent surge of the ocean's surface calmed to more predictable currents. A single, massive railway connected the two cities, and one ship traveled along it: the *Luminosity*.

Once the deep-sea ship disembarked, there was no turning back.

Nix drew a short breath. Fury curled like black smoke in her soul. "What part of 'go fuck yourself' was unclear?"

Kessandra's lips twitched imperceptibly. "Perhaps it was the enunciation."

Lumos below.

"This isn't a joke. Why are you so desperate to get me back to the mines? Just because a squad was murdered?" Nix tossed her long, brown hair over her shoulder, scowling. "Newsflash, Nines. Soldiers die in the mines more often than the primarch cares to admit."

Kessandra flinched at the nickname. The motion was barely noticeable, but as long as she got that reaction, Nix would keep using it to cause pain.

"These soldiers didn't die in the mines," Kess replied, slipping back into her jacket. Her shivering slowed, but not enough that her words weren't stiff with cold. "They were killed in the Dive Room."

Oh.

That vivid image smashed into her again: a room of metal walls and flickering incandescent bulbs, cave-like, lined with utilitarian lockers and dive suits. In the center, a single pool, shockingly blue, deceptively deep.

Nix's chest felt tight. "Not underwater?"

"They hadn't even suited up. Something ripped them apart." Kessandra's brow knitted together, her lips pursing at a problem she hadn't solved. She cast a glance over Nix's shoulder, but they were still alone, flanked by two concrete walls. "It's possible Triolan spies infiltrated our ranks somehow. Or it could be something less nefarious: a soldier loses his mind in the depths. It's happened before. But—"

"A dive squadron has fourteen soldiers." Nix frowned.

"Each highly trained in combat."

"So how the hell did a couple people, even if they *are* Triolans, manage that?"

"Exactly." Kessandra snapped her fingers, and for a moment, it felt like old times. They smiled at each other, ever-so-briefly, before Nix remembered what was happening here. This wasn't a clandestine meeting. This was an assault.

Nix crossed her arms, burying her piqued interest. "I'm not going back to the mines. You swore the same thing, so why the change of pace?"

Kessandra's face smoothed. Her ichoron eye glowed eerily, and her words were measured. "The primarch asked me to investigate."

A lie. Nix scowled. "Asked? Or told?"

"The details are unimportant. My passage on the *Luminosity* is booked. My excuse is a winter vacation to 'enjoy Fall.' After a few public appearances, my time will be spent investigating our army base, its command, and the remaining dive teams."

That would include Leon. The idea of him stationed at the Crypt was bad enough—him stationed there with *Kessandra* lurking on the edges made Nix's skin crawl. She was quickly losing the ability to refuse this special assignment.

"Then where do *I* come in?" Nix drew out the last word, a lingering threat. "We both know you don't need a bodyguard. What's so important that you'd blackmail me with my father's health?"

The subarch closed her eyes—and when she opened them again, her raw gaze nearly made Nix's breath catch.

"You're the only one I can trust, Nix."

Something shifted in Nix's soul. She shoved it down, deep down, recalling Quian's bloated face when she finally found him in the mines. He was so pinned by rock they couldn't even haul out his body, but Nix never forgot the way his corpse had been frozen in a scream.

Her voice trembled. "Ironic, because I can't trust you at all."

There wasn't a glimmer of remorse in Kess's gaze. She lifted her chin. "That's your prerogative. But something is killing our soldiers in the mines, and we need to find out what before more people die." Nix winced, and Kessandra's tone softened. "You don't have to believe me, Nix, but this was my *absolute* last resort."

The ancient promise hung between them. After the tunnel collapse, the return trip on the *Luminosity* felt never ending. The whole time, Kessandra grew more distant, the love they'd cultivated over months fracturing at the seams. Quian's absence was everywhere, and the anguish of losing him was too much to bear.

It was worse after they disembarked in Valkeshia.

Kessandra cornered her in the army tower, expression calm as anything.

This was a mistake. You have no place in my life. Kess's cool words, so measured against Nix's devastation. She'd stepped into the elevator, uncaring about the shattered mess she was leaving behind. Her final promise rang in Nix's mind: *Don't worry. You'll never see me again.*

Liar.

For a long moment, neither of them moved. The sarrant was heavy in the sheath on Nix's back. To her left, far below the rusted railing, waves crashed against the cliffside. In the distance, the Ever-Storm churned over the open ocean, rumbling with thunder, flashing with lightning.

And far below it, somewhere in the depths, was the Crypt.

How many of them would die there this time?

"Fuck," Nix muttered, pressing her palms into her eyes. But her mind flashed back to her father, to Melana's grim confirmation. Nix could refuse again. In a few days, Kessandra would board the *Luminosity* and be gone—probably for good.

But her father wouldn't be long to follow without that medicine.

There really wasn't a choice. So Nix held up two fingers: two demands. "If I agree, do more than give my father medicine. I want the entire Marr casten taken care of—medicine, food, supplies. They think you're one of them, the peoples' princess, so act like it. Whatever they need, you provide."

"That will be costly. The primarch would notice those supplies and question—"

"I don't *care*. You're smart." An understatement. "There are black market channels all over the city. I'm sure with your resources, you can establish a trade shipment from your private funds."

Kessandra's forehead furrowed, but she finally nodded. "I will make the arrangements, then. What's your second request?"

"I want my own room this time. On the *Luminosity* and in Fall."

Now the subarch's lips twitched upwards. "Whatever do you think I'll be doing to you, my dear?" Unlike Nix's pet name, Kessandra's rolled off her tongue, a silken promise. Just like everything else.

Irritation flared. "Don't call me that." Nix shoved her shoulder and stomped back to the alley's entranceway. "I'll be at the dock in three days. I don't want to see you until then. Acknowledge?" The military statement cut through the air.

Kessandra mock-saluted, the motion crisp with subtle sarcasm. "Affirmative. And Nix—this assignment pays *very* well. I made sure of it. Once we return, you'll have the life you always wanted. An honorable discharge, spirescraper living—anything."

Nix spun on her. "You have no idea what I want. I'm a soldier, not your pet. Tell the commander I'll be on special assignment, but I expect a full reinstatement when I return." A pause, a third finger. "And make sure Ensign Leon Dirk's family gets his Fall deployment stipend early. His sister's having a baby, and they need it."

She watched Kessandra carefully, but the subarch just tilted her head. "One of your ensigns is deploying too? Hmm. At least there will be another familiar face nearby."

"Don't compartmentalize my squad like pawns on your chess board."

Kessandra tucked her hands in her pocket. "Everyone is a pawn… but this isn't my board."

The fact that "yet" seemed to linger in that sentence chilled Nix to the bone.

Kessandra continued, blasé: "Either way, consider it handled."

Nix appraised her, waiting for the catch. When Kess offered none, she muttered, "Great working with you. Try not to get attacked on the way back to your fancy tower," and stalked back to her family's apartment.

6

THAT EVENING, NIX WENT TO SEE THE COMMANDER.

That wasn't the way she'd planned to spend her final days in Valkeshia, but something was niggling at the back of her mind. She entered an army spirescraper elevator and pressed the heavy button for the two-hundredth-seventh floor. This high up, the elevators had soldiers checking tags; they required both that and her ichoron sarrant for admission.

The hallway here was just as plush as the level she trained on—thick red carpets, papered walls, ichoron accents. Huge windows offered a stunning view; they were high above the clouds now, and the Grand Palace gleamed in the crimson sunset. Beyond, the snow-capped peaks of the Sveltal Mountains were tinged purple.

Nix didn't look up, or out. Instead, she stepped to the window, ignoring the way her palms sweat on instinct at the drop, and peeked *down*. A layer of dark clouds, perpetual this time of year, obscured her vision—but she knew the Marr casten's shortscrapers were very, very far away.

How easy it would be to forget they existed at all.

Nix set her jaw and stalked through the corridor until she reached a long hallway of living suites. Higher ranking officers lived and worked on the same floor for convenience, so when the commander didn't answer her knock on his office door, she strolled to his living quarters instead. His name was displayed beside an eye-catching golden door decorated with a triangle pattern.

She rapped on it, hard.

And then again when he didn't answer.

After a long moment, the commander opened it, lips pressed in disapproval. "Marr? I hardly take house calls. What are you doing here, Sergeant?"

Beyond him was a luxurious apartment of marble floors, spacious rooms, and expensive décor. Considering Nix had a bedroom and bathroom—and *that* was luxury compared to the shared barracks offered to ensigns—a flash of envy hit her chest. A dark whisper came unbidden: *you could've had this someday, if Kessandra hadn't interfered.*

It hardly mattered now. If Nix ever saw Valkeshia again, it'd be a miracle.

Swallowing past the lump in her throat, she gestured inside. "I need to speak with you about... earlier. It probably shouldn't be in the hallway."

That made the commander stiffen. He cast a

surreptitious glance over her shoulder, then stepped aside to admit her. The door closed with a heavy *thunk*, and he locked a brass deadbolt into place. Neither of them spoke until they were deeper into the apartment, until he'd gestured at a leather couch and Nix took a seat.

"Brandy?" he asked. "Or is valloch your preference?"

"What's the difference?"

The commander looked aghast. "Brandy, then. Only the finest chemists can distill a suitable tank of valloch. It's expensive."

Nix felt a bit snubbed at that. "Looks like you can afford it." At his glower, she hastily tacked on, "Ah, Commander."

He did have a name—Tylon—but no one knew his surname. The ensigns theorized he was from a shortscraper casten, and ditched that part of his identity for a faster promotion. Regardless of the truth, "Commander Tylon" was far too informal, so everyone just called him "the commander" instead.

He didn't seem to mind.

The commander grumbled something and stepped behind a bar in the far corner. He poured amber liquid into two crystal glasses, gave himself double the pour, and carried them over. For an awkward moment, Nix wasn't sure if she should offer her glass for cheers, but the commander sank into the armchair across from her and took a deep swig of his beverage.

"You're going to Fall," he said. It wasn't a question.

Nix swirled her drink, daring to take a sip. The liquor

was sharp, heating her throat all the way down. "How'd you know?"

"The subarch has a reputation for getting what she wants. And she specifically requested your squad." The commander leaned forward, resting his arm on his knee. "She's going to need your help, Marr."

The warning in his voice set her nerves on edge. "What the hell are you so *worried* about? If she dies, isn't that one fewer subarch we have to deal with?"

"Don't *ever* say that out loud again, Sergeant." His voice was authoritative, and the façade of two soldiers enjoying a drink shattered. Nix sat up straighter, setting her jaw against the commander's stern gaze. "Kessandra isn't just a subarch; she's the only royal actively attempting to stop this Lumos-damned war."

That made Nix freeze. Even with the warmth of the brandy, even with a fire flickering merrily in the hearth beside ichoron-tinted windows, she was cold. "She's —what?"

The commander drew a slow breath. "When Valkesh separated from Triol, our ancestors failed to look forward at what our nation could become. Without land, we can't grow the crops to survive. With every firstborn promised to the military, our citizens are in discontent. Fall was an experiment, but the cost of manufacturing that dome and building an underwater city was absurd. Maintaining it is proving even more difficult."

"I'm aware our resources are limited," Nix said.

"That's why we're fighting to invade Triol. Capture more land on the other side of the mountains."

The commander laughed, rough and hollow, and she suddenly felt like a child. His words weren't condescending, however; merely stating fact. "We can barely get a foothold in Sveltal Pass. What makes you think we could hold land that's been in Triolan hands for centuries?"

Nix took another sip of brandy, suddenly wishing she had a double pour, too. She'd been so focused on keeping her ensigns alive that she never stopped to consider the bigger picture.

But, of course, that was Kessandra's specialty.

"If we stop fighting, we'll be overrun." Nix gripped her glass tighter, her knuckles white. "Valkesh will be reabsorbed into Triol. Our entire culture will cease to exist."

"Our culture is an offshoot of Triol regardless," the commander admitted, but he didn't sound happy about it. "But there's a bigger issue here. Did you stop to consider *why* the Triolans are pushing so hard to break past the mountains?"

That answer, at least, was easy. "Ichoron. The mines." They taught that on day one of boot camp.

The commander nodded. "The mines. Ichoron is only found below Fall. The Triolans have created islands that fly—but imagine what they could do with access to those mines. And with a few more decades, our military won't be at such a disadvantage. Ichoron weapons are just the beginning."

Nix contemplated that. Her sarrant had been propped against the couch, but it was just one of many ichoron-enhanced weapons. Kessandra used a custom ichoron pistol. They buried ichoron spears attached to chains in the metal bellies of the Triolan islands to anchor them for boarding. It wasn't a stretch to think more could be coming.

"Then we hold out a few more decades," Nix said fiercely.

But the commander was already shaking his head. "We may survive that—at great cost to our citizens. But Kessandra is working on a solution: a trade route. Ichoron for necessary supplies. Instead of battle, we make treaties, and war becomes a distant memory."

It was shocking to hear a career soldier saying that... but then again, none of the royals watched their friends massacred. None except Kessandra. Realistically, a soldier had all the motivation in the world to stop a war.

Nix wasn't sure how she felt about all this. But global politics were hardly her concern, not when her next deployment loomed. "So, the primarch is sending her to Fall to... what? Get her out of the way?"

"War is about control, and the primarch has long enjoyed his hold over Valkesh." The commander massaged his brow, finishing his brandy. He pushed to his feet, the movement almost laborious, and stepped to the bar for another pour. "One week ago, Kessandra requested a briefing with me and several other ranking officers. The next day, she was given this special assignment."

"And you think she's in danger."

"I think Kessandra has a following that could rival the primarch's, but her goals don't align with his. And I think that terrifies him."

The words lingered between them. The commander could be stripped of his rank for voicing that kind of thing, and it added a heavy weight to the admission.

Nix finished her brandy in a single shot. "I think I'm ready for the valloch, now." She stepped to the bar, offering her glass.

The commander smirked humorlessly and pulled a gold-tinted bottle out of a cabinet. He gave her a generous pour this time, sliding the crystal tumbler across the polished wood countertop. "If you're going down there, I'll make your orders clear. At all costs, you are to protect Subarch Kessandra. She's too important to lose. Confirm, Sergeant."

Nix wanted nothing to do with Kessandra—but she was going to the Crypt regardless. And at least now, she knew why.

She saluted crisply, and duty settled into her bones. Just like that, Kessandra became another soldier in her squad—and Nix hadn't lost a soul to battle in years.

"Affirmative, Commander."

This time, they did tap their glasses together, and the *clink* was heavy with promise.

AFTER THAT VISIT, Nix's mind was too wired to sleep. She perused her squad's barracks and found it empty. And no wonder; days of leave didn't come often. There was no question where the sixty-first had gone tonight.

And so, Nix ventured to the "street" level of the spirescrapers, a huge walkway suspended between four different towers—the Grand Palace, the army spirescraper, the university's Valkeshian campus, and the engineering spirescraper. The path was entirely outdoors, studded with expensive restaurants, lavish shops, and equally gilded people swathed in heavy fur coats, fluffy earmuffs, and sleek boots.

The spirescraper citizens walked right past the alley Nix delved into now, boots smearing the snow as she stepped between the army tower and engineering one. Her destination was nearly impossible to find—just a simple metal door painted in faux rose-gold to match the walls on either side.

But she knew exactly what she was looking for.

When Nix pushed inside the cozy tavern, she was greeted with raucous shouts of welcome. She lifted a hand, left her ichoron-edged sarrant in a designated stand by the door, and trudged to the bar.

Lanskin, the bartender, quirked an eyebrow. "Well,

look who it is. Been waiting for you, kid. What're you having?"

She perched on one of the thin stools, scanning the occupants—noting her squad clustered in back, same as always. "Whatever Leon is having."

"Funny, he came in ordering 'whatever Nix usually gets.'"

"He's got good taste." Nix smirked, sliding two coins across the table. They were simple copper chips stamped with the primarch's insignia: a domed city perched before the iconic spirescraper skyline of Valkeshia. And over it, a humanoid figure loomed. The primarch, obscure enough to be the current one or any primarch long passed.

She tried not to look at the domed city on those coins.

Lanskin swept the coins away, then fetched a glass and filled it with amber ale from a spigot by the bar. As they pushed it towards her, they smirked. "Good to have you back, kid. I missed your stories."

"They'll be a lot less frequent in a few days," Nix muttered, and took a deep swig of her beer. "Thanks, Lan. I'll stop by on my way out."

Lanskin tipped their tri-point hat and moved down the bar to serve another soldier. Nix, meanwhile, pushed through the dense crowd. Despite the late hour, Lanskin's unnamed pub was one of two popular spots for soldiers, so the place was packed. Nix elbowed through the crowd, stopped to salute two other sergeants and one lone lieutenant, and wrestled a chair to her squad's table.

"Well, fancy seeing you here." Claire slapped the table

in satisfaction. Her ivory cheeks were tinged pink from the liquor, and she lifted her glass before draining it. "Didn't think you'd make it tonight, Marr."

Off duty, and *only* off duty, they were allowed to call her by her casten name. Only Leon, so far, had earned the right to a first name—and he'd quite literally saved her life on Island B3D, when she'd been swarmed by Triolans while trying to destroy its power supply. She figured an act that stupid deserved a reward.

Her eyes cut to Leon, who was wedged in the back corner sipping a matching glass of amber ale. Had he told them about Fall yet, his impending deployment? Or was he basking in the normalcy for a few more hours, same as her?

Hardly mattered. Nix shrugged against Claire's teasing, settling in with her drink. It was cold and bitter, and burned her throat all the way down—but in a much different way than the commander's valloch. Her head was fuzzy now, so she felt a bit looser with her speech. "Well, the commander's extra assignments don't stretch into my days off."

"'Extra assignments,'" Zarl drawled. He was sitting with his arm around Claire's shoulders, so apparently, they'd reconciled this week... but that could change by tomorrow morning. "That's a fancy way of saying 'cleaning duty.'"

"Hey," Nix said without venom, even as the rest of her squad roared with laughter.

Garith sniffed, sipping gin from a clear tumbler.

"Listen, we all know why the sergeant said what she did to Subarch Kessandra."

Nix leaned her chin on her palm. "Think carefully about your next words, Garith."

But they were her youngest ensign and hadn't yet learned the benefit of keeping their damned mouth shut. "She's in love with her, same as all of us."

Claire snorted. Beside her, Zarl choked on his drink. He spoke first: "'All of us' meaning *who?* I'm not in love with—" and his eyes cut to Claire. When she took a demure sip of her drink, her own gaze averted, he shoved away from her. "You?"

"She's *gorgeous*. And famous. And rich." Claire patted Zarl's cheek. "You're lower on the hierarchy, sweetie."

So, clearly tonight would be an off-again night.

Zarl swelled, but Leon smoothly diverted attention. "Ah, I have an announcement. I'm deploying to the mines. In three days, I'll be boarding the *Luminosity* for Fall."

The sudden topic change landed like a rotting fish in the center of the table. For a moment, everyone just stared. Nix sipped her ale, tracing the beads of moisture on the side of the glass with a finger. It was a struggle to keep the dread out of her expression.

Hails, a quiet kid with a wicked right hook, spoke first: "Fall? How hasn't the sergeant killed you already?"

And then every pair of eyes swiveled to stare at Nix.

She drained her beverage, feeling lightheaded and oppressively warm. "Listen, I don't control you folk. I've

71

issued a warning—and he's choosing to ignore it. My job's done."

Across the table, Leon grimaced.

The squad all straightened in their chairs, primed to launch into intensive conversation about Leon and his bold choice—but Nix held up a hand and silenced them before they could. "And with that, I should let you know that I've accepted Subarch Kessandra's special assignment. I'll be on the *Luminosity* in three days as well."

Now there was no silence. Their table *erupted*—to the point that other squads in the tiny tavern began shouting at them to quiet down and Lanskin themself stomped over to swat Nix with a red drying cloth. "Keep your squad appropriate, Marr," they barked, but a glimmer of amusement flickered in their eyes. "How about refills for the inconvenience?"

Everyone raised their glasses, dropping coins in their outstretched hand. Lanskin pocketed them and strolled off, chuckling.

Sneaky.

"I thought Her Esteemed Subarch hadn't picked a soldier for the assignment," Leon said, his words measured.

Everyone fell silent, watching with rapt attention.

Nix tossed her long hair over her shoulder. "She spent a while mulling it over, then made me an offer I couldn't refuse." Bitterness flavored the words, and she moved on quickly. "Regardless, I spoke with the commander. He'll be reassigning Sergeant Yatasha Pilon to your squad. She was my best ensign two years ago, and just earned her promotion. I trust her—but never forget what I taught you."

"Keep ourselves alive. Keep our squad alive," a few of the more sober ensigns dutifully repeated back.

Nix raised her glass. "Don't do anything I wouldn't do."

"Shit," Garith muttered.

Leon, meanwhile, had set his jaw, and once conversation resumed around them, he flicked two fingers and moseyed towards the bar. Nix waited a few minutes for Lanskin to deliver her replacement ale, then followed, but Leon was already exiting the tavern.

Ah. That kind of conversation, then.

She took the glass outside; Lanskin knew she wouldn't steal it. It was bitter cold now, the sun long-since set, and the wind normally absent in the lower levels was cutting up here. She pressed against the spirescraper's tall wall and hunched deeper in her jacket. "Surprised?"

Leon was standing a few feet from the door, and he crossed his arms against the wind. "You're not doing it for me, are you? Following me down there?"

It was a fair question. Nix's protective nature with her squad was renowned. She offered a rough chuckle. "Don't take this the wrong way, Leo, but you would never be enough to get me back to Fall."

"It's that bad?" His lips pressed into a thin line.

Nix contemplated him, weighing truth versus empty warnings. But he wasn't just an ensign she was trying to scare anymore—he was an ally she may need to rely on later. He deserved the true story. "My best friend died down there. In the Hectron Tunnel Collapse."

"What?" Leon exclaimed, eyes widening. "You said you deployed at nineteen. That incident happened after—"

"I deployed twice. Once at nineteen. I survived, kept my head, and was stupid enough to think it was easy money." Nix couldn't look at him. She stared up, tracing the spirescrapers looming over them. "I deployed again at twenty-one... and this time, my best friend came with me. We met Kessandra on the *Luminosity*. She and Quian went into the mines together that day."

"And he died there." Leon scrubbed a hand over his messy black hair. He wasn't wearing a coat, but he seemed to savor the icy air after the heat of the tavern. He wouldn't feel that way in the Crypt, sodden and wet and miles from any natural sunlight, but Nix kept that thought to herself.

She nodded curtly. "I know that place better than anyone. If you think you're safe... you're probably wrong."

Silence lingered between them. For the first time, Leon looked appropriately unnerved.

He cleared his throat. "So—are you going to be staying in Fall, or going to the Crypt with us?"

Us. The soldiers of his new dive team. He'd clearly received his assignment, and the fact that he'd switched so smoothly from the sixty-first to one of the alphabet was almost insulting.

"It's classified." Nix was ninety percent sure Kessandra wouldn't want the details leaking of their mission—and a hundred percent sure Nix herself hadn't been told the full story anyway. No reason to spread rumors. "But I'll be on the *Luminosity*, and I'll try to help in the mines. I doubt we'll be diving, but—well, keep your head, and know there'll be a friendly face nearby."

Leon's expression relaxed into one of relief. "Affirmative, Sergeant."

Nix forced a smile and turned back towards the bar.

Leon caught her arm. "Ah, Nix. One last thing."

She glanced at him, one eyebrow raised.

"If you need backup with your assignment..." He paused, as if trying to decide how to phrase it. "Protection for Kessandra—or... or *from* her, you know where to find me."

"That's the smartest thing you've said all night," Nix replied grimly. She clapped his shoulder and led him back inside the tavern; one final night of revelry before both of their lives changed.

7

On the western edge of Valkeshia, at the base of a dramatic, rugged cliff, was the dock.

Considering the Ever-Storm rendered the ocean's surface impassable, the dock had been designed for one purpose: the *Luminosity*. Twice a month, the massive ship made its three-day journey to Fall, anchored on ichoron-enforced rods that dove deep into the ocean. Departing days were considered holidays to many merchants—at least the ones lucky enough to secure a space in the shadow of the rose-gold submersible.

After all, most passengers were spirescraper citizens, rich folk adorned in heavy furs and ichoron accessories. The rest were soldiers headed for the Crypt—and they knew this could be their last time topside. All were willing to purchase small comforts if it meant a few minutes of happiness.

Nix rubbed her clammy palms against her trousers as

the elevator descended, its glass walls offering an unobstructed view of the chaos below. She was pressed against the huge windows, a spot she hadn't really wanted, and was trying very hard not to look at the roiling ocean beyond. Even from here, it was menacingly dark, its gray waves crashing against the dock's raised platform with vicious glee.

She was wearing an abbreviated version of her soldier's attire: black pants with a few carefully placed pockets, heavy combat boots that laced to her calves, and a more casual leather jacket over her sleeveless training top. Her camera case was strapped around her thigh, and her sarrant was mostly hidden in its sheath by her duffel bag, strapped like a backpack over her shoulders.

The result of her garment choices was a bunch of very confused spirescraper citizens, ones who clutched pearls and coats tighter as they squinted at her — clearly trying to discern why a not-soldier was in their luxurious elevator rather than the utilitarian lift designated for dive teams.

Nix saluted, and a pair of elderly women tittered in quiet discontent. And here Nix thought soldiers were supposed to be *respected* for their service. Apparently, that only applied when she fit into the nice little boxes society set for her.

Only the elevator attendant by the buttons shared a private glance with her — and he seemed just as exasperated with their crowd. She cracked a wry smile for him, and he winked back.

It was a small courtesy.

With little else to do, Nix faced the window again. They were nearly eye-level with the *Luminosity* now, the elevator halfway down the cliffside. The oblong ship nearly obscured the ocean, it was so large.

Not even Nix could deny the *Luminosity* was a work of art. With its rose-gold ichoron plating, expansive tinted windows framing the ship's hull, and massive clamps securing its roof to the undersea railway, the entire thing was an engineering masterpiece. It was meant to fit three thousand souls comfortably and entertain them during the trip: a casino, greenhouse, theater, and promenade ensured the interior was even more spectacular. In fact, it represented everything forward-thinking and fantastical about Valkesh.

Last time she'd descended these elevators, Quian had been at her side. He'd elbowed her and grinned and drawled, *"You didn't say it was so ostentatious."*

Nix had snorted into her canteen of water, accidentally sprayed it over two soldiers who would become friends, and they'd laughed all the way to the ground. Those soldiers died during the Hectron Tunnel Collapse.

All of them.

Kessandra hadn't been in that elevator. Nix didn't meet her until disembarkation, because of course a subarch had a *private* escort onto the *Luminosity*'s upper decks.

"Ground level. Enjoy the shops, folks. The *Luminosity* disembarks at sunset, so make sure you're on board by then." The elevator eased to a halt, and the attendant pulled a crank to prop the doors open.

Nix waited until they'd all filed out, then waved at him. "Thanks."

"Be careful in Fall." The attendant's tone was oddly heavy.

That was when Nix remembered that they brought dead soldiers back in metal boxes and transported them up these elevators after all the passengers left the docks. His knowing look made a lot more sense now.

"It's not my first visit," Nix said. *Or my second.*

The attendant sighed, his expression haunted. "It hardly matters."

Nix's heart pounded. She drew a slow breath through her nose.

She'd be back. This was just a temporary assignment.

It didn't feel like it.

She stepped out of the elevator and he closed the doors behind her, beginning the climb back up for more passengers. Along the cliff, six other glass and gold elevators made a similar vertical trek. To her left, a metal freight elevator with tiny windows emptied soldiers in a back alley, where they could choose to either board the *Luminosity* right away or dive into the rows of stalls first.

Nix adjusted the straps of her duffel bag and merged into the crowd.

It was *frigid*. This close to the ocean, this late in the year, icy wind swept onto the platform. The air was scented with salt. Huge windbreaker walls had been constructed, which helped a little, but people still hunched in their luxurious coats. Their laughter pealed over the wind as they strolled through the market.

"Sergeant," a familiar voice called, and Nix glanced over her shoulder at Leon. Unlike her, he was clad in a proper military uniform, complete with a strict jacket, copper tags on display, and a sarrant on his back. He'd even decided to wear the hat, which was a running joke among their squad—useless in battle and ridiculous in formal settings.

Nix flicked it off his head when he got close. "None of the sixty-first will let you live that down."

"I'm trying to make a good impression," he said, cheeks coloring. He fitted it back on his head, a bold move with the wind. "I didn't realize Fall offered so much."

Suspended on steel cords, huge billboards flashed black and white films of excursions, local inventions, luxury hotels—anything someone might want to experience in the domed undersea city of Fall. The university was just the beginning of a long list of attractions. Nix watched them for a moment, then shrugged.

"You won't have time to explore it." Her tone was teasing, but laced in truth.

Leon chuckled humorlessly. "Are you going up the soldiers' entrance, or the passengers'?" He jerked a thumb at the two staircases—one on either end of the *Luminosity*. One towering set climbed to the underbelly, the spirescraper citizens' playground. Another led to the upper decks, cordoned off for soldiers during the three-day trip.

"Kess will be on the lower decks, and transitioning between them is... tricky." Nix grinned. "Not impossible, though. I'll find you during the trip and show you a few things."

"You're a bad influence," Leon said, rolling his eyes.

Nix winked.

They started walking, milling through the shops. Merchant stalls were hawking everything from silk robes and leisure suits to mouthwatering dishes of shrimp and fish. Nix and Leon were hardly tempted—both were here for a reason, and it wasn't spending hard-earned coin.

Of course, they hadn't made it five steps without a distraction. A middle-aged woman with heavy black glasses and skin the shade of sun-touched sand, snatched the ear of a boy running past.

"I saw that," she said, loud enough that Nix could hear.

The boy batted her away. "I didn't do anything." He had the posh accent of the spirescraper citizens.

"What are you doing to my son?" another woman snapped. She strode up, flipped a mink scarf around her neck, and seized the boy's arm.

The older woman released him, her gaze scathing. "He's yours? Excellent. You can pay the merchant for the piece he stole." Now she gestured pointedly at the jewelry merchant behind them, one who immediately gaped at his wares in horror.

"My diamond bracelet—" he exclaimed.

The boy shoved his hands in his pockets.

The mother sniffed. "He would never steal. We have dozens of diamonds at home."

"Sounds like you're adding another to your collection." The woman with glasses held her leather suitcase's handle casually, lifting her chin, standing her ground. "This merchant probably worked his whole life to pay for that one. Do the right thing, or I'll call the authorities."

The mother puffed up indignantly, as if she might argue.

Nix strolled up to them, crossing her arms. "*I'm* the authorities. Sergeant Nix Marr, bodyguard to Subarch Kessandra Marie Vendermere Biltean III. Empty the boy's pockets, please."

Her voice offered no apologies, no room to budge on the order. It was a tone that commanded soldiers in battle, and coupled with Kessandra's name, the mother's alabaster face flushed. Flanked by Leon, there was no argument. She quietly reached into her son's pockets— and pulled out a diamond bracelet.

Her shocked gasp was covered by the satisfied, "I knew it," of the woman with glasses.

"Mmm." Nix gestured at the merchant. "Her Esteemed Subarch will be pleased to hear about your generosity, should you decide to pay for that piece. If not, the merchant can determine if it was damaged by your son's greedy hands."

The woman's ears were red now, even as she

contemplated the piece. "I did intend to purchase a gift for my sister before our visit." She stepped to the merchant and tugged out three ichoron coins stamped with the primarch's insignia. Her voice was quiet, begrudgingly remorseful. "Please accept my apologies on behalf of my son. I truly don't know what he was thinking."

The merchant seemed just as frazzled, but graciously accepted the payment. "I can box it for you? Wrap it, for your sister?"

"That would be lovely."

Nix left, gesturing for Leon to follow her.

Seamlessly, he stepped alongside her, lips tilted in amusement. "Pulling the subarch's name out awfully fast, aren't you?"

"She might as well be good for something," Nix muttered.

On her right, the woman with the leather suitcase and thick glasses bounded up. She had light brown hair that fell in curly waves over her shoulders, and her dark eyes were alight. "Fabulous. Are you really the subarch's bodyguard?" Her hand wrapped around Nix's arm, feeling the strong muscles underneath her jacket. "A stunning specimen. Of course, I expected nothing less from Kessandra."

"I'm not her toy, or yours," Nix growled, wrestling her arm back. "What do you need?"

"Ah, trust me; it's purely scientific. I hardly have time for that type of thing." The woman smirked, pushing her round spectacles further up her nose. "I'm Doctor Hallie Jesko."

Nix stiffened, cursing her earlier tone. In the army, doctors were highly respected—they kept her squad alive, after all. Earning the title required extensive study at one of Valkesh's university campuses: either in Fall, or Valkeshia proper. And considering that "Jesko" wasn't a casten, it must be a family name... which meant this woman was a spirescraper citizen through and through.

It was too late to backtrack on her tone. Embarrassment heated her skin.

Luckily, Leon was there to save face. He tipped his ridiculous hat. "It's a pleasure, Doctor Jesko."

"*Lumos*, Doctor Jesko was my mother. I'm only forty-two. Call me Hallie."

Nix cleared her throat. "Ah... how can we help you, Hallie?"

"You military folk. Always so polite." Hallie readjusted her grip on the suitcase. Based on how she carried it, it looked heavy. "Subarch Kessandra is a friend of mine. I'm just introducing myself."

The commander's warnings flared in the back of Nix's mind. Friends and foes—and not everyone would be so easily identified. Nix skirted the line between polite and cautious. "I'll pass your regards along to Subarch Kessandra." A pause. "Thanks for pointing out that kid. You'd best get on board before the crowds form a line."

Hallie contemplated her for a moment, then smirked. "I appreciate your suspicion. Kessandra will need someone like you." It sounded vaguely like a threat—but before Nix could pry, Hallie waved and strolled for the passenger staircase. Within seconds, she vanished into the crowd.

Nix watched the area longer than necessary, neck prickling, until Leon cleared his throat.

"Is there a reason you're suspicious?" He paused, rubbing the back of his neck. "It might be useful to know a doctor while we're in Fall."

"She seemed a little too interested in the subarch. This isn't as black and white as the army spirescraper." Nix crossed her arms.

Leon chuckled, but now he sounded nervous. "Great. Maybe take some pictures before you board; you might need the stress relief." His eyes cut to the military staircase. "I'm going to meet up with my dive team. They, ah... they put me in Dialta."

"It's a good one. Dialta has a reputation for being a cautious team."

"My speed, then." He waited, but Nix didn't offer her old teams—either of them. With a sigh, he clapped her shoulder. "See you on board, Sergeant. Try not to murder a royal before we disembark."

Nix snorted. "No promises."

He waved and strolled in the opposite direction, and Nix was alone yet again.

8

WITH LITTLE ELSE TO DO, NIX MOSEYED HER WAY TO the passenger staircase. Hallie was long-since gone, but a steward met her at the base, holding up a hand. His eyes skimmed her military duffel, the sarrant strapped underneath it, and he jerked a thumb across the market. "Soldiers board over there. You're restricted to the upper decks for the duration of the journey."

"I'm here under Subarch Kessandra Marie Vendermere Biltean III's orders." Nix could die just reciting her stupid title. It took far too much air—but it did the trick. No shortscraper citizen would wave a subarch's name around without expecting consequences.

The steward frowned. "Ticket, please?"

She handed it over, a heavyweight paper ticket embossed with actual gold. *First class*, it read in cursive lettering. *Admit: one. Deck one.* A steward had delivered it to her room last night as she packed, tucked inside an unmarked envelope. She'd rolled her eyes, because on the *Luminosity*, the rich stayed low, middle-class workers slept in the ship's center, and the soldiers resided in the upper decks—but deck one was reserved for royalty and their personal guests.

Seeing the ticket made this much more real.

Now, the man squinted at the ticket—*deck one*—then at Nix. His frown deepened. A line was forming behind them, but the steward didn't allow her access to the staircase. Instead, he raised a signal flag at his kiosk. Far above, footsteps echoed on the metal staircase, and minutes later a stern-looking woman arrived. She was wearing a fancier version of his crimson uniform, one with rose-gold trim meant to emulate ichoron.

"Deck one," the woman said, studying the ticket. She tested the edges, attempting to tear it. It didn't rip, which told Nix the paper itself must have been crafted with ichoron drops. That alone made the woman hesitate. "Which royal are you escorting?"

Because Nix had to be escorting someone. The primarch's family was extensive: there were no fewer than eighteen subarchs—direct descendants and their blood families—and many more tertiarchs below them. Despite that anonymity, the royals maintained a certain air: they held themselves like there was a stick up their asses.

Kessandra fit perfectly. Nix didn't.

For a moment, Nix considered lying just to fuck with

her. Naming a royal that almost certainly wasn't on board, or telling the steward the ticket was counterfeit. That would give her every opportunity to abandon this dangerous assignment and return to—

—what? Her father needed that medicine. The commander had already pushed the weight of this assignment. Nix was leaving, no matter what.

Maybe she should have taken a few more pictures of Valkeshia before she left.

Too late now.

"Subarch Kessandra," the steward, meanwhile, whispered to the supervisor.

Behind them, the impatient crowds were beginning to murmur at the hold-up. The senior steward glanced at them, pressed her lips together, and gestured for Nix to follow her up the staircase.

"Right this way." The supervisor spoke over her shoulder as they climbed—she must do this walk several times a day, considering she was barely winded. "I apologize for the confusion; we didn't realize Subarch Kessandra had hired security. I'm thrilled to welcome you aboard and will provide a personal escort to the subarch's suites."

Suites. Plural.

Nix better have one all to herself.

The staircase was ten stories tall, which was easy compared to the soldier's staircase to the upper decks— that one stretched three times as high. At the top, a perilous metal platform extended to the ship. Even the steward was breathing hard when they arrived, but she composed herself quickly and gestured at the entrance.

Nix stopped, eyes widening.

The last two times she'd boarded the *Luminosity*, she'd entered the soldiers' side: cold, utilitarian hallways, small rooms with four bunks each, and a single mess hall to occupy them for three days.

Here, the difference was almost laughable.

Another steward perched in a pressure chamber beyond the metal door, offering a rose-gold tray of champagne. The tray couldn't be ichoron—*couldn't* be, because what an absolute waste—but it sure looked like it. Beyond him, the next room opened like a massive cavern. It was easily as big as the Tertiary Training Room, but instead of housing multiple army squadrons, it was a promenade of shops. The ceiling curved six stories above them, lined with restaurants, cafes, spas, and anything else that might suit a spirescraper citizen's whim.

"The architecture of the *Luminosity* is the pride of Valkesh," the senior steward said cheerfully, leading Nix inside. "The color palette is the primarch's favorite: the black walls indicate our oppression from all sides, but as you can see, we still find beauty in the interior design. Every rose-gold accoutrement you see is actual ichoron."

"What a waste," Nix said, without thinking.

The steward nearly tripped. Her happy mask faltered, but she replaced it immediately. Her hand tightened around Nix's ticket. "Well, ichoron symbolizes the power of Valkesh. There's plenty of utility in how it reinforces the submersible under the immense pressure of the ocean."

Nix considered the champagne for a long moment, then left it behind. Drinking every time the royals' choices horrified her would be a slippery slope.

The architecture *was* breathtaking. Like in the army tower, everything was accented by marble and ichoron. Sleek lines pulled the eye upward, drawing note to the towering ceilings. Geometric moldings—squares, hexagons, triangles—adorned every surface. Railings were gold, statues were gold, and there were so many leafy plants that Nix felt like she'd stepped into a greenhouse.

"I was under the impression that Our Esteemed Primarch offered the same luxuries to his military that he did to his upper-class citizens. Clearly, I was mistaken." Everything about this place reminded her how far removed from Kessandra she truly was.

She'd seen it before, of course, but what had seemed spectacular at twenty-one was now bloodied with the deaths of fellow soldiers—old friends. She'd honestly forgotten how absurd this ship was.

"Oh, the primarch offers equally accommodating living quarters to his soldiers—" the steward began to say, clearly a well-rehearsed speech. But Nix raised an eyebrow and the woman clamped her mouth shut. "Ah, never mind. This way, please."

They wove through the sparse crowds and bypassed a bank of ornate elevators. Instead, the steward led Nix around the corner, to a set of crimson-and-gold double doors. She inserted a heavy brass key, and the doors creaked open to reveal a luxurious elevator.

"This elevator is for deck one's personal use." The steward beckoned her inside. "Your keys are inside your staterooms. We offer royalty and their venerated guests all the privacy they require."

Nix took position in the elevator, watching the steward carefully. Once the doors closed and they were alone, she said, "What's your name?"

"I—" the woman stopped short, hesitating. "No one has asked me that before."

"That's because they're assholes. But I'm interested."

"It's... ah, it's Josie Reslet."

The Reslet casten wasn't far from the Marr casten, so her face flashed acknowledgement when Nix replied, "I'm Sergeant Nix Marr. Call me Nix." A pause, a curious question: "Are you happy doing this?"

Josie blinked. "Of course."

"Really? Because this just seems like a slap in the face to most of Valkesh."

Josie's mask slipped, and her tone was lined with exhaustion. In the elevator's lighting, the stress lines on her fair skin were obvious. "I'm glad to travel. My life in the shortscrapers wasn't great. But it *is* hard to smile around them sometimes."

Finally, they were getting somewhere. Nix's lips quirked. "Trust me. I know."

Josie laughed. When the doors opened into a wide hallway, her pleasant demeanor was back in place, and she continued as if they hadn't spoken. "Originally, the engineers wanted to place the ballast tanks on this level — massive tanks we slowly fill with water to weigh the ship. It helps us descend along the rail. But our last primarch rejected the idea, considering the beauty of the depths."

"Where are the ballast tanks now, then?" Nix raised an eyebrow.

"Oh, they're sequestered away between decks eight and seventeen, where they won't bother anyone." Josie gestured over the walkway. "This is the result: the *Luminosity*'s iconic glass bottom. You might have noticed it from the market below."

The floor *was* glass: reinforced with the rose-gold haze of ichoron, but still. Far below them, people swarmed between the merchant stalls like ants. The bitter wind was a memory now, but it had started to snow again. This close to the ocean, the fluffy white flakes had no problem cutting across the docks in a dizzying display. A long line waited to board the *Luminosity*, people desperate for a reprieve from the cold.

Nix hadn't given much thought to the people who'd be boarding this ship, but now she vaguely wondered who made up the majority. Spirescraper citizens looking for a vacation? Shortscrapers hoping for work? Or a mesh?

"Come along." Josie ignored her contemplations, striding forward.

A walking platform was suspended over the curved glass, complete with heavyset rose-gold railings. It looked sturdy enough, but Nix stepped lightly as she followed Josie over the walkway.

Josie kept talking: "Once we reach the bioluminescence of the deep sea, you'll have a remarkable view of the fall."

She wasn't referring to the city this time.

"Has anyone at that fancy university figured out what sea creature died there?" Nix asked, only mildly curious. The ancient creature's bones were as big as mountains and spread over most of the ocean floor. As a result, its carcass supplied sustenance to a thriving bioluminescent ecosystem around Fall, the city. The only comfort was that the species itself was long gone. After all, if animals that big were still lurking in the Deates Sea, someone would have noticed.

Scientists were "87% certain."

Now Josie chuckled. "The most recent venture is a mapping expedition to ascertain the scope of the leviathan's corpse. They attached equipment to the bottom of the *Luminosity* to capture images as we move over the ocean floor. I'm sure the university will release a statement when they know more."

"That's dandy." Nix was 87% certain she'd be alive to hear their theories.

Josie led her past a huge lounge in the center of the deck, one where the carpet ended and the suspended walkway itself shifted to glass and the world seemed to bottom out beneath them. Luxurious velvet armchairs and low-top tables framed a bar carved of wood, although the space was empty now.

"How many royals can I expect on this deck?" Nix asked.

The steward lifted her chin. "Oh, not many this trip. Subarch Kessandra is the most notable, although she's accompanied by Tertiarch Polaris and his guards."

Hmm. Nix hadn't heard of Polaris.

"I should warn you that the ship pressurizes slowly over the next three days—by the time we dock in Fall, we'll be breathing the same chemical mix they do. But if you begin to feel ill along the journey, please visit our medical ward on the nineteenth floor."

Nix hadn't remembered feeling sick over her last journeys on the *Luminosity*. She frowned. "Has that always happened?"

Josie smiled politely. "Since the inception of the ship, yes. The ocean is incredibly heavy, Sergeant. Without pressurizing the ship and the dome, even ichoron would have a tough time withstanding the increased atmospheres. But the chemists are quite proficient—the air may feel heavier, but you shouldn't notice any substantial change."

They stopped at a set of double doors on the opposite side of the lounge. By Nix's estimate, there were ten suites on deck one. Well, eleven, if she counted the huge doors at the end of the walkway, which clearly led to the primarch's private suite. But that would be off limits, and this primarch rarely left Valkeshia.

Josie cast one last glance at Nix's ticket, then rapped on the double door. She seemed abashed now, but she held her ground as she called, "Subarch Kessandra. We have a visitor for you: Sergeant Nix Marr."

Nix had to laugh at the casual way Josie double-checked the authenticity of the visit, even after leading Nix into the belly of the beast—as if she didn't trust that Nix belonged here. Which was reassuring, but also ridiculous.

"Josie, if I was planning to hurt the subarch, I'd have done it years ago."

The steward flinched, her face paling. "Ah—it's just that we didn't know you were coming."

"That's because I'm disinclined to inform the entirety of the *Luminosity*'s staff about my private security," a smooth voice said from down the hall. They glanced left to see Kessandra standing in the doorway of the suite next door. "Your rooms are here, Nix."

Nix planted her feet. "I'd rather take the suite you *aren't* in, thanks."

The sheer fact that Kessandra reserved individual rooms, then *moved right in* was an egregious overstep. If Nix didn't quell those now, she might as well make herself a doormat in Kessandra's life.

Josie looked horrified at her tone.

Kessandra's gaze hardened, her ichoron eyeball icy gold against the deep bronze powder dusted on her eyelids. Instead of acknowledging her snark, however, Kess's gaze shifted to the steward. "Thank you for bringing her, Josie. You are dismissed."

The fact that Josie stiffened told Nix she truly didn't expect anyone on this deck would know her name. Her words were rushed: "The disembarkation dinner begins at sunset; the chef sincerely hopes you both attend." She handed Nix a brass key, bowed hastily to the subarch, and turned for the elevator.

Silence followed in her wake. They were alone for the first time since the alleyway conversation. Kessandra met her gaze, rolled her eyes—in the most dignified manner one *could* roll her eyes—and stepped back into the suite, leaving the double doors open.

The emptiness of deck one was oppressive. Through the glass bottom, visible over the nearby railing, the market was swathed in snow. Merchants were already beginning to pack their wares, and the line waiting to board the *Luminosity* was very long now.

Leon would already be settling into his bunk, flanked by his new dive team.

For a moment, Nix entertained the idea of fleeing the ship. Taking the elevator to the promenade, muscling through opulent crowds, shoving her way down the staircase. She could be back in the army tower—or better yet, back home—in an hour or two.

Back to her dying father. Quian's grieving mother. A squad who'd already said their goodbyes.

There was no option left, and Kess knew it. Grimly, Nix trudged through the double doors into her suite, closing them behind her.

9

THE PRIMARCH FAVORED BRIGHT LIGHTS, BOLD contrast, and solid lines in his décor, and the geometric shapes etched into the doors were no different. They were also heavy, clearly reinforced; it was a miracle Kess heard Josie knock on the other suite's door at all. Either that, or she'd seen Nix through the windows and somehow timed how long it'd take to get to deck one.

Nix wouldn't put it past her.

After stepping inside, she locked the doors on impulse. As much as she hated Kessandra, she was a professional — and the commander made his orders clear.

"Take a seat," Kessandra said primly.

Nix didn't move. Instead, she surveyed the rooms.

There seemed to be three: similar in setup to the commander's quarters in the army spirescraper, but far more lavish. The living room was pressed against a huge, curved wall of reinforced glass. Tasteful leather couches faced each other, and a long, low table was anchored between them. Kessandra's custom pistol—black and ichoron-touched—was holstered, but within easy reach on the low table.

Against the back wall was a small kitchenette with marble countertops. A nice spread of cheeses and jams had been laid out, chilled atop an oblong bowl of ice. Even the little fork used to pick slices of cheese was tinted rose gold.

The rest of the suite consisted of a room with a single, ridiculously large bed, and an adjoining bathroom. Nix squinted at the toilet, a porcelain piece with a polished wooden seat and an ichoron handle.

Kessandra noticed. "Were you expecting a chamber pot?" Her tone was dry.

Nix ignored that. Even the shortscrapers had upgraded to communal restrooms for sanitation reasons: the previous primarch had instituted the change decades before Nix was born. Still, a private restroom on a *ship* seemed shocking—and yet knowing the royals, it was hardly a surprise.

"Just wondering why someone would waste ichoron on a toilet handle."

"Rose-gold paint exists, you realize."

Nix raised an eyebrow. "Is that painted?"

Kessandra pursed her lips.

"Thought not," Nix drawled. She stepped into the bedroom, dropped her duffel bag and sarrant by the doorway, and tossed herself onto the bed. It was so wide, she could spread out like a starfish in any direction. On her right, the windows were round portholes—probably to manage the glare from the bioluminescent ocean. Tough for rich people to sleep against huge swaths of blue light, she supposed.

There was a stick telephone on the bedside table, and she picked the receiver up with one hand. A click, a moment of static, and then a pleasant female voice said, "Hello, Sergeant Marr. Who are you trying to call?"

Nix stiffened, scrambling for the base piece to speak into the microphone. "Uh—who are you?"

"I'm the switchboard operator." She sounded a bit perplexed, like she expected Nix to know this. Like Nix used a telephone on a regular basis. "Royal guests have direct access to our head chef, the ship's captain, any of the storefronts, or the Luminosity's travel advisor, if you're more interested in planning activities once we arrive in Fall."

Nix frowned. "What's your name?" She already hated that the default here seemed to be "anonymous help."

The woman paused. "Ah, Ramona."

"Thank you, Ramona."

"You're... you're welcome, Sergeant Marr. May I direct your call?"

Nix shrugged against the mattress. The telephone's cord rested against her cheek. "Nah. I was just curious. Thanks again." She hung up, twisted to set the telephone back on the bedside table, then stared at the ceiling.

How grand.

"Are you quite finished?" Kessandra called.

Nix groaned, but hauled herself up and trudged back into the living room.

Kessandra was leaning over a set of documents, written reports stacked between black and white photographs. Her braided hair was tied in a thick bun, but she was wearing casual attire: a simple white shirt, suspenders, and black slacks. Her freckles were hidden yet again beneath a smooth mask of powder foundation.

"Are you friends with Ramona too? Or did you just memorize all the staffs' names before boarding?"

Kessandra lifted her eyes, and her ichoron eyeball pinned Nix in place. She raised one perfectly shaped brow. "Why do I feel like this is a lose-lose scenario for me? I haven't been on the *Luminosity* in years; obviously, there's been some turnover. However, some of these people have been serving my family since my infancy. What would you like me to say, Nix?"

Nix huffed. "Josie told me no one asks for her name."

"And naturally, you assumed that included me."

The neutrality in Kessandra's tone made Nix pause. It wasn't some form of emotional manipulation to make Nix sympathetic or pull on her heartstrings. It was cataloging, like Kessandra wasn't certain where they stood anymore. That alone made Nix swell with satisfaction.

If Kess didn't already know that answer, Nix would keep that mystery going as long as possible, just to spite her. "Yes. I did."

"Well, then. I'm deeply sorry to disappoint. Josie was

promoted last year, but she was my family's personal steward when I was young. Ramona has been our switchboard operator for decades. She used to direct my calls to the chef at midnight when I wanted cookies, after my mother told me no."

"Sounds like a nice life." The sarcasm in Nix's tone was devastating.

Kessandra drew a slow breath and pushed to her feet, striding to the bar attached to the kitchenette. Clearly, she needed a drink.

Nix could relate, but she was far too stubborn to ask for one. So, she stood awkwardly while Kess chose a tall, stemmed glass and uncorked a bottle of wine. It was deep red, and she offered the bottle to Nix after she poured.

"Wine isn't my style," Nix lied. Normally, she'd drink anything—but for now, the desire to stay sharp and attentive won over the urge to dull the edges of this insufferable expedition. Liquid courage was a fool's game when someone like Kessandra lurked on the edges of her sanity.

Kessandra's expression was tinged with mild exasperation. "I see. Then I can presume the night in the atrium, where we stole this exact type of wine and hid below the observation deck—that was just a fluke?"

That night had faded so far into Nix's memory, she'd almost forgotten about it. Now it came roaring back, heating her face as she remembered how fast they drained that bottle, how light and warm they felt afterwards. How their eyes met, how Nix had whispered, "Can I?" as she traced Kess's arm. How Kess had breathed, "Always," and then Nix was trailing down, feathering along Kess's abdomen, lifting her shirt, touching hot skin. Kess's gasp —Nix's soft laugh. The way they both went silent as her fingers dove further south.

There had been something intoxicating about making Kessandra, the notoriously composed subarch, lose *all* composure in a public place. Something that even now made Nix entire body twinge with desire.

Maybe Nix *did* need a drink.

"That was a long time ago." Nix hated that her voice was strangled. She cleared her throat. "Are you going to give me the briefing or not?"

"Hmm." Kessandra's lips were tilted ever so slightly upward. It was infuriating. Nix glared, daring her to protest, but the subarch merely took a smooth sip of her wine and pushed the folder across the table.

Nix reluctantly eased onto the opposite couch, opening the folder to parse through the files inside. There were handwritten notes, a few reports drawn up with a typewriter, and—images. All thoughts of the atrium vanished as she flipped through the photographs.

"Lumos below," Nix breathed.

"You can see why I needed your help," Kessandra replied, taking a longer sip of her drink. Any amusement was gone, replaced with grim discontent. "'Terrible' doesn't begin to describe this."

For once, she was right. Six identifiable bodies—and countless mounds of flesh that couldn't even be guessed.

Sightless eyes and spilled intestines made Nix's stomach churn. Chunks of hair and gore smeared over the Dive Room's wooden benches, bits of it sticking out of the vents of a few lockers.

Nix had killed on the front lines, it was true; spilled Triolan blood like water in the ocean. But this... this looked like an animal had ripped their soldiers apart.

"Any chance the Crypt Keeper is real?" Nix asked, only half joking. She flipped through the reports, skimming the testimonies: the commander who managed the Crypt, the other dive teams, the doctors who conducted autopsies. She'd read this in-depth later, but for now her eyes lifted to Kessandra.

The subarch had finished half her wine and was swirling the rest in its glass. "I don't chase myths. Nothing can live in the mines—not even a humanoid creature with glowing red eyes. The water is too saline."

That was true. Even in heavy dive suits, swimming in the mines felt more like floating. It was an eerie experience. But considering Nix had seen those eyes firsthand, she wasn't inclined to dismiss rumors so fast.

Nix's brow furrowed. "Then what's your theory?"

"The same as always. People."

She'd have believed it before seeing the photographs. Now, Nix wrinkled her nose. "There's no fucking way one person did *that*."

Kessandra tilted her head. "Are you familiar with dethalos?" When Nix just raised an eyebrow, the subarch folded her arm over her leg, wine glass perched between long, slender fingers. "I thought not. It's kept very hush-hush—the primarch doesn't want to scare people. But I've investigated every report, which is why my great-uncle sent me on this assignment."

That was directly at odds with what the commander had implied: that Kessandra hadn't had a choice, that the primarch was sending her on a dangerous mission to put her life at risk. Nix's voice was cautious. "Okay."

"Dethalos is a disease characterized by the sudden onslaught of violent impulse. The symptoms preceding the outburst include headaches, nausea, and disassociation. Eventually, the person won't respond to their own name." Kessandra tapped the photograph of the carnage, drawing Nix's eyes down again. "The final stage is outward aggression. Those infected become almost animalistic in their desire to kill or maim."

Nix stared.

Then she started laughing.

Kessandra watched her coolly. "This is amusing to you?"

"Look, I know you think I'm an idiot. But come *on*, Nines." She spat the nickname, inwardly cheered when Kessandra stiffened.

The subarch drew another long sip of wine. It briefly tinted her burgundy lipstick crimson. "Nix, you're one of the most observant people I've ever met. Which means you'll draw the same conclusion: that no human in their right mind could accomplish this." Now she spread the photographs out for Nix to see. One after the other of smeared blood, gore, *corpses*, glistening in the cold lights of the Dive Room.

Experienced soldiers, all of them. As close as family; dive teams would die for each other. That alone prickled Nix's suspicion.

And more, she examined the images from a photographer's perspective. Whoever was taking these pictures didn't want to get close. Most were done from a distance, as physically far as they could be without losing the shot. If even the army investigators hadn't wanted to approach... the real scene must have been a sight to behold.

"No one's managed anything quite this devastating after being infected. But there's no doubt in my mind that *this*," she tapped the table hard, "is dethalos. A disease."

That should scare Nix more—but all she focused on was the immediate problem.

"So, you think there's a crazed killer running loose in the Crypt?" Nix waved a photograph for emphasis. "And no one's noticed who it is? Or tried to stop him?"

"No. I think the killer did what everyone afflicted with dethalos does—he died, violently. Seizures, or suicide, or his heart exploding in his chest. The methods vary; the result is the same."

Nix wasn't laughing now. "*Lumos*. You're serious, aren't you?"

Kessandra's gaze softened, and her voice was quiet. "My dear, I would never have troubled you for less."

Fuck. Nix leaned back on the leather couch, running

her hands through her hair. She stared up for a moment—even the ceiling was paneled with rose-gold accents—and drew a short breath against her pounding chest.

As if the Crypt wasn't bad enough.

"How does it spread? Are we walking into an outbreak?"

Kessandra leaned back in her chair, crossing her legs. Closing herself off. "You won't like it."

"Come on, Kess. I'm already here. Just tell me."

The subarch sighed, tapping her right temple. Indicating her implanted eyeball. "I have reason to believe that it spreads with ichoron. That this material is somehow poisoning our population."

It landed like a bullet to the head. Nix felt like she'd been electrocuted with a lightning strike from the Ever-Storm. On reflex, she glanced at the door—but of course, they were alone. "You think—Lumos below, Kessandra, can't you stop lying for—"

"Nix." Her tone was chilling. "This isn't a lie. I've spent my entire life gathering empirical evidence to prove it, and the results are clear. Everyone infected with dethalos has had extended exposure to ichoron."

Extended exposure.

Gooseflesh pebbled Nix's arms. "S-So my father—"

"It's possible, but unlikely. Cases seem more common in Fall. While the occasional citizen in Valkeshia has been affected, it's concentrated below the ocean—near the mines." Now she drew a sip of wine, tasting the flavor.

"For example, I've shown none of the symptoms, despite my eye. Your father will likely be fine."

"Comforting."

"As comforting as this gets. If it wasn't passable for the majority, ichoron would have been blacklisted centuries ago."

Her tone was deadly serious, and it was pissing Nix off. She shoved to her feet. "Your calculations are wrong. Ichoron can't be poisoning people."

"An unknown substance we scooped out of the deepest crevices of the ocean and smeared over everything in our lives? Something that's allowed us to hold our own in a persistent war—and as a result, it's never been properly tested?" Kessandra examined her perfectly manicured nails. "Ah, yes. Whatever could be the problem with that?"

"Someone would have noticed," Nix snapped.

Kessandra heaved a tired sigh, standing as well. She strapped the pistol's holster to her hip, checked the clock mounted to the wall, and finished her wine. "I don't have the stamina to argue with you tonight. Dinner is next on our list; you'll find everything you need in your stateroom. I expect you to dress appropriately."

With that, she strolled for the door adjoining their suites, her heels clicking smartly on the marble floor.

"Hey, Kess," Nix called.

She paused, glancing over her shoulder.

Nix could barely keep the derision out of her tone.

"Don't intrude on my rooms again. You want entry—you knock. And maybe I'll answer."

"Hmm." Kessandra lifted her chin. "All right, then. When we venture into the general public, I expect *you* to conduct yourself appropriately. You are my subordinate and will offer me the respect a subarch deserves. Is that clear?"

Nix scowled.

"Confirm, soldier," Kessandra said.

Tit for tat; Kessandra's favorite fallback. Humiliation and anger swept over Nix. She was ever-aware of the power imbalance between them, ever-aware that Kessandra only needed a sentence to destroy Nix's life. It had fury surging up Nix's throat, mixing with the miserable acceptance that she was truly submerged in Kessandra's web of lies, now.

Nix clenched her jaw so tightly it ached. "You're an ass."

"I'm aware of your opinion."

"As long as we're on the same page." When it became apparent that Kessandra truly wasn't leaving until she responded in kind, Nix muttered, "Fine. Affirmative."

"Thirty minutes. Meet me in the lounge." Kessandra stepped through the door into a suite identical to Nix's. The door shut resolutely behind them, and a moment later a heavy lock clicked into place.

Nix flipped off the door. It was wholly unsatisfying.

She risked another glance at the photographs on the table, her chest cold. Her eyes roamed over the ichoron décor, settled on the cheese platter with the tiny rose-gold fork. Somewhere above them, her father was taking medicine laced with the stuff. Her squad was training in a room painted in it.

It couldn't be true. Kessandra lied about everything; this was just another manipulation on her long, long list.

Ignoring her twisting insides, Nix stepped into the bedroom. She had time for a nap before dinner.

10

KESSANDRA LOOKED *STUNNING*, AND NIX WAS MILDLY pissed about it.

She lounged in the center of deck one, alone except for a bartender who'd apparently been stationed here exclusively for her private use. He cleaned the bar with a white hand towel, the picture of professionalism, as Kess sipped a fancy drink with an orange peel in a crystal tumbler. "Excellent, Dominik," she was saying. "You're right; the absinthe gives it a nice punch."

"Just a tad." He laughed, tapping a tinted bottle with a finger. "Too much, and you'd be on the floor."

Nix wasn't much into the bodyguarding side of this assignment, but her senses still prickled at the comment. She scowled when the bartender acknowledged her, crossing her muscular arms.

"That had better be a joke, Dominik."

His eyes lingered on her sarrant, clearly ichoron-edged and sheathed on her back. It looked ridiculous, considering the outfit Kessandra had placed in her closet: formal black slacks, a button-down white shirt, and a tight black vest that severely restricted movement. Nix had rolled the sleeves to her elbows, then tied her hair into a side ponytail that draped over her right shoulder. Now she let him stare at the sarrant; let him digest what, exactly, that meant.

"It was a joke," he said, stumbling over the words.

"Hmm. Have you known the subarch long?"

At the nearby table, Kessandra sipped her drink, watching the exchange with mild interest. Based on their history, this might actually be turning her on. Kess always loved the moments Nix seized control.

Nix remained focused on what was important: that if Kessandra's drink *was* poisoned, her life would be a lot less complicated.

The bartender folded the towel into a neat square, but his eyes flicked to Kessandra, as if waiting for her help in the interrogation. "Ah—not long, no. We just met."

"Great." Nix stepped forward, narrowing her eyes. "Next time you make a drink for the subarch, you'll make one for yourself, too. Same pours, same bottles. Square?"

"O-Of course, sergeant."

So, he already knew her rank. Good. That would make things easier. She patted the bar in satisfaction. "Nice to meet you, Dominik." As she walked away, she gave him a full view of her sarrant.

Meanwhile, her eyes roamed over Kessandra, who'd smoothly pushed to her feet. Kessandra offered a sardonic smile. "Well, that was something." And—yep. There was an underlying purr to her tone, a heat Nix could never miss.

And damn if that dress wasn't helping. Gone was Kess's military uniform; in its place was a sequined crimson dress that clung to every curve. It cut low over her chest to display smooth mahogany skin, and ended at her knees in black tassels that brushed her calves.

Impractical. Stupid.

"Who drinks from a random bartender when there are sealed bottles in your room?" Nix snapped quietly. "Don't you have any sense?"

Kessandra finished the drink in one shot, smacking her lips in satisfaction. Her tone was *not* quiet. "Wonderful, Dominik. Thank you for not killing me." She winked at him and left the glass on the table, then strolled for the elevator. As Nix drew alongside her, she murmured, "He was a plant from Tertiarch Polaris. It'd be a fool's game to kill me with the entire army outside. Best to wait until we're deep in the ocean, after my guard's down."

There were days—not many, but some—where Nix wondered how the hell she'd ever snagged Kessandra in the first place. And on the heels of that question came the lingering thought: where was *Nix* on Kessandra's chessboard? Because this was some cunning shit.

It still left the very obvious problem. "What if he'd

poisoned you tonight and stashed your body in that room? We'd be submerged before anyone realized."

"That's why you're here, my dear." Kessandra smiled prettily.

Maybe she should strangle Kess herself and save Polaris the misery. "This isn't a joke."

Kessandra kept her pace measured, her voice soft. "Ichoron is remarkably useful for building a poison tolerance. I've been protected against most poisons since I was a child." Now her gaze went distant. "The process was... less than pleasant."

Nix winced. They stopped at the elevator, and she gestured for Kessandra to step inside, then followed. Her boots—shiny black things that were uncomfortable as shit —sank into the thick red carpet inside, and she leaned against the golden railing to take her weight off them. "I'm still concerned about the fact that you think Polaris is a threat."

She tried to keep the fear from her voice, but after a few minutes in public, Kessandra's safety already seemed compromised. Nix's skin crawled with the prospect.

Kessandra pressed the button for the promenade deck. "You misheard; *he* thinks he's a threat. I know better. He's my fourth cousin, a miserable bobble of a man." She chuckled. "He always fancied himself one murder away from the title of subarch. With me removed, he believes his bloodline is strongest to take my place."

"That's not how royalty works," Nix said. Then she paused, analyzing Kessandra's face. "Is it? I was told the subarchs are immediate family to the primarch, a title shuffled whenever a new primarch rises to power. He'd have to kill the current one to have a chance."

"Unless our primarch lies to him, offers gilded promises in exchange for an act of loyalty."

Nix stared.

Kessandra examined her nails, perfectly painted for the evening. She didn't seem at all fazed by this revelation.

Nix, meanwhile, was *very* fazed. Sarcasm dripped from her tone. "Oh, that's dandy."

"Polaris is inconsequential, dear. His determination falters whenever he's facing true strife—which is the difference between a subarch and a tertiarch. The guards with him, however... they *are* dangerous. Ex-Elites."

Elites were the highest-ranking special assignment. Most soldiers only ever lasted a year in the Elites, simply because the assignments—infiltrating Triolan inner circles, culling brutal enemies in combat—were so deadly. To have retired Elites in his service was a statement in itself.

Nix pulled at her collar. "How did he get higher-ranking bodyguards than you?"

"Why? Are you worried?" Kess leaned against the railing opposite Nix like a model—the picture of ease.

"They're *Elites*."

"Mmm. The primarch offered me their services first— and after I refused, they arrived on this vessel anyway, flanking Polaris." Kessandra pinned Nix with a cunning gaze. Her ichoron eyeball seemed to blaze with fire.

"You're here because the vultures are circling, and I don't intend to become their next meal."

A chill swept up Nix's arms, prickling her skin. She rubbed her forearm, but determination quickly replaced unease. This was no different than any other military assignment: identify the threat and eliminate it. Even if they were Elites.

"Fine. But if I'm keeping you alive, you'll need to stop taking stupid risks."

Kessandra's lips tilted upwards ever so slightly. "I think you're forgetting who the commanding officer is here."

"And I think *you're* forgetting who's going to be leaping into battle on your behalf." *Against Elites*, Nix's mind supplied.

Retired ones, but still.

She'd need to find Leon on this ship sooner rather than later. The upper decks were a bit of a hike, but if she could coordinate a rotation somehow, at least she'd feel comfortable grabbing some sleep. It would be less important to watch Kessandra every waking second, more vital to identify the Elites and separate them from Kess in the first place.

After all, Kessandra could handle an opponent on her own. If Nix ran interference on the dangerous ones, Kessandra would survive long enough to regroup.

Nix's mind was already running options, so she almost missed the way Kess purred, "Ah, my hero. That suit is doing you every favor, by the way."

The doors dinged open.

Nix barely heard them, acutely aware of Kessandra's gaze on her muscular shoulders, the way they lingered at the vest that showed every curve of her waist. She opened her mouth to—what? Object to the gaze? Or say something *truly* ridiculous?

But Kessandra ended the moment before it began. "Smile, Sergeant. It's time to act." She strolled into the promenade like she was a peacock amongst pigeons.

With a groan, Nix stalked after her.

THE DINING ROOM was strategically designed to bid farewell to Valkeshia. The room was a massive bubble at the back end of the *Luminosity*, bulbous steel accented by wrap-around windows that displayed the cliff—and above it, looming over them, the fabulous spirescrapers of the city. The angle was wrong to see the shortscrapers, but that had probably *also* been intentional.

The lower dining room, the place where every guest except royalty and soldiers ate, was a massive, circular area filled with white tables and formal settings. Along the back wall was a buffet table. The huge space swarmed with people; there must be at least two hundred eating here, and these were just the guests who'd chosen to attend the disembarkation dinner. There were more lounges spread around the ship for everyone else, and many would be watching through their stateroom portholes.

The moment Kessandra stepped into the dining hall, a hush fell over the room. Nix tensed, anxiety spiking as all eyes seemed to fall on her charge, and then excited murmurings filled the air like buzzing bees.

"Can you try to be more subtle?" Nix muttered to Kessandra.

"Absolutely not. It's important they see me here: healthy and alive. Just in case."

That made Nix wince. "Nothing's going to happen."

Kessandra smiled brightly at the crowds, ever the politician, even as she said, "I believe you'll try your best to avert it. But even I cannot plan for every contingency."

She dipped her head in gratitude as a steward unclipped a velvet rope to a circular staircase. The steward bowed smoothly. "Your table is prepared, Your Esteemed Subarch. The venerated Tertiarch Polaris is dining nearby, but you'll have total privacy. I do hope it's to your satisfaction."

"I'm certain it will be a wonderful meal," Kessandra said.

The steward clipped the velvet rope behind them, and his eyes burned Nix's back as she followed closely. At the top, the view was even better—here, the windows climbed all the way to the domed ceiling, offering an unobstructed view for the moment the water would wash over the vessel.

Nix was slightly bitter about the whole setup. Lumos forbid royals eat with the common folk. Oh no. They had to have the best seat in the house, high above everyone else.

How typical.

"Who even are these people?" Nix asked, her voice quiet. "All the passengers."

"A mix, I'd imagine. Workers, educators, vacationers. Others, too—we need chemists and biologists and nutritionists to ensure a domed, underwater city isn't a death sentence. Fall has one-quarter the population of Valkeshia; it's hardly surprising we fill the ship every time."

It sounded so logical when Kessandra said it. Nix still had trouble wrapping her brain around a thousand passengers visiting a random city. Especially when *she* had no reason to leave Valkeshia, aside from military deployments.

Kessandra had moved on. "There's your competition." As they crested the staircase, she nodded graciously at a man seated at a table about thirty feet away.

After describing him as a "bobble of a man," Nix expected the tertiarch to be soft from a life in the palace. But the royals valued military prowess, and it was clear someone from the army had trained Polaris in private. He sat straight and rigid; from a distance, he looked more like the primarch than Kessandra did. After all, both Polaris and the primarch had oak-toned skin that seemed bleached by the sun, a direct contrast to the mahogany complexion Kessandra inherited from her mother.

Polaris's gaze, however, was familiar—the same calculating expression Kessandra often wore. Maybe it was a royal trait.

His escorts weren't eating with him. They flanked either side of his chair, hands clasped behind their backs. Everything about the Elites screamed military, from their hardened bodies and expressions. Up close, Nix was amazed to see the rose-gold sheen along their skin. Ichoron sarrants, identical to Nix's, gleamed. One had hers strapped to her back, but the other had commissioned a hip sheath. An odd choice for a weapon with such a long hilt, but Nix had no doubt he could use it.

"They look fun," Nix drawled.

Kessandra snorted. It sent a shock of satisfaction through Nix's chest—but irritation followed close on its heels. She didn't care that she could still make Kess laugh. It didn't matter that *she* was the one standing beside the subarch, while spirescraper citizens ate far below and looked up in awe.

It couldn't matter.

"Please don't stand behind me like that," Kessandra said. "I want to present a united front; let's eat together."

Without warning, Nix was thrown back to the day she'd first talked to Kessandra. They were in the *Luminosity's* mess hall, surrounded by soldiers—Quian at her side, elbowing her, pointing at the subarch. *"She's eating alone,"* he whispered. *"Now's your chance."*

"She's probably waiting for someone," Nix had snapped, face flushing.

She acutely recalled Quian's amused look: the way his lips tilted, the way his teeth showed when he laughed. *"No one's talked to her since we boarded. She's lonely. Bring her over here and let's all eat together."*

That was Quian: always grabbing strays.

"Nix?" Kessandra's voice was uncharacteristically soft.

"Don't," Nix replied stiffly, taking a seat across from Kessandra. Devastation made her chest tight, dredging up feelings she thought she'd left behind long ago. She placed her sarrant in easy reach against the table, and turned her attention to the city, seizing the opportunity to breathe deeply and redirect her thoughts.

The market was completely clear now, and the sun was setting over the Deates Sea. It cast the city in a brilliant red glow, lighting the ichoron plating on fire. Valkeshia gleamed.

Absently, Nix undid the clasp of the leather satchel at her thigh, tugging out her camera. A waiter approached while she set up the shot, but Kessandra didn't interrupt her—she simply placed an order of sparkling wine for both of them. The conversation was background noise, muted by Nix's sudden desire to capture this grand city before they left it... maybe for good.

She lined up the shot, peered in the viewfinder, and snapped the picture.

"Can I see the photo?" Kess asked.

Nix contemplated her for a moment, then leaned back

to allow her access. Kessandra peered through the viewfinder, her tight braids falling gently over her ears, partially hiding her eyes. "Beautiful composition."

Cheeks heating, Nix rubbed the back of her neck. "Thanks." Her neck prickled, and she glanced over her shoulder—Polaris was moving with his bodyguards toward their table. Without thinking, Nix tapped Kessandra's hand, their fingers brushing for just a moment.

Their eyes met.

And the moment passed. Kessandra straightened, steepling her fingers, instantly ready to receive the company. When he neared, she smiled politely. "Tertiarch. I was wondering when you'd say hello."

"I expected you to do the same," Polaris replied, his tone clipped.

"Mmm. I didn't care to waste the steps. Especially since you've always been bold enough to approach me without an invitation." Kessandra took the flute of sparkling wine offered by the waiter, who placed a second in front of Nix wordlessly. Kessandra sipped the wine and smiled. "A bit dry, considering even our greenhouses are subject to the harsh soil here. What do you think, Sergeant?"

Nix seized the cue. She was, after all, used to commanding a squadron—and serving a subarch placed her ahead of some tertiarch with murderous thoughts. She drew a long, even sip, savoring how it dried her tongue in the aftertaste. "The citrus notes are surprising."

Polaris appraised Nix. His Elites stood behind him, silent and unmoving as the tertiarch said, "When the primarch told me you'd chosen a private guard, I expected someone higher-ranking than a sergeant."

Well. That hurt.

Nix raised an eyebrow. "Are you planning to test my skills? Because I could use a workout."

"I wouldn't waste the time," Polaris replied, cold as the snow swirling around Valkeshia.

Kessandra drew another sip of her wine. "Polaris, if you take that tone with my guard again, she won't have to fight you. You'll already be dead." The two Elites stiffened, reaching for their weapons, but they looked bit unsure. Kess's ichoron eye narrowed—it allowed her to zoom into details, shuttering like the aperture of a camera lens—so she definitely identified their hesitation.

Nix leaned back in her seat, smirking. It was a *little* fun, watching Kess work.

Polaris, meanwhile, spluttered. "Verbal threats in a public place?" He cast a glance over his shoulder. "I knew you weren't the photo-ready image of a royal everyone seems to think you are."

"Far better than a veiled attack in the secrecy of my stateroom. I sincerely hope you aren't that audacious, but you've done more foolish things." Kessandra smiled over her glass, brushing her lips against the flute. "Did you need something else, Polaris?"

He stiffened, floundering for words.

Nix casually pushed to her feet, smoothly retrieving

her ichoron blade. Her eyes cut right past Polaris to the Elites on either side of him. Up close, their skin shimmered like gold dust—no one knew exactly how the Elites gained the hue, but the forefront rumor was a specialty oil, or maybe a lotion. Either way, their skin looked as impervious as they were.

It was nerve-wracking.

Nix didn't let it show. "You two are army, so I trust that your loyalty for a fellow soldier," at this, she gestured at Kessandra, "runs deeper than his ambition. But I guess only time will tell."

She's one of us, Claire had said. The commander reiterated it. Time to test how loyal Kessandra's potential following truly was. Just in case, though, Nix rested her sarrant on her shoulder; the stance was casual, but left plenty of opening to defend if the Elites attacked.

The Elites kept their faces professionally smooth, but Nix knew the look in their eyes. It was the same one her ensigns got the first time they realized killing a Triolan meant taking a life—even if they were the enemy.

Mental or physical… there'd be consequences.

Across the dining hall's upper level, the waiters were perched with arms laden with food, staring wide-eyed at the confrontation. At Nix's blade, a clear display. Over the banister, people were busy gawking at the windows as the ship prepared to disembark—but it was only a matter of time before someone noticed.

Polaris seemed to realize it, too, because he rubbed a

gold ring over his thumb. A nervous tick, maybe? His tone was final. "Enjoy your dinner, Subarch."

Kessandra didn't respond. She simply waved a hand in dismissal and turned back to the windows. Nix, on the other hand, didn't sit down until Polaris and his Elites had left the dining hall entirely. Only once the velvet rope was clipped back over the staircase did Nix sheath her blade and take a seat.

Neither addressed the conversation.

Soon after, the waiters filled their table with food, and the chef came out and personally greeted Kessandra, offering full-bellied laughs at her inquiries about his family. After they chatted for a bit, he left. In the remaining silence, Nix dipped a cracker-like crisp into her bowl of thick orange soup. The sunset was almost over, and Valkeshia was barely visible amidst the gentle snowfall and darkening night sky.

"Have you done photography long?" Kess asked, taking a delicate taste of her own bisque.

Conversation, like they were old friends reconnecting after a long sabbatical. It almost made Nix laugh out loud —except that Kessandra *also* knew Quian was fascinated with photography. Kessandra had been the one to sneak him into the *Luminosity*'s darkroom after they first met. She'd paid for professional photos of the three of them, although they'd disembarked the ship before they could retrieve the developed images.

Nix tried to keep the irritation out of her voice. "About two years. I needed—something—after Quian. And you."

She tried to keep her voice light, but anger seeped in. Her camera was still out on the table, and she collapsed the lens, flicking the latch to secure it. It slid seamlessly into the leather pouch at her thigh.

"I am sorry about Quian."

It was too soon. She wanted an apology, but—not like this. Not with that tone.

"I don't want to talk about it," Nix muttered.

Too late: she was back in the Dive Room, the day of the tunnel collapse. The dripping water and the hiss of decompressing dive suits, the groans of sixteen soldiers—Osaga and Betalan dive teams—the ones who survived. Nix lying on her stomach by the pool's edge, ready to inch back in, ready to swim until she died if it meant finding Kessandra and Quian.

They'd gone in together. They had to be together.

And then, just as she tried to slip into the murky water... Kessandra surfaced. She wrenched off her helmet right there in the middle of the pool. Nix couldn't remember her expression or tone—not with certainty.

But she remembered the words. They never left her mind.

"Quian didn't make it."

The memory passed in a breath, merely a second in the present day, but it left Nix reeling.

"I miss him too, Nix. More than you realize." Kessandra's tone was soft.

Was she trying to fix this? Right now, on this ship,

after manipulating Nix into coming here at all? It was too much — the walls were closing in.

Nix slammed her fork down, her whole body stiff.

"You knew him for two months. He was my best friend. And now he's gone." Her voice broke on the last word, and Kess was staring at her with such Lumos-damned sympathy it made Nix want to scream. Who the hell was she to offer pity, after everything? Who was she to stare at Nix like a child might clutch their beloved toy, broken beyond repair?

If Nix was broken, it was Kessandra's fault. Her words were vitriolic. "He's dead, and that's on you."

Kessandra scowled. "I didn't cause the tunnel collapse — "

"You didn't *save him*."

"That's because he shouldn't have needed saving!" Kessandra hissed the words, and they pierced like one of her bullets might.

Silence.

"What are you implying?" Nix's fingers wound around her fork, as if she might use it as a weapon instead. She leaned over the table, blind with fury — Kessandra was all that existed. "Think *long* and hard about your response."

Kessandra's face rearranged into a neutral mask, although her fingers trembled against her glass. She drew a short breath. "I'd hoped we could resolve our history, but perhaps it's best we leave our ghosts in the Crypt. You are dismissed, Sergeant. Cool off and rejoin me in the morning."

Nix barked a hollow laugh. "Isn't that typical? Pulling rank to avoid the hard conversations."

"You are compromised, and we haven't even left Valkeshia." Kessandra narrowed her eyes, all business now. "If you can't separate our past from the current issues, you have no position at my side."

The intercom crackled, and a polite voice came on the intercom:

"Attention, guests of the Luminosity. This is Captain Navaan. Our journey to Fall is commencing; please prepare for the dive."

The ship jerked, and everyone below them laughed and squealed as the *Luminosity* began to move along the metal rails. Through the windows, the docks smoothly slid away, and the entire ship began a gentle incline towards the ocean.

Kessandra held her gaze, lips pressed into a tight line. "You are dismissed, soldier."

Nix briefly wondered about Polaris, about the Elites, about Kessandra being left alone. The commander was clear: protect Kessandra at all costs. But the ship was moving now — she was officially trapped on the *Luminosity*.

No going back.

Nix's chest tightened, and she felt hot all over. Fury made her want to scream; terror made her want to cry. She would have been excited to watch the ship submerge, but she remembered Quian last time, pressed against the glass with anticipation bright in his eyes.

"*We'd better hope it's watertight,*" he'd said, not bothering to hide his wonder as gray water slid up the portholes.

Nix had laughed and shoved his shoulder. "*If it isn't, we'll go down together.*"

Her heart was breaking all over again.

Kessandra hadn't moved. Her gaze was hard, unforgiving.

Without a word, Nix fled.

11

SHE HAD NO PARTICULAR DESTINATION IN MIND—JUST *away*.

It wound up being a difficult task. The ship could carry a thousand passengers, and it seemed like all of them were out and about. Nix wove through crowds as dense as the army mess hall during dinner, ignoring gasps as people realized she was armed—murmurs of confusion when they saw the ichoron tinge of the sarrant's hilt.

It faded into the background, muted chatter that became a gramophone looping amidst the chaos in her mind.

To drop something like that—to imply that Quian was an incompetent soldier—for Kessandra to *pardon herself* from the guilt of his death... It was too much. Nix had half a mind to march back to the dining hall and rekindle that fight, but she was still a soldier—and a dismissal wasn't something she'd challenge.

The last thing she wanted was to see that asshole again tonight.

Nix exited the other end of the promenade, where a grand staircase swept to another bank of elevators, and guest staterooms spread in three long hallways through the center of these decks. Nix marched right into them, because at least here she wasn't facing *people*—frivolous spirescraper citizens shopping for ichoron jewelry while soldiers high above them prepared for death.

Nix's chest was tight. As she passed two teenagers, one asked, "Hey, are you alright?"

She was sweating, she realized, her heart thudding in her chest. The world had narrowed to a singular directive: *get away*.

But there was nowhere to go.

"Fine," Nix gasped, and broke into a run.

The claustrophobic hallway of staterooms opened into the back end of the ship—which would become the front end as they neared Fall. And here, *finally*, she found what she'd hoped for. The library, a massive room identical in size and shape to the dining hall. Water had already washed over them—the glass dome high above was black as night, the stars already gone.

They were descending into the Deates Sea now.

The library's lower level operated as a reading lounge. Ornate pillars and curving archways formed divided seating areas, tastefully decorated with chaise lounges, armchairs, and couches. A few bookshelves were bolted into the walls, but the actual library was on the upper level, accessible through a massive staircase curving in the center of the room.

Stewards swept through the crowds—sparser here, thank Lumos—and offered after-dinner cocktails off rose-gold trays. The people here were a quieter sort, more intent on muted conversation and soft laughter than anything boisterous.

Nix wearily climbed the staircase to the upper level, slipping past the drapes that adorned the archways. Out of sight, she braced against a cool marble pillar near a long stack of bookshelves, pressing her forehead to the stone, drawing deep breaths.

She needed to get a grip.

Quian was gone. *Kessandra* was alive—but if Nix didn't control her anger, she wouldn't be for long. And that would have sweeping ramifications not only for Nix's family and career, but the entire future of Valkesh.

But she swore she felt Quian's eyes watching her from the shadows.

Tears slid down her cheeks, and for once, she let them. Her gasps turned into shuddering sobs, and the breakdown felt like a massive relief. But it was too vulnerable—she was too exposed here.

Blind with grief, she staggered away from the pillar, deeper into the maze of bookshelves. Unlike the main entrance to the library, the lighting was softer here—just bright enough to read the books' spines. And no one was grabbing novels yet; the atmosphere of the *Luminosity* was too new, too exciting.

In a few days, this place might be packed, but for now it offered an anonymous reprieve.

The circular wall that enclosed the bookshelves had a few portholes, and as she stumbled along it, she found a pair of armchairs facing a slightly larger window. No one else was around, and it was well-hidden from any prying eyes. Nix whispered thanks to Lumos or anyone else listening, and sank into the armchair.

And here, she allowed herself to unravel.

Shortscraper citizens didn't put much stock in the concept of "fair," but Nix couldn't help the fury that set off another wave of tears. Because Quian hadn't done anything wrong. He'd been goofy, fun-loving, with an infectious smile and an eye for detail. He'd shared his passion for all things with the world, and even the camera at Nix's hip felt like an echo of something real.

Lumos blessed, she missed him.

And now she was in this ship for the fifth time, trapped, descending to the depths of the ocean with a woman who didn't even *like* her anymore, not the way Nix needed, and it was all too much. Her rigid control disintegrated, and she wept.

And of course, that's where Doctor Hallie Jesko found her.

"I keep telling the primarch that we need to build psychological analysis into our military training. Does he listen? Nooo."

The older woman plopped into the chair across from Nix, displacing her thick black glasses to massage her eyes. "Don't worry, Sergeant. I'm not going to report that you're unstable." Nix recoiled, but she held up a hand, clearly trying to reassure. "It's okay. This is a very natural response to all you've seen."

Her bedside manner was shit.

Normally, Nix respected doctors. Today, she found it hard to muster a polite tone. Nix swiped her eyes, glowering. "The fuck are you doing here?" She didn't need anyone hinting that she was unstable. This was a moment of weakness, one Nix thought she'd endure in private. It had her temper balancing on a knife's edge. "Leave me alone."

"My job is to aid recovery. Most of my cohorts take that literally, but I find value in the psychological aspect." Hallie tapped her temple. "Our brains are our greatest strength. Did you know we can measure electrical impulses in a brain even *after* death? They're incredible."

Nix didn't want to think about death, or dying, or a brain surviving after someone was gone. If she stayed here, she'd say something inexcusable to a doctor who clearly prioritized Nix's fellow soldiers.

She pushed to her feet, spinning to stalk through the row of bookshelves.

Hallie caught her arm, pulled her back. "Hang on, hang on. I'm sorry, alright?"

"You didn't do anything wrong, doctor," Nix muttered. "But I'm not in the mood right now."

"Because of something Kessandra said?"

It stilled Nix, made her remember that this woman could still be a threat. Instantly, her body slid into assessment mode, every nerve tight, every sense on alert. Hallie was clad in a modest blue dress and heels, with a string of pearls around her neck. She wasn't wearing any ichoron, which was surprising for someone of her status. Her hair had been coiffed into a fancy up-do, and her glasses looked bigger than ever.

Nothing about her screamed that she could do damage, but Nix wasn't stupid. Enemies came in all shapes and sizes.

"The subarch is none of your concern," Nix said tightly.

Hallie gestured back to the seat. "She'll be *your* concern, if you don't stop and listen to me."

That piqued her attention. After tonight, Nix was looking for any reason to write Kessandra off entirely. Slowly, she sank back into her armchair. Her cheeks were still wet, and she wiped them on her shoulder.

Hallie pretended not to see. Instead, she gestured at the window. "I always hate this part of the journey—the darkness feels so oppressive. But by tomorrow, the ocean will begin to brighten. We'll reach the leviathan fall by midday, and by tomorrow night, the bioluminescence will be as bright as daytime."

It was pitch black out the window. Nix folded her arms. "Is this some kind of metaphor? 'Things get better,' is that what you're saying right now?"

"No poetry in your soul, hmm? You have a camera—I expected an artist's spirit."

Nix brushed the leather satchel at her thigh. She forced her tone to remain measured. "You expected wrong. What do you need?"

Why are you here?

Hallie leaned forward, hands laced over her knees. "Your charge is making enemies, and it isn't going to get better once you reach the Crypt."

Her use of the word had Nix blinking in surprise—typically, that was a soldier's term. Civilians just called it "the mines," or something similar.

But Hallie noticed her reaction and smiled grimly. "I've treated *many* soldiers who have crawled back from that place. I know it has that reputation for a reason—and I know Kessandra's suspicions about what we're mining there."

This material is poisoning our population.

Nix had dismissed it in their suite, but now the doubts came roaring back. She cast a glance over her shoulder, but they were alone. Downstairs, people laughed quietly, talked freely, but they'd found a private corner of the world. Hallie clearly intended to use it.

"Is it true?" Nix breathed.

Her father, taking that medicine every day. The Elites, fellow soldiers corded with ichoron muscles, strengthened by its sway. This entire ship, flaunting their ichoron like jewels. Nix's gaze slid to the sarrant propped at her chair, and dread inched along her spine.

"That ichoron is toxic?" Hallie tilted her head, considering. "It's possible, but it's affecting people at such a slow rate we're unable to identify it as a definitive cause. For a Valkeshian citizen, it's like saying the air we breathe is dangerous. It'd taint us from day one, so any results would be skewed."

Relief spread through her veins. Nix leaned back in her chair, a vicious smile crossing her lips. "Then Kessandra is wrong." She delighted in saying the words, delighted in how they tasted on her tongue.

Except Hallie wasn't smiling. "Subarch Kessandra is rarely wrong... and the longer this goes on, the more inclined I am to agree with her original assessment. She collected research, and at *eleven* years old, she presented her findings to the primarch. He dismissed them, then called in a panel of doctors—including myself—and told us in no uncertain terms that we were to 'find fault in her report.'"

Of fucking course he did. Nix gritted her teeth. "I figured the primarch would want to know."

"That his winning card is killing him slowly? Come on, Sergeant. You understand this game."

Nix shouldn't be surprised at how the primarch spent his time, not anymore. It didn't stop anger from flaring through her, hot as an inferno. She took a few moments to draw deep breaths, trying to calm her racing heart. It barely worked.

She wasn't angry at Hallie, not anymore, but it came

out that way. Accusatory. Tense. "Did you? Find fault in her report."

"My colleagues did. Fabricated results out of thin air, confident reassurance that ichoron is as safe as wood or stone." Hallie puffed an exasperated sigh, waving a hand. "But we're hardly *ingesting* wood or stone. We don't use it for implants, or give it to our soldiers as a serum. I handed the primarch the report he wanted—and then visited Kessandra for the first time."

Nix couldn't think about the primarch—about this monolith she couldn't fight, couldn't change. It felt like it was crushing her, same as the pressure of the depths. Kessandra was the threat available to combat, so Nix redirected.

"And you've been buddy-buddy with her since? Because I've never heard of you."

Hallie snorted. "That's because I value my life. I only performed her eyeball implant surgery at sixteen at her behest: a way to solidify our loyalty through public commitment to ichoron advancements, while offering us private data on its effects."

A human test subject. Nix scowled. "Seems like a stupid risk."

"A dethalos diagnosis is incredibly rare—so far, Kessandra hasn't been affected by it, obviously. But that implant does allow Kessandra to monitor herself." Hallie set her jaw. "I wasn't happy about it, but she was quite determined."

"Glad to hear you two are buddies. Is that why you

boarded the ship? To help us in the mines?" Suspicion laced Nix's tone. She still didn't quite trust the doctor's claims—not until she could get confirmation from Kessandra. In the meantime, she'd keep the details of their mission private.

Hallie laughed. "No. If the primarch found out I was lurking around that investigation, he'd have me killed. However, if there's a possibility of it linking with our research, I need to know. By official standards, I'll be revising curriculum at the university."

"And clearly, I'm vital to that." Nix couldn't help her sarcasm.

"You're responsible for protecting Kessandra. I'm here to confirm your suspicions."

Nix kept her voice neutral. "I don't have suspicions."

Hallie tapped her cheek, contemplating. "Somehow, I doubt that. I'm sure you've talked with Kessandra at some point, and I'm sure you'll stroll back to her to verify this. So, let me be as clear as possible." The doctor's tone lowered, deadly serious now. "The primarch can't control Kessandra anymore. His next goal will be to bury her under the weight of an entire ocean, just like he tried to do four years ago."

Four years.

The Hectron Tunnel Collapse.

Nix's chest tightened, and she shoved to her feet. "I don't want to talk about the collapse."

Hallie watched her carefully, cautiously. She pushed her glasses up her nose. "Sergeant. It is vital you realize this: that 'accident' was nothing of the sort. Kessandra is a queen on a board of pawns, and she's moving faster than the king can control. If you aren't careful, history *will* repeat."

Nix couldn't handle this… this implication that Quian was murdered just for being an innocent bystander in some bigger scheme. If Nix hadn't sat down with Kessandra at that lunch table the night the *Luminosity* disembarked, would he still be alive?

A hot, dangerous fear ignited in her soul. Because Quian was gone, but someone else was lingering on the outskirts of this political game.

Leon.

She couldn't lose another friend. She couldn't find Leon's bloated body crushed under rubble, face frozen in a scream. Maybe Kessandra didn't think these soldiers needed protecting, but Nix knew otherwise.

Her friends. Her squad. She hadn't lost a soul in years.

And she wouldn't. Not again.

Cold determination settled, quelling her trembling hands and washing over her like the icy Deates Sea. She needed to find Leon. She needed to protect him.

"I'll keep the warning in mind. Thank you for taking the time." Her words were biting, forcibly polite. The doctor watched her carefully, as if assessing her response to this information.

Maybe this was carefully planned. Maybe Hallie genuinely felt Nix should know. Either way, Nix was done entertaining Kessandra—or any of her supposed "colleagues."

"If you'll excuse me, doctor." Without waiting for a response, Nix left.

And this time, Hallie didn't stop her.

12

GONE WAS THE PANIC—THIS TIME, NIX MOVED through the ship with unwavering purpose: reach the upper decks.

While many had retired for the evening, others were just getting started. She wove through the promenade. The shops were closed, but the many lounges were abuzz with jovial conversation. Four photographers had set up shop in the promenade's center—a large "outdoor" café surrounded by leafy plants—and were capturing the memories as fast as their shutters would allow.

That reminded Nix she'd need to get more film soon. The darkroom was along the ship's other side, a few decks above the library. Surely Josie, the lead steward, could give her the code to develop her pictures in privacy.

A conundrum for another time.

She joined a stream of people climbing into elevators going up: either to the gambling hall, the theater, or another late-night attraction. The people here had clearly enjoyed the evening *too* much, since most of them were hunched together, giggling, murmuring. A few reached out to feel her sarrant, and she swatted their hands away.

"Military only," she said to one particularly drunk guest.

The girl squinted back at her. She couldn't be older than nineteen. "Aren't military supposed to be upstairs?"

She slurred the word "supposed."

Nix smirked, crossing her arms. "Aren't you supposed to be drinking age before getting wasted?"

"I'm—" the girl paled, covering her mouth. "Gotta go —" and she bolted from the elevator as the doors dinged open. She didn't make it far before doubling over a huge potted palm, puking into the soil. A few other guests on the elevator dissolved into laughter. One distinguished young man rolled his eyes.

Nix wrinkled her nose. "Lovely."

"Indeed," he said drily.

The doors slid closed again, and they left the girl to her misery. At the top floor, deck nineteen, anyone leftover filed out and delved into a long, luxurious hallway that opened into a wide gambling hall. It echoed with bells and whistles, shouts and cries. Patrons enjoying themselves — and the *Luminosity* staff enjoying their coin.

Nix nodded to the man. He strolled to a poker table, and Nix pivoted towards the stairwell that led to the military decks. Normally, the stairs were sealed off with a heavy door—one designed to stop water flowing between decks in the event of a breech. But Kessandra had revealed a weakness: the circular lock had an override switch at the base of the door.

Nix bent there now, feeling along the edges until she found a familiar cover. She popped it off, flicked the heavy toggle inside, and smiled as a *click* echoed in the small stairwell.

Time to go home. Or as close to "home" as Nix could find on this ship. She spun the handle and opened the heavy door, slipping through it in seconds. It sealed behind her, leaving no evidence she'd intruded at all.

Straightening, Nix continued into another world.

Unlike below, where everything was designed for aesthetic first, utility second, the army decks were absurdly simplistic. It was the difference between a spirescraper and a shortscraper—the cold, metal walls devoid of any ichoron touches almost made Nix feel like she was back in the Marr casten.

Almost.

Half of these decks were devoted to the ship's necessities—power, water, sewage. There was an entire deck dedicated to the air machines, which circulated oxygen through the ship. In Fall, they produced oxygen with plants, and twice a year pumped in air from the surface. On the *Luminosity*, though, the ship opened its windows to grab fresh air anytime it docked at Valkeshia.

The rest of the upper decks was a mockup of everything that lay below. A mess hall mimicked the dining room, a lounge would transition into a gambling hall or theater or anything else the soldiers desired. Barracks offered little privacy, but privacy was hardly the point for dive teams.

Dive Team Dialta, Leon had said. Nix mentally oriented herself and walked with confidence toward the mess hall. They'd all still be up. The first night on the *Luminosity* was always set aside for drinking and socializing.

Of course, she didn't make it fifteen steps down the long hallway before she came upon a viewing area. The old rocking chairs were still there, hard pieces that were beaten with age and use. They faced a window—one of the only big ones up here. Nix's breath vanished.

Quian hadn't brought his camera to Fall, but she remembered him tugging out a piece of parchment and a set of charcoal. Just like they used to in the Marr casten, he'd dropped to the ground and began to sketch.

Nix remembered craning over his shoulder, squinting at the huge black splotch on the center of the page.

"What is that?" she'd drawled.

He'd grinned. *"Depends on what you're looking for. I say it's a masterpiece."*

"Looks like a porthole."

"That's the beauty of abstract. It can be anything you'd like." And he'd scribbled until the splotch became a porthole, identical to the ones littered around the ship. He signed it with a flourish, handed it to Nix. *"A Marr original. Keep it in the family."*

She'd misplaced that picture, somewhere in the chaos of a whirlwind romance with Kessandra and a harrowing journey to the mines. When she remembered to look for it after—well, after—she found it missing. Lost to time.

Her heart ached. Nix absently tugged out her camera, flicked the latch open, and unfolded the lens. In a few seconds, she snapped a picture of the old chairs, illuminated with yellow light against a black window.

"Sergeant?" a disbelieving voice said from the entrance to the mess hall.

She glanced down the hallway to see Leon flanked by two other soldiers. One was a short woman with rich brown skin and a curious smile. The other was a bulky man with tan undertones who moved with a dangerous grace. They straightened imperceptibly at her title—most of the people who deployed to the Crypt were ensigns.

"Nice outfit," Leon drawled, folding his arms.

Nix glanced at her button-down shirt, the formal vest, the black slacks, and wrinkled her nose. "Not my choice, trust me." She pocketed the camera, striding over. "I told you I'd come say hello."

Meanwhile, her eyes roamed over him—but of course, he was in one piece. It was still a relief; she hadn't realized how much the good doctor had rattled her. Seeing Leon alive and well put her fears at ease and made it easier to smile in earnest.

Leon grinned back. "Missed me that much, huh?"

"More like the pomp and circumstance down there is a pain in the ass, and I needed a breather." Nix saluted the two other ensigns, satisfied when they mimicked the motion in crisp unison. "Sergeant Nix Marr. I'm on special assignment in the lower decks."

Most of Nix's other ensigns—Garith, definitely; Claire, probably, and at least three others—would have blurted Nix's mission simply for bragging rights. Luckily, Leon wasn't one of those ensigns. He kept his mouth shut, letting Nix decide how much to reveal.

Right now, she wasn't feeling very proud of her position guarding Kessandra, so she stayed quiet.

"Ensign Jakart Helsyon," the bulky soldier said.

The girl beside him stood stiffly. "Ensign Riles Reslet." She fidgeted with long hair tied in a tail at her neck.

"A pleasure," Nix said. "Are you both Dialta?"

Jakart puffed with pride. "Yeah. The rest of our dive team is in there, but Riles wanted some quiet."

"Leon said he did too!"

"He's being nice," Jakart teased.

Riles flushed, ducking her head. At her side, Leon chuckled, clapping her back. "I wouldn't mind a breather. Been a long day, huh?" Now his eyes cut to Nix, and a meaningful look passed between them. "But maybe you two can give us a minute? I'll see you back at the bunks."

Jakart and Riles waved at Leon, saluted Nix, and strolled toward the staircase. Only once their heavy footsteps were gone did Leon rock back on his heels.

"Everything okay, Nix? You look… less than solid."

"It's fine," she lied. "How are you settling in?"

Leon smiled, gesturing over his shoulder. Behind him, dozens of soldiers were enjoying their night. Several were playing cards, a few others were arm wrestling, but most were just sitting around chatting. Meeting each other, forming those vital connections, bonding over what was to come.

It made Nix acutely aware that she had no place on these decks, now.

"Things are great here." Leon shrugged. "This is a lot more fun than you implied."

Nix narrowed her eyes. "You know this part isn't what I meant."

His expression sobered. "I know, Sergeant."

It was kind of rude, tossing him into the future when he was trying to enjoy the here and now. She fumbled for a topic change, settling on: "Where's the lieutenant?"

There was always a lieutenant in charge of supervising the dive teams over this three-day journey. She'd hoped for more information—maybe a name to see if it was the same crotchety bastard from her last tour—but Leon just glanced around the mess hall.

"Ah, upstairs, I think?"

Awkward silence passed between them.

"I—guess I'll go. You can get back to your dive team," Nix said, gesturing up the stairs. "They seem nice. Smart."

"Jakart has more kills than any ensign in the sixty-first, if you can believe it. And Riles kicked my ass in a practice fight." Leon rocked back on his heels, his gaze softening. "I'm okay, Nix. You don't have to worry about me."

Nix spluttered. "I'm not—"

Leon quirked one eyebrow, lips tilting upwards.

It was so achingly familiar that Nix cut herself off, started laughing instead. "Okay, maybe a little." She rubbed her neck. "It's a tough habit to break, but I'm glad you're settling in well. Before I go, come with me. I need to show you how to access the lower decks."

"You think you'll need backup?" he asked, following her seamlessly. Just like old times. "Is the subarch really in danger? Or... is she the danger?"

"Tough to say." Without hesitation, she offered an abbreviated version of everything: Polaris, the Elites, Hallie's warning. The only thing she kept secret was ichoron's volatility—no reason to scare anyone until they knew for sure.

Nix still didn't really believe it.

She couldn't believe it.

Over the course of explaining, Leon's expression shifted from interested to disturbed. Near the stairwell, he stopped, his jaw clenched. "So, Doctor Jesko thinks the Hectron Tunnel Collapse happened because the primarch was trying to kill Subarch Kessandra?" His words were whispered, barely audible, but forceful enough to make Nix grimace.

"That's her theory."

Leon shifted his weight. "I'm shocked the primarch would willingly destroy a section of the mines."

Hearing it out loud formed a lump in Nix's throat. She couldn't hear "mines" without thinking "Quian," and the implications of this weren't something she cared to unpack right now. His dream camera felt heavy in the pouch on her thigh.

She didn't have any pictures of Quian. Only a few existed, and she hadn't felt right taking them from Melana. Now, she desperately wished she'd been more selfish.

No. What she really wished was that Kessandra never met them to begin with. Never brought a country's worth of political coups with her. Then Quian would be safe. Her voice was flat and dull. "I think he'd do just about anything to maintain control. Ichoron would be a small price to pay."

Leon's brow knitting together. "Even kill good soldiers like your friend? That goes against everything he stands for."

"I don't..." the words stuck in Nix's throat, and she had to force them out. "I don't think he was an intentional death." Admitting that out loud was hard, because it almost absolved Kessandra of blame. An accident. Everything in Nix recoiled at it; "an accident" was too clean. Too simple. The primarch may have organized the collapse, but *Kessandra* was at fault. She'd been positioned at the entrance, funneling soldiers to safety.

Why didn't she pull Quian out?

He shouldn't have needed saving.

Anger and sadness swelled in her chest, but Leon was watching, so she stuffed it down again. Now wasn't the time. A few slow breaths calmed her nerves, steadied her voice. "The Hectron Tunnel was mostly tapped out anyway. Its loss barely affected Ichoron output."

"Convenient," Leon muttered.

Nix crossed her arms, almost hugging herself, and glanced around the hallway. They were alone, of course. The upper decks had a much smaller population in a similarly huge space, so in some ways, it was more relaxing than everything below their feet. "It would have been an easy excuse to kill Kessandra without any questions."

Much as she loathed to admit it.

Leon firmed his resolve. "Okay. I believe that he wanted her dead. Now my question is *why?*"

Nix couldn't answer that without voicing Kessandra's concerns about ichoron. She shrugged. "I mean, she's an ass. I can't blame him."

Leon was startled into a laugh. He clamped his mouth shut, but his eyes still wrinkled in mirth. "Sergeant, you're going to get in trouble, talking like that."

Nix grinned back, feeling a bit lighter.

Amicable silence now. This was a lot closer to her hope for this visit.

"Come on," she said. "There's an emergency latch on the bottom of this door. It's well hidden, but once you know about it, transitioning to the lower decks is easy."

She led him to the door, walked him through the technique. Once the door was open, she stepped onto the other side—the side to the gambling hall, the fancy elevators, the promenade. Kessandra. Where she belonged, now.

It pulled at her heart. In that moment, she'd have given anything to follow Leon to his dive team's rooms, toss herself onto a tiny bunk, and chat the evening away with new friends. But of course, that wasn't her reality anymore.

"Just stay alert, all right?" She clapped his shoulder. "If I need you, I'll send word... somehow." Maybe Ramona could call one of the phones here in secret — she didn't want the lieutenant knowing she was stealing one of his soldiers.

"Same to you," Leon replied, his tone grim. "I'll try to swing by the promenade tomorrow night, after everyone is asleep. Maybe we can reconnect there."

"Affirmative," Nix replied.

He saluted, the picture-perfect ensign.

Lumos, she missed her old life.

She gripped the door, easing it closed. Before she shut it entirely, her eyes met Leon's over the threshold. "I'm glad you're here, Leo. It's nice to have a friendly face nearby — even though it was a damned stupid move, picking this deployment."

"I learned from the best," he replied, grinning.

A sadness lingered in his eyes, though.

Nix sympathized. She saluted and closed the door. A quick spin locked it again, sealing her away from her backup. Nix drew a breath, stared at the ceiling while she composed herself, and turned on her heel to head for the elevators.

It was probably time to go find Kessandra.

Lumos, she was tired.

Still, when she approached the bank of elevators and movement caught her gaze, Nix dodged on instinct — and a sarrant's ichoron blade whistled past her head, slicing a few hairs.

An attack.

She ducked out of the way and unsheathed her own sarrant in one fluid motion, spinning to face her opponent. And dread crept along her bones — because the man staring down at her was one of Polaris's Elites.

Fuck.

They were perched between six elevators, with the stairwell to her right and the gambling hall opening on their left. Several nearby card tables were surrounded by patrons tossing ichoron chips into the center like they were candy. A few strolled past the entrance with drinks in hand, but anyone who glanced their way was quickly distracted by the bells of winners across the hall.

Still, *someone* would be intervening soon. Right? They'd call a steward, or the ship's security, and put a stop to the fight.

But one look at the Elite proved it wouldn't happen fast enough. Not with his swift movements. Not with the drunken distraction and noise of the gambling hall.

She was alone... for now, at least.

Nix tensed, circling the Elite. His sarrant was clearly custom, a brutal variation of their typical blade-spear. The hilt was slightly shorter than usual, wrapped in leather—but the blade was easily twice the width of Nix's and sported wicked serrations near the base. With its ichoron edge, he could probably cut a body in half.

"Not even a hello?" she drawled, feigning more confidence than she felt. "This is a pretty bold place for an attack."

The Elite narrowed his eyes. "I have my orders. No one will question me."

Orders... from Polaris, no doubt.

"They might if I'm bleeding on the carpet. Look, there are easier ways to know if I'm a threat. You could *ask*, for one." Nix paused, considering. "I mean, the answer would be 'yes,' but it's politer than trying to decapitate me." She shifted her grip towards the pommel of the sarrant's hilt. Holding further from the blade meant losing some of the fine control used for short, piercing motions, but gave her more reach and power.

Something told her she'd need it.

His lips tilted upwards. "In another life, we might have been friends. In this one, you're fucking with the tertiarch, and now he's questioning *our* loyalty." Any humor vanished. The Elite spun his sarrant casually, and it moved like an extension of his own arm. "Soldiers follow orders. So, here's yours. If you want to survive this trip, stay out of our way."

"Mmm. Pass."

"Shame." Without warning, he lurched forward, blade glinting in the incandescent lighting. He moved like a creature possessed, dangerously fast. She barely saw his blade fast enough to roll out of the way—and then he lashed out with a vicious kick and knocked her to the ground. Her breath left in a wheezing gasp, which only doubled when he slammed a foot into her stomach. Nix was left gasping for air that never came, agony ringing in her ears.

She was barely aware of screams from the gambling hall. Barely aware of anything but that rose-gold blade piercing towards her chest.

Numbly, Nix swept her own blade on instinct, metal clanging metal. His sarrant cut into the plush red carpet near her shoulder. Every nerve alight, Nix slammed her foot out, her fancy dress boots mercilessly cracking into his kneecap.

He grunted, doubling over.

There must be steel toes in these boots, then. How very like Kessandra to commission something so polished—and so dangerous.

Nix didn't waste the chance. She twisted into a kneeling position, simultaneously drawing a desperate, ragged inhale, and elbowed his face.

Bone crunched bone. A spurt of his blood splattered her face: direct hit to the nose, apparently. She leapt to her feet, gasping in pain, dancing away. He followed suit, blindly squinting in her direction—apparently even ichoron enhancements couldn't stop the physiological reaction of tears after a nose injury.

His sarrant was still buried deep into the carpet. As he

moved to wrench it free, she slashed at his wrist. He released the blade immediately, narrowly avoiding amputation. Nix seized the chance to drive him back from the sarrant, separate him from his weapon.

He grinned, blood staining his teeth. He seemed unsteady now, his eyes unfocused. "You could have been an Elite."

"I'll keep it under advisement," she wheezed. Pain from his kick had exploded in her side, but adrenaline kept it from coloring the fight. A distant part of her brain wished Leon had left the upper decks with her—at least she'd have someone watching her back now.

Too late.

His hand drifted to his side, and then a short, wicked dagger emerged from the folds of his shirt. She couldn't leap away fast enough this time. The short blade stuck in her shoulder, cutting deep into the muscle, nicking bone.

His hand clamped around her mouth, silencing her cry. His eyes were wild, almost unhinged.

"You'll die first. Kessandra is next." His hot breath brushed her cheek.

There was nothing amicable in his expression now.

A shot of fear lanced down Nix's spine—her mind already running options to escape, to survive—and then salvation came from a panicked shout. "Let her go!"

A gunshot echoed, inciting a round of screams in the crowd.

13

It was the interruption she desperately needed.

Even with her vision swimming and her breath shaky, Nix didn't take her eyes off the Elite. While he glanced at the sound of the gunshot, she bit his hand hard enough to taste copper. He recoiled, and she lashed out like a woman possessed.

If someone was dying today, it wouldn't be her.

Her sarrant buried in his side, cutting flesh like butter. Hot blood poured around the wound, but she withdrew quickly, staggering backwards.

His knife was embedded in her shoulder. It was an ichoron knife—rose-gold glinted beneath crimson. In a panic, she wrenched it out, pressed a hand against the bleeding wound. It stained her pretty white shirt a vivid red, darkened the black vest.

She must be a sight.

The gunshot had come from the gambling hall, where a dense crowd had formed. Most were hanging back, but one particularly bold guest—a spirescraper citizen, by his accent, with a pistol he clearly knew how to use—strode forward. The older man's gaze was dark as he looked between the two bleeding soldiers.

His eyes settled on the Elite. The guest must be ex-military, because he hesitated upon seeing the ichoron dusting the man's skin. Realization flashed in his gaze. Not good—between them, Nix would never rank higher than an Elite.

She contemplated pleading her case, but it was moot anyway. If this fight continued, she'd be killed. If the guest turned public opinion against her, equally dead. Nix did not love those odds, so while the bleeding Elite was distracted, she sprinted for the stairwell.

She thought about going *up*, but the only soldier she could trust there was Leon.

And if this Elite was attacking Nix... where was the other one?

Kessandra.

Nix catapulted herself down, down, down, gasping for breath, blood soaking her shirt. She was leaving a crimson trail right to deck one, she knew, but it hardly mattered. The Elite could very well be an intentional distraction, which meant Kessandra's only hope was Nix reaching her fast enough.

Kessandra was a solid fighter, but she specialized in

range—and these Elites clearly preferred an up-close-and-personal attack.

Her entire body felt cold with the thought. The staircase ended at the promenade deck, and Nix twisted into the elevator bank like the Elite was hot on her heels. From what she could tell, he wasn't—but that didn't mean much.

A few passengers, fatigued from the night's events, yelped as she barreled past. Their yelps shifted into gasps of horror when they saw the blood, but then she was gone, skidding to a halt in front of the private elevator to their deck. The brass key was heavy, smearing with red as she fumbled with one hand to insert it and summon the elevator. Her left arm wasn't responding well after that dagger wound, but it was a problem for another time.

It took an eternity to open, moments where her harsh breathing filled the hallway, where spots danced in her vision as she glanced over her shoulder. Her sarrant remained out and ready for an attack, and the Elite's blood dripped off it, too.

He didn't show.

The elevator doors opened, and she leapt inside, jamming the button for deck one. Only in the safety of the elevator did she slouch against the wooden wall and seize a calming breath. She was starting to shake, the reverberating effects of shock, but her mind was calm.

Protect Kessandra.

Nothing else mattered.

When the doors dinged open, Nix strode across the walkway, murder on her mind. The lounge in the deck's center was empty—Dominik was gone to who knew where—and Nix arrived at Kessandra's suite without incident.

She slammed a fist on the door. "Kessandra! Open up."

Nothing.

Fear sliced into Nix's mind—*you've failed; she's already dead*—and it solidified into something dangerous. Without warning, Nix kicked the door in. All the fancy ichoron locks in Valkeshia couldn't stop her from splintering the wood around it, and after a few tries, it shattered around her boot. She muscled inside, expecting the site of a massacre—

—and found Kessandra, wrapped in a towel.

Her skin was glistening, so she'd clearly just stepped out of the shower, but she already had her pistol in hand. Her ichoron eye narrowed at the pupil, and her gaze lingered on the crimson stain over Nix's left shoulder, the way it trailed down her shirt, tainted her sarrant.

Kessandra lowered her pistol. "Well. At least you're still standing."

Nix didn't even have the energy to roll her eyes. She simply began a sweep, room by room, checking every feasible spot an Elite could hide. When she dropped to her stomach to check under the couch, Kessandra sighed, like she was irate Nix was smearing blood on her carpet.

It was tough to stand again, but Nix managed it.

"There's no one here," Kessandra said, stepping into

the bathroom. A soft *thump* as the towel hit the floor. The water turned back on. Nix couldn't see past the bathroom door, but surely—*surely*—Kessandra wouldn't be stupid enough to continue showering.

But after Nix finished her sweep, closed the front door as best she could, Kessandra still hadn't resurfaced in real clothes. Irritation creeping into her mind, Nix peeked into the bathroom. The lights in here were bright, bold enough to illuminate Kessandra's silhouette behind the linen curtain. Steam curled near the bulbs above the mirror.

"Are you fucking *kidding* me?" Nix growled. With Kessandra alive and the Elites absent, Nix's mind had shifted to priority two: barricade themselves somewhere safe.

The subarch was making that *very* difficult.

Nines, indeed.

They needed to get into Nix's suite, with undestroyed doors that locked. Then, *maybe*, Nix could relax and treat her wound. The Elite's knife had cut deep, and her left arm was basically useless now, slick with blood and very cold.

"You're the one who interrupted," Kessandra said, as blasé as if they were chatting about the weather. "I highly doubt whoever attacked you will be stupid enough to try a second time tonight, but if you're concerned, feel free to stand watch." She began to hum, her dark silhouette reaching for a bottle of some kind of soap.

Nix slammed the door closed, staggering to the living room. Fucking royals.

Her gaze cut to the destroyed front door, and she groaned. In hindsight, it was a stupid move—severely compromising the safety of Kessandra's suite. Which meant they'd be stuck in hers tonight. That wasn't a bad call, just in case Polaris tried anything else... but the idea of spending nine solid hours with Kessandra was grating.

With little else to do, Nix towed one of the couches in front of the damaged door—at least that'd slow the Elites down. The very motion exacerbated her wound, which gushed with fresh blood. She bit her tongue before she could scream, or cry, or something. She needed to bind that injury, and fast.

If Nix had been smart, she wouldn't have removed his knife at all. She lectured that to her ensigns. The sixty-first would be laughing if they saw this.

The sixty-first. Shit, she'd forgotten about Leon. Could she get word to him? Would it matter, or was he safer away from her? If she called, she might pinpoint him as an ally—and then the Elites could find him next.

No, better to meet him tomorrow night, as planned.

With the front door barricaded, Nix staggered to the door adjoining their suites. She performed a similar sweep of her own rooms, but everything here was undisturbed. With shaking fingers, she undid the clasp on her camera's satchel, wiping her hands so she didn't damage the leather with her blood.

At least the camera hadn't broken in the fight, thank Lumos.

A distant roaring echoed in her ears now. She desperately wanted a nap.

Her breaths were hard to draw, and she carefully stripped her vest, then her bloodied shirt. It was a shame to use the suite's embroidered towels to staunch blood, but Nix was out of options. She shoved a hand towel against her wound, whimpered as it sent a wave of pain through her body.

She would never get used to being stabbed.

Bracing the towel with shaking hands, Nix stepped in the bathroom to inspect her side. Already, her stomach was blossoming in deep purple bruises. Damn, that Elite packed a solid kick. At least she broke his nose—probably —because he definitely cracked a few ribs.

She was rummaging through the bathroom drawers, hunting for a medical kit, or *something*, when a door closed in the living room.

Nix stiffened, lurching into the room. Her sarrant had been propped by the bedroom door, its sheath discarded beside it, and it was in her hand before she comprehended Kessandra strolling into her suite.

She was dressed in a blue nightshirt, but pulled on slacks for decency. Her long braids were twisted into a loose bun on the top of her head, and her green eye glinted with irritation. She gestured at the couch, locking the door adjoining their suites behind her.

"Take a seat, dear. You're about to fall over."

The nickname summoned their last conversation, and suddenly Nix wanted to be *anywhere* else. Her fingers could either hold the sarrant, or the bloodied towel draped over her shoulder, and she reluctantly released the weapon in favor of the alternative. "Don't talk to me like that."

Kessandra's tone hardened. "Fine. Sit down, soldier. Now."

An order.

Nix should have known.

Still, she couldn't exactly argue. Like Hallie said, Kessandra was rarely wrong—and the adrenaline from her fight had worn off. All that remained were vicious chills that wracked Nix's body, and the icy caress of air against her blood-slicked skin.

She contemplated the couches, but it was impossible to get blood out of leather. Every piece of furniture here probably cost more than a year's salary; Nix couldn't stomach it. Feeling dizzy, she sank into one of the wooden chairs beside the kitchenette's small round table instead. The cheese and meats were gone, the counter swept clean for the next day—so clearly *someone* had been here while she was gone.

Josie? Or another steward?

There were too many breaches of security on this ship. Nix's mind spun with deadly possibilities. She'd have to tighten all of it if they were going to survive.

Kessandra took the seat beside her, twisting in the chair to have access to her wound. She'd brought a heavy metal case from her quarters, and unclasped it now. Inside was a simple medical kit, complete with bandages, antiseptic, and pills for pain and fever.

"That could have saved your towel," Nix muttered, lifting it halfheartedly.

"Bite this." Kessandra offered a thick leather strap—a belt she'd folded over. As Nix wedged it between her teeth, Kessandra gently removed the towel, peeking at the wound beneath it. "It's deeper than I thought," she murmured, and tugged out a bottle of antiseptic. It drenched one of the thick squares of gauze in seconds.

Kessandra pressed it against the wound with little mercy.

Nix groaned into the belt as fire swept up her arm.

"—few more seconds," Kessandra was murmuring when awareness seeped back. The room reoriented itself as the flames faded, as Kessandra left the wound alone to tug out a needle and thread.

Nix spit out the belt, gasping for breath. "Stitches? Really?"

"Ichoron stitches, in fact. Unless you'd prefer to be bleeding from this wound the next time an Elite attacks?"

"How'd you know it was an Elite?" Nix grimaced as Kessandra struck a match, lit the nearby oil lamp. Considering the whole ship ran on electricity, they must have stocked the royals' rooms with those for ambiance. Quaint. Nix's words were laced with exhaustion, straining for humor. "Maybe I just picked a fight with a spirescraper citizen for fun."

"If you picked a fight with anyone, it'd be me. And the only one reckless enough to attack you would be operating under Polaris's orders." Kessandra almost

Rebecca Thorne

sounded amused. She held the needle over the flame.
Once the tip was red-hot, she waved it for a few seconds
before tugging out a tiny spool.

She was right; the thread gleamed rose-gold in the
lamp's flickering light.

"Is that a good idea? The ichoron?" Nix asked, fear
lacing her tone.

Kessandra raised one slim eyebrow. "I thought you
didn't believe me?"

It was almost *masterful* how Kessandra evaluated
people.

Nix held her gaze, jaw tight, gray eyes battling green
and rose-gold. "Don't fuck with me, Kess. I'm not in the
mood. Hallie told me she was working with you. She told
me that the primarch staged the Hectron Tunnel Collapse
to kill you."

For a moment, it looked like Kessandra might actually
answer. Her eyes drifted to Nix's, long enough to confirm
that she did, in fact, know this information. Long enough
to confirm that everything Hallie said was true—which
meant Quian *was* killed because of some political ploy.
Long enough that Nix began to think this was the moment
Kessandra would make amends for his death.

Instead, the subarch replied, "That's classified
information."

Betrayal was a bitter pill to swallow.

"Everything is, with you."

Kessandra's gaze dropped to the wound. Her jaw was
tight, her voice stiff. "There's a reason for that, Sergeant."

She sounded so frustrated that Nix couldn't even argue—not that she had the energy to try, anyway. She just watched in grim silence as Kessandra threaded the needle, as expertly as if she'd done this dozens of times before. They learned basic medical aid in the military, but even Nix wasn't comfortable with stitches unless it was necessary.

"Maybe we should call Hallie," Nix said.

Kessandra's lips twitched. "We can, if you'd feel more comfortable. If she's speaking so carelessly to you, I'll need to chat with her regardless. But I assure you, I'm fully capable—and I'd rather my bodyguard not lose more blood while we wait."

Plus, the Elites could be lurking in the hallways. Better to keep the doctor safe by keeping her *away*. Nix winced. "Fine. Do it."

Kessandra handed her back the belt, and Nix bit it again. She leaned against the table, her fist clenched as Kessandra bent over her wound. She wanted to pay attention, but the last of her adrenaline had faded away, and her shoulder was a burning mass of agony that pulsed in time with her heartbeats. The antiseptic seemed to have lit every nerve, and pain cut straight to the bone.

Her groan as the needle bit flesh turned into a muffled scream, but Kess didn't stop. On the second pull, Nix's vision faded. On the fourth, everything went blissfully blank.

She came to slowly, vaguely aware of Kessandra waving something foul-smelling under her nose. It made her gag, the vitriolic scent so strong it pierced the back of her throat and lingered, stirring nausea.

"We're done." Kessandra pulled the scent away, thank Lumos. Nix tried to focus, but exhaustion was pulling at the edges of her mind. It would be so nice to fall into bed, sleep this awful day away.

Maybe when she awoke, Nix would be very, very far from here.

Someone was patting her cheek. "Sergeant. Nix. Wake up."

Kessandra didn't even sound sympathetic. Nix groaned, forcing her head up, forcing herself back to reality. "Fuck off. I wouldn't even be *in* this situation if—" the words faded, and she groped for new ones. "—if you weren't... you." Was she slurring? It felt like she was slurring.

The subarch rolled her eyes. "Eloquent." With little regard for her patient, she looped an arm under Nix's uninjured shoulder. Kessandra was strong in her own right, and she had no trouble hauling Nix to her feet. "Come on, dear. I'll want a full report tomorrow, but for now, I think you've earned a rest."

Nix wanted to argue, but apparently she'd lost more blood than she thought. Her vision was blurry, and everything seemed like it was under water.

Heh. Because they *were* underwater.

At the windows, the vaguest hint of blue colored the glass. As Kess eased her onto the huge mattress, Nix stared at the inky black brightening beyond the porthole.

Everything felt fuzzy, but relaxing was hard when a threat still loomed. "The Elites —"

"We're well-barricaded in your suite. I've already alerted the *Luminosity*'s captain to your physical state — security is sweeping the decks for Polaris's Elites as we speak."

"They might attack the staff —" Nix breathed, pushing upright. Her stomach screamed protest, her knife wound throbbed, and she fell back against the cushions. "Josie could —"

"Josie wouldn't be stupid enough to confront an Elite alone." A threat lingered in that sentence, but Nix couldn't quite read into it. Kessandra breezed past. "If needed, Captain Navaan will mobilize the soldiers in the upper decks to help the hunt."

Nix relaxed a bit. That sounded better.

Now Kessandra's lips tilted in amusement. "It's quite impressive, what you've managed in just a few hours. Polaris was bound to make a mistake, but I didn't expect it so fast. You must have rattled him at dinner."

Nix unconsciously swelled at the pride in her voice — even as a niggling thought in her brain screamed, *that isn't a compliment, you moron.*

With Kess, it was hard to tell the difference.

"Glad to be of service," Nix mumbled, letting her eyes drift closed. "Wake me when they find him."

Those words were definitely slurred.

For a moment, it felt like Kessandra's fingers ghosted over her forehead, smoothing sweat-slicked hair from her face. But of course, that must have been a fevered dream, because when Nix opened her eyes next, the lights were off, and the room was empty.

Her eyes drifted shut again, and this time she slept until morning.

14

Nix awoke to a stern conversation in the living room.

It took her several minutes to realize why that was a problem. Her head felt like it had been wrapped in a blanket, smothering the outside world. It took a concentrated effort to pry open her eyes, and even more energy to process the ceiling of this place. It wasn't her army bedroom, or her father's apartment, so where —

The *Luminosity*. Fall. The Crypt.

Right.

Nix pushed herself upright, groaning softly. She was alone in this room, the door closed for privacy, and beyond the porthole, the ocean glimmered with soft blue light. They'd reached the deeper waters, then. It was pretty, shining like stars in the midnight sky — except every soft blue speck moved gently with the currents.

The conversation in the living room got a bit louder. Kessandra wasn't alone.

A spike of alarm propelled Nix to twist out of bed. Standing was perilous, considering how deeply her head pounded, how wildly her vision swam. Gripping the bed, she pressed a palm to her forehead—and paused.

She could move her left arm again. Painfully, but still. It was a welcome surprise.

Nix peeled back the bandages over her left shoulder, squinting at the wound. They used ichoron in the army spirescraper after bloody sparring matches, so this was nothing new. The ichoron stitches were doing their job; what had once been a vicious mess of skin and blood was now a thin scar.

This time, it made her skin crawl to see the rose-gold embedded in her body.

Lumos, she wished she hadn't come on this stupid mission.

Dried blood flaked down Nix's arm, stained her stomach pink. The sheets were flaked in it—if she'd had half a brain last night, she would have scrubbed down before falling to the mattress. Nix wrinkled her nose and gauged priorities. The conversation didn't sound urgent, although it was concerning Kessandra wasn't alone.

Her personal hygiene would have to wait.

She tugged a loose shirt over her bloodstained brassiere, retrieved the sarrant propped by the door, and strolled into the living room. Her steps were wobbly, but she'd dealt with enough battle situations to regain her head quickly after an injury. Now, her entire mind was focused on the intruder.

A well-dressed woman with deep bronze skin and minimal makeup was perched on the couch opposite Kessandra. She wore a hat pinned over thick hair, its green velvet fold adorned with an ichoron medal. Upon closer inspection, it was stamped with Valkesh's national insignia: Fall, Valkeshia's spirescrapers, and the silhouette of the primarch.

Her uniform was formal, almost militaristic, but deviated just enough that Nix couldn't pinpoint who she was looking at.

The woman glanced up, and her stern expression had Nix bristling. "Ah. The murderer awakes."

Across from her, Kessandra narrowed her eyes. It was an eerie motion with the ichoron eyeball, and lasted only a breath before her expression smoothed. She dipped a teabag into a porcelain cup. "Alleged murderer, Captain Navaan. Sergeant, why don't you take a seat?"

"I'd rather stand," Nix replied tightly. Her head was throbbing—it felt like someone had gouged her eye with a spoon. Because of the blood loss... or something worse? "What the hell do you mean, murder?"

"Hmm. Interesting that you don't know." Captain Navaan tilted her head.

Nix scowled. "I don't know because I was *unconscious* half the night."

At the couch, Kessandra's lips quirked, the barest motion of amusement.

Captain Navaan heaved a laborious sigh. "Well, then. Let's take a trip to the site of the incident, and perhaps that will jog your memory." She pushed off the couch, smoothed her uniform, and started for the door. The first aid supplies from last night had been tidied, the kit stowed in the armoire beside the door, but there were still bloodstains in the carpet. She paused for a moment, examining them, but didn't say a word.

Nix's eyes cut to Kessandra, who'd also stood. It didn't look like she'd slept much, considering the bags under her eyes. Most would never notice—the royals always looked impeccable—but Nix saw right through it, and guilt prickled in her chest.

Maybe it was the fact that Kessandra had helped her last night. Maybe it was the uncertainty of a new enemy, a new problem. Either way, Nix had a grudging respect for Kessandra in that moment. It felt, finally, like someone was on her side.

Because of that, Nix played the part Kessandra wanted. The perfect soldier.

At least this way, they'd present a united front.

"On your orders, Subarch?"

Kessandra scrutinized her for a moment, the ichoron eye zooming onto her wound, flicking to her face. It made Nix's cheeks warm, made her wonder if she should have changed or cleaned up a bit first. But with Captain Navaan at the door, clearly waiting for them, there wasn't time for much else.

"Bring your camera, Sergeant. That way no one can

compromise the evidence." Her tone held no accusation, but Navaan rolled her eyes nonetheless.

Nix couldn't blame her, though. Swiftly, she buckled the leather case around her thigh, checking that the camera inside was still safe. Her sarrant went over her back, same as always—Kessandra must have polished it overnight, because it was clean of any blood.

Captain Navaan led the way. They didn't speak as they passed the empty lounge, journeyed along the suspended walkway to the elevator.

Beneath their feet, the glass dome offered a stunning view of the ocean floor, maybe a quarter mile below them. The railway lifted them high above any obstructions, although they were still a distance from the leviathan fall. Soon, they'd see magnificent and terrible creatures from the deep awash with glimmering blue light—but here, it was mostly algae blooms that drifted in the currents.

Seeing it brought back stunning memories—memories of Kessandra, her face younger, illuminated by cerulean light as she brushed her lips against Nix's. The way even her ichoron eye seemed to soften in the glow, and suddenly it was just the two of them, a pocket of happiness in a dark, cruel ocean.

Nix's eyes lingered on the back of Kessandra's head. Last night didn't change things—not their history, not her feelings—but she'd seen firsthand how spirescraper citizens could upend a shortscraper's entire life. Nix could only hope Kessandra valued her enough to negotiate for her freedom.

Otherwise, Nix might well be fucked.

"Who died?" Nix asked as they stepped into the elevator. Surely, she hadn't hurt the Elite *that* much. He'd been alive when she left—but with a wound like that, it might not mean much. There were a lot of important, squishy organs in the stomach. It wasn't a stretch to think he'd bled out.

Maybe she did kill him.

It was self-defense, but word would travel if an Elite died… and she doubted anyone was paying attention to the beginning of that fight. The odds of a witness testifying that she hadn't *started* it were minimal.

Sweat prickled along her forehead. Every breath was a shuddering wheeze, and Nix had to favor her bruised side as she moved, or her ribs started screaming. There was a strong possibility she should have stayed in bed, because she'd be useless in an attack right now.

Across from them, Captain Navaan stepped away from the blood smears Nix had left the night before. The doors closed, and instead of answering, she said, "You left a convenient trail to follow straight down from the gambling hall." She emphasized the word "convenient" in a way that made Nix bristle. The woman moved on before she could argue: "Would you like a picture of this too, Kessandra?"

"*Subarch* Kessandra," Kessandra replied coolly. "You're in command of this vessel, Captain, but patrons of the *Luminosity* still follow our laws. One more slip, and my security won't be under your scrutiny… You'll be under mine."

Captain Navaan set her jaw.

The rest of the journey was spent in tense silence.

They exited the royals' elevator and stepped briskly through the promenade. Guests were out and about—it must be late morning, based on how Nix's stomach was grumbling—and if anyone else heard about the murder, they gave no indication of it. People milled from store to store, perched at the café, admired the bioluminescence out the window.

They walked past, entering the long hallway of staterooms Nix had crossed last night. Except instead of approaching the library, Captain Navaan entered another elevator, this one made of glass and iron. It opened above the library, in the atrium at the front of the ship.

This time, the door was sealed off, and two soldiers were posted at either side. Security on the *Luminosity* was a deployment all its own, viewed as a cushy retirement job for the soldiers who never desired more. They saluted the procession, but their expressions were grim.

Nix frowned, mentally bracing for what was inside.

But as they entered, it looked exactly like it had before: a huge observation platform that faced floor-to-ceiling windows. Barely visible through the windows were dual rails that disappeared into the abyss—the *Luminosity*'s track, a steel wonder that would lead them all the way to Fall. At the speed they were traveling, glowing algae blooms and deep-sea floaters slid past the windows at a dizzying rate.

Inside the atrium, it was another world. Tall trees and

dense flora occupied a veritable garden that sloped down from the platform, manmade and meticulously maintained. The air here was slightly humid and warmer than the rest of the ship. The railing at the edge of the platform was big enough to slip through, and Nix knew from personal experience there was plenty of space below it to relax in private.

And do... other things.

But the memories fell from Nix's mind the instant they approached the platform's edge. Because here, the scent of dirt and leaves was poisoned with acrid copper. The aches in Nix's body vanished as she realized the extent of the scene.

This wasn't just a murder.

It was a massacre.

Down the sloped path of soil and foliage, pieces of a body were strewn haphazardly. It was impossible to identify who the person—people?—had been, but it was obvious they'd been hacked to bits. Blood stained the dark ground, splattered on bright green leaves, painted yellow flowers crimson. A jaw, half-covered in flesh, caught her attention nearby. Its teeth were bloodied, and the head repulsively absent.

She'd seen a lot of death, but this still made her stomach churn.

Beside her, Kessandra had lost focus. Her eyes were fixated on the mess, but not in her normal, calculating manner. This time, she just seemed stunned, utterly disconnected from reality. And that scared Nix a lot more than the body beneath them.

Captain Navaan clasped her hands behind her back. It almost looked militaristic, except she was definitely a private spirescraper citizen. Army deployments were protection assignments, not commanding a pleasure cruise.

Still, she sounded like every army officer Nix had ever met. "Sergeant Nix Marr. Where were you last night? I want to know every detail."

"I —" Nix hesitated, still watching Kessandra.

The subarch hadn't moved.

Captain Navaan noticed too, now. She snapped her fingers. "Subarch. I figured, with your military background, you'd be fine facing this carnage. However, if it's upsetting your constitution, you may return to your suite."

She made no such promises for Nix.

That seemed to snap Kessandra out of it. She massaged her forehead, blinking hard, and glanced at Navaan. "It's not your place to worry about my constitution. I'm counting two distinct bodies. One is obviously an Elite. That leaves me to assume the other is Polaris."

Silence.

"You think two bodies are down there." It wasn't a question; Captain Navaan's tone was simply stating fact.

Kessandra put one hand on her hip, the picture of ease now. Her ichoron eyeball appeared cold and unfeeling.

"Considering how quickly you jumped to the conclusion of my bodyguard committing this crime, I'm unsurprised at your investigation skills. Retrieve Doctor Jesko; she'll confirm two separate corpses."

"We have our own doctors aboard the *Luminosity*."

"Yes, but none of them have hands-on experience with dethalos." Kessandra waited, scrutinizing Captain Navaan's gaze. When no recognition flashed, she tilted her head. "If you're unfamiliar with the concept, consider it another reminder that your control doesn't stretch further than this ship, Captain."

Brutal.

Nix stood ramrod straight behind Kessandra. She'd wanted Kess to fight for her freedom, but this wasn't a fight—fights implied an even playing field. This was a verbal slaughter, where Captain Navaan opened the door and Kessandra stepped out with her pistol raised.

The two women faced off against each other, tense and quiet.

Finally, Navaan smiled tightly. "I would not have wasted your time on circumstantial evidence, Subarch Kessandra." She flicked two fingers at a thin stairwell on the side of the platform, one so well-hidden Nix hadn't noticed it before. They stepped down it, planting feet on ground level, and moved toward the carnage.

"Sergeant," Kessandra said, gesturing at the bodies. A pointed hint that Nix had a job here—and it wasn't tagging along for a pseudo-investigation.

Nix tugged out her camera. Hopefully, she had enough

film to capture all this. There'd be utility in these images — especially if Navaan thought *Nix* had committed the crime.

For once, she was grateful she'd spent the night in Kessandra's company. Grateful to have an alibi. If the primarch really was out to get Kessandra, destroying the reputation of her chosen security was a solid way to start.

If Captain Navaan locked Nix in a cell for the rest of this journey, Kessandra would be exposed to the real killer — and if this *was* Polaris scattered at their feet, things got a lot more dangerous.

Mutely, Nix began snapping pictures. The jawbone, a scrape of scalp with short dark hair, a finger bone poking out of the soil. Down here, the smell of blood was nauseating, almost sickly sweet alongside the perfume of the flowers. She used an age-old army technique of breathing through her mouth and disconnecting from the idea that, just a few hours ago, this had been a living, breathing person.

People.

Whatever.

Meanwhile, Kessandra paused, kneeling beside a particularly disgusting lump of desiccated flesh. Navaan snapped to get her attention. "Over here, Subarch."

Kessandra rolled her eyes, but pushed to her feet and dutifully followed Captain Navaan to the base of a towering pine tree. It was identical to the kind that flanked the Sveltal Mountains, but nothing about it reminded Nix of home.

"Look up. But don't step underneath the branches—it's still dripping."

Kessandra wrinkled her nose and tilted her head, squinting into the boughs.

Nix edged closer to see what they were looking at. It was a head, impaled fifteen feet off the ground. Its jaw was missing, but the sightless eyes couldn't be mistaken: the male Elite who'd attacked her last night.

She never even got his name.

Nix felt cold all over. Her head was still pounding, and her shoulder ached. Every breath felt like fire, but she was *still* having a better day than that guy.

"He was *alive*," Nix said, without thinking. "Did you interview the witnesses? They must have seen him standing after I ran."

Kessandra massaged her brow, but didn't silence her.

Captain Navaan, meanwhile, narrowed her eyes. "Witnesses saw you flee—and him follow. I can't find conclusive evidence of what happened after that. Blood trails split between deck one and the atrium. But further inspection of the body—"

"Bodies," Kessandra corrected.

"… bodies… revealed that these cuts were made with an ichoron blade."

Now Captain Navaan's gaze settled on the weapon strapped to Nix's back.

Nix burst out laughing. "That's it? That's all you have? You know three people on this ship have ichoron blades.

Four, if you count the lieutenant supervising ensigns on the upper decks."

"Yes, but this man certainly didn't kill himself, and getting a blade from a highly trained Elite is nearly impossible. Except, apparently, for *you*—since eyewitnesses reported you separated this man from his sarrant during your scuffle at the gambling hall." Captain Navaan was unmoved, convinced of her theory. "Polaris's Elites had a longstanding history of service; one wouldn't massacre the other. And I've already confirmed the lieutenant was confined to his quarters all evening."

"Why?" Kessandra asked sharply.

"Excuse me?"

"Forgetting Marr for a minute—why was the lieutenant in his quarters?"

Captain Navaan's tone was laced with suspicion. "He came down with a stomach bug. It was quite apparent that he couldn't have left the upper decks last night."

"Nausea." Kessandra glanced again at the Elite's head, which was slowly dripping blood into the soil below. "Captain, this isn't a murder. This is an epidemic. I will personally attest that the sergeant was in my quarters immediately following that fight, bleeding out over her dining room table. She could never have made it all the way to the atrium."

Captain Navaan scowled. "You'll forgive me if I don't—"

"I'm under no obligation to forgive you—but if you act

quickly, you'll regain my respect." Kessandra stepped into Navaan's space. They were roughly the same height, but the urgency in Kessandra's gaze clearly made the captain uneasy. "You're wasting time pursuing my security for this crime. The attacker here was the other Elite, the female one. Clearly, the Elites met Polaris here, and she massacred them both."

"That's speculation."

"Huh. Speculation. Where have I heard that before?" Nix drawled, feeling spiteful.

Captain Navaan scowled. "Even if that were true, this is an isolated incident. Hardly an epidemic."

"*This* means you have a murderer on the loose—and if you consider the strength of an Elite, and the physical prowess of Tertiarch Polaris, you'll realize that only another Elite could have ripped them apart like this. So, Captain. Where is the female Elite?"

Silence.

"We haven't located her," Captain Navaan said, grudgingly.

"And you won't—all you'll find is the trail of corpses in her wake. Dethalos is an illness that incites violent rage in its victims. If it's reached your vessel, no one on the *Luminosity* is safe." Kessandra's tone was dark. "I recommend immediate quarantine—every civilian locked in their quarters. If you can, stop forward progress. Return to Valkeshia for military intervention."

Captain Navaan stared at her, as if waiting for a punch line.

She didn't receive one.

"The *Luminosity* can't be stopped, Subarch Kessandra. And considering this is the first time I've heard of 'dethalos,' I'm starting to wonder what's real—and what's a protective instinct to save Sergeant Marr from incarceration."

Kessandra exhaled a frustrated huff. "Check on the lieutenant and find out. Cross check my claims with Doctor Jesko. And when all the stars align, come find us on deck one." Now she lifted her chin, her ichoron eyeball piercing. "You are at a crossroads, Captain Navaan. If you value the life on this ship, you *will* take action."

Kessandra didn't give her the chance to argue. She spun on her heel and stalked toward the staircase.

15

THE SOLDIERS POSTED OUTSIDE LET THEM LEAVE THE atrium.

Nix was almost expecting them to grab her arm, forcibly detain her, then toss her in a cell somewhere in the upper decks. But they just saluted Nix, silent, maybe a bit curious. Kessandra didn't even look at them as she strode for the elevator, moving so fast a burning pain slid up Nix's side.

"Hang on," she gasped, staggering into the elevator. "I got the shit beat out of me yesterday, Kess. One second."

Kessandra barely looked at her, jabbing the button for the library's level. Only once the doors slid closed did she reply, "I need you to promise me something."

It made everything inside Nix prickle. Her mind slammed back to the mines, to the two of them crouched on her thin bunk, whispering promises that could never survive beyond the damp hallways of the Crypt. Nix leaned against the elevator's wall, pressing one arm against her side to mitigate the pain.

"That *highly* depends on what it is."

Kessandra considered her tone and heaved a sigh. The bags under her eyes seemed very pronounced now. "Never mind. I don't have the energy to argue with you today. Before Navaan locks down the ship, we'll need to get some errands out of the way."

"Errands—" Nix cut herself off, grimacing. "You really think she'll do a ship-wide lockdown because of one murder?"

"Two murders." Kessandra tugged a small rose-gold ring from her pocket, tossing it over.

Nix turned it over in her hands, vaguely recognizing it. "Polaris was wearing this at dinner. He rubbed it right before he left." She hadn't even seen Kessandra retrieve this, but she'd clearly found it in the atrium, based on the blood staining it.

"There are too many tertiarchs to track reliably. The primarch distributed those rings as a symbol of their royal standing."

"Naturally, the subarchs are too fancy for this shit." Nix handed it back.

Kessandra swelled a bit. "Well. I certainly don't need one. Regardless, it confirms my suspicions: Polaris is dead."

"Excellent. That means my job here is done. You're safe." Nix kept her expression impassive, humor nudging the edges of that statement. "Drop me off at the next stop, if you please."

Kessandra's lips quirked upward. "Cute." The doors dinged open as the elevator settled on the bottom floor, and she strode out with little regard for Nix's pulsing ribs. "I want you to develop those photos and bring them to our suite."

"*Our* suite?"

"You kicked my door down," Kessandra said stiffly. "Or did you forget that in your panicked haze? The stewards will be replacing our bedding and replenishing our fridges, but repairing a door will require a service order. I doubt approving that will be high on Captain Navaan's to-do list now."

"Can't you pick *another* suite? There's almost a dozen down there."

Kessandra stopped moving, pinning Nix with a serious expression. "Do you realize what's about to happen on this ship, soldier?"

Nix stiffened.

They were in the massive, circular entryway near the library now. People milled about, chattering about the bioluminescence through the windows, their future activities in Fall, or the book they'd read to occupy the day. Inside the library's lounge, someone started playing a grand piano, and the music covered Kessandra's next words.

"Anarchy." Kessandra hissed the word, gesturing at the guests nearby. "Look around. This entire vessel is filled with ichoron-enhanced people. The security is bare minimum, minus the soldiers on the upper decks. What do you think will happen when they're slaughtered where they sit? How do you think the survivors will react?"

A chill slipped down Nix's spine, freezing her to the spot. That—what Kessandra was talking about—was end-of-the-world shit. It was as ridiculous as the idea of Triolan forces flanking them through the Ever-Storm, as ridiculous as the Crypt Keeper hauling itself out of the waterlogged mines for a cup of tea.

Nix laughed, but nervousness filtered into her tone. "Come on, Kess."

Kessandra stared down her nose at Nix. She looked like a statue, cold and immovable. "Fear can propel someone into dangerous decisions. You, of all people, should know that."

She started to move again, but Nix grabbed her arm, spun her back. Someone across the hall stifled a gasp, and Nix realized too late she'd manhandled a subarch. She released Kessandra, but her tone was heated. "Hang on. You said 'ichoron-enhanced' people." Her shoulder twinged, and she swore she could *feel* the ichoron thread embedded in her skin.

Kessandra folded her arms, waiting.

Nix's gray eyes shifted to Kessandra's ichoron eyeball, which looked even more inhuman in the incandescent lighting of the library.

"*You're* ichoron-enhanced." Nix's words were breathy, and for once, true alarm filtered into her tone. Because if this illness affected Kessandra as well—if she went mad with violence—Nix wasn't even sure what she'd do.

Dethalos was a death sentence. Kessandra said no one afflicted with it survived, one way or another.

Despite everything, ugly fear took root in Nix's chest.

Kessandra, meanwhile, had a smooth mask over her face. She must be terrified, bitter, hurt... but her tone was devoid of emotion. "An astute observation, Sergeant."

"An astute—" Nix dug her hands through her hair, pacing away and back again. They were attracting attention, so she stomped to a nearby steward and snapped her fingers. "We need somewhere private. Now."

The steward flinched. "Uh... t-there's a lounge for royals and their guests upstairs. Behind the mythology section." He tugged a key off his pocket, unclipped it. His eyes were wide as she snatched it from his grasp.

"Great." Nix started up the curved staircase, and Kessandra followed like she was the guest of honor at a royal ball. It didn't take long to find the lounge, tucked on the opposite side of the library from where Hallie had confronted her the night before. It was a simple room with six armchairs and a bar—empty now.

Nix ushered her inside, checked the hallway for any lurking guests, and quietly shut the door. Only once it was locked did Nix spin on her charge.

Kessandra cut off her rant, her tone amused. "I can see you're angry."

So blasé.

Everything in Nix ignited.

"No *shit*. You knew about dethalos when you were a child. Doctor Jesko said you asked for the implant at sixteen. Lumos, Kessandra, what were you playing at?" Nix couldn't keep the fury from her voice. How fucking *reckless*.

Kessandra settled into one of the armchairs, resting her chin in her palm. "The primarch removed my ability to investigate claims of the disease. He destroyed my credibility in the circles that mattered. So, yes. I asked Doctor Jesko for the next best thing—a first-hand analysis of the most extensive ichoron implant we had at the time."

"The kind they reserve for soldiers who *lose their eyesight in war*."

"You should be glad they only recently released the newer surgeries. These days, they're replacing internal organs, plating bones, lacing veins." Kessandra wrinkled her nose. "All experimental, of course. Still horrific."

Nix paced the room, then stalked behind the bar. Now she needed a drink. "I don't care about those. You're seriously telling me that you asked for an artificial eye, on the researched assumption that it might turn you into a possessed monster."

"I requested an artificial eye knowing the risks, and preparing to document the reality of what happened, yes." Kess leaned back in her chair. "An educated decision— which is more than most of these surgery recipients are allowed. Did you think I implanted it for aesthetics?"

"A bit, yeah," Nix snapped. A gold-tinged bottle

caught her eye—valloch, like the commander was drinking in Valkeshia. *Expensive*, he'd said. Tough to distill. With vicious pleasure, she wrenched the cork out.

Kessandra sighed. "If you're playing bartender, I'd also like something."

Silence thrummed between them as Nix poured one drink... and begrudgingly added a second glass to the bar top. Kessandra didn't deserve the fancy liquor. Instead, Nix found a simple bottle of gin and a mixer of lemon soda inside the polished cabinets—lemon and gin would blend into something almost palatable.

Frankly, the taste of Kessandra's might be easier to swallow. Valloch was strong, bitter stuff. But knowing how expensive it was, and that someone in Valkeshia would be aghast at a shortscraper drinking it, had Nix drawing a spiteful swig.

She handed off Kessandra's glass, then slumped into the chair across from the subarch, trying not to wince at the methanol taste of the valloch. "So, what now? We take your eyeball out?"

"That's an extensive surgery. I can ask for Doctor Jesko's help, but it isn't something she can prepare for today. And if Captain Navaan follows my orders, we'll all be on lockdown soon enough." Kessandra swirled her drink. She surely noticed Nix's beverage choice, but instead commented: "The lemon was a nice touch."

"Don't. Don't try to be friends, Kess. I'm not in the mood."

Kessandra heaved a sigh and leaned forward, resting

her arms over her knees. "Then let me make this hyper-clear for you, Sergeant. I didn't summon you for some lovesick trial. This is not a romantic reunion. The moment I saw those photographs, I knew dethalos isn't as contained as we thought. The primarch was hoping to kill me on this journey, but a firsthand investigation of that site is necessary for my research regardless."

Nix numbly sipped from her crystal tumbler. "And now Polaris is dead, and his Elite is rogue."

"Precisely. The primarch is no more a threat to me than a butterfly in the greenhouses of Valkeshia." Kessandra tapped her right temple, indicating her ichoron eye. "But dethalos? That's what I've feared since I was a child. The sickness is spreading, and I suspect that the closer our proximity to the mines, the worse it will get."

"Sounds arbitrary." Nix prayed she was wrong.

"Everything is arbitrary—we have no idea why this happens. We only know it's linked to ichoron."

"So, what proof do we have that it'll get worse near the mines?"

Kessandra took a daintier sip, as if mulling over her next words. "How's your head after using those ichoron stitches? Are you feeling nausea? Dizziness?"

Nix stiffened. "Kess, you asshole. You didn't put those in to help me. I was another Lumos-damned experiment to you."

"You are *never* an experiment to me," Kessandra swore, and her fervor stunned Nix into silence. She pushed to her feet, drew a measured breath. "You were bleeding, and I knew we'd be able to remove those stitches today. You can use your arm again, can't you? It was a calculated risk."

Nix felt like she wanted to claw the stitches out of her arm. Her head suddenly seemed to pulse more vividly, and she could imagine the disease spreading into her bones. "Don't *ever* fuck with me like that again. I'm not you. I won't use my own body as an experiment."

"Noted," Kessandra replied stiffly.

They both finished their drinks—Nix in one long, bitter gulp, Kess a bit slower. A double *clink* sounded as they set their glasses on the polished bar top. Valloch spread through her veins like fire, simultaneously igniting Nix's determination and steadying her nerves. "I'm going to find Hallie and get these removed. Finish your 'errands' yourself."

"Before you go," Kessandra stood in front of the door, blocking her in. "About that promise."

"I thought you didn't want to fight."

"A bit late for that, dear, isn't it?" Despite the nickname, Kessandra's gaze pinned Nix to the spot. "The symptoms of dethalos are headaches, nausea, disassociation. I won't notice they're happening—not fast enough to react before awareness fades. If you see these symptoms progressing…" She tugged out the ichoron pistol strapped to her hip, attempting to hand it over. "Kill me. I don't care how you do it—but fix the problem. You can't let me hurt anyone."

It was all Nix had dreamed of since stepping on this

ship. But hearing it presented so neatly, almost clinically, had her recoiling.

"*Lumos*, Kess. I could just tie you to a chair or something."

The fact that she didn't laugh made Nix's heart pound. She stepped away from the pistol, pointedly refusing it.

Anger seeped into her tone. "You wanted to know why I brought you, Nix. This is it. No secrets, no fuckery. *This* is why you're here: because of anyone, you wouldn't hesitate to kill me if I presented the chance."

Nix hated this entire conversation. "I dunno. Those Elites would have too, based on Polaris."

"And they wouldn't have wasted any time. I'm not ready yet." Kessandra released a breath, and it might have been Nix's imagination, but it sounded like her voice trembled. She holstered the pistol. "You have a purpose here. When I'm dead, your priority will shift to protecting Doctor Jesko and our research. Until then, I have to utilize every minute I have left. The future of Valkesh depends on a truthful analysis of this disease."

She was talking in absolutes, like there was no way to stop this. Nix scowled, anger flaring again. "I'm not killing you, Kessandra. Shit."

"You don't have a choice, soldier. This is a direct order."

"*Fuck* your orders," Nix snarled.

For the first time, Kessandra's eyebrows shot up, surprise painting her face. It wasn't often Nix could catch her off guard. It was empowering, and fueled Nix's maelstrom of emotion. Without giving herself time to second-guess, Nix strode into Kessandra's space. Kessandra opened her mouth to object, but Nix slammed a hand on the door, much like she'd done in the alley in Valkeshia—pinning Kessandra to this conversation.

It was different this time. The air between them charged with energy. Nix could see every shaky inhale that passed Kessandra's burgundy lips.

"All your calculations," Nix hissed, leaning in close. She focused on Kessandra's organic eye, smoky green and bright with—what? Anguish? Desire? Or something else? It hardly mattered. "All your meticulous plans, your precious chessboard, and you forgot. I'm not a pawn. I'm a Lumos-damned knight, and I'm not killing my queen."

The words hung between them.

Nix's mind whispered insidiously, *Quian is dead. How many times have you imagined doling her the same fate?*

Nix's heart laughed and laughed and laughed.

When Kessandra didn't reply, Nix pushed back, giving her a bit of breathing room. She was still standing inordinately close, near enough that Kessandra's perfume —lavender and orange—seemed intoxicating.

"Keep that in mind, Nines, because it's not changing." The nickname, for once, was reminiscent of old times: a caress, calloused fingers against smooth skin.

Finally, Kessandra reacted: the barest tilt of her lips, a smile that, for once, reached her eyes. She smoothed it quickly, but it was the kind of mask that seemed moments from breaking. Like one tiny breeze could send her into a fit of affectionate laughter.

It was satisfying as hell.

At Nix's smug smirk, Kessandra lifted her chin. "I suppose I should have known better than to rely on you for logic."

"Ouch." Nix crossed her arms.

"If you insist on being stubborn, I can hardly stop you. But I need you to be watching... and intervene when necessary." Her tone was pained. "I don't want to hurt anyone, Nix."

It broke Nix's heart.

"You won't hurt anyone."

Kessandra contemplated her for a moment, as if gauging her sincerity. But she'd chosen well—Nix wouldn't kill Kessandra, but she was fully capable of subduing her. The idea of it being necessary made Nix's gut twist, but that was their unfortunate reality.

She pulled back her shoulders, her voice hard. "I promise, Kess. I'll keep you contained."

The words held weight to Nix, but sadness lingered in Kessandra's eyes. The subarch moved like she wanted to reach for Nix—her hand twitched at her side, her eyes drifted to Nix's shoulders, the wrapped wound—but she seemed to think better of it.

Even without physical contact, their proximity ignited every nerve in Nix's body.

Kessandra smoothed her jacket to hide the twitch. "Lucky for me, dethalos takes time. Before there's a lockdown, I need to check on the lieutenant: he has an ichoron rod in his leg from an earlier surgery, if I remember correctly. Doctor Jesko can remove your stitches. Once she's done, I need you to visit the darkroom and develop those photos."

"Is that a priority, all things considered?" Nix forced herself to focus.

"A historic event is unfurling before our eyes; how we document the next several days will alter the future of Valkesh. Yes, dear. It's a priority." Kessandra drew a breath, recentering herself. Gone was the amusement, the hint of fondness—in its place, the coolly professional subarch had returned. "When you're done, meet me on deck one. Captain Navaan is stubborn, but she values control... which means this ship is hours from lockdown. Move quickly."

A dismissal.

Nix reluctantly gripped the door handle. Then she paused, glancing over her shoulder. "Kess... is it just ichoron-enhanced people? Or can proximity to ichoron cause this?"

Nix's head throbbed, pain pulsing in time with her heartbeat. It took a moment to realize she was terrified of the answer.

Kessandra shifted her weight. "It's inconclusive. But for our sakes, I hope it's merely the enhanced. Otherwise, no one in Valkesh will survive."

16

DELVING BACK INTO THE LIBRARY NOW FELT LIKE DIVING into another world. The guests were still milling about, soft laughter and muted conversation as they enjoyed their short vacation, but now everything seemed to have an edge. Nix found herself squinting at every passenger, analyzing the ichoron accessories they wore.

A rose-gold tooth in that woman's smile. Rose-gold tubes that curled over that man's ears. One woman proudly displayed a rose-gold prosthetic leg, a common sight in the army spirescraper and beyond. They were stronger and more comfortable than a metal prosthetic, with the added benefit of being a fashion statement within higher society.

Most of the passengers just *wore* ichoron—their outfits studded with it, their jewelry gleaming in the bright lights. But even a desperate majority might not be able to stop a handful of ichoron-crazed people attacking with little regard for their own survival.

She'd seen the massacre upstairs. They'd be ripped to shreds regardless.

Nix hurried past. Priority one was removing these stitches. Ridiculous to think something they'd used regularly in Valkeshia was so dangerous here, but Nix wasn't about to test it. Not if Kessandra was relying on her like this.

Nix grimly strolled through the long hallway of staterooms between the library and promenade. Cleaning carts were perched here and there, stewards bustling around empty rooms replacing bedding and cleaning towels. A few saw her sarrant, still strapped to her back, and hastily bowed—the rest were too busy to look up.

None of them knew what was coming.

Part of Nix wanted to go hunting, find that second Elite before she killed anyone else. If she stopped her in time, maybe they wouldn't have to lock the ship down. Maybe they could make it to Fall, utilize the military presence there to cordon off the ichoron-enhanced folk before it became a problem.

Kessandra would be included in that.

"Fuck," Nix muttered, aggressively massaging her forehead to mitigate the ever-present headache. Her stomach still ached from the Elite's kick, and it made her movements stiff and sluggish. She couldn't fight an Elite in their *right* mind in this state, much less one ravaged by a violent disease.

She'd have to trust that Captain Navaan would mobilize the military to help.

Which, of course, meant Leon.

Nix felt shaky with the things she couldn't control. Protecting Kessandra, Leon, Hallie. Sure, fine. But she was just one soldier, and this... well, this felt a lot bigger.

She was so engrossed in her thoughts that she'd reached the promenade's center before realizing it. Five stories of shops and restaurants spread above her, the huge space feeling like another atrium. Nix shuddered, moving swiftly through the crowds to—where? She paused at the grand staircase, gasping for shallow breaths.

Did Hallie even have a doctor's office here? Or was she just researching this disease in the privacy of her stateroom? Nix had never even thought to ask.

That was when a familiar face passed her: Dominik, the bartender from last night.

She grabbed his arm without thinking, wrenching him back. "You."

"Ah—yes?" Recognition flashed on his face, and panic tinged his tone. "Shit. Look, I'd never hurt the subarch. The tertiarch just wanted me to watch her and report back—"

"It doesn't matter," Nix replied curtly. She almost said, *the tertiarch is dead*, but it felt a bit premature to admit it out loud. Best to let Captain Navaan break that news. "You're familiar with the passengers here, right?"

Dominik stuck his hands in his pockets. He wasn't wearing any kind of uniform, so his work shift must start a little later in the afternoon. "There are a thousand passengers on this ship. I don't know them all."

"But you know the important ones, right? Like Doctor Hallie Jesko?"

Now he frowned. "I've heard the name. If you need a doctor, the medical ward is opposite the gambling hall. Deck nineteen."

"I don't need *a* doctor. I need *that* one, specifically." Maybe it was the urgency of the situation, but this seemed like pointless waste of time. Nix heaved a sigh. "Look, where's Josie? I assume she's your boss."

"She's everyone's boss," Dominik said, a tinge of irritation in his tone now. "Her office is over there." He pointed at a nondescript door half-hidden behind a large potted plant.

"Great. Thanks." Nix strode off, leaving Dominik to his day.

She rapped on the door, then tried the handle and let herself inside. Josie's office was actually fairly large—but of course, she managed quite a few people on this ship. It seemed like there was one steward for every three passengers, considering how prevalent they were around the *Luminosity*.

Nix's stomach twisted, and she prayed Kessandra was exaggerating. Because if the ship dissolved into anarchy, it would fall on these folk to maintain order—and they were all just trying to survive.

Josie was seated at a desk adorned with potted plants. She glanced up when Nix entered, and her eyes widened in recognition. Immediately, she swept her papers away and gestured at the seat across from her. "Ah, Sergeant Marr. It's a pleasure; I wasn't expecting you." Unlike Dominik, she embodied cool professionalism at all times. "Did Subarch Kessandra need something?"

Nix wanted to grab her, bundle her in a closet, and lock the door until they reached Fall. Somewhere safe, somewhere protected. Instead, she forced a smile. "I need to find Doctor Jesko. Ah, Hallie Jesko. Did you offer her a workspace?"

It took Josie a moment to place the name. She tapped her desk with a long finger, lips pursed in thought. "Forgive me; we always have several doctors on board. Fall's university campus is the premier spot for a medical education."

"She has thick black glasses and a nosy personality."

Josie snorted, then covered her mouth. "I always forget how refreshing it is to have military down here." Still chuckling, she parsed through a few files near her desk, tugging out a long passenger manifold. A few moments of hunting and she triumphantly tapped the thick paper. "Here we go. I didn't personally meet her, but it looks like she placed a request for a private medical bay."

"Is that common?"

"Well, common enough that we have the facilities prepared. The subarch herself approved the request, so Doctor Jesko's workspace was in order before she boarded." Josie scribbled the location on a piece of paper and slid it across the table. "I hope everything else is to your liking?"

Nix took the paper, guilt churning in her gut. "It's… fine. But Josie. When—*if* the captain makes an announcement later today… do me a favor?"

Josie tilted her head, awaiting the request.

"Hide."

The steward hesitated. "I—I'm sorry?"

Nix pushed to her feet, pocketing the location. "Things might get dangerous on this ship. Don't be a hero; close yourself off somewhere safe and *don't leave*. Not until we dock at Fall." Her tone was firm, the same tone she used to order her squad in life-or-death situations. "Do you understand me?"

She half-expected an "affirmative, Sergeant," and a crisp salute—but of course, Josie wasn't a soldier.

The woman swallowed. "Is something wrong, Nix?"

Josie would never believe what was really wrong—and Nix couldn't afford to waste any more time. She breathed a sigh. "I hope not. Just… don't forget what I said."

She left Josie in her office and tried not to look back.

DECK EIGHTEEN WAS A WORKING DECK, apparently. Offices lined the halls, clearly meant to be rented out to the more business-minded guests. Three days of relaxation was apparently too much for the rich, prolific spirescraper citizens. This deck was far less crowded, although a few office doors were open, and the clacking of typewriters reverberated off the paneled walls.

It didn't take long to find Hallie's office. It was in a hallway with other specialized workstations—places offering welding, fabrication, carpentry, and drafting tables. At the very end was a set of medical bays, which were more equipped for laboratory research than patients. The other two bays were empty, but Hallie's door was closed.

Nix rapped on it, hard, and held her breath.

A few moments later, the door wrenched open and Hallie huffed. "I told you, I don't want lunch—" she paused, swallowing the rest of her sentence. "Well, well. I knew you'd swing by eventually. When is Kessandra going to mosey her way up to say hello?"

"Subarch Kessandra is busy," Nix said, and stepped past Hallie into the private bay. There was a single window on the far wall, but it was big enough to see the ever-brightening bioluminescent algae floating past. Coupled with the incandescent lamps in the corners of the room, the whole place had a cozy glow.

"Sure. Come on in. Interrupt my research." Hallie closed the door, locked it, and took a seat at the far table. The chair squeaked as she sat in it, scooting it back to examine Nix. "You look like shit. No offense."

Clearly they'd moved past the point of politeness. Nix

rolled her eyes. "In what world wouldn't I take offense to that?"

Hallie dismissed her exasperation with a wave. "So, what's Kessandra doing that's so important?"

"Someone's been murdered. Just like the dive team — but it happened late last night."

That caught the doctor's attention. She smirked grimly, bracing her elbows on her knees. "Let me guess. Polaris's Elites were infected with dethalos."

Nix knew they were researching this exact phenomenon. It still stunned her to hear it stated so casually. "If you knew they were a threat, why didn't you and Kessandra *contain* them?" Nix's voice heated up. "Polaris and one of the Elites are dead; Lumos only knows where the second Elite is. People could die —"

"Don't pretend like this is my fault," Hallie said sharply, and her tone silenced Nix immediately. "I'm just a doctor. And frankly, my standing with the primarch is precarious as it is. If he figured out what I've been doing the last decade, he wouldn't revoke my license. He'd have me killed."

There was a chair in the opposite corner of the room, wedged between two workstations. Nix sank into it, grimacing as the motion pulled at her abused ribs. Her head still hurt, and it was starting to make her a bit nauseated.

Or maybe that was this entire situation.

"Sorry," Nix said, quietly. "This is just… a lot."

Hallie tilted her head, heaving an exasperated sigh.

"Trust me, I know. You winced when you sat down, so I'm beginning to think you look like shit for a reason. Are you bleeding out?"

"Not anymore." Nix pulled her shirt back, revealed the bandages. "Kess is shockingly good with emergency medical aid."

"She's a soldier who's spent a lifetime experimenting on her own body." Hallie didn't sound impressed. Instead, her tone was deeply sad. "In another life, she'd have passed medical school with full marks, and would be revolutionizing my industry."

That only made Nix more determined to protect her. She slipped out of the shirt, carefully undoing the bandages with one hand. "Well, she used ichoron stitches, and now I have a pounding headache. I want them gone."

Hallie rolled her eyes, pushing to her feet. "Calculated risks, that one. Give me a moment." She began perusing the equipment on the far wall, gathering the supplies necessary to remove the stitches. As Hallie hunted, she said, "I presume you've made the connection between her eyeball and dethalos."

"We talked about it." Nix still wasn't sure how she felt about that discussion—or the underlying tension. Part of her fell so easily into what she remembered: Kessandra's body against hers, the sound of her laugh, the safety of knowing someone competent, capable, beautiful, was looking out for her.

The rest of her was struggling. Dethalos on its own was a lot to stomach, but partnering with Kessandra, even grudgingly, felt like disgracing Quian's memory. It was ridiculous; if he were still alive, he'd beg her to let things go, move on, find happiness.

She wasn't even sure what happiness looked like now.

"I want to know parameters," Nix said, forcing her mind to the task at hand. "Who's at risk? How fast will they turn? Is it just ichoron-enhanced, or can medicine do it? Proximity to ichoron?"

"You sound like Kessandra." Hallie produced a set of tweezers and a short, curved rose-gold blade, then rounded out her collection with a bottle of sterilizing solution. "And I'll tell you the same thing I told her — which has only been confirmed so far. We have no fucking idea."

Nix felt cold. "I thought you spent years researching this."

"Oh, we did. And the answer is, it's random. It doesn't act like a normal illness. Most of the people affected had ichoron enhancements, but two in the last century didn't. We suspect it's worse near the mines, but even that is a tenuous connection at best. We can't predict anything at this point."

That... was not the answer Nix wanted to hear. "How can we be sure Kessandra will succumb, then?"

"We can't. But she's a prime candidate." Hallie rolled her eyes. "That's why Kessandra requested the deployment four years ago in the first place, before the Hectron Tunnel Collapse."

Nix stiffened. "You've got to be fucking kidding me."

"Sergeant, this is nothing I'd joke about." Hallie deposited her items on the table beside Nix's chair, then tugged her own seat over for better access. Her expression was exasperated. "For the record, I advised against both the surgery for her eye *and* the deployment. But at that point, the primarch was closing in—it was the mines, or a mysterious death on the front lines."

Nix was going to kill him.

No, first she was going to kill Kessandra... in a less-than-literal manner. Then she'd find the primarch and slit his throat, in a *very* literal manner.

"I didn't know." Nix's words were tense, spoken through clenched teeth.

"Well. She's not very forthcoming." Hallie rolled her eyes. "This shouldn't hurt too much, but you'll feel a tugging sensation."

Nix braced herself against the chair as Hallie swiftly snipped the meticulous knots at either end of her ichoron sutures. Only ichoron could cut ichoron reliably, but her blade made short work of it.

It didn't take much to tug out the thread. What remained was a thin, puckering line. Hallie swiftly wiped it with antiseptic and admired the wound. "She did great work. Maybe next time she'll ask you before putting poison in your body."

"We discussed that too," Nix grumbled, then pulled her back to the topic at hand: "If proximity causes a dethalos infection, why didn't Kessandra try to kill us four years ago? We were in those tunnels every day, and she didn't show these symptoms."

Hallie wrapped up the bloodied thread and dumped it into a nearby trash can. Her tools went into a sterilizing solution. "No idea. Maybe some people are immune. Maybe the disease gets worse over years. Maybe we're completely off base." Hallie sounded as frustrated as Nix felt. "This isn't a neat little box, Sergeant. 'These people are safe, and these ones aren't.' Records of dethalos's symptoms are slim, and no one pieced together their relation until Kessandra."

"And now it's increasing at a faster rate." Nix grimaced as the doctor pressed the wound again with antiseptic. It burned a bit, but nothing like the pain from last night. In all honesty, those sutures were probably a good call.

"We started getting twenty cases in five years. Then two years. Now the primarch is hiding reports every time the *Luminosity* docks. The military is struggling to keep these people contained, but Fall citizens are starting to whisper about the murder rates—about folk vanishing in the middle of the night." Hallie wrapped the wound in a tight bandage, tying it off with a thin metal clamp. "Things are unraveling faster than anyone cares to admit. But if something happens to Kessandra—or me, really—no one will know why."

"Nothing will happen to Kess," Nix swore.

Hallie smirked. "She said you two had a history."

"It's not—" Nix swallowed her defense, glowering. "She's the reason my best friend is dead."

The doctor didn't deny that Kessandra would be capable of something like that. She just raised an eyebrow. "Huh. Well, maybe not, then."

Yeah. Maybe not.

"Either way, I expected the Elites to lose their minds as we approached Fall. That branch of the military is essentially our testing ground for ichoron soldiers, and I'm loath to say it's been a success." Hallie tapped Nix's side. "Lift your shirt. Let me see why you were wincing."

Nix rolled her eyes, but dutifully raised her shirt to show the heavy bruising along her stomach. Hallie whistled appreciation. "There's a battle scar for you."

"It'll fade," Nix said. It had better, and soon. "So, the entire ship is at risk now?"

"Maybe. It depends on how dethalos spreads. But if even five people succumb to it, the death toll will be unimaginable." Hallie's tone was soft now, even as she prodded Nix's ribs. She paused when Nix inhaled sharply. "Cracked. Not broken, though."

"Dandy."

The doctor rolled her eyes. "Not much I can do about those. I'd say 'rest,' but I'm not sure that's in your vocabulary."

Nix let her shirt drop. "Not when the guests are about to start murdering each other."

"Mmm." Hallie pushed to her feet, but her gaze pinned Nix in place. "Sergeant, the next most dangerous person on this vessel is Kessandra. With her military training and that ichoron eye, she's a threat to everyone."

Nix wanted to argue… but there was nothing to say. Instead, she took a different approach. "Then you'd better prepare for surgery."

Hallie considered her. "You want me to remove it."

"No shit." It was abrasive, but Nix was beyond pleasantries now. "I figured that'd be your first step, doctor."

Hallie massaged her face with both hands. "It's an intense procedure. She won't be functional for a while afterwards. And her old eye is gone — she'll be half-blind."

Nix pushed to her feet as well, lips tilted downwards. "Better than dead. How long do you need?"

Silence as they stared at each other. Then Hallie smirked. "Lucky for you, I've grown quite fond of that child. Preparations are already underway. The big question was, 'how can we do it without anyone noticing,' but now that Polaris is dead and the ship is poised for lockdown, it won't be a problem. Get her here tomorrow, and try not to let her kill anyone in the meantime."

"You can't do it sooner?" Nix's voice was harsh. She hated begging, but this entire situation scared her.

"It's *major surgery*, Sergeant. If you want me to move faster, you'll stop wasting my time." Hallie gestured at the door. "You've got your orders."

Nix huffed, but headed for the door.

Of course, she hadn't made it two steps before Hallie said, "One final thing. How's your headache?"

Nix had forgotten. Now she paused, assessing. Dread slid through her veins.

"It's gone."

"Hmm. Don't waste time finding Kessandra. Something tells me this situation is about to go from bad to worse."

Nix clenched her jaw, nodded stiffly, and strode for the elevator.

17

NIX MOVED QUICKLY, MIND WHIRLING. AS RIDICULOUS as it seemed, she was aching for the time when *Kessandra* seemed like her biggest threat. It was obvious why Kessandra had been so insistent that day in the training room, when she'd pinned Nix to the mats. The desperate way she'd whispered, *"There's been a murder,"* and the weight those words now held.

How much weight did Kessandra carry on any given day?

When would it crush her?

Nix stepped into an empty elevator and jammed the button for the library level, taking a slow breath to calm her thumping heart. She was excellent in intense situations, could channel everything to fighting when necessary. But this panic wasn't a simple moment of fight or flight—this was long-standing anxiety that built in her chest until it felt like every breath was a labor.

She wanted off this ship. She wanted to go home to her father, her squad, Lanskin's pub. Hell, she'd even take another deployment to the front lines if it kept her far from this mess.

But "this mess" was all around them. It was waxed on the marble floors and infused in the glass windows and shaped into the metal railings. There was literally no escape—not from the *Luminosity*, not from ichoron. Nix felt claustrophobic, and had to clench her eyes shut before her breathing could slow.

The elevator dinged open, the sound cheerful, and Nix opened her eyes. A glamorous couple stood opposite her, eyebrows raised in unison. One of them—a person who could have been any gender—frowned, casting a questioning glance at their partner before saying, "You look pale, kid. You okay?"

"Fine," Nix gritted out, pushing past them. "Might be a good time to get back to your staterooms."

The pair watched her go with mystified expressions.

The library was bustling now. People perused the bookshelves upstairs, choosing tomes with little regard for tracking what was taken. Some of them tucked into the lower level's lounge chairs, taking fancy drinks from the stewards, while others hobbled back toward the staterooms with stacks of leather-bound books.

The darkroom was attached to the lower level, down a long hallway framed with sepia-tinted imagery. Technically, it was open for guest use—although only the passionate photographers took advantage. Everyone else relied on the professionals to capture their time on the *Luminosity*; the film would be developed and mailed to them upon reaching Fall.

The hallway itself burgeoned into a secondary observation deck directly below the atrium. The darkroom was quickly forgotten when she realized just *who* was on the deck, pressed against the windows.

"Leon?" Nix asked, striding into the space. Like the atrium, it featured floor to ceiling glass and a multitude of plants. But this room was significantly smaller, and its hidden location meant it was empty, aside from a few tufted chairs.

Leon glanced up from where he'd been kneeling, his body half-hidden by the foliage planted near the windows. "Oh, Nix! Hey. I was hoping to find you around here somewhere." He pushed to his feet, dusted his pants off. His military uniform was gone, replaced with more casual attire, but he wasted no time saluting. "You just missed a bioluminescent fish. It was tiny, but—well, we must be getting closer to the leviathan fall."

Nix's brain couldn't quite process the whiplash of his topic, and the thoughts in her own head. She blinked, crossing her arms. "What are you doing down here? I thought we were meeting in the promenade tonight."

"I got bored." His expression was sheepish.

Boredom. Nix *wished* she had that problem.

It reminded her that the darkroom awaited, and Kessandra had given her a clear task. She gestured with two fingers, moving back into the hallway. "Follow me. I have to develop these photos."

"Sure," Leon said easily, and fell in step beside her. As they walked, he squinted at her posture. "You're walking stiff. Did something happen?"

"Got into a fight. He lost." Eventually.

Leon frowned, but Nix didn't want to elaborate here.

She led him into the photography workroom. It was separated into two sections: a preparation area, and the actual darkroom. A round lightbulb was anchored over the darkroom's door—indicating whether visitors could enter, or if doing so would destroy any developing photographs.

Even though there must be *dozens* of images to develop after last night's festivities, no one was here. Maybe the staff only used this place after hours.

Regardless, Nix was glad for the isolation. Less to explain, fewer people to panic about. In fact, with Leon watching her back, she felt safer than she had all day. She led him directly into the darkroom, locking the door, flicking on the "occupied" light outside.

The darkroom was cast in an eerie red glow, courtesy of tinted glass over the lightbulbs. Anything stronger would ruin the photos. Still, the light threw dim shadows over Leon's face as he leaned against the door and watched her tug out her camera.

"Where's the subarch? I figured you two would be together."

Lumos, that was a loaded statement. Nix grimaced, rewinding the used film with a brass key attached to the bottom of the camera. "She's visiting the lieutenant." She double-checked the red lighting before flicking the switch at the camera's base. The bottom panel popped off, revealing two spools and the film strung between them. "You didn't see him today, did you?"

"No, and we thought that was odd." Leon frowned, crossing his arms. "Is he alright?"

Nix tugged the spools out of the camera, carefully unwinding the negatives. There were several trays already set up along the table—Lumos forbid a rich photography enthusiast would have to mix their own solution—and she quickly identified the stop bath. Her words were grim. "I doubt it. But he won't be our biggest problem soon."

She could have lied. Hid the truth from Leon to spare him, especially if Captain Navaan somehow *did* manage to get this crisis under control. But dethalos felt like a gun pointed at Leon's head—and if he died from the effects of this, Nix might as well have pulled the trigger.

She couldn't stomach it.

So, as she seesawed the strip of negatives into the stop bath, drenching the film, she said, "I wasn't honest with you before. About why I'm here—and what Kessandra's uncovered."

His eyes widened. He glanced at the door, checking to make sure they were truly alone. "What do you mean?"

And so, Nix told him everything. His carefree attitude

turned somber, then horrified, as she revealed all the details: ichoron, dethalos, Polaris, Kessandra, Hallie and the surgery, and the fate of this ship.

By the time she was done, the negatives were rinsed and hung to dry. It left her hands free for a minute, but time felt agonizingly slow inside this room. What was happening beyond the doors? Was anyone losing their minds yet, or would that be a more gradual shift?

Leon was silent too. Finally, he said, "I—I'm sorry. You're telling me ichoron is poisoning people?"

"You didn't get an ichoron tattoo, did you?" she joked, but it was laced with seriousness. ichoron tattoos were expensive and considered taboo in proper spirescraper society—but for that reason, many ensigns gravitated towards them.

A few kids in the sixty-first talked about getting one. Nix prayed that hadn't happened.

Leon drew a shaking breath. "It always felt like a waste of money. I don't understand. If this stuff is dangerous, why hasn't anyone noticed before?"

"Cover-ups at the highest level." Nix squinted at the negatives as they dried, hunting for which images to develop. Her eyes settled on the picture she'd taken of the outcropping in the Marr casten, the one where she and Quian used to sit. She hadn't let herself think about it— about the Hectron Tunnel Collapse, about the truth behind it.

With everything she knew now, Kessandra suddenly

didn't seem like the villain she once was. Although her words in the dining room last night were lodged in Nix's brain: *He shouldn't have needed saving.*

Everything about Kessandra felt like ichoron: pretty on the surface, useful in practice—tinged with poison.

Leon watched her carefully. "Like the Hectron Tunnel Collapse."

She nodded, still examining the negatives as they dried.

"Okay." He paused, like he was trying to decide what to say next. "Okay. I think—"

Her eyes settled on the image of the rocking chairs on the upper deck—the one she'd taken out of nostalgia right before finding Leon and his new friends. Inside the image, near the window... she couldn't tell, but it looked like...

"Hang on," she breathed, adrenaline spiking. She ripped the negatives from their clips, snatched a pair of metal scissors, and cut that image out. It was barely bigger than a coin, too small to see the details, especially in the red glow of the darkroom.

"What's wrong?" he asked, stepping closer.

She ignored him, slipping the negative into the enlarger—the machine used to transpose a negative onto photo paper. It had an accordion-style lens like her camera's, but much bigger, which faced down toward a wooden baseboard. Her hands were shaking as she slid paper underneath the lens.

"I think I saw something," she said to fill the silence, flicking on the light inside the enlarger. It shone onto the negative, which amplified onto the photo paper. She held her breath, waiting for the image to form.

Quian always loved this part. He used to have a contest while they waited: who could hold their breath longer. They'd always burst out laughing at the end, because nothing could compete with the minutes it took to develop the image. But by the time they recovered from their laughing stint, it was usually finished anyway.

Now, her heart clenched as she stared at this picture.

At the hallway, gradually taking shape. The rocking chairs, crisp and clean. The window and the dark ocean beyond. The ichoron mechanisms inside the camera meant everything was in perfect focus.

Which meant they both saw the pair of eyes, looming over the rocking chairs — staring right at Nix as she snapped the image.

Her body washed with cold.

"W-What is that?" Leon asked, his voice barely a whisper. "Dust on the lens?"

"It's not dust." Nix's heart pounded, the hairs on her neck prickling.

In the orthochromatic image, the eyes appeared to glow white amidst a background of black and gray. Except they weren't white in real life… they were blood-red. She never thought she'd see them again, but this was undeniable. They loomed over the rocking chair, glaring at the camera, promising death in the barest tilt of their slitted pupils.

Suddenly, it felt like she was back in the mines,

chipping away at the rock to collect the ichoron that oozed out. Quian would tap her shoulder, point at the crag walls, and she'd know the Crypt Keeper was lurking. If they didn't meet its gaze, it'd leave them alone... but everyone knew what would happen if curiosity won out.

The soldiers who followed those eyes into the depths were never the same. Some never came back at all.

"—nt Marr. *Nix.*" Leon was shaking her shoulder, and she gasped, tensing, ripping her gaze away from the developing image. Shit. The image was still developing. She immediately shut off the enlarger's light, casting them back in that crimson glow, and dunked the photo into the fixer tray.

"Sorry," she breathed, shuddering. "I just—I've seen that before. It's the Crypt Keeper."

"That's a myth," he replied tentatively. "Isn't it?"

They both looked at the photo soaking in the solution. Nix didn't even want to remove it—if she touched it, pulled it out of this tiny room, it was admitting that this *thing* lurked on the ship. Waiting to strike.

She believed in ghosts.

She was starting to believe in possession, too.

"It has to be a trick of the light," Leon said.

Nix reluctantly set the image under the water, rinsing it off, and clipped it to dry next to the other negatives. Her hands were shaking. "I always thought it was a hallucination. Too much time without sunlight, working in total darkness. Easy to see things. No one's ever caught it on camera before."

"Is that really what it looks like? The Crypt Keeper?"

She nodded, swallowing past the lump in her throat. "It lurks behind you, waiting for you to turn around. You can feel it—sense it. Sometimes it would caress you *through* the dive suit, like fingernails trailing up your spine."

Now Leon shuddered, scrubbing his face to anchor himself. "And now it's on this ship."

"We need to find Kessandra," Nix said, examining the other negatives. She couldn't look at the photo of those eyes, not without feeling like she was drowning. The early negatives had emotional weight—the outcropping in the Marr casten, the shining spirescrapers of Valkeshia from the dining hall—and then it dissolved into bloodstained smears in the atrium.

Nix cut them out, but there didn't seem to be enough time to develop them. Not with this… this *thing* lurking in the *Luminosity*.

Maybe it wasn't poison after all. Maybe it was something supernatural.

She wasn't sure which option she preferred.

"Come on," she said, stuffing the negatives into her camera's case, pocketing the one developed photo in her trousers.

They made it into the hallway before a crackling voice came over the loudspeakers:

Attention, guests of the Luminosity. *There has been a security breach. This ship is on lockdown until further notice—all guests will return to their rooms immediately and remain there until my next announcement. All soldiers, report to the promenade for your newest assignment. Repeat. All soldiers, report to the promenade.*

Shit. This was progressing right on Kessandra's schedule—and for once, Nix had prayed she'd be wrong.

Leon set his jaw. "Then you weren't lying."

"Did you *think* I was lying?"

"Sergeant, don't take this the wrong way, but... I was hoping." Leon drew a slow breath. "Stay safe out there. Don't go hunting something you can't fight, okay?"

The glowing eyes. Nix wanted to object, but he was right—the Crypt Keeper was an incorporeal threat. The infected Elite was the immediate danger, and it must be severe if Captain Navaan agreed to a full-ship lockdown *and* military intervention.

She smirked grimly. "Oh, don't worry. I'll be fighting real threats first."

"Considering you're basically limping, that's far from comforting."

She clapped his shoulder. Already, she felt restless; she needed to reconnect with Kessandra immediately, just to reassure herself the subarch was safe. "I'm not here to comfort. Enjoy patrolling the hallways, Leon. Stay alert, and try not to die."

He saluted, but the motion was tinged with sarcasm.

Nix had a feeling it was the last time she'd see him for a while. She only hoped when they met again, it was with better news. A cure, maybe, or a battle plan against this lurking specter. And yet, as she merged into the crowds of confused guests streaming back to their rooms, fear settled like a cold lump in her stomach.

It felt like wishful thinking.

18

THE SHIP WAS CHAOS.

Perplexed stewards took varying forms of control, directing guests back to their staterooms. A few of the senior stewards were addressing irate passengers, spirescraper citizens clearly unused to being ordered around. Nix watched it all distantly, weaving through the crowds to one of the elevators. The promenade would be a guaranteed nightmare for a bit, but if she could get to the upper levels near Hallie's lab, she could cut through the gambling hall and reach the upper decks that way.

"Hey," a steward said, huffing. He stepped in her way, narrowing his eyes. "Didn't you hear the captain? The ship is on lockdown. Return to your stateroom."

Nix quirked one eyebrow and turned slightly, showing her ichoron sarrant.

The steward hesitated. "Ah, a soldier. You're supposed to be in the promenade. That way."

"I'm on special assignment." When that didn't seem to register, she heaved an irate sigh. "For Subarch Kessandra."

He gauged her—but finally stepped aside. "Just... don't be in the hallways long." Nervousness laced his voice, and Nix wondered how much he'd been told.

Anything was too much for someone unequipped for combat, as he clearly was. Sympathy swelling, she stepped past him. "Trust me. I won't." And she strode into the glass elevator, jamming the button for the nineteenth floor.

As the elevator rose steadily, the atrium level came into view. The soldiers guarding it were gone, and a simple sign on a metal post had been positioned in front of the locked doors. It was hard to read from this angle, but the cursive word *Closed* was visible.

Such a prim and proper way to say, *there's a massacre inside*.

Nix clenched her jaw, turning away from the windows. Find Kessandra. Nix was bouncing on her feet, ignoring the twinge of her ribs as she stepped onto level nineteen. Even the medical bay had been closed. Here, a similar sign was positioned that politely stated, *Call if you need medical assistance*, with a three-digit number.

Was Ramona safe inside her office? Ah, switchboard room?

Nix could only hope so.

Past the medical bay was another lounge, and Nix stopped short on seeing the bioluminescence out the windows. It was bright blue now, another light in an already bright space—but now the water's murkiness had cleared somewhat. A massive shape in the distance caught her eye, so tall it was nearly level with the *Luminosity*. The long, thin shape was fractured at the center, tilting at a precarious angle, but there was no mistaking what it had once been.

A bone. They'd reached the leviathan fall.

Before Nix could contemplate that, a crash echoed in the gambling hall.

Nix stiffened, hand reaching for the sarrant over her shoulder on instinct. She strode swiftly through the wide entrance, shifting to a painful jog as screams echoed in the huge room. Far beyond the tables of slot machines, a panicked thrush of people were shoving for the far exit.

They were, of course, hitting a wall of soldiers trying to do the exact opposite.

And in the room's center, surrounded by shredded corpses, was the female Elite. Nix sized her up in seconds —the bloodstains on her torn uniform, the inhuman snarl on her face, the strands of hair in her crimson teeth—and then realized who was squaring off against her.

Kessandra. Because *of fucking course* she'd be here.

The subarch stood between the Elite and the passengers scrambling to escape. As the Elite lunged towards them, Kessandra fired her pistol. Ichoron bullets ripped through the woman's flesh, but she kept coming, jerking unnaturally before lurching forward with renewed vigor.

"Kess," Nix shouted. "Run!"

"Not possible." Kessandra was perfectly calm, a true soldier. She lunged sideways as the Elite reached her, narrowly dodging the woman's swiping hands. The Elite glanced at the crowds, but Kessandra called, "Hey! Focus on me," and punctuated it with two more bullets—this time, to the skull.

Blood spurted from the wounds, flesh and bone flying, but despite the holes in her head, the Elite's deadened gaze locked on Kessandra. One of her eyes was just a cavity from Kessandra's bullets, but it didn't seem to slow her.

The panic behind Kessandra grew more frenzied. If they didn't move this fight away from the bottleneck, more people would die... and it wouldn't be from the Elite.

The Elite leapt again, arms outstretched. Crimson blood dripped from her fingers—the woman's sarrant was still strapped to her side, utterly unused. Kessandra fired one final shot, then rolled behind a slot machine. The Elite slammed into the side of the heavy machine. It teetered precariously, tipped seconds after the Elite hit the plush carpet, and crashed on top of her. Ichoron coins spilled out of the bottom tray, scattering like snow as the pinned Elite thrashed under its weight.

Kessandra holstered her pistol right as Nix reached her. "That was my last bullet. I had to shoot the lieutenant, although he didn't get back up again."

The fact that Kessandra went against two of these things in an hour sent a spike of panic through Nix's veins.

She should never have let the subarch out of her sights. Her voice was clipped. "After this, we are going to have a long talk on acceptable risk."

"We've had that talk before, and it never ends well for you," Kessandra replied. "I'm afraid I can't get close without a weapon. If you retrieve her sarrant for me, we can cut her to pieces."

For the love of Lumos below.

"There is no *we*," Nix hissed, grabbing Kessandra's arm and shoving her behind another row of slot machines. In a breath, she surveyed Kess for wounds... but aside from a few scrapes on her cheek, she seemed okay. "There's me, and the mess you've made. Go *hide*."

"Hide?" Kessandra repeated, indignation in her normally composed voice. "Who do you think I am?"

The Elite was stirring, clawing her way out from the machine's grip. Nix readied her sarrant. "I think you're the runner-up in our Duel in the Depths. And you're out of your league, Subarch."

It was a low blow—the Duel in the Depths had been a makeshift competition with their dive team on day two of the *Luminosity*'s journey to Fall. Already bored and tense with anxious energy, they'd faced off in a tiered contest to see who could conquer the others with their sarrants.

Nix and Kess were the final contenders.

Nix won.

Kessandra's face twisted into exasperation. "You—"

The Elite snarled and threw the slot machine aside.

Several of her teeth were chipped or gone, and the remaining ones were coated in frothy blood. Her eyes—or the one not blown to bits—was a watery brown, and the white around it was stained with burst capillaries.

Kessandra raised her fists like she was going to try hand-to-hand combat against an ichoron-sick Elite. Nix snapped, "Kess, for the love of Lumos," and shoved herself in front of the subarch just in time.

The Elite lunged with a strangled scream, and Nix slashed at her chest.

A finger went flying.

The Elite didn't seem to notice. She connected with the flat of Nix's sword, prying for Nix's face. Only Nix's sarrant held her back; Nix craned out of reach, gasping against the fiery pain in her side. The stab wound had mostly healed, but a cracked rib would take longer.

All of it was a setback in a fight.

With a desperate grunt, she shoved the Elite to the side, slicing toward her head. It didn't work—the woman was unnaturally fast. Her ichoron-dusted skin gleamed as she twisted on her back, setting her sights again on Nix.

At least she was easily distractible.

"The sarrant, Nix," Kessandra ordered.

"*Hide.*" Nix spat the word, grunting as she dodged the Elite's swipes. She'd thought there might be some glimmer of humanity inside this woman, but it was clear the longer they fought—nothing remained but a monster.

For a moment, a breath, those glowing red eyes

intruded on her senses. She imagined seeing them hovering above the maddened Elite, and it sent a true shot of fear down her spine. She hesitated, eyes flicking from the real threat to a perceived one—and that was the only opening the Elite needed.

The woman tackled Nix to the ground, slashing at her clothes, her face, her chest. Her nails weren't sharp, but she tore into Nix's skin with relentless animosity. Nix swallowed a scream, writhing to dislodge her—

—and then a metal pole slammed into the woman's head.

It was enough force that she went flying, skidding to a stop several feet away. Nix gasped for breath, feeling blood trickling down her neck—hers, or someone else's? —and then a hand appeared in her vision.

Nix clasped Kessandra's hand, allowing the royal to haul her to her feet. She swayed unsteadily, but readied her sarrant again.

Her ribs were agony. Her breath felt short.

And Kessandra plucked the sarrant from her hands before she realized it.

Nix lunged for the weapon, but Kessandra easily danced out of range. "Try the pole," she said, but there was no humor in her tone. "It's apparently quite effective." She stepped forward, moving like a dancer on a stage, ichoron blade flashing as she swiped ruthlessly at the Elite.

Several soldiers had broken free of the crowds, sprinting toward the carnage with sarrants and pistols.

Nix recognized Jakart briefly, shouted at him to stay back, but in the chaos, no one seemed to hear.

The Elite had recovered and tried to attack again — but enough of her body was damaged that it wasn't functioning properly. Her lunges were slow, uncoordinated, and her guttural screams were more of a gurgling sound now. Kessandra sliced at her appendages, severing what she could, and then went for the head.

Before her strike could land, a gunshot rang out.

The soldier had been aiming for the Elite. It was obvious by the horror in his face, the stiff way he lowered the gun — he'd made a mistake. The gunshot silenced those remaining in the gambling hall... all except Kessandra, who inhaled sharply.

Blood blossomed at her side, staining her white shirt.

A graze. *Please let it be a graze*, Nix thought desperately.

Kessandra stepped out of the Elite's reach, pressed a hand to the wound, examined the blood. For a moment, she seemed to fade, staring at the blood long enough that the Elite began inching toward her again. Then, her eyes fell on the mangled human — and she sliced the sarrant one final time.

The Elite's head rolled on the ground. This time, her body went limp.

"I-I'm so sorry, Subarch," the soldier stammered.

Nix swiftly stepped beside Kessandra, peeling up her shirt. The royal was swaying — from shock or pain, it was tough to say — and she refocused when Nix gripped her shoulder tightly. "You shouldn't have stolen my fucking sarrant, Kess."

"You s-shouldn't have made it so easy to grab," Kessandra replied faintly.

Asshole.

Nix squinted again at the wound—it looked like a graze, but it was deep. Thank Lumos these soldiers didn't have access to ichoron bullets, or Kess might be dead. She pressed Kessandra's hand against the wound, wiped and sheathed her sarrant, and fumbled for a strategy.

She couldn't let Kessandra collapse here. Not if she was going to lose her mind when she awoke—not with all these witnesses. If anyone here was still under the primarch's thumb, there'd be no easier target.

The next obvious choice was Hallie's office, but it hadn't been set up for patients. There was no way Kessandra could perch in that hard chair while Hallie stitched this wound. For a moment, Nix questioned if she should even summon the doctor, or if that would remove her focus from surgery preparation.

But the surgery couldn't happen if Kessandra died of blood loss.

Shit.

"Doctor Hallie Jesko," Nix said harshly. "Find her and send her to deck one. Her office is on the eighteenth floor, below the medical bay."

"You can stitch this. It isn't worse than your stab wound," Kessandra said, exasperated.

Exasperated.

Nix rolled her eyes, unable to believe how fucking ridiculous this woman was. "Considering how I felt last night, that's not encouraging." When Kess wrinkled her nose, Nix added, "Besides, I'm a hell of a lot messier with sutures. Keep pressure on that."

"I'll... I'll send the doctor," the soldier stammered, eyes wide. "I'm so sorry, Subarch Kessandra."

He hurried away, and Jakart tentatively approached. "Do you need help getting her somewhere, Sergeant? I think the medical bay is closed, but—"

"Yeah. Help me get her downstairs." Nix glanced past him at the panicked crowds, who'd foregone the elevators and had now mostly fled down the staircase. "You folk are needed in the promenade. This wasn't a one-time thing."

That made the soldiers pale. They gripped their weapons a bit tighter, staring at the carnage in the gambling hall. Overturned card tables, discarded slot machines, and the bodies of the guests too slow to escape before the attack.

"What should we do with—um, her?" Jakart moved to take Kessandra's other arm, supporting her weight, but the soldier's eyes were on the dead Elite.

Nix didn't glance at the mess. She couldn't stomach it now, not with her adrenaline wearing off. "Leave her. Someone can tell Captain Navaan later, but I think she'll have more pressing issues in the meantime. The lieutenant is dead; who's the next highest-ranking soldier?"

"Uh... you, I think," Jakart said.

Great.

Kessandra grimaced, readjusting her grip on the wound. "Sergeant, I hate to hurry things along, but I may need to sit down."

"Yeah, I bet," Nix muttered, and they began the careful trek to the elevators. The soldiers parted, some saluting as they passed. Jakart seemed unnerved by the attention, but he took his part in helping Kessandra seriously. The elevator doors slid closed, and he cleared his throat.

"What do you mean, it's not a one-time thing?"

Nix assessed Kessandra, who seemed to be struggling to focus. Blood coated her side, and her hand slipped off the wound. Nix pressed her own hand there instead, frowning as Kess swallowed a groan. "It's—complicated. Something infected her, and we think it will infect others."

Jakart stiffened. "So, anyone could become like—that thing?"

He sounded one step short of the trigger-happy ensigns that ran into battle and promptly got themselves killed. Fear was a powerful motivator, and Nix wasn't about to let it control Jakart—especially not when Kessandra was so close to coming under fire.

"That thing was a person, once," Nix replied curtly. "A soldier like you. Don't forget that we're here to protect, ensign. Not hunt."

"You'd have been a lovely commander," Kessandra drawled, but her words were slurring now.

The elevator dinged on the promenade level. Nix ignored Kess, gesturing at the promenade. "I can get her to safety. Find Leon and let him know what's happened. Tell him I'll meet up with him soon."

"Right. Are you taking command after that?"

Nix winced. "I have other priorities. Follow the captain's orders; she's still in charge of the ship. Enforce the quarantine and stay alert."

"Affirmative." Jakart detached, his uniform smeared with blood now. He saluted, whispered, "Feel better, Subarch," and jogged into the promenade.

Nix hauled Kessandra into the royals' private elevator. Hopefully Hallie had a key too, or this would be a painfully long night.

By the time they limped into Nix's suite, Kessandra was barely conscious. Her wound was nasty, but Nix couldn't shake the niggling fear that this went deeper. Her mind flashed back to the deadened gaze of that Elite, the way she looked without seeing—exactly like Kessandra had done when she saw the blood.

She eased Kess onto the couch, leather be damned.

"Don't move. I'll grab some supplies." The medical kit had been carefully tucked into a cabinet near the sink, and Nix was fumbling for it when Kessandra spoke, her tone almost wry.

"You're worried."

"Not about you," Nix replied stiffly, snatching the kit and returning to the couch. "Maybe I should take a shower to prove it."

Kessandra pried open her eyes—one cold ichoron, one smoky green—and her gaze flicked to Nix. "That's not a bad idea. Is t-that my blood, the Elite's, or someone else's?"

"No fucking clue." Nix's entire shirt was splattered with crimson, ripped from the Elite's claws. Truthfully, she wanted nothing more than a long, scalding shower. But she couldn't risk it — not with Kessandra in this state, not with her skin almost ashen, her lips too pale.

Kess chuckled, then hissed as the motion jostled at her side. She seemed to be faring better now that she was lying down, but it still wasn't *good*. "The wound isn't serious. It's just a shock to my system."

"I'll believe that when you aren't on the cusp of fainting."

"You forget, Nix. While you've been fighting on the front lines, training as a true soldier… I've wasted away in my ichoron tower." Kessandra's lips tilted upwards, but her amused expression was overtaken by a groan. She shifted to examine the crimson coating her hands. "I haven't bled in years."

It left a sour taste in Nix's mouth. "How nice for you." Nix flicked open the medical kit and parsed through it for bandages. Her eyes fell on the ichoron-laced ones. With too much force, she shoved those aside.

That was the last thing they needed now.

Kessandra knitted her brow. In the soft light of the bioluminescence, she seemed almost… sad. "I'm sorry about what I said. About Quian."

"It's still too soon." The words were pained.

Kessandra clenched her eyes shut, but for once, she listened.

It didn't stop the guilt from prickling Nix's mind. She worked mutely, mopping the blood and applying firm pressure to the wound. The silence around them seemed deafening until a sharp knock echoed at the door.

The doctor was here.

19

"WOW. IS THIS HOW YOU ARE AT PARTIES?" HALLIE strolled past Nix with an appraising glance at her attire, the scratches on her face. "Glad I skipped the invite."

On the couch, Kessandra wheezed a laugh.

Nix rolled her eyes, casting a suspicious glance past Hallie. But of course, the spacious deck was empty. The only way Nix had seen to access deck one was the elevator, but there was no way of knowing who had keys down here. It was lucky Hallie had one—although that was almost certainly forethought on Kessandra's part. Everyone else was a security risk.

Hallie breezed into the room, pushing her glasses further up her nose. Her humorous tone dropped when she assessed Kessandra's physical state. "Why am I not surprised that you went and found something dangerous?"

Behind her, Nix folded her arms, although her lips

tilted upward. She wasn't surprised either, honestly. Annoyed, maybe, but hardly shocked.

Kessandra cast a very unimpressed look at them both. "You make it seem like I *sought out* an ichoron-crazed Elite."

"Looked that way to me," Nix said.

"She passed me as I left the upper decks, and promptly started tearing people to shreds in the gambling hall. What was I to do? Board the elevator and leave them to it?" Kessandra puffed exasperation, which made her grimace again. "Doctor, I'd appreciate if you didn't delay. My vision is waning."

Leave it to Kess to have a stick-up-her-ass way to say, *I may faint*.

"Yeah, yeah," Hallie replied, swiftly tying her poufy hair back. She tucked her thick black glasses in her pocket, then pulled a similar pair from her leather bag. This set had extra-curved earpieces, something to keep them on her face while she worked.

Relief swept through Nix without warning. Thank *Lumos* Kessandra made friends with a doctor early on. Granted, it was probably a necessity for Kess, but it still let Nix relax a little. And considering the adrenaline crash —the way her hands were trembling, the way fatigue slid through her bones—she was incredibly grateful for Hallie.

Kessandra was watching her carefully, pinning her ichoron eye to Nix despite her obvious exhaustion. As Hallie tugged out an entire menagerie of medical supplies, arranging them on the table with practiced ease, Kessandra said, "Sergeant, you're dismissed."

"Like hell I am," Nix grumbled.

"You need a shower, fresh clothes, and a few minutes of peace." Kessandra let her eyes close, let her voice slip into *just* that realm of begging. "Let yourself unwind. Doctor Jesko is more than capable of addressing this."

Hallie glanced at Nix, quirking one eyebrow. "I'd prefer that over dealing with *two* patients today. Although we'll need to clean those scratches before they get infected."

"Take care of Kess first," Nix said automatically. "Uh, Subarch Kessandra."

"Shedding protocol already," Hallie smirked.

On the couch, Kessandra hadn't opened her eyes. Her breathing was pained, rasping, and it looked like she might have fallen asleep. Nix watched her for a minute, wrestling with duty over the desire to finally wash away the blood and grime.

A few minutes of peace would be a welcome shift.

"She'll be okay. And I brought a sedative if she tries anything drastic," Hallie said quietly, and made a shooing motion towards the bedroom and bathroom.

Drastic. Because even though Kessandra was lucid now, that would change. Nix drew a slow breath to calm her pounding heart and nodded. "Call if you need anything. *Anything*, Hallie. You hear me?"

"Affirmative," Hallie said sarcastically.

Nix might lose her mind before Kessandra did.

She stepped into the bedroom, peeling off the blood-stiff shirt and pants. Her motions were uncoordinated, and she hissed as her rib throbbed. A distant part of her wished there *was* something to take—something ichoron-based—to heal faster. The rest of her remembered the Elite's inhuman snarl and decided the pain was preferable.

With her sarrant carefully set by the door and her camera stowed on the bedside table beside the telephone, Nix stepped into the bathroom and finally surrendered to a nice, hot shower. For several long minutes, she just stood under the spray, watching the blood rinse down the drain.

It took a long time to realize tears were there too.

Nix massaged her eyes, her face, and stared at the black ceiling. Even the overhead tiles were accented with rose-gold intersecting triangles. She laughed bitterly and muttered, "Why the fuck am I here?"

No one answered, of course.

Nix used whatever was in the fancy brown bottles to scrub her skin and hair. It felt good to wash everything away, even if a few of her scrapes had started bleeding sluggishly at the attention. She moved methodically, and when everything was clean, she still didn't want to turn off the shower.

Apparently, she needed the moment of peace more than she knew. Nix closed her eyes and slowly lowered herself into the porcelain tub, resting for a moment. Her rib screamed in protest at the position, but the pain slowly faded into a dull thrum. Time passed at a crawl as her tense muscles relaxed, her pounding heart slowed, and her strength returned.

It was only late afternoon. Why did it feel like an eternity had passed? Nix could have easily fallen into bed and slept the rest of the day away—but she feared what she'd awake to find.

With that terrifying thought, Nix finally peeled herself out of the bathtub and turned off the water. Her damp hair would take a long time to dry, so she tied it into a messy bun for now. She glanced at the outfits Kess had slipped into her wardrobe on the first day—more suits, because Kessandra certainly had a type—and forewent them all for something with flexibility: her army training uniform.

It was wrinkled from days inside her duffel bag, but the black sleeveless top and loose pants felt freeing. It felt like a shield, like it was centering her back where she belonged. Not fancy parties and enticing outfits: a battlefield, where she took command.

Nix almost felt like her old self as she cracked open the bedroom door.

And just as she took a step into the living room, the phone in the kitchen rang.

Kessandra jerked awake, then gasped in pain, reflexively pressing a hand to her side. Hallie grabbed her wrist and snapped, "Not *yet*, I'm working." The doctor hunched back over the wound as Kessandra craned her neck to see Nix.

"Who's calling?" The words were slurred.

Clearly during the half hour Nix had spent relaxing, Kessandra had also rested. It now meant the subarch was in a rare state of utter incompetence, which almost made Nix grin. Kessandra *hated* feeling incompetent.

Almost delighted, Nix waved her off. "I'm sure it's for me. I'm a stunning commodity on this ship, apparently."

"Stunning is right," Kessandra murmured, eyes slipping closed again.

Hallie snorted.

Nix should have expected the rejoinder, but it still had her face burning. She quickly turned for the telephone so they wouldn't see her reddening cheeks. The obnoxious ringing ceased when she picked up the earphone, lifting the candlestick base to speak into the transmitter. "Hello?"

Like before, Ramona's voice filtered through the phone. "Hello, Sergeant. Glad I finally tracked you down. How's the subarch?" Fear laced her tone, and Nix immediately knew this wasn't a house call.

"She's recovering. What's wrong?"

Ramona released a breathy laugh. "Order is breaking down. Captain Navaan wants Subarch Kessandra on the bridge immediately. It's on the upper decks, accessible through an elevator near the atrium."

Nix glanced over her shoulder. Hallie had taped a square piece of gauze over the wound, but now she unraveled a roll of it and murmured something to Kessandra. The subarch nodded, prying open her eyes, taking Hallie's hand as she eased her into a sitting position.

The very motion had the rich shade of her skin paling. She bit her lip to keep quiet, but leaned heavily against the couch's back as Hallie swiftly wrapped the bandages around her waist and secured it. Sweat was trailing down her forehead when the doctor gently lowered her back onto the couch's cushions.

"Not possible," Nix said firmly. "The subarch is injured. She won't be visiting the bridge."

That got Kessandra's attention. She tried to push upright again, but it didn't quite work. "I-Is that Ramona?" Kessandra clenched her eyes shut, then drew a fortifying breath. "Tell her I'll go. I'll—"

Nix lowered the mouthpiece to spare Ramona her next sentence: "Kess, I swear to Lumos and the depths of the abyss that if you leave that couch, I will kill you myself."

"Y-You can try, dear," Kessandra retorted.

"It won't be hard, Nines. You're nearly comatose."

Nix gave Hallie a commanding look, and the doctor smirked understandingly, slipping a pillow under Kessandra's head. Satisfied Kess wouldn't leap up on her own accord, Nix tuned back into Ramona's response.

"—captain is very insistent." Ramona paused, and the silence was filled with terror. "People are losing their minds, Sergeant. I—I don't know what's going on." Her voice trembled.

Lumos, this wasn't fair to her or anyone else. Nix swallowed past the sudden lump in her throat. "Are you safe right now?"

"In the switchboard room, yes. It's on the upper decks, opposite the soldiers' side."

Considering the soldiers were all in the promenade, that made it one of the safest places on the ship. Nix nodded curtly, even though she couldn't see it. "Stay there, Ramona. Lock the door, and keep as quiet as you can."

"I can't keep quiet. My job is to connect calls." Ramona hesitated. "It's important, Sergeant. Especially now."

Nix's heart ached for this woman. She massaged her forehead. "I know. Stay there. Tell the captain I'll be there soon—and once I've talked to her, I'm going to bring you a pistol. Three knocks, a pause, three knocks, okay? Don't open the door for anything else."

"Okay," Ramona whispered.

"You're doing great," Nix said softly. "Just keep your head for now. We'll get through this."

She hung up the phone and stared at the rose-gold plating the earphone for a minute. Disgust and anger prickled the corner of her mind, fury at the fact that this stuff was so prevalent. If it spread from ichoron-enhanced folk to anyone in proximity, the entire nation was doomed.

One thing at a time.

Nix drew a grounding breath, slipping into her bedroom for a jacket and her sarrant. Kessandra had already stocked the closet with a spare pistol, since Nix didn't really use one. It wasn't ichoron-built, but it'd help. Maybe. She holstered it for Ramona.

Then Nix contemplated the camera. It'd be safer here, and considering she might need it for images later, she wasn't inclined to risk its safety right now. Seeing it reminded her of the eerie image, which she fished out of the bloody pants she'd left on the carpet.

The pair of glowing eyes stared back at her. Nix suppressed a shudder, stepping back into the living room.

"I'm going to the bridge—" she paused, watching Hallie withdraw a needle from the crook of Kessandra's arm. Kess was unconscious now, her face finally smoothed, her breathing evening out. "Medicine?"

"Sedative. A light dose; she'll sleep for a few hours, but should be awake tonight." Hallie pressed a square of gauze to the injection site, then tucked the used syringe into a special bag on the table.

It was probably a wise idea. Nix didn't trust Kessandra to realize she was gone and not try to follow.

She didn't trust Kessandra for much, truth be told.

Hallie lifted her eyes, met Nix's gaze. "It's spreading, then."

"The Elite was just the first," Nix confirmed, massaging her forehead. She tossed the picture on the table. "I meant to ask Kessandra about this, but—well, I'll have to do it later. Have you seen this before?"

Hallie stepped away from Kessandra, stretching her back, and replaced her glasses with her original set. She squinted at the image, frowning. It took a moment for comprehension to flicker over her expression. "Only from eyewitness accounts. A specter from the mines. The Crypt Keeper, you soldiers call it."

"Not a very scientific name... but then again, we're not the most scientific bunch." Nix gestured at the image. "That's the first time I've seen it outside the mines. It has a reputation for killing the people who meet its gaze. They go mad—or they swim deeper into the mines and drown."

"Dethalos," Hallie muttered.

"Is it possible that thing is causing this?"

Hallie rubbed her chin thoughtfully, casting a dubious glance at Kessandra. "More likely it's a hallucinogenic side effect of the toxic material inside ichoron."

"Doctor, we're not hallucinating looking at that image."

That seemed to quell her. Hallie's jaw clenched, but she looked again at the image. "Three decades ago, no one thought ichoron was dangerous... so anything is possible. We don't know what we don't know."

The statement lingered between them, baneful and dangerous.

"I'll stay and watch her. Just in case." Hallie sighed, taking a seat on the opposite couch. "This will delay the surgery, Sergeant. I hope the captain's call is worth it."

Then the doctor still felt the surgery could progress, even with this new injury.

Nix breathed a sigh of relief and rolled her shoulders, loosening the joints. She did feel better after that shower. "The captain isn't worth my time. But if there's a way to stop dethalos from spreading on this ship, we need to take it—and it sounds like Ramona is in trouble. Do you think we can move the surgery down here?" It'd certainly be safer than Hallie running back and forth.

But the doctor snorted. "Absolutely not. I need extensive equipment for that surgery. I was already planning to hijack the medical bay, now that it's closed. All the doctors on the ship are making room calls right now, although I warned them that won't help." Hallie sighed, contemplating. "If you can get me back to my office tonight, I'll make sure we're prepped by tomorrow morning."

Day three—the day they were supposed to arrive in Fall.

What state would the city be in? If this spread on the ship, were the citizens there at risk too? Granted, the military presence in Fall was immense. Hopefully they'd gain a measure of control. Hopefully what was happening here was an isolated incident… because if it wasn't, Nix doubted any of them would survive.

Hallie seemed to be thinking the same. "There's a possibility we can turn the ship around and head back to Valkeshia. But then we'd have to survive three more days with everyone here… and the scientist in me needs to see how extensive this plague has become."

"We'll figure it out," Nix said with a confidence she didn't feel. "Stay here, and I'll grab my friend Leon to escort you back to your office later tonight. You met him before we boarded."

Hallie smiled. "Ah, yes. Strapping specimen. I do love

working with military folk." She winked, then plucked a book off the table beside the couch. Where she'd found that, Nix had no idea, but she was clearly content to settle in. "Give Captain Navaan my regards. She doesn't know me yet, but I'm certain she will."

Nix snorted. "Duly noted. Stay safe. Call Ramona if there's a problem."

Hallie waved her off. On the couch, Kessandra drew slow, steady breaths, still fast asleep. Ignoring the fear in her gut, Nix strode out the door.

20

THE SECOND THE ELEVATOR DOORS DINGED OPEN ON the promenade, Nix realized what Ramona meant: it was a different world above deck one. The promenade was deserted, tables of the café upturned, silent as death. Soldiers had probably been divvied out into patrol groups, but the ship was huge and it clearly wasn't enough coverage.

An inhuman snarl echoed through the cavernous space. Someone was losing their senses a couple decks above — Nix saw him lurching toward the banister, clutching his head. She crept through the shadows to avoid his attention, mostly because she didn't trust him not to catapult himself over the railing to reach her.

He'd probably break most of the bones in his body... but similar injuries hadn't stopped the Elite.

On the opposite side of the promenade, she reached the long hallways of staterooms. A quick glance down both corridors proved the passengers were tucked away now. A squad of soldiers moved through one of the hallways — five that she could count.

Good. Five meant they'd have a chance against one of the infected.

Nix's eyes darted to the hidden door behind the potted plant. Thinking of Ramona, she stepped quickly towards it, rapping on the door. "Josie," she hissed, rapping on the door. "It's me. Are you there?"

A long silence. Nix tried the handle, but it was locked. She knocked again, as loud as she dared considering the snarling two decks up. No one answered.

Good. If Josie was there, it meant she was smart. If she wasn't there, hopefully she'd found safety.

With renewed determination, Nix stepped through the other hallway, the one not patrolled by nervous soldiers. After the mishap with Kessandra, she wasn't prepared to test their trigger response — and she couldn't afford further injuries. Not with Kess laid up right now.

Her ichoron sarrant was a comforting weight; dried blood still smeared the edges of it, but it was as sharp as ever. Her other hand drifted to the knives sheathed at her hip. Might be good to have an off-hand weapon today.

Another squad was congregating in the library, which was in shambles. Two soldiers were bleeding out on the ground, and the other three had cornered another man at sarrant-point. Except this victim didn't seem to be ichoron-infected.

Nix paused on her way to the elevator, huffed in

Rebecca Thorne

exasperation, and shouted, "Hey. Sergeant Nix Marr. What the hell are you doing?"

"He snuck up on us—" one of the ensigns said viciously.

"His buddy killed Riles and Kaltas."

Nix's blood went cold. "Riles?"

The second ensign jabbed a shaking finger at their dead comrades. Both were in one piece—mostly. One had his neck snapped, and Riles—*Riles*. Lumos, she hadn't stood a chance. Her back was ripped to shreds, her hair taken out in chunks. Apparently, some infected used weapons, because a polished pen had been jabbed in her neck.

It clearly punctured something vital.

Nix wondered if Leon knew.

Was Leon even *alive*?

Cold fear gripped her, but now wasn't the time to break down. She pushed it aside and refocused on the squad. She'd had years commanding ensigns, and it infused her stance, her tone, her words. "Lower your Lumos-damned weapons, *now*." She waited as they weighed the request, waited until their eyes fell to her ichoron blade.

Reluctantly, they stepped away from the passenger. He was hunched into himself, sobbing hysterically.

Nix approached, glaring at the ensigns. "Stay put. Let me handle this."

They grumbled, but obeyed.

"You." Nix waited until the man squinted up at her.

His face was a mess of blood and tears. "Do you have a headache? Nausea?"

"N-No," the man hiccupped. He was clearly lucid, and his eyes flicked to the soldiers. "They were going to kill me. M-My husband—*Lumos*, what happened to my husband?" His eyes glazed over, and he broke down into another round of sobs.

"Your husband was sick. The best way to avoid the same fate is to quarantine," Nix lied. She wanted to tell the truth, but this little interlude proved these soldiers were too young, too reckless, to differentiate friend from foe. Until Kessandra woke up, Nix wasn't inclined to make their tenuous knowledge public. "Where's your stateroom?"

"On the f-fifth floor."

"Get there. Now. And don't open it until the captain makes another announcement."

He staggered to his feet, then flinched when the ensigns readied their weapons again. Nix held a hand to stop them, then gestured at the elevators. The man didn't move. Instead, his eyes drifted to the body behind him, one Nix hadn't even noticed. It was clearly an infected— the man had an ichoron prosthetic. He'd been thrown into the furniture near the windows and impaled, but even so, he was twitching like he might stand back up.

It was so unnatural. Only her extensive training kept her voice level now.

"He's already gone. Hurry up." *I'm sorry*, Nix wanted to say, but this man was clearly fragile enough as it was.

With a choking sound, the man fled, sprinting for the elevators. Once he was gone, the soldiers relaxed—but only a little. Nix glanced again at Riles, then strode to the infected. She couldn't risk him attacking anyone else.

"Rest in the depths," she murmured.

His glazed eyes found her, and he started clawing weakly toward her face.

She drove the ichoron blade across his neck, slicing deep into the muscle and veins, and she swore she felt it in her bones, too. Blood spurted, and his breathing became a gurgling gasp, then went silent. Swallowing her devastation, Nix wiped her sarrant on his clothes, then stepped back to the squad.

"This is the moment you decide what kind of soldiers you are." Her gaze was cold, her tone unforgiving. "If you slaughter everyone in sight, that will always be your legacy."

Two looked at their boots. The third swelled, although anguish tinted his voice. "But he came at us so fast—"

Nix held up a hand to silence him. "That's how you'll know *who* to fight. Shore up, ensigns. We're not on the front lines anymore." She cast another glance at Riles's corpse, regret settling over her shoulders. While she'd showered, people had died. Her resolve hardened; she needed to reach the captain.

There had to be a way to regain control.

"Continue your patrol. Watch each other's backs. And if you can, merge with other squads. Three of you will be at a disadvantage, and we don't need any more fatalities."

Nix clapped the shoulder of the one who'd protested. "Now's the time to prove yourself, soldier."

He nodded numbly, tears shining in his eyes. Under her hand, he was trembling.

Nix forced a smile. "Good luck." And she stepped toward the elevators, following in the passenger's steps. The squad lingered in the library, and one soldier watched her as she rose in the glass elevator, past the atrium, into the depths of the ship.

The nineteenth floor was empty. Lights beamed over upturned furniture and bloody carpets, but the gambling hall was deserted. Nix didn't spare it another glance. Instead, she turned for the staircase, identical to the one across the ship, and found the switch on the heavy metal door.

The door creaked open into a utilitarian hallway lined with rooms—similar to the passenger staterooms below. When they first met, Kessandra mentioned that the captain and essential crew lived opposite the soldiers on the upper decks. Nix just hadn't seen it before; a huge bulkhead partitioned the crew from the soldiers.

Straight ahead was another staircase to the *Luminosity*'s highest levels, which undoubtedly housed the boilers, air filtration systems, furnaces, sewage tanks and everything else needed for a ship this size. On her left was a steel wall with a single door labeled "bridge."

Ramona should be nearby, and Nix wasn't in a rush to see Captain Navaan before helping her. Nix scoured the empty hallway, scanning doors... and sure enough, there was the switchboard room. Nix cast a surreptitious glance down the hallway, then rapped three times, paused, and offered three more knocks.

The door creaked open, and Ramona peeked out. Nix wasn't sure who she was imagining, but she wasn't prepared to see an aged woman who was as elegant as she was determined. Her gray hair was pinned in a stately bun, and her ivory skin was a similar shade to Nix's.

Her dark eyes were fearful, and she glanced down the hallway before urging Nix inside. "I think it infected one of the navigators," Ramona whispered. "I heard screams a few minutes ago."

The switchboard room was dark and small. It consisted of not much more than a tall board of flashing lights—each light labeled for a different area of the ship— with a single telephone connected to it. Every phone on the *Luminosity* seemed to have a light, and it was dizzying to track it all.

Luckily, that wasn't her job. Nix closed the door firmly behind her, sheathed her sarrant, and tugged the pistol out of its holster. "It's loaded. It won't stop them... but it might slow them down long enough for you to escape."

"Them—our passengers. Our crew." Ramona's lip trembled, but she drew a fortifying breath and took the gun. Despite clearly being a spirescraper citizen, Ramona held it like she was familiar with weaponry. "Sergeant, what's going on? Why is this happening?"

Nix massaged her forehead. This wasn't some ensign with the order of protecting civilians. Ramona's entire job was communication—so it was best to have her informed. "Be discreet with this information." She waited for Ramona to nod resolutely before continuing. "Subarch Kessandra believes ichoron is poisoning the passengers. Anyone ichoron-enhanced."

Ramona stiffened. "Welanna—ah, the navigator—they take ichoron medicine for tremors. Does that mean—?"

"It might." Nix couldn't think about ichoron medicine turning people. Easier to imagine implants or prosthetics —not ingested ichoron. It was a dangerous slide into panic if she imagined her father complaining of headaches, sick with nausea. She couldn't let herself picture what the Marr casten might look like if this reached home.

Bloodied walls. Shredded corpses. Empty apartments.

Nothing would be the same.

Nix drew a trembling breath. "Was Welanna on duty? Would they be in the bridge?"

"T-They were about to report." Ramona clenched her eyes shut. "I told the captain to barricade the bridge, but she insisted all hands on deck. Lumos, that's why she didn't answer the call."

Fuck. Nix was suddenly glad she deviated to Ramona first.

It was a true testament to the switchboard attendant's courage that she squared her shoulders and lifted her chin. "How can I help, Sergeant? What can I do?"

Nix didn't want this responsibility. She prayed Captain Navaan was safe, if only to continue commanding the ship. But for now, she had to do *something*, so she glanced at the switchboard and cataloged her options.

"Do you have a ship-wide announcement option here? Or is it just individual calls?"

"Only calls. Anything more would overstep the captain's authority." Ramona carefully set the pistol on the table beside the switchboard. She had an empty glass beside it, and a half-eaten sandwich of meat and greens. It looked like roasted turkey, spiced to perfection if the scent was any indication. Nix's stomach growled—she hadn't eaten all day, and she hadn't even noticed until now.

Later.

Nix frowned. "Okay. Can you patch me to my room?"

Ramona swiftly took her seat, fingers moving too fast to follow. After a second, she handed the earpiece and mouthpiece to Nix, then leaned back while Nix took the call.

Hallie answered quickly. "Yes? Sergeant Marr's room."

"It's me," Nix said. "There's a bit of a problem. I'm with Ramona, but the bridge may be compromised."

"What do we need a bridge for anyway? The ship's on a rail. It only goes to one location."

Nix snorted. "Tell that to our captain." If she was still alive. "I'm going to scope it out, but if I'm delayed... just know I'm coming back. No matter what."

Hallie paused. "Shit. Stay safe, Nix."

"You too." She didn't ask how Kessandra was—she assumed there'd been no change, that Hallie wouldn't be joking if there had been. Still, as she hung up the phone, Nix desperately wished Leon or Kessandra were here to watch her back.

Too late for that.

"Keep an eye on the calls, and keep the door locked tight. No one enters until we dock at Fall, all right?" Nix glanced around the tiny room. "Do you have everything you need in here?"

"For three days, this room is all I am," Ramona admitted, and a flash of humor entered her tone. "I have rations, a chamber pot, and a cot folded in that closet."

Nix smirked. "You'd have made a great soldier. Stay here, stay hidden. When this is over, I'll come get you, okay?"

What she'd do with all these people, Nix had no idea. But she couldn't leave Ramona to the sharks. When the woman nodded agreement, one hand resting on the pistol, Nix let herself out. A few seconds later, the lock thudded into place behind her.

The hallway was too empty. Too quiet. Nix should have noticed it before.

With trepidation, she stepped toward the bridge.

21

This floor was closest to the heavy anchors attaching the *Luminosity* to the long undersea railway — while it was mostly a smooth ride, there was a whining undertone of metal-on-metal that grated on Nix's nerves.

Or it could be her own fear, amplified by the otherwise eerie silence.

The bridge stood alone, a single doorway set against an otherwise smooth metal wall.

Nix didn't knock. Sarrant brandished, she spun the handle, breaking the seal on the bridge's pressurized door. It hissed open, and she shoved it the rest of the way, stepping into the bridge as if she were stepping into a warzone.

Ten minutes ago, that might have been true. Now, the bridge was smeared in blood, and only Captain Navaan and a few of her crew were left alive, gasping over the gurgling corpse of, Nix presumed, Welanna. It only took a second to scrutinize the bridge itself: the blood splattered over the massive windows on the front of the ship, the broken handles where someone smashed into the helm, the panel of indicator lights now smashed to bits.

The room was large, but facing the shredded bodies of at least six crewmembers, it felt very small.

"What—the fuck—is going on?" Captain Navaan wheezed, pressing a hand to her thigh. Blood stained her crisp black slacks; it glistened in the bright lights. She turned wild eyes on Nix, who met her gaze unapologetically.

"Exactly what Kessandra warned you about," Nix said, assessing the other crew. There were three left standing aside from the captain. It wasn't clear what their purposes were on the ship, but they had enough ichoron medals adorning their uniforms to prove they were important.

Nix disregarded them with ease, sheathing her sarrant.

Captain Navaan, meanwhile, had processed what Nix said. She was holding a pistol similar to Kessandra's, and her eyes cut to a crewmember who'd clearly died from a bullet wound to the neck.

A ricochet?

With all this metal, Nix wouldn't be surprised.

The captain shoved the pistol back into a holster at her hip, clenching shaking hands into fists. *"Kessandra* knew about this too early. I knew there was a fucking reason the primarch wants her gone."

Nix stilled, eyes narrowing. "Say again, Captain?"

She pulled the title through gritted teeth.

But Navaan was clearly done with games. She rounded on Nix with the fury of the Ever-Storm, eyes dark and wild. "Your precious subarch is coordinating a strike against the throne. You can't expect him to take that lightly."

Nix pulled her shoulders back, her own anger flaring. "You're working with him. Did you coordinate with Polaris, too?"

"We work *for* the primarch, not *with* him. I didn't even know Polaris was supposed to be on board until he showed up," Navaan spat. She looked one second from wringing Nix's neck, her chest heaving, her face splotchy. "But the primarch made my directive clear. Kessandra was never supposed to make it to Fall. And now I know why— she's done something to my Lumos-damned ship."

Nix shouldn't have been surprised that the primarch employed multiple people to kill Kessandra, but hearing it confirmed set every sense on high alert. Captain Navaan was no longer an irritation to be tolerated. Now she was a threat—and Nix didn't take kindly to those.

It made vivid sense why Navaan had attempted to pin Polaris's murder on her.

Nix was suddenly grateful for Kessandra's intervention there.

"Kessandra didn't make your navigator lose their mind." Nix's words were tight, and her fingers curled around her sarrant's hilt. "In fact, the subarch is the only one trying to *stop* what's happening here. You might realize that if you pulled your head out of your ass for a few minutes."

Captain Navaan stiffened. "Don't you dare. I invited Kessandra here for a conversation, but if you test me, you'll be in chains the rest of this trip."

"Good fucking luck," Nix replied.

A stalemate.

In the corner of the room, a stifled sob caught their attention. Both of them glanced toward the windows. The view from the bridge truly was immaculate—floating blue algae finally giving way to the bones of the leviathan, and the thriving ecosystem the leviathan fall created. Bones emerged from the sand like mountains, and bioluminescent fish darted between them, chewing the decomposing flesh. Nix thought she caught a glimpse of one of the Deates Sea's abyssal sharks, but it was gone before she could tell.

But the surviving crew pressed against the windows stole their attention. One of them looked vaguely sick, clamping a hand over their mouth and nose as they stared with watery-eyed horror at the carnage. The other two were hunched together, shaking with whole-body sobs.

In shock. All of them.

Nix set her jaw. "You can try to arrest me, but you won't get far. Or you can focus on what's important here: damage control. Because like it or not, Captain, your ship is teetering on the edge. Kessandra is the only one who can help you."

Captain Navaan stared at her crew longer than

necessary. For several seconds, the sound of her heaving breaths filled the room. She scrubbed her face, and for a second, it looked like she was hiding tears.

When she spoke, her voice was strong. "Fine. What the hell is dethalos?"

Well, at least this was progress. Nix stepped to the body of the navigator, kneeling beside them. Welanna had been a young soul, and it pained Nix to see the way they'd bled out from the captain's bullets.

But at least this meant the Elite's never-ending stamina had been a special circumstance. Normal infected could be killed with bullets. Kessandra would be interested to know that... eventually.

"Kessandra has evidence that ichoron is poisoning our population—and dethalos is the result. A disease that ravages the mind, turns it violent." It still felt like a bad dream to voice out loud... but then again, the last two days on this ship already felt like a nightmare.

Nix couldn't quite forget the glowing eyes, though, the suspicion that something more supernatural was at play here. But if anyone on this ship was going to survive, she needed to provide the captain with researched facts, not speculation.

"Ichoron—" Captain Navaan cut herself off, shaking her head. "But this has never happened before."

"It has. The primarch just doesn't want to admit it." Nix's bitterness was unfiltered now. "Trust me, Captain. It'd be an impressive conspiracy if Kessandra had poisoned Welanna in her current state."

Navaan wiped her bloody hands on her pants, sinking into the captain's chair. She grimaced, pressing one palm into the wound on her thigh. "The fight with the other Elite. Ramona has been keeping me updated on the ship's proceedings—she receives the calls first."

Nix was mildly pleased that Ramona had taken the time. The *Luminosity*'s switchboard attendant was truly a credit to her profession.

"I heard." Nix closed Welanna's eyelids, then pushed to her feet. "Kessandra saved lives at the expense of her own safety. Keep that in mind as you decide your loyalty." Now Nix scowled. "And don't think she'll be an easy target, either. I promise you'd go through me first."

As it stood, they clearly had bigger problems.

Captain Navaan stared at her, exhaustion creeping into her gaze. "I signed on to command the greatest vessel in Valkeshian history. I never wanted to murder a royal."

"Good. Do your part and we might still get out of this." Nix stepped to the other crewmembers, offering a hand. Her rib twinged as she pulled the nauseas-looking one to his feet. "You don't have any ichoron enhancements, do you?" she asked him, point blank.

He numbly shook his head. "I just—don't do well with b-blood—" His eyes ghosted along the chunks of flesh smeared across the wooden floor, and his face drained of any remaining color. "Sorry," he gasped, and retched into a nearby trash can.

Nix grimaced at the sound, stepping away to give him space.

The other two crewmembers weren't much better off. One was clearly trying to keep her head on, but her partner was a shaking mess. Nix sighed, and a deep part of her wished she could afford a similar breakdown.

She couldn't. Instead, she faced Navaan. "Do you have communication to Fall?"

"No. There are undersea cables between Valkeshia and Fall, but radio contact doesn't go far underwater from a moving ship." Captain Navaan's leg didn't seem to be bleeding much anymore. She'd found a handkerchief somewhere to apply to the wound; it was bright red, but not saturated.

"So, we have no idea what we'll find there." Nix had *really* hoped they could call ahead.

Navaan's gaze sharpened. "You think Fall is facing this same problem?"

"I think this problem is stronger near the source of ichoron. There's a reason no one was sick on the surface." The crewmember was done retching, which was a small blessing, but he still looked sick. Nix considered him for a moment, but if he didn't have any ichoron enhancements, he was probably just unprepared.

She couldn't blame him there.

Nix squinted into the abyss, but although the water was bright and clearer down here, visibility still wasn't great. "How much longer until we reach Fall?"

"We'll dock midday tomorrow."

"And there's no way to turn the ship around?" Nix asked.

Captain Navaan laughed coldly. "No. The ballast tanks are already filled, and we've pressurized too much. All our downward momentum will be gone if we empty those tanks. Fall has a special mix of ultra-light air that lets us climb back up the rail, but we have to dock there first."

Nix knew that, but she'd been hoping for a secret override switch, some internal mechanisms on this massive vessel that could miracle their way back home. No matter what, this was a one-way trip.

She just had to pray they'd find something favorable inside that glass dome.

Captain Navaan was squinting at her sick crewmember. "You asked him if he'd had ichoron enhancements." Her tone was contemplative, dark. "And dethalos is an ichoron infection."

Nix frowned. "It's not like other sicknesses—we can't trace exactly how people are getting infected. A quarantine is the safest way to ensure everyone's safety."

"Quarantine. Right." Captain Navaan pushed to her feet. "Lyso, Jules. You two may return to your quarters. I can handle things for now—go gather your wits."

The shaking crewmembers staggered to their feet, cast one final glance at their ill cohort, and stumbled to the door. The one Nix presumed was Jules wept as she inched around Welanna's body, stepped over pieces of people she'd clearly known well. Lyso was silent, numb, as they followed.

The door closed behind them. The remaining crewmember hauled himself to his feet. His face was dangerously pale, but his eyes were alert, and he swallowed hard. "A-And me, Captain? I'll—I'll be okay. It's just a s-shock." He stumbled over the word, gasping as he accidentally looked down at the bloody floors again.

Captain Navaan watched him carefully, her expression pained.

"Dethalos infects those who have ingested ichoron," she murmured.

"We don't know that—" Nix tried to say, but in the next breath, a gunshot cut the air.

The crewmember glanced down at his chest, blossoming with blood. His hands shook as he clawed at his shirt, gaping like a fish, tears streaming down his face. "C-Captain—" he gasped, but the word cut off with two more gunshots.

He fell.

It only took a second to process what had happened, and then Nix had her sarrant out, the blade pressed against Captain Navaan's neck. "What the *fuck*, Navaan?" The ichoron sliced skin, a clear warning.

"I can't take the risk of another crewmember losing their mind." The captain dropped the pistol in her hand, her voice thick. "If you kill me, we'll all die. I'm the only one who knows the docking procedures in Fall, now."

"You—" Nix trembled with rage. "You killed him. *He wasn't infected.*"

"He was showing symptoms, and that's enough."

"*How?*" Nix snarled. How could she discard a life so carelessly?

Navaan wasn't listening. "That's dethalos, isn't it? Ichoron-enhanced are the ones murdering us." The captain laughed, her voice teetering on the edge of hysteria. "What's really happening with Kessandra, Sergeant? Something tells me she's not laid up with injuries."

It hit too close to home. Nix pressed the ichoron blade a little deeper, cold satisfaction sliding through her veins when Captain Navaan hissed in fear. "The only reason I'm not killing you now is because we have bigger problems... and someone has to dock us in Fall."

"Yes. I do." Captain Navaan held her breath, but Nix pulled away with a derisive huff. The woman pressed a sleeve to her neck, checking the wound Nix had left there.

Nix, meanwhile, kicked her gun away. It slid across the bloodied floor, well out of reach now. Right past the corpse of the crewmember Nix didn't know to save. Blood pooled around his corpse, but he was unnaturally still.

Shit. Nix didn't sheath her sarrant. "You have one fucking job now, Navaan. Get us to our destination—and pray to Lumos there's mercy for you there."

With one final glance at the crewmember's dead body, the other corpses in the room, the murderer left standing, Nix stalked out of the bridge.

The door slammed behind her, and a moment later it locked from the inside. Nix sheathed her sarrant with a shuddering sigh. "What the fuck," she whispered, her voice breaking as she stared down the empty hallway. Her eyes skirted to Ramona's switchboard room, but the woman was well-barricaded and equally armed. She'd be safe for now, and they may need her expertise.

Kessandra was Nix's next focus. She pivoted for the staircase, boarded the elevator back to the library.

She'd just stepped into the empty room when an announcement came over the ship's loudspeakers. Captain Navaan's voice was clear and controlled—no sign of fear or doubt as she spoke.

"Attention, passengers, soldiers, and crew. This is an urgent update on our quarantine situation. The threat lies not with a single assailant, but with any ichoron-enhanced person aboard this ship. Repeat: ichoron-enhanced people are succumbing to a disease that sends them into a violent spiral. To protect yourself, you must separate from any ichoron-enhanced person.

"Soldiers. Keep the peace... through any means necessary."

Nix stopped short as the elevator doors closed behind her.

"Are you fucking kidding me?" she shouted at the ceiling.

Of course, Captain Navaan wasn't there to hear it. But at her words, a snarl echoed down one of the long stateroom hallways—and instantly, gunshots echoed. Screams filtered from the staterooms as passengers began turning on each other. They grew more panicked as the soldiers turned on *them*.

With one fucking announcement, Navaan had lost control of her own ship.

But of course, that was how she justified her own Lumos-damned fear. It wasn't murder if everyone was doing it—the ethics of survival were unfocused on a battlefield.

Nix should have slit Navaan's throat when she had the chance. Agony clenched her chest as she surveyed the elevator, imagined riding it back to the nineteenth floor, climbing the staircase, barging into the bridge, cutting the woman down.

It wouldn't help now. Navaan made an error—but Nix had guided her down that path.

All the blood that spilled on this ship was Nix's fault, now. Did Kessandra know the captain would lose herself like this? Is that why she kept her suspicions of dethalos close to her chest this morning, rather than revealing the disease to Navaan early?

Probably. Kessandra thought ahead. Nix didn't.

And now everyone was paying for her own damned mistake.

Nix's throat was closing. She couldn't breathe around her pounding heart. Fuck. She moved rigidly, unsheathing her sarrant, stepping through the long hallway of staterooms. Behind the doors, more screams, panicked shouts, pleading, begging. How many ichoron-enhanced were on this ship?

How many *would* have turned, if given the time?

And how many wouldn't have?

The world was closing in. Everything felt muted—like she was watching from someone else's eyes. In the promenade, four troops of soldiers were engaged in combat: some with passengers, some with each other. High above her, someone shouted about an ichoron tattoo, someone else pleaded it was small, clearly she wasn't sick, why would—and an anguished scream as gunshots echoed.

Sticking to the shadows, Nix flinched, choking on a sob. She wanted to intervene, but this felt too big. Like leaping into a battlefield without a plan. Everything was dissolving, spiraling out of control, and Nix needed to get somewhere she could breathe again.

The elevators. Deck one. Kessandra.

But as Nix rounded the corner, trembling, shuddering, someone clamped a hand over her mouth.

22

PANIC SEIZED HER.

Nix reacted on instinct, grabbing her assailant's arm, spinning them over her shoulder. Leon thudded to the ground in front of her, the air leaving his lungs with a *whoosh*. He gaped, gasped, and wheezed, "Fuck, Nix. It's *me*."

"D-Don't sneak up on me," Nix snapped. She tripped over the first word and hated herself for it.

His expression twisted into one of sympathy. He rolled onto his hands and knees, taking her proffered hand. The second he stood, a *thud* caught both their attention. They spun, weapons ready—but the person who had tipped over a banister and crashed to the marble floor, gutted and bloody, was definitely dead.

Nix stared too long, covering her mouth with a hand.

Leon was the one who hauled her behind a huge potted plant, hiding them from view. His voice was clipped. "Tell me you're going to deck one. It might be the only safe place on the ship right now."

Deck one.

Kessandra. Once she woke up, she'd know what to do.

Nix nodded, fumbled for the key. Her shaking hands couldn't quite get it in the lock, so he took it from her, swiftly opened the metal grating and ushered her inside. Only once the elevator doors had closed did he slump against the wall.

"What the fuck was the captain thinking with an announcement like that?" Leon ran his hands through his hair. "Everyone was already on edge. It didn't take much to tip them."

"It's my fault," Nix breathed, and her words dissolved into a sob.

Leon watched her, expression pained. After a moment's hesitation, he pulled her into a hug. "You weren't holding a gun to her head, forcing her to say that. Come on, Nix. This is so much bigger than you."

His words were weighted, and she couldn't even argue with him. His embrace was strong and comforting, even though she was his commanding officer, the experienced one, the one who faced battle and kept her head.

Except on the front lines, everything made sense. Find enemy, fight enemy... kill enemy.

Here, she didn't even know who the enemy was.

She pressed her forehead into his chest for a few short breaths, savoring this moment of quiet. The elevator doors dinged open, and she pulled away with a shaky breath and a forced smile. "Sorry."

"You haven't done anything wrong, Nix," Leon said quietly.

He looked a hundred miles away, his expression distant and sad. Nix could relate. It was more and more likely they wouldn't survive to see the surface again. Sunlight, spirescrapers... family, friends. They'd die down here, and no one would know why. It'd take another decade to build a new ship and travel the rail to find their remains.

If Fall was safe, they might have a chance.

But Nix was doubting that more and more.

"I wish you hadn't accepted that assignment," Nix said, regret in every syllable.

Leon squeezed her arm. "Funny. I was thinking the same thing about you."

Nix laughed, rubbed her face, and pulled her shoulders back. Carefully reassembling the pieces, shoving anything too emotional into a little box. She could deal with it later—if they survived. There were more important things at stake, and she couldn't afford to lose her head for long.

Tremors still wracked her body, but they faded into forced determination. "Well, I'm glad you found me. I know your orders are to patrol the ship, but I have new ones... if you're willing."

Leon saluted crisply. "Our lieutenant is dead, and I

don't take orders from a captain who never served in the military. What do you need, Sergeant?"

Relief filled her soul. Nix nodded crisply, leading him down the empty walkway of deck one. The glass below them gleamed with blue bioluminescence, and the lights here were dimmed for the evening. It cast everything in a quiet cerulean hue. The lounge sat in empty silence, and as they passed it, Nix wondered what happened to Dominik and Josie.

She hoped they were okay.

She somehow doubted it.

"Doctor Jesko is watching Kessandra right now. She needs an escort back to deck eighteen. Get her there, then stay with her and keep her safe." Nix spoke as they walked, glancing over her shoulder at Leon. He was distracted with the views of this deck, but he righted himself as she addressed him. "Hallie is preparing a surgical bay to remove Kessandra's eye. It's the only way we can keep her from —" Nix cut herself off.

Leon understood anyway. "Is she already showing symptoms?"

Nix nodded. "She's under no illusions it won't happen."

"And she suggested the surgery?" Leon frowned. "Does she really want to be incapacitated right now?"

Nix rolled her eyes. "No, *she* suggested that I kill her. I forced the surgery."

"Keeping her alive, because you're such a good

bodyguard." On the surface, it was a factual statement—but there was a hint of amusement lining his voice.

"Shut up." Nix's cheeks were flushing as she stopped at her door, rapping sharply on the wood. "Hallie, it's me. I brought backup." She reached for her key, but the door clicked open.

Kessandra was on the other side. "Ah. Excellent timing."

She was standing. Awake. Nix had only been gone a few hours—Kessandra shouldn't have recovered so quickly. Nix craned past her to see Hallie relaxing on the couch, fully alive and clearly untouched, reading her book like nothing was wrong.

Suspicion flared. Nix glanced back at Kess. "You're supposed to be unconscious."

"I *was* unconscious, thanks to a sedative from the good doctor." Kessandra narrowed her eyes, like she hadn't approved of that tidbit of information. "Luckily, I woke up. What happened with Captain Navaan? I was just about to head to the bridge when we heard her announcement."

"You were—" Nix shoved past her into the room, glaring at Hallie. "Some doctor you are."

"She's a notoriously terrible patient," Hallie said, flipping to the next page in her book.

Leon filed in after them, closing the door behind him. He saluted Kessandra. "Subarch. A pleasure to see you again."

"Leon." She appraised him, a queen studying her pawn. "You're in excellent health. That bodes well."

"Uh, thanks?"

Nix stepped in front of him, shielding him from view. "*You* should be sitting down. You were bleeding out on my couch earlier today." Anger flared, and she stiffened. "You didn't."

Kessandra's expression was coolly neutral.

Not confirming.

Not denying.

"You *asshole*," Nix seethed, striding towards Kess, ripping up her loose shirt. The stitches were tightly wrapped, but she felt along Kessandra's stomach for them. As predicted, the sutures were stiffer than a normal set. Not thread. Ichoron.

"As much as I missed your touch, this is hardly the time," Kessandra said.

"Take them out," Nix spat, whirling on Hallie. "Lumos, when did you even put them *in*?"

Hallie pushed to her feet, carefully bookmarking her page. She slipped her book back into her leather medical kit. "While you were showering. I originally refused, for the record, but she's quite persuasive."

"This is no time to be laid up." Kessandra smoothed her shirt. Moving made her wince a little, but compared to how she'd been hours ago, it was a marked improvement. A stupid, ridiculous improvement.

Nix wanted to scream.

"I saw the image you collected, and I have a theory

about your ichoron lens. All the photos I've reviewed haven't shown those eyes—but none have a lens like your camera. If it's ichoron-specific, there's a possibility it's able to transpose the hallucination of the Crypt Keeper into the film somehow." Kessandra tilted her head, contemplating. "It's only a theory right now, of course. We'd have to test it with a normal camera to be sure. But it is an interesting piece of evidence—"

"Don't talk to me about evidence," Nix hissed.

Kessandra sighed. "I recognize you're concerned, but Doctor Jesko is leaving two more sedatives. You'll be able to subdue me if you're still too soft to finish the job. In the meantime, I can't afford to spend my final hours unconscious."

Final hours. Like she was on her damned death bed. Nix clenched her jaw and stomped to the kitchen, wrenching a cabinet open. "I'm not *soft* because I won't kill you." Her words were bitter, and she snatched a jar of pecans. Her stomach was not happy after an entire day without food, although now she almost felt too sick to eat. "I won't kill you because you're important to Valkesh and this cause."

And me, Nix's heart whispered.

"I know," Kessandra said quietly.

Oh.

Hallie cleared her throat. "Sedatives are over here. One shot anywhere on her body will work, but use both if you *really* have to knock her out. If Leon can get me to my lab, the surgery will be ready tomorrow morning."

Nine hours from now. Nix nodded numbly.

Kessandra, meanwhile, pinched the bridge of her nose. "We talked about this. I'm not partaking in that surgery."

At the door, Leon shifted awkwardly. "I'm... ah, gonna wait outside. Come find me when you're ready, doctor." He slipped out the door with a wave.

In his absence, Hallie snorted. "You're hardly prepared for the alternative, Kessandra."

"I'll be half-blind."

"Better than all dead," Nix snapped, crunching on pecans. The texture felt like wax in her mouth, the flavor dull. "We're running out of options here, Kess. Stop thinking you're replaceable, because you aren't."

It came out vitriolic, poisoned with the anguish of the past.

Kessandra drew a measured breath. "Doctor Jesko, you may leave. Be safe getting back to your lab."

"Sure," Hallie replied, shouldering her bag. "Don't kill her." It wasn't immediately clear who she was talking to. She stepped out the door, closed it softly behind her.

Silence lingered in her wake. Nix angrily stuffed more pecans in her mouth, but her adrenaline was wearing off and anguish was hitting hard. She wasn't surprised to feel tears pricking her eyes, or see her hands shaking.

Kessandra sighed, stepping lightly toward the couch.

She wasn't going to start the conversation. Upstairs, people were massacring each other, fighting for their lives against a disease no one could identify. In the sudden emptiness of the suite, Nix couldn't find the energy to argue. Instead, she diverted the topic.

"You think my camera might identify the Crypt Keeper?"

"My ichoron eyeball sees it every time." Kessandra tugged the file on the coffee table closer to her, reviewing the images yet again.

"What?" Nix stiffened, glancing around the room. "Is it here? Now?"

Kessandra grimaced as she leaned forward, plucking the developed photo Nix had taken out of the pile. Even from here, Nix could see the malicious gaze peering over the rocking chairs in the black and white image. "No, it isn't among us now. Frankly, I assumed it was a hallucination... but only my ichoron eye could see it. By capturing it on camera, you've proved it's real. Ichoron finds ichoron."

Nix popped a few more pecans in her mouth, speaking around them. "You think that thing is related to this."

"I think it's a byproduct. A flare-up of the poisonous substance, maybe?" Kessandra frowned, letting the picture fall back to the table. "We can't break ichoron into basic elements. There's nothing else like it. It wouldn't be unreasonable to assume we're seeing a chemical reaction in real time."

It didn't make sense, and judging by the frustrated look on Kess's face, they both knew it. Nix chewed slowly, swallowing. "Have you considered ghosts?" She wasn't joking.

Spirescraper citizens didn't share their superstitions... probably because rich folk died in cushy rooms under the supervision of a doctor and loved ones, usually from natural causes like old age. No one starved in the spirescrapers, not like they did in the castens below.

Nix expected some derision at that suggestion.

But Kessandra didn't laugh. "Of course, I have. Unfortunately, the pseudo-science on identifying specters is notoriously unreliable. It can hardly be presented as evidence to a panel of educated scholars."

Nix set the jar of pecans back on the counter. "Have you tried killing that thing with an ichoron sarrant?"

"Beg pardon?"

"The ghost. The Crypt Keeper. Whatever you call it, ichoron finds ichoron." Nix gestured at the sarrant she'd left by the front door, propped near a coat rack. "What if we try to kill it?"

"It's incorporeal. I'm not even convinced it's real, despite photographic evidence." But Kessandra's eyes cut to the sarrant, and her expression turned thoughtful. She was sitting perfectly straight, shoulders pulled back, chin lifted—even with the mess of her uniform, she somehow still looked regal.

Dressed to the nines.

Fuck.

"You have to get the surgery, Kess. Please."

Kessandra appraised her, clearly unsurprised by the pivot. Her ichoron eye glowed softly, her smoky green gaze immensely sad.

She was still going to refuse. Nix leapt into another tirade before she had the chance. "I can't lose anyone else. Quian almost killed me. Then you left, and I've spent four years trying to piece myself back together." It didn't seem convincing enough. She was trying to persuade Kessandra to give up her literal eyesight. Nix wracked her brain for what might work. "And—and you have an obligation to the citizens of Valkesh. If you die down here, they—"

"Nix."

She stopped.

Kessandra spoke softly. "The citizens of Valkesh aren't owed more than I've already given. Not right now. But I will get the surgery."

Oh. Nix swallowed past a sudden lump in her throat.

Kessandra sighed, rubbing her arm. "I probably should have done it years ago. It'd have made more sense than cramming it onto this short trip. But there were... complications. The palace can be a dangerous place."

Nix searched her face, finally seeing the truth. "You were worried about being incapacitated. Of what the primarch might do to you while you recovered."

Kessandra flinched, the motion so subtle Nix almost missed it.

Nix crossed the room, sitting beside her.

"Shit." She thought about everything she'd learned on this trip, about Kessandra experimenting on herself, skirting a ruler who wanted her dead, playing the perfect subarch to the public and a deadly game of politics behind closed doors. All for Valkesh. "You really have been trapped in an ichoron tower, haven't you?"

Kessandra massaged her brow. "The Hectron Tunnel Collapse changed everything. I had the return trip—just a few days—to determine my next move, or be killed some other way. So, I twisted the story, presented myself as a hero. If the army's darling went missing, people would notice."

She was right, as always.

The subarch's gaze shifted to the ceiling, like she couldn't look at Nix. "The one thing I didn't consider... was you."

A devastating sadness washed through Nix's body. She was suddenly back in the army tower, pleading with Kessandra to stay. The days after the tunnel collapse were filled with cold, distant words that hinted at something irreparable—especially at a time when Nix was sinking into grief.

Kessandra hadn't stuck around long once they reached Valkeshia. She stepped into the army tower's elevator and never looked back.

Nix knew. She'd waited for one final glance.

"Yeah. I noticed." Nix's words held none of her old anger. This time, it was a neutral statement.

Numb.

Kessandra's fingers wound through Nix's for a bare moment, tracing the back of her hand before pulling away. Where she touched, Nix's skin burned.

"You misunderstand. You're all I've cared for since we

met… and the primarch knew it." She pulled back, one hand pressed to her side over the ichoron stitches. Her voice was pained. "Once he realized he couldn't touch me, you were the next logical alternative. And not just you — your father. Your casten. Everything you love, he would have destroyed if I didn't comply."

An icy shock of fear slid down Nix's spine. "What?"

"That's why I severed our ties. No matter what, I needed you safe."

If Kessandra was hoping for sympathy, she was looking in the wrong spot. Fury replaced fear in the span of a heartbeat, and Nix tensed, rigid. "Are you *fucking* kidding me?"

That seemed to throw Kessandra off balance. "Beg pardon?"

"Oh, shut up." Nix shoved to her feet, pacing the room. All of this. Everything in the last four years — a ploy. She was promoted to sergeant, probably because sergeants had a higher survival rate, and the primarch couldn't lose his leverage. Then she was barred from further promotions because they give Nix too *much* power.

A carefully constructed game. Keeping Nix leashed in Kessandra's sights, a permanent reminder of her obedience.

Nix would snap the primarch's neck in two. He'd better pray they never made it back.

But he was far, far away, and Kessandra was right here. The perfect channel for her ire. She spun back, fists clenched. "Everything in the last four years, all the things you said—you did it to protect me? Do you even fucking *know* me?"

Kessandra stiffened. "I know you're impulsive and occasionally reckless. A lowly officer facing the might of a nation."

"Gee, thanks," Nix snapped.

"You cannot fathom what he might have done, Nix. With one order, he could have wiped out the Marr casten —and made it seem like an accident." Kessandra's voice was cold. "That building beside yours, the one that collapsed? Did you ever stop and think what *they'd* done to his predecessor?"

Shit.

Nix hated him. She hated them all. She dug her fingers in her hair, spun toward the windows. The bioluminescence wasn't calming right now. It was oppressive, a reminder that it was either the weight of an ocean... or the weight of a dictator.

"I don't need your protection. You're not responsible for me and mine."

"I disagree. My very presence placed you in his sights. I never should have accepted your invitation that first night on the *Luminosity*." Kessandra's words were tense. "But I did. And after, there was no move. No counter." Now her voice trembled. "No escape."

Nix felt cold. The idea of losing Kessandra, even if it got Quian back—she couldn't stomach it. Regardless of what had happened since, she wouldn't trade those stolen nights in the Crypt for the world.

A quick breath, and Kessandra's composure was back. She pushed to her feet, the movement smoother than it should have been. "I let you think it was easy to leave. Nothing could be further from the truth."

Nix didn't buy it. "So, for four Lumos-damned years, you just... what? Played his game? Couldn't have gotten a message to me any sooner, huh?" Nix stepped into her space, close enough to feel the heat between them. "It sure seemed easy for you. Sitting in your tower, convincing yourself this was the right move."

"What was the right move, then? Tell me," Kessandra hissed.

Nix held her gaze. It felt like she might ignite at any moment. "We work together. I'm your knight, Kess. *Use* me. You're not alone on that board."

It hung between them, electrified.

And to Nix's surprise, tears sprung in Kessandra's eyes—even the ichoron one. She scrubbed her face, drew a trembling breath. "I couldn't use you. Not after Quian."

Nix stilled.

Because there was the final hurdle between them.

Kessandra backed away, knees hitting the couch, and braced herself on the armrest. Like she couldn't bear to be too close to Nix anymore. Her words came out in a tumble. "You weren't the same after, and that was my fault. But I swear on Lumos and the depths, Nix. I *tried* to save Quian. The moment I realized what was happening, I tried to get him out."

Nix's throat closed, and fighting past it was a struggle. "We don't have to talk about this."

"Please. Just listen." Kessandra sounded so desperate that Nix didn't have the heart to silence her again. "Boulders were crashing around us, closing passageways. He thought you were deeper inside. I used my oxygen tank to prop open one of the tunnels... but then I was trapped near the entrance, pulling soldiers through the opening. Quian—he was panicking."

Nix didn't want to imagine Quian and Kessandra hovering at the entrance to the mines. She didn't want to imagine Kessandra sacrificing her air supply for the other dive teams.

She didn't want to imagine Quian delving into a death trap to save *her*.

"Tell me you stopped him," Nix breathed. Her body was chilled.

They both knew how this ended.

Kessandra shuddered. "We had *no* idea you were on the surface already. He swam away before I could grab him—and without my oxygen tank, I couldn't follow."

Tanks were attached to the individual dive suit. There was a spare breather for emergencies, but it was a temporary solution. The ichoron-enforced metal tanks were quite literally life or death to dive teams.

Following Quian without one would have been a death sentence.

"Please. Tell me what else I could have done." Kessandra's words were pleading, begging for atonement.

She buried her face in her hands, her shoulders shaking. "I've replayed it in my head, over and over, for years. I don't—I don't know what else I could have done."

Just an accident. Of course Quian would dive back in to save Nix. Of course Kessandra would have followed if she could. The world was literally caving in around them, and a second passed—and the wrong choice was made.

But it wasn't Kessandra's wrong choice.

It was Quian's.

"Why didn't you tell me?" Anguish painted Nix's voice.

"I tried." Kessandra sunk into one of the dining chairs, misery in every line of her body. "Lumos, Nix, I tried, every single day on the *Luminosity*'s return trip. But I *let him die*. How could I tell you what happened? All the things I didn't do?" A shudder ripped through Kessandra's body.

Nix clenched her eyes shut, drawing slow breaths.

Quian. *Quian*. Her best friend; that stupid, heroic boy. Diving into a bad situation to save Nix—and she hadn't even needed saving. And he died that way, crushed under the weight of his heroism. The injustice of it pushed tears to her eyes, too. She'd spent years crying over his death, and now she mourned everything he was in his final moments.

Brave. Stupid. Fantastic.

Lumos below, she missed him so fucking much.

Kessandra didn't say another word, not as the minutes passed. Not as Nix paced, sorting out her feelings. Quian's ghost seemed to fill the space, his presence suddenly so strong Nix swore he was standing beside her like always. But it would never be that way, not again.

It took a long time to realize Kessandra, for once, wasn't looking for excuses. She wasn't fumbling apologies. She sat on the dining chair like she was awaiting an execution—and had utterly accepted her fate.

Like she deserved everything Nix had handed her.

Except she didn't.

"It wasn't your fault," Nix said.

It took everything to drag out the words, but for once, they were true. She'd spent years hiding behind anger, fear, hatred. It was easier to blame Kessandra than try to understand her, and that was something Nix couldn't stomach anymore. If she continued this cycle of judgement instead of forgiveness, they would never survive this.

Upstairs, the ship was chaos. Here, the tumult was quieter, but no less dangerous.

"If that's the truth, then it wasn't your fault, Kess." Nix faced her, nearly pleading. "You know that. Right?"

Kessandra was utterly broken. She inhaled, trembling. "My great-uncle gave me the perfect excuse to leave you behind. And because I'm a coward, I took it. All I know, Nix, is that since I stepped into that elevator and left you behind, I've hated myself more every day."

Nix's protective barrier shattered.

"You're not a coward," she swore, striding forward.

Kessandra rose from her chair, bracing for a hit.

Instead, Nix pulled her into a fierce hug.

She wasn't mindful of her strength, and Kessandra's arms wound around her shoulders instantly, squeezing back like Nix was the only port in a storm. The embrace was everything Nix wanted in the last four years, every breath they'd failed to exchange together.

Quian was dead, but he'd made his choice. It was brave, it was reckless, and it was his. Kessandra shouldn't have spent years atoning for his mistake, trapped in that tower while dodging a cunning tyrant. Nix shouldn't have spent the same time loathing her from afar.

Mistakes were made. The past was over. But today, right now... maybe they could make amends.

Nix pressed a desperate kiss to Kessandra's lips. Then another.

Comfort shifted to urgency.

Their tears mingled as they crashed together.

23

Nix had her fun with people before Kessandra. There was the girl from the Marr casten, when they were just old enough to explore themselves without pressure. One time, she'd kissed Quian, just to see how it felt—like kissing a brother, nothing either of them cared to repeat. Another time, a fellow sergeant courted her for months, blowing off steam after the perils of war.

And then, Nadine. Everyone remembered Nadine.

None of them had been recent, and time meant that every touch from Kessandra lit her body aflame. They'd barely started and it was almost too much—but each caress held the passion of desperation. Every searing kiss was years they lost, every heated whisper a promise that filled a void in Nix's chest.

She couldn't get enough.

Kessandra couldn't either, apparently. Her lips were insistent as she urgently lifted Nix's shirt. She softened her touch only when Nix hissed in pain, feathering against the sensitive bruise near Nix's cracked rib—but then her touch was so gentle the pain shifted into something new. Kess dove in for another kiss.

An alarm blared overhead.

It sounded like a siren, but a warning one. *ATTENTION,* the mechanical voice intoned. *ATTENTION. PLEASE RETURN TO YOUR STATEROOM.*

"Shit," Kessandra gasped.

"It's anarchy upstairs. Didn't I mention?" Nix stretched her arms as Kessandra stalked to the door. The separation gave her a bit of breathing room, but the cool air against her skin only made it pebble with goosebumps. Everything in her body pulsed, and Nix still didn't want to stop.

She had to get a hold of herself.

But then Kessandra jammed a red button hidden behind the doorframe—and the alarm cut off abruptly. It still blared in the distance, muted and persistent, but now it felt like they were in their own little bubble.

"Royals can silence ship-wide announcements?" Nix wasn't even surprised.

Kessandra strode back to her. Her eyes were still rimmed in red, but the anguish had been replaced with desperation. Passion. "We're already in our stateroom. And there's nothing we can do for the chaos." Her hands trailed again under Nix's shirt, but this time they slid higher.

Higher.

Nix hissed through her teeth. "We could still—"

"What? Get ourselves killed?" Kessandra scoffed, her eyes searching Nix's. Her hand traced the swell of Nix's breast under her brassiere, but she didn't move further just yet. Despite that, something tense wound between them, tight as a gear ready to spring loose. "We'll go out. But there's no way two people can stop what's happening. May I?"

Nix should say no.

She should insist they try to save a few people, at least.

But Kessandra was inches away for the first time in years, and Nix swore she couldn't breathe. Nix recaptured Kessandra's lips and murmured against them: "Fine. You win."

"What a surprise," Kessandra breathed, and her hand squeezed Nix's breast, her fingers running along the sensitive nipple with expert motions. It made Nix feel faint, weak in the knees, and it absolutely wasn't fair that Kessandra still had this hold on her—even after years.

But Nix wanted her hands all over Kessandra, not the other way around.

"Uh uh. You're first, not me." Her voice was fierce, leaving no room for argument—something Kessandra absolutely adored in these moments. Already, Kess's breath quickened in anticipation, and she pressed harder against Nix's body as she withdrew her wandering hand.

Nix kissed her again, almost aggressively. "Are you up for it? With everything?" Now Nix's fingers trailed along the bandages on Kessandra's side, applying light pressure.

Without Kessandra's hands all over her, she could think more clearly.

Not by much, but it was something.

"I—" Kessandra took a moment to formulate her thoughts. "I asked for ichoron stitches for a reason, dear."

"*This* was the reason?"

"One of them. I plan for most contingencies."

That caused a spark of irritation. Nix took Kess's wrists in her hand, pinning them over her shoulder as she pressed two fingers between Kessandra's legs. "I'm not a fucking contingency, and you'd do well to remember it."

At her touch, Kessandra melted against her, burying her forehead in the crook of Nix's neck. "H-Have I told you the thrill I get whenever you call yourself my knight?"

Satisfaction slid through Nix like an elixir. She rubbed hard, tight circles, delighting in the way Kessandra ground against her. "I'll remember that. You're not going to last long tonight, are you?"

"Four. Years," Kessandra gritted out.

"You're telling me you haven't met anyone else that whole time?" It was unfathomably long for Nix—even if the other encounters meant nothing in the long run.

Kessandra's chest was heaving. She was close already, a little too stimulated by Nix's touch. "What can I say? I have a type."

That sent a flush down Nix's entire body. She forcefully hiked Kessandra up. The subarch immediately wrapped her legs around Nix's waist—a practiced motion Nix thought neither of them would remember.

"Bedroom," Nix growled.

Heavy kisses made it difficult, but Nix managed to navigate past the couches, moving quickly for the bedroom. Carrying Kess sent a shot of pain through her rib, but that faded when Kessandra nipped her ear, tangled her fingers in Nix's long hair.

Hallie wouldn't approve.

Nix didn't give a shit.

They didn't make it far into the bedroom. The bed suddenly seemed too far away, and Nix was rather enjoying this vertical approach. She shoved Kessandra's back against the wall by the door, pinning her in place. Her hands tightened around Kess's ass as she reveled in the way Kessandra shuddered against Nix's body.

Nix lifted her higher, using the wall for leverage as she pulled away from Kessandra's lips, trailing the curve of her neck. Kessandra's head fell back against the wall, her eyes closing, her breath short.

"You were always good at this." The words were strangled. "I missed—" she cut off with a sharp gasp when Nix scraped her teeth against her throat. "T-That."

"That," Nix agreed. It was too warm in this room. "I think we're done with pretenses. Get these off." Nix let Kess stand on her own feet, then ripped open her bloodstained shirt. Buttons bounced along the floor, and Nix tackled the brassiere next. It was lace, of course, a dainty white piece that buttoned in front for convenience.

And it was, indeed, convenient.

"You never disappoint, Nines." She tore off the button

without a thought, then pressed her lips to the space it vacated.

Kessandra arched against her. "Keep destroying my clothes, and you'll—"

"What? Be paying for it?" Nix pulled away the brassiere, revealing breasts she'd unwillingly remembered in the darkest hours of night. A shock of desire lanced through her. Stunning. "I'm counting on that."

Her lips pressed against Kessandra's nipple, and she was rewarded with another stifled inhale. Perfect. Fire burned through Nix as her tongue circled the smooth flesh, tasting salt and a hint of lavender. Her teeth tugged the tip for a moment, waiting until a moan slipped from Kessandra's lips.

Nix pulled back, smirking.

The moan shifted into a groan. "Damn it, Nix."

Ah, sweet music, hearing the stoic Subarch Kessandra Marie Vendermere Biltean III unravel beneath her. Nix pressed another hard, fast kiss to Kessandra's breasts before trailing downward, her hot breath pebbling the skin over Kessandra's toned muscles. "Time to be patient." Her voice was lilting, drenched in promise. "It's a good thing sergeants get their own rooms. It let me get... creative."

"Creative," Kessandra breathed, a fire lighting in her smoky green eye. She seemed acutely aware of how low Nix was delving, but even as her body shivered, desperate intrigue colored her voice. "How creative?"

"Mmm. Let's just say I spent some money on the

camera… and some more on that vibrator the engineers built last year."

Kessandra's breathy sigh proved she was imagining it already. "The greatest contribution to society." She blocked Nix's hands just as they latched onto her belt. "Enough. Shirt off. Pants off."

"Oh, Nines." Nix surged upward, pinning Kessandra's arms against the wall. The motion was so fast Kessandra's eyes widened, her gaze shifting into hungry desire when Nix whispered heatedly, "I'm not taking your orders tonight."

"I see," Kessandra breathed, stealing another passionate kiss.

"You will," Nix bit Kess's lower lip, slipped her knee between Kessandra's thighs for a mere moment—just to offer a taste. Kessandra wasted no time grinding onto it, delicious friction that had Nix's own center throbbing.

Without preamble, Nix wrenched Kessandra's pants down and dropped to her knees. In a swift motion, the button was undone, silky underwear revealed. They were soaking, which was a lot hotter than Nix expected. She ran her finger along the sodden silk a few times, her lips pressing to the smooth skin above the line of Kessandra's underwear.

Kessandra was barely holding it together. "Nix—" she gasped, her hand weaving into Nix's hair.

Four years *was* a long time. As much as Nix wanted to savor this, they both wouldn't last long tonight, and she knew it. With a final motion, she pulled down the underwear, revealing the source of Kessandra's pleasure.

Kessandra was beautiful everywhere, but here, her upbringing was obvious. Where other women had messy curls, Kessandra kept herself groomed all over. Nix loved that no one else knew it.

Nix again rubbed soft circles, applying steady pressure, moving faster as Kessandra began writhing against the wall. It really wasn't taking much, and Kessandra's eyes were already slipping shut, her fingers tracing the wallpaper, her stomach, Nix's hair, like she didn't know what to do with them.

"Talk to me, Kess," Nix said, partly because she loved hearing Kessandra lose control, partly because she knew it would take immense concentration—which might buy them some time. Nix picked up speed, then pulled her hand away entirely.

Kessandra inhaled through her nose, her fingers tightening against Nix's scalp. "You're a f-fiend."

"Rude." But she was talking, so Nix rewarded her by lowering her lips to Kessandra's hot folds. She knew exactly how to trace the tiny bud with her tongue, how to nip at just the right ferocity to keep Kessandra moaning.

Nothing had changed, and it was delightful.

"I—oooh, Lumos. You're a fiend, but you're—*very*—fuck —" Kessandra breathed, her chest heaving, her injury utterly forgotten. Alarms were still blaring in the distance, but they seemed even further away now. Her hips thrust towards Nix involuntarily, and already her thighs were shaking. "That's excellent. Right there, dear, p-please don't stop—" her words dissolved into a groan, and she clenched her eyes shut.

Nix scraped the flat of her tongue against Kessandra one final time before pulling back.

"*Nix*," Kessandra nearly snarled.

"Touchy." Nix kissed her inner thigh. Giving her a minute; after four years, that felt far too fast. She kissed near, just close enough to incite Kessandra, but never gave in. "I brought the vibrator, you know." Another kiss, another shudder. "Didn't expect to see Valkeshia again, so I figured I might as well have a few good nights in Fall."

Kessandra was dazed, her breaths forcibly evening out. "You don't say." It was an act. She was still wound too tight, but she'd do anything to try and convince Nix to continue.

That's how Nix knew she was too far gone—and it was intoxicating.

"I doubt I'll need it now. Ready for more?"

"Dear, you never have to ask," Kessandra groaned.

Excellent. Nix slipped one finger in, a thrill running through her as she felt Kess's arousal—she was clearly waiting for this. Nix added a second finger, making sure to circle Kessandra's sensitive entrance before curling inward. Finding *that* spot.

Kessandra stiffened, nearly slamming her head back against the wall. "Lumos below, Nix. I—I need—"

"Tell me," Nix said. Her fingers pumped, slow at first, then more. Her lips joined, and Kessandra's hands drifted up, past the bandages to squeeze her own breasts. She was quickly losing the ability to stand. They might need to move to the bed after all.

Or the shower. Nix couldn't decide.

"T-That," Kessandra breathed. "Please, *that*. Don't stop—"

This time, Nix didn't. Her tongue swirled, her fingers pumped, and she watched beauty unfold as Kessandra started shuddering beneath her. Nix's own center throbbed viciously at the private show. The bioluminescence painted Kessandra's skin in tones of blue, and her face was flushed, and her breaths were short, and the longer moans became fervent cries, which grew in intensity until finally, *finally*, Kessandra cut off with a strangled gasp.

Nix savored everything. The way Kess's whole body trembled, shuddering in waves of pleasure. The way her hands squeezed herself, the way she shifted her hips to get a better angle, the way every issue faded from this beautiful woman's mind.

For just a moment, just a breath, Nix could let Kessandra forget the world on her shoulders.

For just a moment, Kess was allowed to be selfish.

Nix had never found anything more beautiful.

She came down slowly, and Nix caught her. Kessandra braced herself on Nix's arms, shivering in the afterglow. Her weight was heavy, her ability to stand long gone, and that was pleasing too.

"Well?" Nix whispered, still tasting Kess on her

tongue. She kissed Kess again, sharing the experience. "Feel better, Subarch?"

"Leagues, Sergeant," Kessandra breathed against her lips. "Although it's wholly possible I've pulled a suture."

Nix chuckled, but her fingers feathered along the bandages just in case. The ichoron thread felt intact, but she hated that it was sewn into Kess's skin at all. "I can try to restitch them with normal thread. They've healed up enough." It was exactly the opposite of what Nix wanted —while the hot passion seemed to have cooled on Kessandra's side, Nix was on fire.

Kessandra searched her face, seeing it, and a wry smile tilted her lips.

It didn't help matters.

"Later, dear. Looks like it's my turn."

Kessandra kissed Nix again, then walked her to the edge of the bed and pushed. Nix fell to the mattress, her body screaming protest. She felt like desire might eat her alive, shifting the pain of her rib into pulsing pleasure— but despite everything, Nix hesitated. "Are you sure you're up for this? I can handle myself—"

"With your vibrator, correct? An excellent idea." Kessandra left Nix on the bed, rifled through her duffel bag with practiced ease. Nix's cheeks flared in embarrassment—even though the vibrator was the most embarrassing thing *in* there.

They'd never used something like this before. The anticipation, the vivid memory of what just transpired, it had Nix squirming. Her hand itched to delve lower, but

304

she managed to refrain. She squeezed her thighs together, telling herself she wouldn't be as fast to satisfy.

Her body laughed at that. Kess could kiss her once right now, and Nix might explode.

Kessandra resurfaced with the vibrator, a sleek black device with a rounded cap attached to a rod at one end. It was meant for massaging sore muscles, technically, but Nix was sure the engineers knew *exactly* what they were doing when designing it.

Kessandra plugged it into the wall, then flipped it on to test. A humming sound filled the room as the rounded cap bounced off her palm. The look she shot Nix was scheming, and it sent a wave of agony over Nix—anticipation warring with desperation.

This was either a brilliant idea... or a very, very bad one.

Nix couldn't wait to find out.

Kessandra shut the vibrator off. In the resulting silence, she asked, "You remember our call-off word?"

The words were so unexpected that it took several seconds to catch up. Of course she did. Deep in the mines, it became a joke, but now Nix pushed upright. Her eyes flicked to the vibrator. "Can't we come up with something better than 'commander?' I'm only ever thinking of one person now."

"Same. Which is why we'll both take it seriously." Kessandra pressed a fierce kiss to Nix's lips, easing her back onto the bed. She left the vibrator on the bedside table, positioning herself on her hands and knees over

Nix's form. Her shirt and brassiere were still open, her pants still gone. She was a *sight*.

Lumos, it was so hot in here. Nix shuddered, staring.

"Clothes off," Kessandra ordered, and this time, Nix tugged off her tank top, slipped out of her pants. It took a bit of maneuvering with their positions, but Kessandra seemed to enjoy watching her wriggling.

Every touch against Kessandra's skin was lightning. The empty air between Nix's throbbing center and Kessandra seemed insurmountable in the most frustrating way.

Once they were both bare, Kessandra let herself fall against Nix. She *finally* positioned her thigh between Nix's, offering a spot of much-needed friction as her lips ravished Nix's neck, breasts, stomach, moving slowly lower. Nix wasn't shy about grinding against Kessandra, desperate with desire, her whole body pulsing with heat.

Just as the friction between her legs shifted from "that feels good" to "fuck, I need more," Kessandra lifted her leg. Nix's hips followed, but when it was apparent Kessandra wasn't coming back, she thumped back to the bed, swallowed a groan of her own. Admitting her frustration would just feed Kess's amusement... and draw out the torture.

Nix should have known everything she did would come back around. Tit for tat—that's how life was with Kessandra.

Nix clenched her thighs together, her own hand reaching to finish the job. Her words were breathy, punctuated by the throbbing in her center. "At least I'm not a tease." Her rough fingers were well-practiced, calloused in all the right ways, and she swallowed a gasp.

Lumos, she really wasn't going to last long, was she?

And worse, Kessandra seemed content to watch her touching herself. That sent a new wash of flame over Nix's whole body, and pre-climax shudders wracked her.

"N-No intervention, huh?"

"Oh, it's rude to stop a lady's pleasure," Kessandra said silkily, and draped herself back over Nix's body. The heat of Kess's skin, the pressure of her form, her passionate kisses—they only made Nix rub herself faster, the tight circles growing more and more frantic.

And right as Nix was sure she'd finish like this, Kessandra pulled away and blocked her hand. "Ah, ah. Not yet."

"Damn it *all*. What happened to stopping a lady's pleasure?" Nix might murder her after all. Everything pulsed, alight with pleasure denied. Long, agonizing seconds ticked by where she was tempted to muscle out of Kessandra's grasp and satisfy herself, but the subarch's grip was firm, and neither voiced the call-off word.

All part of the game.

Right now, it was a shitty game.

Kessandra forced her back from the edge, no contact until Nix's body cooled, until she wouldn't combust from the next touch. As Nix relaxed a bit, frustration edging her expression, Kessandra's lips tilted into a sly smile. "There we go. Beautiful."

Nix flushed, because it was wholly obvious Kess meant it.

"Are you ready?" Kessandra traced her stomach, the solid lines of her toned abdomen. The bruise was beginning to fade, but her rib twinged when Nix shifted — except now, she hardly noticed the pain.

Nix's response was harsh. "Nines, if you don't do something soon, I'll be ready without you."

It wasn't a lie.

Kessandra chuckled, and finally, *finally*, dove deeper. Her lips circled Nix, and even though Nix thought she could handle it, she absolutely wasn't prepared for the wave of pleasure that washed over her. Her sensitive clit pulsed with growing intensity, and violent shivers cascaded over her body. Kessandra was merciless too, her tongue twisting in all the right directions, lips sucking in random bursts of sensation.

Nix loved to hear Kessandra talk, but Kess thrived on the opposite — the short, breathy moans, the sharp inhales, the feeling of Nix's body and mind shattering under her attention. Nix knew this and played it up, which wasn't hard after a point.

"*S—hit,*" Nix breathed. She wasn't even sure when her eyelids had drifted shut, when her head tilted back against the mattress, but not much mattered beyond *feeling* what Kessandra was doing.

Lumos below, it was as close to true bliss as Nix might ever get.

It was frankly a fucking miracle she'd lasted this long.

"Kess—" she breathed. "If you want that v-vibrator," her breath hitched as Kess's tongue hit *right there*, and when her senses returned, she tried again, "you'd better move—*now*." The final word was a strangled groan.

Kessandra pulled back—which was both good and *fucking awful*—and traced her fingers up Nix's stomach, right to her bellybutton. Her light touch made Nix tremble. "Oh, dear. You seem to think I'll be stopping at one."

Dread and anticipation washed over Nix—and then Kessandra's lips were back in place, and she forgot about much else. Everything built, piling inside her chest like a tight coil about to spring apart. Her hips twisted against her lover, her hands fisting the bedsheets, and without much preparation, she climaxed in an explosion of pleasure.

Nix whimpered, too far gone to care about much but the shockwaves rolling through her. Stars burst behind her closed eyes, short-circuited her brain, and then it was just a dissolution of *wow oh my god yes fuck yes, that, that, Kessandra, shit*—inside her mind.

Not that she could voice any of it.

She was vaguely aware of Kessandra's tongue slowing to guide her through… and then everything seeped back into existence. Nix slowly noticed of the soft bed beneath her, the gentle caress of Kessandra's fingers through her sweat-slicked hair, the blue glow from the windows.

Reality.

Right.

"Tell me how you feel," Kessandra said. Another order.

Nix obliged. She always would. "Fucking fantastic. Lumos, I missed this."

Kessandra seemed to glow with pride. Her smile was nearly blinding. "Excellent." And with a grimace of her own, she pulled off the bed. Nix didn't miss the way she swiftly checked her stitches, but she seemed determined to keep going. The vibrator was waiting.

Nix wasn't sure she could take it, after that, but she wasn't about to tell Kessandra *no.*

But when Kessandra picked it up, she stilled.

Nix pushed on her elbows, frowning. Kessandra had frozen, staring at the vibrator, eyes distant. Her ichoron eyeball was perfectly still, its artificial pupil fully dilated.

Fear crept into Nix's blood, washing away the last vestiges of satisfaction. "Kess?" It was too soon. She wasn't supposed to lose her mind yet—not like the other passengers. Not like the Elites. She had to hold off until after the surgery.

Lumos, couldn't they have one fucking night?

"Kessandra," Nix said, panic making her voice sharp. She pushed off the bed, taking Kess's arm.

The physical touch seemed to shock the subarch out of it. She dropped the vibrator, and it bounced off the thick carpet. They both stared at it, and Kessandra pressed a hand to her forehead. "It's getting worse."

"Nausea?" Nix asked, pulling Kess's shirt tighter around her shoulders. She suddenly wished she hadn't ripped the buttons off. Kessandra hugged it against her like a shield, even though the fight was happening in her own body.

"It comes in waves. Nothing incapacitating yet." Kessandra undid the bandages around her waist, proving that she had indeed pulled a few stitches. Blood gleamed crimson against the rose-gold stitches. "Can you take these out? I think I'm done weighing my sanity against my functionality."

Nix breathed a sigh of relief. "Finally."

They left the vibrator on the floor, shifting to other matters. Nix removed the stitches just like Hallie had earlier that day, and whispered a prayer of thanks that the wound was healed enough to just require a bandage now. Kessandra mutely slid into dark slacks, a black tank top, and that crisp white military jacket. It was far too formal, like she was dressing for her own fucking funeral.

Nix aggressively tugged on a sleeping shirt instead. But when she offered Kessandra a pointed look, the subarch's anguished expression stopped the comment tipping Nix's tongue.

Without discussion, crawled into bed together.

They curled against each other. Kessandra's forehead rested against Nix's chest, and Nix tucked her chin over Kess's long braids. For several moments, Nix catalogued the small things: the gentle creaking of the metal ship, the sway of the currents—much less intense down near Fall, the way Kessandra's steady breaths felt less like a prison, more like a comfort.

It was too soon.

"Don't let me hurt anyone," Kessandra whispered.

"There's no one down here to hurt," Nix replied quietly. Her grasp tightened on Kess's arms.

Kessandra was crying again. Nix felt the tears dampening her nightshirt. "I could hurt you." Kessandra's words were barely audible, but they were filled with so much anguish that Nix nearly broke.

"You won't, Nines. Get some rest."

It took a long time, but Kessandra's eyes finally drifted shut, and her breathing evened out.

Nix stayed awake, holding her, trying to ignore the sick feeling of fear in her chest.

SEVERAL HOURS LATER, Kessandra awoke. Her body was hot with fever, her eyes wild with violence.

Nix had been waiting for it, but it didn't stop the dread that slid through her veins like poison. Neither of them spoke. Nix wasn't sure she could anyway, even though her mind raced with pleas to Lumos. *Not Kess. Please. It's too soon. Not like this.*

Too late. Kessandra's muscles were unnaturally rigid. Her eyes searched Nix's, her tongue traced her lips, which were a bit swollen from last night. The silence felt oppressive, smothering Nix until she couldn't breathe.

A snarl erupted from Kessandra's lips, and she lunged at Nix's face.

Feeling dead inside, Nix buried the syringe in Kess's arm.

Once Kess slumped back to the bed, unconscious, Nix pushed to her feet, mutely slipped into her training uniform, buckled her camera to her thigh, shouldered her sarrant and holstered Kessandra's pistol.

Then she scooped Kessandra, still dressed to the nines, into her arms—and they left their suite behind.

One way or another, everything ended today.

24

THE SHIP HAD DESCENDED INTO CHAOS—AND THEN, sometime overnight, calmed down. Not in any *good* way, though. Nix braced for screaming, gunshots, gurgling cries, but as the elevator doors opened, all that met her was cold silence. Dread slipped through Nix's veins as she hoisted Kessandra's limp form closer, rounded the corner, and assessed the damage.

Somehow, the ghost of her expectations was worse.

The promenade was a wreck. Shop fronts had shattered windows, the contents pillaged—which was a surprise, because Nix truly didn't expect anyone to be focused on stealing when survival was on the line. The café didn't seem to have a single piece of unbroken furniture. Decorative banners hung from the second story had been torn, and plants were upturned, soil spilling over the marble floor.

Worse was the blood. There weren't hints of a

massacre; it was bold strokes, cutting through any chance of dismissing this as a different disaster. It splattered on walls, smeared across the ground. Handprints scrambling along doorways, painting the promenade's tables, tinging the banisters of the grand staircases. The bodies weren't far behind—some were intact, clearly deaths of friendly fire. Some... weren't.

The smell of dried blood and cooling meat nearly made her gag. She was no stranger to it after her tours to the front lines, but the *Luminosity* was pressurized, contained, and the air only circulated so much.

Nix didn't enter the promenade. Everything felt numb, but she had a mission—and she wasn't going to sacrifice Kessandra's safety for a faster path to the medical ward. Her fingers tightened around Kessandra as she hunched in the shadows, peering through the leafy foliage of a potted fig.

It was unnervingly silent... but when she strained to hear, she could identify the quiet moans and snarls of infected. They weren't nearby, clearly, but she traced one sound to the staggered steps of a soldier two stories up.

Clearly, the infected had won this fight. Any surviving passengers or soldiers had retreated into private rooms, leaving the hallways unguarded.

Nix couldn't even blame them.

The path to the library—and up to Hallie's office—was dangerous here. There were two hallways beyond the promenade, but staterooms lined those walls. Nix couldn't risk being ambushed from two directions here, not carrying Kessandra like this.

Lumos, she should have called Ramona and had Leon sent to meet her.

She hadn't been thinking.

Nix drew a slow, quiet breath and backed away from the promenade, turning instead to the elevators. This would also be a risk, but a managed one. At least on the higher floors, she could fight from the elevator's doors, and no one would be sneaking behind them.

She pressed the button to call one closer. It dinged, a sound that pierced the empty quiet. Nix flinched, holding her breath. Long seconds ticked past, and then she heard a responding snarl.

Two.

Three.

"Fuck," she muttered, bouncing on her toes as the elevator doors inched open. A clattering sound, and she glanced left to see two infected scrambling toward the elevator. Fear shot up her chest, and in her arms, Kessandra stirred. No. No, no, no. The sedative wasn't supposed to wear off this fast.

Desperation had Nix muscling into the elevator, discarding Kessandra on the back floor as she unsheathed her sarrant. The infected from the promenade were nearly on her, and she sliced the hand of one that got too close. Her ichoron blade cut the bones like butter, and the hand plopped to the carpet, twitching.

The infected—an elegant man in a ripped suit—

screamed, and renewed fury lit his deadened eyes. His companion scrambled over him, lunging for the doors just as they slid closed. She managed to get her arm inside.

Nix stabbed her through, then kicked her out of the way.

The doors closed.

"Fuck," she breathed, slamming the button for the nineteenth floor. Hallie said the surgery would take place there, in the abandoned medical ward. It was a known evil; at least in the gambling hall, there'd be places to hide.

The elevator lifted away from the promenade. Heart pounding, Nix turned back to Kessandra. As a precaution, she'd tied her wrists and ankles with the rope previously used for the living room drapes. Now, Kessandra blinked awake, wrenching at her bindings.

She was still bleary from the sedative. Too late, Nix realized she'd left the second one in her suite. "Great going, Marr." Nix's derisive mutter was barely audible, and she sheathed her sarrant as they climbed.

She couldn't be tempted to use it. Not against Kessandra.

"Kess? Are you... you?"

Nix wasn't expecting it. She hadn't seen anyone rediscover their humanity once the violent impulses set in. But then again, she hadn't watched anyone succumbing to this as closely as Kessandra. Hope flickered in her chest, a dangerous thing.

Kessandra groaned, reaching for her forehead with

bound hands. "I'm—" she cut off, grimacing. "I'm afraid I don't—what happened...?"

Nix dropped to her knees beside Kessandra, casting a quick glance at the floors as they passed. Tenth floor now. They couldn't stay here long, but this felt precious. "Thank Lumos, that asshole primarch, and all the other royals in Valkeshia. Kess. Look at me. Is it really you?"

She blinked blearily, and her ichoron eyeball seemed to glow. Nix imagined the rose-gold replaced with red, malevolent and dark, and couldn't contain her shudder. It took far too long for Kessandra to place who she was looking at.

"Nix," she finally said. All at once, relief painted her features, but it was quickly replaced with abject fear. "My dear, I'm—the bonds won't be strong enough. It's in my head. I can feel it rummaging around my memories, plucking what's important to use later."

It. The ghost, the specter, the Crypt Keeper—that thing following them around this Lumos-forsaken ship. Nix drew a short breath, taking Kessandra's hands. She didn't undo the bindings. "We'll be in surgery soon enough. Just hang in there, Kess. A few more minutes."

Sixteenth floor.

Kessandra squeezed her hand, hard. "Please, Nix. You promised."

"I'm not going to kill you," Nix spat.

"Then I'm g-going to kill *you*," she replied, choking on a sob.

There was no doubt in her words.

A chill slipped down Nix's spine, and the doors dinged open. Nix spun to face the elevator bank, unsheathing her sarrant in one smooth motion, but the space was empty. This floor had emptied out hours ago.

Nix prayed it stayed that way.

"That's not happening." But when Nix turned back around, Kessandra bared her teeth like an animal, eyes glazed and furious. She tried to lunge, but the ropes stopped her from standing, and she topped over.

Anguish slipped through Nix's chest. Fuck. For a moment, she thought about pleading, begging Kessandra to resurface, to stay with her. Nix was less and less convinced it was an illness at all, less and less convinced dethalos even existed.

If it was a possession, Kessandra could fight it.

And Kess always won her battles.

But ultimately, it would be a waste of breath—and if her words summoned other infected, Nix would be left fighting them while trying to protect Kessandra. Injuries would happen, and Nix couldn't live with herself if Kessandra died from her own actions.

And so, she went the merciful route—and slammed her sarrant's blunted pommel on Kessandra's head.

Kessandra's possession—illness, or whatever—must not be that far along, because it worked like a charm. She crumpled into a pile at Nix's feet, silent, still. Nix knelt beside her, gently felt for the wound. It was bleeding sluggishly where her sarrant had connected, but that was better than any alternative right now.

Nix *really* should have remembered that second sedative.

"Don't hold that against me," Nix muttered, mostly to herself. She sheathed her sarrant, scooped Kessandra up a second time, and stepped out of the elevator. This time, there wasn't any hint of snarls or footsteps; the gambling hall was empty. Only the corpses of those killed by the Elite remained.

Nix moved swiftly through the large space, stepping over bodies and around upturned card tables. Revulsion swelled in her throat as she caught a glimpse of the Elite's decapitated head. Even back then, things had seemed simpler.

How naïve, to think they'd have an ounce of control once this spread.

She almost made it to the other side, almost crossed into the hallway toward the medical ward—when a loud clatter echoed in the space behind her. Nix froze, fully illuminated by incandescent light and the blue bioluminescence filtering through the windows.

A snarl.

They were close to the medical bay. Could Nix make a run for it?

In her arms, Kessandra's breathing was labored. Nix pictured sprinting, slowed by Kess's weight, scrambling to find the right door, praying Hallie and Leon were on the other side. She pictured moving a smidge too slow, being bowled over by more infected. She pictured Kessandra crashing to the ground, waking up again—but this time, there was nothing left of her mind.

Nix pictured being devoured because she didn't have the heart to fight back.

More snarls echoed. She could see them now, a gang of at least four infected homing in on her. They must have just crested the staircase when the elevator door closed. Without wasting time, they sprinted across the gambling hall: three stewards and one soldier. Their eyes were too wide, their mouths hanging open, blood smeared across their skin.

"Don't move," Nix told Kessandra, easing her to the floor out of the way. Then she straightened, setting her jaw, unsheathing her sarrant yet again. "Hey! Over here, you evil bastards."

The four of them picked up pace, crashing over the furniture of the gambling hall. One tripped on a tipped slot machine, another slammed over a circular bar, shattering bottles of booze. But Nix stepped to meet them, because if they were focused on *her*, Kessandra was safe.

One of the stewards reached her first. Nix moved wickedly fast and didn't pull her hits—her ichoron blade sliced through his arm, his chest, digging deep into his heart. He stiffened, blood pouring from the wound, his snapping screams dying into warbled gasps. She kicked him off the end of the blade, and he crashed to the floor.

The soldier hit her next. She tried the same maneuver with him, but his reflexes were clearly still intact. He ducked away from her blade, his blue eyes bloodshot, his face twisted in fury. His sarrant was a normal one, but unlike the Elite, he seemed to remember it. His attack was uncoordinated, like a puppet moving on fraying strings, but she barely had time to parry before the other two were on her.

One bit into the flesh of her arm like she might rip out a chunk, and Nix grunted in pain. Hot blood welled as she twisted violently, wrenching the stewards off, and buried her sarrant in the woman's chest. The other, she kicked off without a glance.

The soldier slashed at her, and Nix leapt backwards, leaving her ichoron blade for a moment. But Kessandra's pistol was still strapped to her hip, and she wasted no time flicking the hammer back, taking aim.

She wasn't as good at marksmanship as Kessandra, but she could hold her own. Especially with ichoron bullets.

The soldier jerked as two sliced through his chest, exploded out his back. Blood sprayed, and he tipped, crashing to the ground.

Nix took aim at the steward who'd bit her, and a chunk of her skull went flying too. The woman howled, but the sound faded as her life vanished. She fell on top of the soldier, a nice pile of corpses.

Gasping, Nix circled for the final opponent—only to realize the steward had noticed Kessandra. Kessandra, who was unconscious, but breathing. Kessandra, who was the easiest target this infected would find. The woman screeched delight and descended on her, and Nix didn't trust herself to fire the pistol without accidentally hitting Kessandra.

She holstered it and body slammed the steward right as she tried to claw Kessandra's face.

The two of them went tumbling into the gambling hall, crashing aggressively into a tall machine that exchanged ichoron coins for cheaper currency. It tipped, the crash echoing in the massive space. If there were any more infected here, they'd be on Nix soon. Nix gasped for breath, spinning on her opponent.

And came face-to-face with Josie.

Josie.

She must have had an implant of some kind, or a tattoo, or took medicine, but either way, her familiar face stopped Nix cold. There was nothing to recognize in her harsh gaze, no hint of the person she'd been.

It didn't matter. Nix felt pinned.

Josie. She'd promised to protect Josie, and Ramona, and everyone else—and now Kessandra was unconscious and Ramona was trapped and *Josie* was here, murder in her eyes. Nix couldn't move, couldn't breathe, couldn't fight. For a long moment, too long, all she could do was stare in horror.

Josie sank her nails into Nix's side, right where her cracked rib was. There was no way she could have known about it, but mind-numbing pain slammed into her nonetheless. A scream wrenched from Nix's lips, and Josie's other hand delved into her mouth like she might rip Nix's jaw clean off.

Nix bit on reflex, slicing flesh, and hot copper flooded her mouth. But Josie was unrelenting, and Nix had given her every opportunity. She moved to gouge Nix's eyes next.

A gunshot rang out.

This time, it wasn't friendly fire. Blood sprayed over Nix, and Josie's body jerked. Her eyes dulled, locking with Nix's for a moment before rolling into her skull. Nix shoved her off, desperate for space to breathe.

Blood—Josie's blood—dripped down Nix's chin. She could feel it staining her teeth, and really thought she might be sick. Dimly, she recognized a figure approaching her, and fumbled for her sarrant. It was still buried in that corpse, nowhere nearby.

But it was an unnecessary effort.

"Sergeant. *Nix*. It's me. It's okay." Leon held up his hands. He carried a pistol in one, and his sarrant was strapped to his back.

Nix choked on a laugh, but blood still dripped down her throat, *Josie's* blood, from the fingers she'd nearly bit clean off—if Leon hadn't intervened, she would have. That thought had her gagging, coughing. It wasn't enough. She twisted onto her hands and knees, her stomach churning aggressively, and when her eyes caught sight of Josie's damaged skull, she started heaving in earnest.

She hadn't eaten much lately, but it all came up. Nix clenched her eyes shut, emptying her stomach, trying not to vomit a second time from the smell alone.

Leon rubbed her back as she gasped for clean air. Somehow, the bitter taste of acid was preferable to the copper of Josie's blood. Nix spat a few more times and pushed to her knees, swallowing a groan. Her voice was hoarse. "It's been a fucking *day*, Leo."

"I believe it," he replied grimly. "You good?"

She'd have to be. Nix swallowed, repulsed by the last ten minutes—well, the last three days, really—and took his proffered hand. He pulled her to her feet, waited while she slipped out of her jacket and wiped her face clean. For a moment, she almost tied the jacket around her waist, but she couldn't bear to think of Josie's blood staining it.

Knowing her victims made it harder to deal with their murder. She draped the jacket over Josie's corpse, hiding it from view. Her hands were shaking. Her heartbeat felt faint.

Leon steadied her, leaving for a moment to retrieve her sarrant. She drew a few more breaths. No time to drop now. Not unless she wanted Kessandra to suffer the same fate.

"The surgery?" Nix scrubbed her trembling hands on her pants, then accepted her sarrant. She didn't sheath it, didn't trust this ship enough to assume anywhere was safe now. "Please give me good news."

"It's ready," Leon confirmed.

"Thank Lumos."

Leon followed her back to Kessandra. He took one look at her and stepped in front, scooping the subarch into his arms with ease. He was taller than her, and Kessandra looked very small in his grip.

They left the bloodied lounge behind, stepping quickly into the hallway with the medical ward. Leon moved with confidence toward the closed door, then rapped on it twice, paused, and three times more.

Hallie wrenched it open, and Nix almost cried on seeing her.

The doctor took one look at them—Kessandra, unconscious, bound—Nix, bloodied, shaking—and pinched the bridge of her nose, right below her heavy glasses. "I suppose now's a bad time for the 'I told you *not* to kill her' joke I had planned."

Nix didn't even have the energy to laugh. She led Leon inside the medical ward, which was a big open room with several partitions for patients, each hidden by velvet curtains. "She was fine most of the night, but woke up mostly infected an hour ago. Getting here was... a struggle."

"Mostly infected?" Hallie perked up, leading them through the empty medical ward to a back room Nix hadn't noticed before. The wall was framed with small portholes, and the area was clearly designed for sick passengers, not massive surgery.

The back room was another story. Hallie must have collected all the best tools on this ship, because expensive medical equipment lined the back wall. She had tools laid out, a bed in the center, and a brace to hold Kessandra's head in place. She'd also included thick ropes to tie Kess to the bed, and that sent a spike of fear up Nix's spine.

"Are you really going to need those if she's drugged?"

Hallie glanced at them, frowning. "Impossible to say how the disease will react. I can't rule out the probability that attempting to remove the eyeball will cause a violent reaction. Which is why I'm interested—what did you mean, *mostly* infected?"

Leon laid Kessandra on the bed, and Hallie gestured at the bonds tying Kess's wrists and ankles. Nix unsheathed her sarrant and cut through them easily, then helped tie Kess in place. "She was gone when we were in my suite. I drugged her. But she woke up in the elevator to this level. She said… she said she could feel it—dethalos, I guess—sifting through her memories." Nix winced, tying a swift knot and moving to Kess's ankles. "She didn't sound fully lucid."

"But talking to you was a good sign." Hallie pressed a hand to Kessandra's forehead, then flicked a syringe she'd retrieved from the nearby tray. Without preamble, she plunged the needle into Kess's arm. "The sooner we get that thing out, the better her chances. Let's not waste—"

She didn't have the chance to finish.

An explosion wracked the ship.

25

IT WAS MUTED, LESS THE SOUND OF AN EXPLOSION, more the violent jerking of the ship. Everyone careened left—Nix caught herself on the bed, but Hallie crashed to the floor. Leon staggered, handling it far better than either of them.

"The fuck was that?" Nix exclaimed, spinning toward the door. The power flickered, and somewhere in the distance, an electric horn blared. Red lights flashed from bulbs Nix hadn't noticed before, mounted in the corners of the room.

"Something hit the ship, maybe? We'd better hope that wasn't the hull being punctured—although I'm inclined to think that didn't happen, considering we didn't all die instantly." Hallie hauled herself to her feet, rubbing her elbow, but she didn't seem injured. She jogged to the window, squinting into the depths.

Only the cold, unmoving bones of the leviathan, speckled with gorgeous blue bioluminescence, greeted her.

"If there's something down here big enough to slam our ship like that, we're fucked anyway," Leon muttered, stepping into the medical ward, squinting into the flickering darkness. The lights couldn't seem to stay on for long, and it was unnerving. Electricity had clearly been disrupted.

"It must have been an explosion, then." Nix scrubbed her face, glancing again at Kessandra. "Doc, come on. Get that thing out."

Hallie spun back to Nix. "Is now really the time?"

"Now's the *only* time," Nix snapped, and silence lingered in her wake. She drew a shaking breath, fighting the sudden lump in her throat. "We're not dead yet. Fall is close. If we can make it to the city, we'll be okay—but either way, Kessandra will die if we don't remove that eyeball. Please, Hallie."

As if on cue, the lights went out. Nix almost cursed, but a second later they powered on again, steady and smooth. The alarm was still blaring in the distance, but here, they were in their own little world.

"Emergency power supply. Thank Lumos they included the medical bay in that." Hallie tied off her unruly hair, then changed out her glasses for the set with curved earpieces.

"Do you need us for the surgery?" Adrenaline raced through Nix's veins, and she glanced again at the door.

The ship could be damaged… and if that was the case, Nix needed to know sooner than later.

There had to be an escape pod on this ship, right?

She suspected not, considering the currents below the Ever-Storm, but there still had to be a backup plan to get them off safely. Either way, she wouldn't find it here, trapped in a medical bay. And frankly, after fighting Josie, her stomach was still churning. She wasn't sure she could watch Hallie removing a literal eyeball—even an artificial one.

"It'd be helpful, but—" Hallie took one look at Nix's face and shook her head. "No, I'll manage. This isn't an organic eye. It's an extensive procedure to ensure I don't damage anything important, but it'll be far easier than the original surgery was."

Nix nodded, trying not to show her relief. "Do you have a key to the medical bay?"

Hallie tossed her one. It was brass, just like the one they used to reach the royals' private deck. Nix pocketed it. "Good. Lock the doors, and don't open them for anyone."

"I'll be a little busy anyway," Hallie drawled, checking the knots Nix had tied.

All right, then. "Leon, with me."

As soon as they exited into the hallway, sarrants drawn, Hallie locked the door behind them. Nix tested the handle just to be sure, but it was solid. Hopefully the infected would walk right past.

With that done, she became aware of a distant, roaring

sound. Water? Had the hull really been breached? The *Luminosity* was ichoron-enforced, able to withstand far more pressure than the depths they visited. But when she strained to hear, there was no mistaking the sound; water was pouring in from somewhere.

But Hallie said they'd have died instantly. So... something else, then?

"What's our plan?" Leon sounded frustrated. "If the ship is damaged, what the hell can we do about it?"

"Then we plan for another alternative." Nix wasn't in the mood for arguing. She met his gaze, her jaw set. With the blood splatters drying on her skin and her ripped clothes, she probably looked a sight. "Are you with me, ensign? Because now's not the time to be questioning."

Leon massaged his forehead. "I'm with you, Sergeant. It just seems futile."

"Let's find out."

Nix pivoted toward the staircase nearby, sprinting up it to reach the bridge. The door between the two levels was closed and locked—and when she pressed the button to open it, nothing happened.

In an emergency, these doors were sealed. Even her override wouldn't help now. Someone had to open it from the inside.

Ramona.

Nix cursed, spinning on her heel. "New plan. We go down."

The lights in the stairwell were flickering, and as they descended, Nix had to dodge a few corpses of passengers who'd tried to escape the carnage of last night. She paused near the doorway to the fourteenth floor, hearing the roaring sound intensify near a door labeled *crew only*. But it seemed louder below them.

"The ballast tanks...?" Josie had mentioned them—they weighed the ship for the journey down the rail.

With water. Lots of it.

Leon didn't answer, his expression grim.

Shit. Those tanks took up the space of nine decks in the center of the ship. Considering all the air the *Luminosity* held, nothing short of an immense amount of water would let it submerge at all. If one of those tanks was damaged, the results would be... fatal.

Chest tight, Nix sprinted down the staircase, fighting every instinct to climb back to the nineteenth deck. The passengers of the lower levels wouldn't have the luxury of climbing to safety, and Nix had to be sure she couldn't help.

As she hit the atrium level, screams filled the air, seeming to come from every deck of the ship. She skidded to a halt, leaning over the banister, with Leon drawing up alongside her. Together, they stared in abject horror at the scene below.

Water was gushing into the library, several decks below them. And it wasn't a slow spill—already, the lowest level was submerged, and rushing water sloshed up the library's curved staircase at an alarming rate. It must have been the ballast tank above the promenade side, because otherwise they'd be facing a torrent of water themselves.

"What the fuck *happened*?" she breathed.

Behind her, Leon didn't look optimistic. His breath came short, his tone panicked. "Nix, we should go back up—"

Before she could argue, a screaming sob cut through the air. Nix craned over the wooden banister, trying to ignore the polite *Closed* sign that had tipped over beside the atrium's locked doors. What was inside was nothing new, now.

Far below, a young woman was fighting the currents, desperately trying to grab something stable as she was ripped around the library. The water glimmered blue while she thrashed against it, clawing her way toward fresh air.

She was going to drown.

Everyone was.

"Stay here," Nix said, shoving the key to the medical ward into Leon's hands. He realized too late what her plan was, but Nix had shed her sarrant, camera, and Kess's pistol in the next breath. Before he could stop her, she jumped the banister.

It was a decent fall, a few stories, and her heart leapt into her chest as she crashed into the rushing water. The currents were coming from all angles—even if the water originated in the promenade, it had flooded with vengeance toward this side of the ship. Now it churned into a vortex Nix could barely fight. She surfaced with a gasp, drenched, the water ice-cold.

Fuck. She hadn't thought about hypothermia.

It hardly mattered. She could save *someone*, at least.

Shortscraper citizens were all taught to swim—especially the firstborns, the ones who'd enlist in the military. The primarch wanted no boundaries between the ensigns and his precious, flooded mines, so there were public pools in every casten.

It was clear the spirescraper citizens hadn't learned the same skill, because this woman thrashed, her motions uncoordinated. Nix grabbed her, began towing her toward the library's staircase and solid ground.

She'd underestimated this woman's blind panic.

She'd underestimated a lot lately, truth be told.

The woman moved with desperation, grabbing Nix, shoving her under in a frantic attempt to reach the surface and stay there. Nix submerged, choking on water, her side screaming, her lungs constricting painfully. She couldn't shout or gasp. Every time she tried to right herself and reach the surface, the woman shoved her back under.

Half-drowned, she barely heard the gunshot echo.

Blood slid through the water like a toxin, fading in the currents. The young woman's entire body went limp. Her claw-like grip on Nix released, and she was pulled away, sucked under the library's staircase.

Everything was dark. Only a deep-rooted survival instinct, the sharp memory of Quian's bloated face pinned beneath rock in a blackened mine, propelled Nix upward.

She'd made his same mistake—she'd swum after someone she couldn't save.

Fuck. She wasn't strong enough to share his fate. She didn't want this.

Except she couldn't remember which way was up. Her brain scrambled to make sense of her new plane of existence, to identify where the oxygen was. Nix picked a direction that seemed right, moving methodically, lungs screaming, her motions growing weak.

She might die here. Truly, honestly, she might die.

She never even said goodbye to Kessandra.

And then something smacked her face. Numbly, she grasped for it, found a thick rope under her hands. She barely had the sense to hold on as it jerked her up—ah, *there* was up—and she broke the surface.

She coughed, water heaving out of her lungs.

"Hang on," a loud voice shouted.

Leon.

Nix's body was functioning, even though her mind was fuzzy. She was vaguely aware of Leon hauling her out of the water, somehow lifting her back to the atrium level. From this angle, she could barely see the pully system he'd set up, where the rope draped over the banister, then wrapped around a nearby decorative pillar. He moved back to the banister with strong footsteps, grunting, and all Nix had to do was hold on.

It was a losing battle. She barely managed to grab the banister, dimly aware of the crashing water below her, aware of how easily it could have become her grave.

It still could, and that thought alone forced her to cling to the banister with numb fingers.

Leon made sure she was anchored, then released the rope and lunged for her. He grabbed her arms, her shoulder, her back, hauling her onto solid ground.

"What the *fuck* were you thinking, Nix?" he snarled, turning her on her side.

Her body felt leaden, and she coughed water, gasping for breath. The roaring in her ears slowly receded, the darkness fading into flickering lights and Leon's furious expression. It took several more seconds to have enough air to respond. He thumped her back a few times, and she coughed more water.

"I—" her voice was a wheeze. "I thought I could save her."

"You can't save everyone." His voice was icy.

Nix knew that. She did, truly. This situation was spiraling out of control, and she knew most of these people were already dead... or would be soon. At this rate, Nix would be impressed if she managed to save Leon, Kessandra, and Hallie.

And Ramona.

Josie was already gone.

Where was Dominik? Did he survive, or was he dragged underwater like that woman had been? And all the others—the steward who'd walked them to their dining table, the chef who'd served their food, the passengers who'd gawked at Kessandra that first night.

They would all die.

"Did you s-shoot her? That woman?" Nix almost didn't want to know. She pushed to her hands and knees for the second time in an hour, drawing shuddering, painful breaths. Every muscle shook with exertion, and she wanted to crawl into a bed and sleep for hours.

She hadn't eaten in days, not in earnest. She didn't sleep last night.

Things were great.

This was fine.

Leon didn't seem apologetic. "Of fucking course I shot her. She was drowning you."

"She was scared —"

"*Sergeant*," Leon snapped, and Nix stiffened. "What's happening on this ship can't be stopped. One person's life doesn't matter now."

Nix lifted her gaze, finally meeting his eyes. His face was worn, the angles harsh in the flickering light. "Then why did you save *me*?"

He went rigid. After a moment, he pushed to his feet and drew a breath. "I don't — Shit, I don't know. You weren't supposed to be here. None of this was supposed to happen, but now it has, and dying isn't as easy as I expected."

"What the fuck are you talking about?"

"We can't *stop* what's happening," Leon replied, anger in his tone.

He made sense, but in the way the Ever-Storm made sense until scientists tried to explain it. On the surface, it was just a large storm — but digging deeper proved it never moved, never changed. On the surface of Leon's comment, she agreed. What lied deeper scared her.

"Leon. What is going on?"

She almost didn't expect him to answer. She almost hoped he wouldn't.

But he did, and it sealed everything.

"Retribution." The word was frigid, and he collected his pistol off the ground. For a moment, she thought he'd point it at her, but he just shoved it into the leather holster at his hip. "You think we wouldn't notice? All that ichoron, smeared over your city like a fucking beacon. We knew you'd found the titanfall. We knew you'd found Lumos."

Titanfall?

They'd always called it a "leviathan fall"—the final resting spot of a sea-faring creature of old. But a titan implied... something older. Something ancient.

But there was a bigger issue: Leon implying he wasn't *also* part of Valkeshia.

Everything she thought she knew shattered.

Nix stared at her friend, the best person she knew these days. Her longtime support. The one she trusted even when she hadn't trusted Kessandra, who followed her into battle, who bought her drinks at Lanskin's pub.

Leon stared back, his expression tinged in fury.

Not the wild fury of an infected—but the cold anger of a person wronged.

"We—we can't have found Lumos. Lumos is our god." It felt so ridiculous leaving her lips; everyone knew who

Lumos was. None of this was adding up and her throat burned from nearly drowning and the water was flooding the second floor of the library now and Nix wasn't sure where it'd stop.

"Lumos is *your* god. And what a shitty role model you all chose."

The entire country worshiped Lumos—all to varying degrees, but there wasn't anything else. Nix stared blankly at him. The only people who didn't follow Lumos's path were... their enemies.

"You're Triolan."

The words felt sour in her mouth.

Leon was tense, every muscle in his shoulders pronounced. "I didn't want you to find out this way."

That made Nix laugh, almost hysterical. "No? How did you want me to find out?" They all knew of the possibility of Triolan spies—every soldier was lectured on the importance of staying vigilant, of identifying threats inside Valkeshia. The fact that one had not only lingered under her command, but had become a true friend over the years was almost too much to handle.

She was so, so tired.

Her sarrant was in reach. Nix's eyes flicked towards it.

Leon saw. He put a hand on his pistol. "Don't. I don't want to kill you."

"How kind."

"You think this was easy?" Devastation leaked into his tone. "Befriending you people, realizing that you're not a monolith of avarice? When I took the assignment, I was told Valkeshians were evil, so entrenched in their own greed that they'd destroy the world to keep it. The sixty-first wasn't like that."

"Now that's a compliment," Nix drawled, sarcasm in every syllable. "Glad we were able to show you that one society has a lot of different perspectives."

Leon clenched his jaw. "There's no nuance to this problem. Lumos is an ancient creature. It might be your god, but it's not a benevolent one. And thanks to your mining operation, it's awakening. You think this—" he gestured around the ship, at the atrium and what lay beyond the closed doors, "—is a disease, but the reality is worse."

A chill swept up Nix's spine. She imagined the glowing red eyes perched over Leon's head, watching her, imagined a vicious, jagged smile curving upwards. "How can the reality be worse than this?"

Unless the Crypt Keeper *did* exist, and it was possessing people like she suspected.

But he killed that thought in a second.

"The bones outside. The fall that created this ecosystem, the spot that seemed *so perfect* for a settlement." Derision cut Leon's expression. "This wasn't a sea creature. There is no leviathan. There were two ancient beings, and Aeris killed Lumos and left its corpse here to rot." Leon laughed, cold and disbelieving, and rubbed a hand over his face. "And then you all went and set up a mining operation in its fucking brain."

Aeris?

Ancient beings?

Nix's entire world was falling apart. Her mind whirled, trying to keep up, trying to sort through this information to find the truth. And all the while, she was acutely aware of the rising water levels, the fact that her sarrant wasn't in her hand. She was unarmed, soaking wet and shivering violently, and her closest friend was nothing of the kind.

Shit.

"Why haven't I heard of Aeris?"

"Because you live in a dictatorship with carefully controlled information," Leon replied, almost exasperated. "Because every book on the subject was burned, and centuries of lies have corrupted everything. Your primarch probably doesn't even know the truth anymore."

Did Kessandra know?

More than ever, Nix wished she were here, because if there was any truth to Leon's claims, Kessandra would have found evidence of it. They couldn't have burned *all* the books. The existence of a second god was... cataclysmic.

Someone would have known.

It was a question for another time. The water had covered half the library at this point, gushing in from the shattered ballast tank. Water he hadn't seemed surprised to see—water he argued they couldn't stop.

Suspicion lingered in the corners of her mind. She'd found him more than once roaming this ship. Knowing he was a Triolan automatically implied sabotage. "Everyone down there is dead. Leo, tell me that wasn't you."

She wanted him to deny it. Pretend it was a freak accident. She could deal if he was Triolan—that was a betrayal, but not anything he could have controlled. He must have been young when he came here. They could come back from that, somehow.

But when Leon didn't argue, she knew this was bigger.

"This wasn't my first choice, or my second, or my sixth." Leon clenched his fists. "But what's happened on this ship proved Lumos is awake, and it's gaining power at an exponential rate. Diseases play by a set of rules—but what's happening here is Lumos, playing with *us*. We've lost the chance for subtlety."

"You're going to kill everyone." Nix wasn't even disbelieving anymore. Now she had a problem—and a duty to solve it. Her fingers curled around her sarrant, and she didn't flinch when he unholstered his pistol and took aim.

"I'm going to *save* everyone." He sounded like he really believed it, too. "The people on this ship are doomed. But Lumos is the titan of chaos and fear. If I cut its supply to those emotions, its progress might not reach Valkeshia."

Her father. Melana. The sixty-first. Even the commander. The idea of them facing a situation like the one unfolding on the *Luminosity* was terrifying.

But he was half the problem for that. Dethalos spurred the initial panic, Captain Navaan sparked the massacre, but *Leon* was responsible for flooding the lower levels. How many hundreds of people did he kill with that single explosion?

She slowly unsheathed her sarrant, brandishing it.

He cocked the hammer on his pistol.

"I don't want to kill you, Nix. I probably should, but... fuck, you're a great officer, and an even better person. Please, don't make me do it."

That twisted her heart. Agony coursed through her, her heart warring with her brain. He was a threat—but he was also Leon, her drinking buddy, the one who'd faced off against a shipful of Triolans on the front lines just to get her out alive.

Lumos, no wonder that escape had been easy.

"Where are the explosives?" Nix ground out.

Leon took a step backward, adding more distance. "They're on a timer. You can't stop it. This ship will be empty by the time we reach Fall."

Not just hundreds of souls. *Everyone* was going to die.

Nix couldn't stomach it. She advanced, moving slowly, plotting escape routes and angles. Her ichoron blade seemed to glow in the flickering lights. The water below the banister churned. She was cold, absolutely freezing, and her fingers were going numb. It hardly mattered.

"Tell me where they are, Leo."

He heaved a sigh, then fired a shot.

Shock—and on its heels, hot pain. Nix staggered, an agonized cry erupting from her lips. Blood welled on her left thigh, and she gripped the wound with one hand, falling against the banister again.

For a moment, it looked like Leon might tip her back over, straight into the churning vortex below.

Instead, his words were pained. "You've got a few hours, Nix. I recommend you get back to Hallie and Kessandra and enjoy the time you have left." Anguish filtered into his voice, which only made her angrier. A tiny clink as he tossed back the key for the medical ward. "For what it's worth, I'm so fucking sorry. You were never supposed to be here."

And he twisted on his heel.

By the time she fumbled for Kessandra's ichoron pistol, he was gone, rounding the hallway near the bank of elevators.

Above her, the flickering power flashed one final time, and darkness descended on the ship.

26

IT WAS A FLESH WOUND.

That didn't mean it hurt any less.

Nix swallowed a gasp, fighting the darkness edging her vision. Exhaustion, lack of food, near-drowning, and now... this. Her cracked rib suddenly seemed very minor in comparison. Agony sliced up her body with every breath, and blood coated her pant leg, seeping into her wet boots. The bullet was still in there somewhere.

Hallie was about to have a second surgery, unless Nix could somehow dig it out herself.

The pain faded as she lurched after Leon. He'd disappeared into another hallway—one that appeared to be blocked off for steward use. Nix only made it a few steps before comprehending what he'd said.

Another ballast tank would blow.

If this much water flooded the lower levels from *one*

tank, the entire atrium would submerge with two. Every spirescraper citizen would perish, unless Nix could find the explosive and disarm it somehow.

With that in mind, Nix pivoted away from Leon.

He'd sealed his fate. She wasn't about to let him decide hers.

But walking proved difficult. She managed to strap the pistol to her hip, the sarrant's sheath on her back, and the camera on her unbloodied thigh. And yet, limping up the staircase was an endeavor. She kept her sarrant out, one final protection against any infected who hadn't been distracted surging to the explosion site.

Sites.

Fuck.

She had to get to floor fourteen, to that *Crew Only* door. If she could reach that, get inside, she might stop the other ballast tanks from exploding. She could prevent the lower levels from flooding further.

It created a singular goal, one she recalled as she heaved herself up step after step. The staircase was almost black, and she nearly tripped twice over shredded corpses. The scent of their death would have made her stomach churn, except she was too numb for that now.

Three more decks.

Her breaths were rattling wheezes. Blood had soaked her leg. Every time she paused to collect herself, her vision grayed, and stars flickered behind eyelids that had somehow slid closed.

"S-Stay together, Marr." She pinched her arm, which didn't help much. Now her arm *and* everything else hurt. The thought almost made her laugh, which almost made her cry, but she didn't have the energy for either.

One more deck. Floor fourteen was in reach.

Her hand slipped on the staircase, and she crashed to an unforgiving step. It dug into her shoulder, and she could barely muffle her groan.

It was a good thing the lights were out. Nix didn't want to see how much blood she'd lost, how much crimson water had dripped from her saturated clothes. She wasn't shuddering now. Her vicious tremors had slowed into icy acceptance.

The ship was doomed. Was Lumos the Crypt Keeper this entire time? And Aeris—who the hell was Aeris?

Nix's mind swirled into a sickening cacophony of paralyzed thoughts. She couldn't sort through them, couldn't follow any thread to a satisfying conclusion. Everything was spiraling out of control.

Stop the explosives.

Nix staggered back to her feet, and the world tipped sideways. She barely grabbed the wooden banister in time, but her sarrant clattered down a few steps. For a long moment, she just stared at it, crushing defeat settling into her bones.

She wouldn't make it to the medical bay, to Hallie and Kessandra, even if she *could* disarm the bomb.

Not like this.

But she had to try for the ballast tanks, at least. She couldn't live with herself if she didn't attempt to stop another catastrophe, even if it swept her into the icy, waterlogged graveyard below. Kessandra would be furious, but Nix couldn't care.

She fumbled for her sarrant and finally sheathed it. Kessandra's pistol was a safer bet with her physical state, anyway.

The fourteenth deck was just a few steps away. Blind, feeling feverish, Nix staggered up them. The *Crew Only* door was sealed like the one to the bridge, but this time, the secret button unlocked it. A heavy *click*, and she could spin the handle.

Apparently, the engineers had cared more about bridge security than these very vital internal systems.

Nix emerged on a gangplank about three-quarters of the way up the ballast tanks. Here, red emergency lights cast the entire place—a room four times as big as the promenade—in an unnerving glow. There were three tanks, each the size of a building in the Marr casten. As she suspected, the one furthest from her, an entire ship away, had been punctured. Water drained violently from the hole, and the floor below it had clearly been compromised.

Dread slipped into Nix's chest. She'd been wrong. The explosives weren't on the fourteenth floor after all. They weren't even on the ninth, the ground level of these tanks.

They were mounted on the *eighth*.

Exactly where Leon had sprinted.

"No." Nix breathed the word, and her energy vanished. She crashed to her knees on the gangplank, tears leaking down her face. It was too much. She couldn't stop an explosion, not from here — and getting back to the atrium felt like an insurmountable task.

Defeat slid through her bones, and for a perilous moment, her vision faded. She pinched herself again, viciously, and hauled herself back to her feet. She couldn't afford this. The passengers on this ship *couldn't afford this*.

Nix had powered through worse.

The eighth deck wasn't that far away, and it was always easier to go down than up.

Nix made it into the stairwell, except now her mind seemed to overshoot her body, careening seven steps ahead of where she physically was. Only immense concentration dragged it back, and then she'd take another step and it'd start all over again. The roaring had restarted again, but this time it wasn't rushing water. Her vision narrowed, but in the darkness, she didn't notice.

She made it to deck eleven.

It was pretty good, all things considered.

Nix collapsed as her boot touched the final step, and she didn't remember hitting the floor.

" — MARR! *SERGEANT*," someone was shouting.

Nix tried to wrench her eyes open, she really did. She could feel someone grabbing her shoulders, physically hauling her up unforgiving steps. Steps to where, though...? Everything was fuzzy. Was she still on the *Luminosity*? Why wasn't she in her stateroom?

Where was Kessandra?

The final thought sent a rush of adrenaline through her veins. Kessandra needed her help. And—and not just Kess. *Everyone*. Nix had to do something. She'd been doing something... the explosives. Leon. Lumos.

With a moan, Nix pried open her eyes. The staircase was still dark, but now rushing water filled the tiny space. Someone had their arms under hers and was hauling her up the staircase. Her feet were freezing, her legs icy, and it took several seconds to realize her lower half was drenched.

Kessandra's empty pistol was soaked. Her camera— Lumos, her camera would be destroyed.

"Sergeant, *please*," the person begged.

Nix's head felt too heavy. She managed to tilt it and look up, see the desperate angles of an ensign's face. Someone familiar... not Leon, but...

"Jakart?" she croaked. Her voice was rough, her throat like sandpaper. She felt hot, too hot, burning all over, and every muscle ached. But she had to get it together, because it was becoming increasingly obvious that Jakart couldn't pull her up faster than the water rising over her legs.

They were about to be submerged, if she didn't help.

"Thank *Lumos* below." In one fierce motion, Jakart hauled her to a clear step, propped her on her feet. She swayed, nearly tipped despite her best efforts, but he steadied her with a firm hold. "I thought you were dead, but I had to check—Leon really liked you."

Leon.

Traitor.

"There was an explosion. Well, three. It looked like you'd seen the first one, but the other two happened right as I found you." Jakart glanced, panicked, behind her, at the rapidly rising water level, and began towing her again. "Come on. We gotta climb."

Nix tried to stumble after him, but the moment she put pressure on her left leg, it exploded in pain. She cried out, buckling under her own weight.

Jakart caught her yet again. "Shit. *Shit.* I was hoping that was an old wound."

"It's not." Nix groaned. The pain woke her up, at least. She managed to take a halting step, then another, and with Jakart's never-ending support, they continued climbing.

She would be dead without him.

"T-Thanks," she breathed as they crested another story.

"This might be faster if I carried you." Jakart huffed, his face dripping with sweat despite the icy temperatures of the stairwell. Nix could sympathize. She felt feverish, either from the wound or hypothermia or both.

Hallie was going to kill her... unless Kessandra did it first.

It took too long to realize Jakart was waiting for a reply — and descending into anxiety when she didn't offer one. "I — can m-manage." But the water was lapping at her ankles again, and she wasn't sure that was true.

"Leon said you were stubborn," Jakart muttered, and bent to offer his back. He wasn't much taller than Leon, but his shoulders were broad, his grip under her legs strong as he scooped her up. She wrapped her arms around his neck. Dizziness swept over her, and the world tilted dangerously.

She could not, in fact, manage.

It was almost laughable to think she could.

Bad timing. All around bad timing. As Jakart positioned her and began hustling up the stairs, Nix wondered if she would faint again.

One niggling thought kept her present. "Are you a Triolan t-too?"

"What?" Jakart puffed for air, spinning around the stairwell for another flight. He was clearly accustomed to climbing stairs. To be fair, most shortscraper citizens were. "Hell no. Who's a Triolan here?" Bitterness crept into his tone. "I should have known they were behind this. From the minute we boarded this ship, everything went wrong."

Nix couldn't bear to admit the truth out loud.

Her mind was so frayed that she couldn't even remember what the truth was. She needed Hallie's help. Kessandra's guidance. Leon used to be her steady shoulder, but he was gone, and Jakart didn't even seem to know why.

Nix didn't realize she'd faded until several minutes later, but Jakart had stopped. They were on deck sixteen, and the soldier was huffing, gasping for breath. Slowly, he eased her to the floor, then mopped his short hair with his shirt. "Fuck. Okay. I think we outran it. Where the hell did all that water come from?"

He was right. At some point, the crush of water had stopped. The lower decks were submerged, but nothing was climbing at the rate it had been. Against the movement of the ship, the sloshing water created a push-pull rhythm that almost lulled Nix into the darkness again. She leaned heavily against the wall, trying to ignore the way her stomach flipped.

"Ballast tanks," she mumbled. It was harder to form words. Nix clawed through the cobwebs of her mind to find what was important. "Nineteenth floor—m-medical ward. Doctor Jes..." her words faded, her mind slipping with it.

Leon shook her shoulders, hard. "Sergeant. You have to stay awake."

Wait. Not Leon. Leon was gone. This was—who was this again?

Nix wanted to sleep for a year. Her face felt so, so hot, her body teetering on the edge of falling, threatening to never resurface. Distantly, she fumbled in her pocket, found the brass key. "Hallie—"

The ensign could have been anyone in the sixty-first. In the darkness, they almost looked like Quian. The thought that he might be there, hovering over her, fretting like he used to, had tears springing to her face.

Maybe she'd see Quian again, after all.

She pressed the key into the man's fingers, and blackness swallowed her.

Nix caught snippets of everything after.

A snarl bouncing off the walls, a muttered curse, the sound of a key sliding into a heavy lock.

The feeling of a soft bed under her shoulders.

The all-consuming fire that seemed to be ravaging her body.

"—a swim in ice-cold water, sure—" a sarcastic voice echoed, but Nix couldn't pinpoint its location in the inky black.

Eyes pressed against her skull, everywhere and nowhere, leering, looming. Crimson pinpricks that made Nix want to scream, to flee, but there was nowhere to go.

She was falling, somehow.

Someone was shouting. Words weren't forming, but the urgent tone couldn't be mistaken. Nix tried to summon herself, to help—she was a soldier, damn it, someone was in trouble, she had to get up—but her body was lead.

A light brightened everything, and warmth washed

over her. A quiet voice, familiar and sad, whispered in her ear, *"Oh, Nix. Please. Not like this."*

"Quian," she tried to gasp, choking on the name.

She hadn't heard his voice in so long. She missed him so much it ached, a literal weight on her chest that made it hard to breathe.

No, not hard. Impossible. That warmth never left, but she was slowly suffocating, gasping for air that never came. It was painful, agonizing. After Quian died, old soldiers in the Marr casten told her drowning was peaceful. Calming. Like going home.

"It's not," Quian's voice was thick with misery. *"Please. Wake up."*

A sharp pain smashed into her chest.

Poison slipped into her veins.

Quian vanished in one swift motion.

And somewhere below her, a malicious voice intoned: *Welcome, little speck.*

Nix jerked away this time, thrashing in the darkness. Something clattered, someone else shouted, and then something metal braced over her nose and mouth. Nix imagined a pair of crimson eyes looming over her body, imagined the pinpricks of fingers sinking against her flesh, digging into her mouth and nose, carving out her throat so she couldn't scream.

A jagged smile, teeth as wretched as a shark's, formed words she couldn't understand. But the intent was clear.

More commands above her, calmer, like she was breathing and well again, not paralyzed by a fever dream.

She heard her name—even if she couldn't remember it now. Muscle memory had her stiffening, stilling.

The air tasted sweet.

The blackness faded into something worse: utter emptiness.

But she wasn't alone there.

27

She came to with a gasp.

"Easy. Easy." Someone put a firm hand on her shoulder, steadying her, careful to avoid the spot where the Elite had stabbed her, where ichoron stitches had wiped any trace of the wound clean. Lumos, that felt like a lifetime ago.

Nix's vision lost its blurry tint, slowly focusing. Incandescent lighting, dim, limited to a few working bulbs. A bright blue glow from the neighboring windows. Two figures standing over her: Jakart and Hallie.

"Kessandra?" Nix's words were hoarse.

Like she'd been screaming.

Was that in her dreams, or had that actually happened? She grasped at the time she was unconscious, but it had washed from her mind like sand through a sieve. All that remained was a looming sense of dread, something she couldn't seem to shake.

Focus on the here and now.

Hallie pressed a hand to Nix's forehead, her cheek, and breathed a sigh. "Kessandra is fine. The surgery went well; she should be waking up soon." Whatever she was checking for, Hallie seemed to find it satisfactory, because in the next breath she smacked Nix's arm. "But when she finds out what *you* did, she may kill you all over again. Blood loss, hypothermia, shock. You two are going to drive me into a watery grave."

"I—" Nix didn't know what to say. She felt... shockingly good, considering all that. It was suspicious as hell. "How am I *alive*?"

Jakart cleared his throat. "I'll—ah, I'll go check on the subarch." And he wheeled toward the back room.

Nix watched him go, rubbing a sore spot on her chest. In fact, there was a bandage there, right over her heart. She lifted her fingers to assess it, and the dread suddenly felt like a toxin in her system. "I'm not okay, am I?"

"Your heart stopped." Hallie sounded exhausted. She settled into a chair beside Nix's bed, and when she pulled off her glasses to clean them, dark bags were smudged under her eyes. "There are adrenal supplements I can inject, but between the gunshot wound and the fever, I was worried it wouldn't work. I had to make a decision."

Nix froze. "Ichoron."

She swore she heard laughter, deep and rumbling. A pair of crimson eyes seemed to hover over Hallie's shoulder, but when Nix blinked, they were gone.

She shouldn't be able to see them at all. They weren't in the mines. She wasn't looking through an ichoron camera lens. But poison was already pumping from her heart to every recess of her body, and there was absolutely no way to stop it. No convenient surgery to isolate the problem.

"Deep breaths," Hallie said firmly, and Nix realized she'd started trembling. She gasped, trying to slow her spinning mind.

"Hallie, I—" *Get it out*, she wanted to say. *Please*, she wanted to beg. But they both knew there was nothing else to do. Nix suddenly and acutely understood Kessandra's fear, why she was so terrified she might hurt someone.

Nix could hurt more than a few people. And if she did, no one in Valkesh would know the truth.

"What do I do?" she whispered instead.

She could leave. Find a quiet corner of the ship and wait to lose her mind. She could shoot herself, but—she just came back from the brink. She didn't want to join Quian like that. Maybe there was a cure, something other than removing implants to stop dethalos.

Hallie leaned over her knees, took Nix's hand, and squeezed it hard. "Listen to me, Sergeant. We are not safer without you. In fact, right now, you and that random ensign are the only people I trust."

Humor tilted the doctor's tone, and Nix swallowed a laugh. "His name is Jakart."

"Thanks for that—he told me, but I was a bit

preoccupied with you. Would have been awkward to ask again." Hallie smirked, but her expression quickly sobered. "Dare I ask what happened to Leon?"

Nix wasn't ready. Her eyes dropped to her bandaged thigh. "Gone."

It was as close to the truth as she could get.

Hallie tugged off her glasses, wiping them clean with her shirt. "Shit. Okay. We're approaching Fall. Captain Navaan is still barricaded in the bridge, and apparently there are explosives on this ship. If one *does* manage to puncture the hull, we all die." The doctor snapped her fingers. "Poof. Crushed into fleshy paste."

Nix grimaced, pushing into a sitting position. "Didn't need that visual, doc."

"I need you to understand what we're up against, Nix. We can't stay on the *Luminosity*—which means we have to reach Fall. But if that city is half as bad off as we are, our fight isn't over yet."

The numb fear was gone, replaced with a weary acceptance. Nix ran a hand through her hair—it was still damp from her dive. With the ichoron coursing through her veins, she actually felt strong. Better than she had in a long time.

For now, anyway.

One thing at a time. That was her mantra, right? One more step, and eventually they'd be okay.

"I'm ready," Nix said, and meant it.

"Good." Hallie glanced at the door. "Because the

surviving infected have migrated upstairs—and unlike you, Kessandra didn't get a shot of heal juice straight to the chest. She's not going to be in any condition to fight."

"Heal juice," Nix repeated, deadpan.

Hallie shrugged. "It's a medical term. You wouldn't understand."

Nix snorted. "No, I don't think I would." She pushed to her feet, realizing her thigh was bandaged tightly over her gunshot wound. Not around her skin. *Over* the damp clothes. "Wow. This is a professional job for someone so well-versed in medical terms."

"Turns out, heal juice to the heart fixes all—even a bullet wound. I'd have cut your pant leg off, but your boots were tough to remove and we were short on time. And as funny as it would be to see you running around in shorts, I thought you might need something warmer."

Nix's cheeks warmed. "Good call." The wound twinged when she applied weight, but that was about it. In fact, every ache she'd accumulated over the last three days was gone now.

Nix didn't want to think about the consequences of that.

One step at a time.

"Ah, folks," Jakart called from the back room. "The subarch is waking up, I think."

Despite everything, Nix's heart thudded in anticipation. As ridiculous as it was, she'd *missed* Kessandra during all of this. But first things first. She glanced sharply at Hallie. "Don't tell her about the shot. Not yet."

"Any particular reason you're keeping secrets?" Hallie asked, quirking one eyebrow.

"She's going to be upset, and I don't think she needs that right now." If Nix knew Kessandra, "upset" didn't begin to describe her reaction—not that Kessandra would have any legs to stand on in *that* argument.

Nix just… didn't want an argument at all. Not right now, not after four years of tense silence followed by days of hashing out everything wrong with their relationship. Not when they'd *just* found a middle ground, rediscovered what they once had.

For a few hours, maybe a few more days, Nix wanted to enjoy it.

Keeping secrets may be selfish, but then again… Nix had learned from the best.

"Please, Hallie," Nix said, quietly.

Hallie appraised her, even as Jakart began speaking softly in the other room. Kessandra must be awake—but this was important. "You may not be able to hide it for long. If something happens to you, Kessandra will be the best one to identify the signs."

Nix clenched her eyes shut for a moment, settling her mind. "I'll tell her soon. But not until she's back on her feet. Okay?"

Out the window, the leviathan's bones—no, not a leviathan… *Lumos*… the corpse of their own fucking god —were so prevalent that it looked like a mountain range.

Huge bioluminescent sea creatures slid around the carcass: squid and sharks and deep-sea whales and every kind of fish one could imagine.

Nix remembered a voice, unbidden: *Welcome, little speck.*

Fear slid into her throat, and she forced a smile. "I promise. I just need the right time."

"Fine," Hallie replied. "I suppose it's all dependent on whether or not we survive the next few hours, anyway." And with a frustrated huff, she strolled into the back room.

Nix stood alone in the main medical ward, pressing a hand to her chest. Feeling the bandage over her heart. If she concentrated, she swore she could feel the ichoron pulsing in her veins. A problem for another time.

Hopefully a much later time.

She followed Hallie's footsteps. The doctor bustled around the bed checking gauges and equipment, and Jakart had taken position near the window. To avoid getting in Hallie's way, Nix leaned against the doorframe, crossing her arms.

"Welcome back, Nines," she drawled, feeling like her old self for a minute.

On the bed, Kessandra was awake enough for a wry smile. Bandages wrapped around her head, obscuring one eye. Despite the surgery, she seemed a lot better off than the last time Nix had seen her... minus the after-effects of the sedatives, of course.

Granted, that wasn't a high bar, but Nix was pleased she met it.

"I hardly think that pet name is fitting right now, my dear." She exhaled the last two words, letting her eye close for a moment.

"Well, your outfit is a little wrinkled, but..." Nix smirked. "You'd be surprised."

Hallie rolled her eyes. "Flirting aside, I need you to stay awake, Kessandra. We'll be moving soon, unfortunately."

It took a moment for Kessandra to reply. "I'm ready anytime. The migraine is... quite potent... but I can stand."

She didn't look like she could stand. Nix pushed off the doorway as Kess tried anyway, struggling to sit upright. Nix watched for a minute, but the attempt went from "well, that's just sad," to "okay, now she might hurt herself" pretty fast.

"Maybe you *don't* leap out of bed two minutes after waking up." Nix pressed Kessandra's shoulder to keep her on the bed. Her fingers lingered, tracing Kessandra's arm before lifting away. "Hallie, this is still the safest place for you two. I'll get to the bridge and speak with Captain Navaan about the damage."

Hopefully no other explosions had caused more surprises.

"The captain—" Kessandra cut off with a groan, pressing a hand to her forehead. "Lumos. Is this head pain normal?"

Nix stiffened, panic slicing through her. Because the surgery was supposed to fix things, not cause the same symptoms. Unbidden, memories of them lying in bed, of Kessandra lunging toward her face, came back in a rush. Her hand clenched into a fist at her side, and she glanced sharply at Hallie.

But the doctor looked wholly unconcerned. "Dethalos doesn't have a monopoly on headaches, Sergeant. You can relax." She lifted the bandages. Kessandra's eye was closed, but the socket was swollen and vivid red when Hallie opened it to check. "Everything looks fine. But you have to remember, your brain has gone from seeing like an eagle to seeing... well, like someone half-blind." She repositioned the bandages to keep Kess's eye closed. "It'll be an adjustment."

"Lovely." Kessandra said through gritted teeth.

Nix couldn't help it. "Wow. Guess I'll be the superior marksman after this."

She was rewarded with a withering glare from Kessandra—which wasn't any less potent with one eye. "Dear, your bedside manner is magnificent as always."

"You weren't complaining last night."

Hallie groaned. "Lumos below. Sergeant, you've said hello. Do everyone a favor and wait in the main room. I'm not sure I can stomach much more of this, and poor Jakart is blushing."

Jakart was indeed flushed with embarrassment, but he waved it off. "It's fine. Leon told me—"

"I know you," Kessandra said. She'd clearly just

noticed Jakart in the corner of the room—which was odd, considering how she normally assessed everything in just a few seconds. How much of that was Kessandra's ability to pay attention, and how much had been the ichoron eyeball?

Nix supposed they'd find out.

"You're the soldier who helped us to deck one after I was shot." Kessandra frowned, pushing upright. This time, she managed it, so clearly the sedative was wearing off. She grimaced, one hand pressing against her forehead. "Where's Leon? He was here, wasn't he?"

Hallie glanced away. Jakart, meanwhile, straightened in interest. Based on his limited information, it wasn't a surprise he didn't know what Leon had done.

Nix swallowed past a sudden lump in her throat. "Leon... he caused the explosion. He flooded the lower levels. He's Triolan."

"He—" Jakart stared, eyes widening. "He can't be Triolan. He's in my dive team. *Was* in my dive team." His voice dropped a pitch in mourning.

But Kessandra didn't even look surprised. "That would explain it."

Ah, how quickly Nix rediscovered her old anger when faced with *this* Kessandra—the one who kept secrets, the one who lied to stay ahead. "What the fuck do you mean, *that would explain it*? Did you know about this?"

"Know he was Triolan? Absolutely not." Kessandra drew a breath, still unsteady. "There are several Triolans in Valkeshia, but they would never board this ship. They're far too scared of the Ever-Storm for that."

Nix felt like Kessandra was speaking another language. "You know *several* Triolans? Our enemies, the ones killing our squadrons to try and invade our city?" But even as Nix said it, she remembered the commander's insight, back in Valkeshia. That Kessandra was attempting to establish trade routes instead of war plans.

Now, Kessandra leveled an unimpressed stare her way. "Sergeant, it is impossible for an entire country to embody 'the enemy.' The people in Valkeshia are ones I've smuggled in; they're helping negotiate for future peace."

Considering Nix had said almost the *exact* same thing to Leon, she didn't even have an argument. She clenched her jaw instead, silent and angry.

"I'm not lying to you, Nix," Kessandra said quietly. "It would take us days to summarize all the things I've set in motion over my lifetime. I truly didn't think a Triolan would show up on this ship—but I was skeptical of Leon after failing to locate his family." Hallie unwound a sensor from her forearm, and Kessandra rubbed the area absently.

"You couldn't find his family?" That had been one of her stipulations, so long ago, and Nix had just assumed Kessandra had handled it. The fact that she hadn't—and then didn't mention it—set off a spark of anger in Nix's chest. "You promised you would."

Kessandra held her gaze. "And trust me, I wanted to uphold our deal, but... his sister doesn't exist." Now her tone softened. "I assumed he wanted to keep the stipend for himself. That kind of fraud does occur, unfortunately."

So, she was trying to preserve Nix's image of Leon. Grudgingly, Nix admitted to herself it was admirable.

She crossed her arms. "No more lies, Kessandra. I'm done with it."

In the corner, Hallie snorted.

Nix's cheeks warmed.

But without her ichoron eye, Kessandra didn't notice Nix's embarrassment. She just rubbed her forehead again and swung her legs off the bed. "Noted, dear. Now, what about the lower levels being flooded? What explosions? I'm afraid I was quite unconscious for most of this."

Nix opened her mouth to respond, but something slammed against the door of the medical ward—and a chorus of snarls carried through the air. More furious slams. Then what sounded like fingernails clawing the wood.

Hallie reached into a nearby drawer and tugged out a surgical knife. It wouldn't help her long, but it was better than nothing. "I told you the infected had retreated here. Kessandra, *no* strenuous activity."

"This is hardly the time," Kess replied curtly. Ironic, considering she still wasn't standing. "Where's my pistol?"

"For Lumos's sake," Nix snapped, striding to the door. "Jakart, with me. You two, stay here." And once Jakart scurried out, she slammed the door to lock Kessandra and Hallie inside.

Against the hallway door behind her, more banging.

Furious howls.

Nix scooped up her ichoron-edged sarrant, glancing at Jakart. "Grab your sarrant. We protect them at all costs."

"Y-Yes, Sergeant."

Together, the soldiers braced for an onslaught.

28

JAKART HAD MORE KILLS THAN ANY ENSIGN IN THE sixty-first, Leon had told her on that first night. Well, it showed.

The door crashed open, and a flood of infected swarmed in. They'd grouped up—passengers from the lower levels, sodden stewards, even a crewmember with a stiff mockup of Navaan's uniform. Nix counted eleven and expected Jakart to balk or flee, but the soldier surged forward alongside her to meet the enemy.

And what's more, he moved with powerful grace, putting strength behind his blows that compensated for the lack of an ichoron blade. Nix tackled the first one, stabbing the infected deep in the chest, but a second slipped around her toward the back door—but before he made it two steps, Jakart dug his sarrant deep into his back.

The infected crashed to the ground, and angry screeching renewed from the doorway. Four more streamed into the space, eager for something to maim. It was a mild relief that, despite arriving together, the group seemed incredibly uncoordinated.

Still, a few circled them, forcing Jakart back-to-back with Nix. Nix was beginning to wish she hadn't waterlogged Kessandra's pistol. A quick glance at the ensign proved he was gripping his sarrant a little too tightly, his posture rigid.

He'd done a good job keeping his head, but clearly this was pushing him into nervous territory—which could be deadly. To distract him, Nix started a conversation.

"What squadron were you in, again?" she asked, eyeing the group, slowly backing Jakart between two of the beds so they couldn't be flanked. One of the infected leapt at her, and she lashed out with equal fervor. Her ichoron blade sliced through the woman's neck, and the head *thunked* dully to the bloodied tile floor.

Jakart averted his eyes. "The twenty-seventh. They— ah, they'd fast-tracked me to the Elites. All I had to do was a tour in the mines, and I'd have been set." Now he laughed, nervousness lacing his tone. "My twin brother and I enlisted together. He was so pissed I beat him here."

"Probably good you avoided the Elites." Nix sliced at another infected. They'd spread around the room by this point, crawling over the medical beds and furniture to reach them. Nix cut a hand off one, but another managed to slash her face. The contact burned; blood dripped down her cheek.

Before she could yelp, Jakart wrenched the attacker off her and tossed them to the ground. He followed it up with a smooth stab to the heart, back into a defensive stance before Nix had a chance to breathe.

He kept the conversation going, shakily. "Well, I definitely didn't know this would be my future. If they've lost their minds, why aren't they attacking *each other* instead of us?"

An excellent question... until Leon told her Lumos fed on fear. It was always scarier to be the hunted than the bystander watching bloodshed. Unease slid through her veins. "I'm beginning to suspect this is all by design." The words felt blasphemous—but also, nothing else made sense. Hallie had tried to tell her earlier that dethalos was unpredictable, not like a normal illness.

Now Nix knew why.

She didn't say that. Instead, she redirected. "I'm glad you're here, Jakart. Even if I'd prefer you be anywhere but this ship."

He forced a smile. "Same. Nice to have backup. Even if you were half-dead an hour ago."

Fully dead an hour ago.

Nix wiped her face, staggering out from the pile of bodies for some clean floor space. The enemies were dwindling, but not fast enough—infected swarmed around her, and two had somehow realized Hallie and Kessandra were barricaded in the back room. They slammed against the door, animalistic in their fury to get inside.

"The door," Nix shouted, holding another infected back as broken nails swiped toward her eyes. They all seemed to have one goal: attack the face.

It was annoying as hell.

Jakart followed her gaze and set his jaw, stumbling over their most recent opponent's corpse. Some of the infected he'd sliced were twitching on the floor, but most were still, severed to the point of immobility.

From an outsider's perspective, there isn't much difference between us and the infected, Nix thought grimly. She pivoted toward Jakart, but there were too many opponents—three more swarmed her, and then she was fighting for her life again.

One of the infected yanked off the door handle, and another slammed into it, cracking the wood. Horror flitted over Jakart's expression as he wrestled with another infected. "I can't make it in time! Subarch, prepare yourself—"

Nix glanced over her shoulder in time to see the infected lunge again, shattering the wood around the latch. The door swung violently inward.

A gunshot cracked through the room.

"Found a pistol." Kessandra was almost smug.

An infected sank her teeth into Nix's shoulder. She cried out, thrashing, but the woman was like a street dog. "Oh, fuck *off*," Nix snapped, and slammed the woman into the nearby wall. Dazed, she released her hold, and Nix grabbed her around the torso and slammed her into one of the hospital beds. Her sarrant followed in the next breath, finishing the job.

Nix's shoulder was bleeding, the scrape on her face burning. But Kessandra hadn't listened—of course she hadn't—and now the two most important people in Valkesh were in peril.

Another gunshot echoed. Another infected fell.

Well. Relative peril.

There were only a few left. Nix rallied herself and dove into the back line, and between Jakart, Kessandra, and herself, they made short work of the remaining infected.

It took a few moments to realize the fight was over. Nix and Jakart were left heaving in a pile of bloodied corpses, and Kessandra was leaning heavily against the doorway to the back room. Hallie stood behind her with that pathetic surgical knife, looking immensely relieved she hadn't needed to use it.

"Nothing to it," Kessandra breathed, and slid to the floor.

"Kess!" Nix surged towards her. She couldn't have been injured—based on the bodies around her, no infected had even gotten close. It didn't stop Nix's heart from climbing into her throat as she knelt. "Shit. Hallie told you, no exertion."

Kessandra gently set the pistol on the tile, like she didn't trust herself to hold it any longer. "I'll take it under consideration when you aren't about to be ripped apart."

"I wasn't—" But then Nix caught the amused look on Kess's face and huffed. "Fuck you." She slid her arm around Kessandra's waist, hauling her to her feet. If she hadn't used those ichoron stitches on the gunshot wound, the subarch wouldn't even be standing right now... but even with them, she rested too heavily against Nix.

For all Kessandra's posturing, she wasn't doing well.

Hallie stepped around them, checking the broken door handle with a sigh. "Well. So much for easing the subarch out of surgery. I suppose we're *all* going to pay a visit to the captain, now."

She wasn't wrong. Claw marks raked the wooden door, scratching right over the geometric designs. The rose-gold door handle had been ripped clean off. And even if it hadn't, the door was compromised—cracked in the middle with a gaping hole from the infected's attack. Even if they barricaded themselves inside while Kessandra gathered her wits, Nix didn't trust it.

Staying undetected was their best survival tactic right now... and nothing about this carnage was subtle.

Nix drew a breath, grip tightening on Kessandra's waist. "Okay. Hallie, help Kessandra. Jakart, take the rear. I'll lead the front. From this moment on, I'll be commanding the evacuation; what I say goes. Affirmative?"

"I'm perfectly capable of—" Kessandra said.

"Kess," Nix growled, silencing her with a stern look. "You can barely stand. We need to move cohesively if we're going to survive, and *you're* my priority right now. I'm here for a reason. You have to let me help."

Kessandra was clearly wrestling with it. She'd spent four years alone, trapped in a tower where control of her surroundings meant survival. Commanding people, issuing orders, it was in her blood—but right now, she physically couldn't handle it.

Right now, Nix needed to step up.

Thank Lumos—or whoever—that the ichoron gave her the chance.

"Please, Nines." Nix's grip on her waist tightened, imperceptible to anyone but Kessandra. A subtle reminder that she didn't *have* to be the perfect image at all times.

Kess breathed a sigh. "Fine. Affirmative. The sergeant is in charge."

"And don't you forget it." Nix smirked.

Kessandra rolled her eye, which only seemed to incite her migraine. She inhaled sharply and didn't waste time leaning on Hallie when the doctor stepped up. Nix extricated herself and glanced at the medical bay.

"Anything we need from here for her recovery, Hallie? I have a feeling we won't be back."

Hallie craned over her shoulder, squinting at the supplies. "My medical kit. The leather bag, over there. And take a few of those bottles in the far drawer. I doubt we'll need them, but better safe than sorry."

Nix obeyed swiftly, pausing only briefly when she realized the "bottles" were ichoron medicine. She suppressed a shudder and set them inside, clipping the medical bag shut. "Can you carry this and Kessandra?"

"We'll manage," Hallie said, taking it in her free hand.

Okay.

The door to the upper decks was still locked, and there was only one method for getting inside: Ramona. As much as Nix hated to coax her into a hallway, they needed the switchboard operator's help.

"Hang on. We'll move out soon." Nix crossed to the phone at a secretary desk near the medical ward's entrance and picked it up. For a moment, she was afraid the loss of power meant it wouldn't work, but it connected with a familiar *click*.

"Room number, please?"

The fact that Ramona was still taking calls in that manner was almost hilarious. Of course, she probably didn't have another option. It wasn't like she could say, *don't bother; no one's alive to answer anyway.*

Nix pushed that reality aside. "Ramona. It's me."

"Sergeant," the older woman breathed. "Thank Lumos below. I thought you were dead. No one's called from the lower levels in hours."

"They're flooded. Everyone's gone."

Ramona was silent for a moment, and when she spoke again, her voice was thick with grief. "What's happening on this ship? This isn't just a disease."

"It's a lot of things. Listen, the subarch is safe, but we need to get to your level and speak with Captain Navaan. Is she still there?"

"She hasn't left the bridge, or let anyone else inside. She should be safe."

Ramona didn't know about Navaan's compromised state, but she would have heard that ship-wide announcement—and was dealing with the ramifications of it. Nix suddenly imagined taking calls from panicked passengers, trying to route their concerns to someone who was dead or worse. And then, to go from all that panic to absolute silence...

It would be unnerving to anyone.

"Okay." Nix glanced at their hodgepodge group. "I need a favor, Ramona. This is important. We'll get to the bridge and coordinate with the captain, but I need you to unlock the door in the stairwell. There's a switch on the bottom that will work, but only from your side."

Ramona inhaled shakily. "There are people in the hallway. I don't... think they're well."

Fuck. Nix clenched her eyes shut. Somewhere deeper in the gambling hall, a snarl echoed, and Jakart lunged to flip off the medical ward's lights. Darkness surrounded them, and Nix reached for her sarrant.

They were out of time.

"I'm sorry, Ramona. I need you to be brave and careful as hell. When you reach the stairwell, I'll make sure you're safe." Nix's words were a bare whisper, but drenched in urgency.

A long silence made Nix begin to think this was the limit of Ramona's courage. Considering how some of the ensigns had acted during this, the older woman had already risen above and beyond her duty. But if she stopped now, they'd be left in an unbarricaded room with no way to exit the ship.

"I'll get there," Ramona said. She paused, sounding regretful. "Please tell the subarch to alert my family if... something happens."

Nix didn't want to think about that. "Nothing will happen. Keep your pistol, and be fast and quiet. We're right downstairs."

"All right." The line went quiet.

Somewhat closer, more snarls filled the air. Another group, meandering in their direction.

Nix left the phone, her heart thrumming with cold determination. "Follow me."

Kessandra kept a hold of the pistol she'd found, but Nix subtly holstered the ichoron one when she passed it. It may not work, but that pistol was as important to Kessandra as Nix's sarrant was to her. Nix wouldn't leave it behind, even waterlogged.

Knowing Kessandra, she'd be able to dry and repair it later anyway.

The dark hallway was empty—though crashing sounds echoed in the gambling hall. More infected were milling through this area. Nix kept to the front and Jakart brought up the rear, as planned. Nix waved for them to hold off, then stepped into the stairwell, scoping the tight space for danger.

Water sloshed several floors below them, but it seemed to be draining further down after the initial rush. Most likely, it was filling any remaining air pockets in the lower levels—otherwise it wouldn't have climbed so high, based on where the ballast tanks were located. Nix shuddered in her damp clothes, and was suddenly very grateful Jakart had found her.

That wouldn't have been a dignified way to die.

Nix motioned them into the stairwell. Once they were safely inside, she eased the door to the nineteenth floor closed; one final defense to ensure they weren't flanked from behind. Of course, it was heavy and metal and screeched loudly the second she tried to push it.

"Fuck," Nix muttered, and slammed it shut with a ferocity that startled everyone. She spun the lock closed against the sudden screams of infected. They'd be sprinting toward the door now, but hopefully the carnage in the medical bay would distract them.

They weren't safe, but for a moment, Nix felt a little better.

In Hallie's arms, Kessandra looked exhausted. Jakart braced against the door. Meanwhile, Nix asked, "You doing okay, Nines?"

"I'll be fine." Kessandra's tone was stiff.

Sure. Nix's lips quirked upward, and she took the lead again.

The bridge's door was still locked. Nix tried the switch at the base, but it didn't work. Below, something slammed against the locked staircase door—then multiple somethings—and inhuman snarls were muted only by the metal.

The infected had definitely heard her slamming that door shut.

"We'd better hope Ramona gets this door open sooner than later," Hallie muttered, easing Kessandra to one of the steps.

"We'd better hope they don't attract infected from lower levels," Jakart said, brandishing his sarrant.

Nix flinched. "She'll be here."

She hoped.

Tense moments ticked past.

Nix stayed perched by the door to the crew levels, rigid as more infected threw themselves against the metal door below them. It held, but that was their only relief. The hallway was icy cold and somehow still humid, and in minutes they were all shivering.

Except Nix. She wasn't cold at all.

It was *very* concerning.

To stay present, Nix counted things. Twenty-eight rivets securing the metal door to the upper levels. Sixteen stairs to the landing, and another sixteen to the nineteenth deck and all the infected. One bandage covering Kessandra's empty socket.

That meant she could appreciate Kessandra's organic eye without the ichoron one stealing all attention. Nix allowed herself to look when Kessandra seemed distracted; even in the flashing red emergency lights, Kessandra's eye was a beautiful shade of green.

Hallie had stepped a few stairs down, squinting over Jakart's shoulder at the door one level below. Jakart stood poised with his sarrant, but for a breath, they were safe.

Nix leaned closer to Kessandra. "It's a good look on you. The eyepatch."

"My natural eye was a better look." For the first time, Kessandra sounded remorseful. She shifted the pistol to her dominant hand, ran her free fingers over the bandages. Her headache was clearly still present, because she grimaced and leaned against the wooden banister next. "It seemed like such a good idea."

Nix draped her arm over Kessandra's shoulders, a comforting weight. She wasn't surprised Kess leaned into her side. "So, the brilliant ideas of a sixteen-year-old aren't so brilliant as an adult. Shocking."

"I grossly overestimated my control on the disease." Kessandra frowned.

Disease.

Nix cleared her throat. "Kess—what if it isn't a disease? What if this is something else?"

Kessandra craned her neck to see Nix properly, then winced at the motion. "What do you mean?"

It sounded too ridiculous to say out loud. Nix almost swallowed the words, wrote them off as the ranting of an enemy trying to poison their minds. Except Leon wasn't shy about murdering the majority of passengers on this ship—psychological warfare didn't mean much when explosives were planted to kill them anyway.

Nix drew a short breath. "Have you ever heard of Aeris?"

Kessandra stiffened.

A *click* echoed, somehow cutting through the muted sounds of snarls and thudding from the nineteenth deck. Their conversation would have to wait.

Nix pushed to her feet, brandishing her sarrant, as Ramona pushed open the door.

29

Ramona leaned too heavily on the door as she pushed it open. She almost fell in, but cast a terrified glance over her shoulder as she caught herself. "Sergeant, you're out of time—" her words cut off as another person slammed into the stairwell behind her.

An infected, wearing the same uniform as Welanna had. He'd clearly been shot, blood drenching his shoulder, but it wasn't anything incapacitating. His nails glinted in the red light as he lunged at Ramona.

She screamed.

Nix smoothly stepped in front of her, slicing the man in half. Her ichoron blade met little resistance as the crewmember fell to the floor, utterly still.

Ramona clamped her hand over her mouth, stifling a sob.

"Ramona, you did—" Nix cut herself off, realizing too late that blood coated the front of the older woman's shirt.

The gifted pistol clattered to the floor as she swayed, and Hallie only barely caught her in time.

Ramona's eyelids fluttered. "T-They ambushed me. I couldn't—"

In the hallway, three bodies lay still. The open door to the switchboard room seemed far, too far.

"She's losing too much blood," Hallie said, peeling back her shirt to reveal a gnarled mess of skin. The doctor inhaled sharply. "They ripped her apart."

It was a miracle she'd reached the door at all.

Nix crashed to her knees, taking Ramona's hand, squeezing hard. The woman was trembling in her grasp, her eyes slowly glazing over. No. No, no, no, Nix couldn't lose another soldier. She couldn't lose another friend.

"Ramona, please—this is a doctor. She can help. Stay with us," Nix begged.

Hot tears spilled down her cheeks when Hallie mutely shook her head.

Then a hand clamped hard on Nix's shoulder, guiding her away. Kessandra filled the space, cupping Ramona's cheek, redirecting the woman's gaze. "Ramona, look at me. Eyes up, please."

Her commanding tone got the woman's attention. She lifted her gaze, her rasping breaths slowing. Her eyes were filled with tears, but when she saw Kessandra, recognized who it was, a soft smile tilted her lips. Her pained wheezing was physically hard to hear. "I always k-knew you would save us."

It was too much. Nix couldn't breathe.

Kessandra, meanwhile, remained calm... almost pleasant. "Ramona, your family will be cared for. I will stop this, and everyone will know what you sacrificed for Valkesh's future."

She always had the voice of a politician—but Nix had never seen it applied like this before. And what was more shocking, it seemed to offer Ramona immense comfort, hearing those words from a subarch's lips.

"T-Thank you." The older woman breathed out, tears glistening on her cheeks. "Thank you, s-subar..." she trailed off, and her eyes lost their focus. Her mouth went slack, her chest suddenly still.

Kessandra waited several more seconds, holding her hand, wiping the tears off Ramona's cheeks, before murmuring, "Rest in the depths." The prayer made Nix flinch, caused a sudden flare of anger at the situation—at their so-called god. Kessandra, meanwhile, closed Ramona's eyes and labored to her feet.

Nix pulled her up the rest of the way, her grip too tight.

Ramona wouldn't have even left the safety of her office if Nix hadn't demanded it.

Jakart lingered behind them, and Hallie carefully took hold of Kessandra again. No one spoke. There'd be time for grieving later, but for now, they had a goal in mind.

The bridge was in sight.

Nix strode up to it, tried the handle. Locked. She slammed her fist against the door, channeling her fury and devastation into something that mattered. "Captain

Navaan. It's Sergeant Marr. Open the door." Several seconds passed, and irritation prickled along Nix's skin. "Let us in, you asshole. We're not going away."

Nix carefully didn't look at the stairwell. At the corpse of the woman who'd died to help them. Guilt and regret might swallow her whole if she had to see Ramona one more time.

She raised her fist to beat the door again—and it clicked, then swung open.

Captain Navaan was on the other side, and she did *not* look good.

Her eyes were frenzied, and she peered past Nix into the bloodstained hallway. "Hurry up. In. *In.*" She almost grabbed Nix's shoulder, but Nix flinched away, leaving her grasping air. The captain's eyes cut to the sarrant in Nix's hand, and she raised her own in a gesture of peace.

Ironic.

Nix scowled and ushered her group inside. Navaan slammed the door shut behind them, resolutely spinning the wheel to lock it again.

The bridge reeked. To be fair, the entire ship was scented with sulfur, sour meat, and the coppery tinge of blood—but this was clearly a closed ecosystem. The crewmember Captain Navaan had killed in cold blood lay on the floor, undisturbed, but the other bodies—the ones killed by Welanna—had been piled in the corner. The result was a macabre stack of corpses, something the captain barely seemed to notice.

Jakart made a disgusted noise and covered his mouth.

"Lumos," Hallie whispered. "Captain, what have you done?"

"What was needed," Navaan snapped.

Captain Navaan's apparent state could be described as "paranoid" at best... and "obsessed" at worst. Her clothes were torn, her hair mussed, her eyes wild. She was nearly twitching as she staggered back to the panel of controls.

Kessandra clearly needed to rest, her own movements tense with pain, but she stepped after Navaan instead. "We need to discuss next steps, Captain." Despite the surgery, despite how she clearly felt, Kessandra's tone was strong.

She wouldn't be able to maintain that ruse for long.

Nix watched her carefully, but then her eyes glimpsed what was outside the massive windows. She expected to see the city of Fall rising out of the ocean's floor, some magnificent view only crewmembers and the ultra-rich received.

Instead, the only thing visible through the blood splattered windows was an underwater mountainside. Fall was perched atop an underwater plateau, but Nix hadn't realized the *Luminosity* dove so far beneath the city. Even more unnerving were the bones jutting from the craggy rock, smooth and white against the bioluminescence.

The leviathan.

No, no. *Lumos*.

Nix suppressed a shudder, squinting through the murk. They were still clearly attached to the rail, but it really looked like they'd be slamming into the mountainside any second. "Uh—should we be concerned?"

"The *Luminosity* has been pressurizing slowly over days," Hallie said, crouching beside the corpse in the center of the room. "Assuming no systems were damaged in the explosions, our atmosphere range should match what's inside Fall. Which means we just need to be lifted out of the water now."

"Uh... how?" Jakart asked.

Kessandra huffed. "There's a tunnel in the mountain. Due to the pressurization inside the dome, the water only goes halfway up—like turning a cup upside-down in a bathtub. We'll anchor to a belt that will pull us out of the ocean and into a docking station." Now she crossed her arms. "Hence next steps, Navaan. Your ship is compromised. There aren't many passengers left, but with Fall's military, we can stage a rescue—"

"I'll dock us on the conveyer belt, get us to Fall. But we aren't opening this ship anytime soon," Navaan snarled.

Silence filled the space.

Nix's grip tightened around the long hilt of her sarrant. "Say again, Captain?"

"There is a *disease* on this vessel. If we unleash it into Fall..." Navaan shuddered, violently. "No. I am still captain. I will anchor us because we have no other choice. The *Luminosity* physically can't return to Valkeshia without repairing our ballast tanks." Navaan's tone dared anyone to argue. "But upon docking, we'll defer to

Subarch Striadas. What he says, goes. Until his decree, no one leaves."

Kessandra's gaze sharpened. Even with one eye, she was incredibly intimidating. "If you think Fall hasn't already seen the adverse effects of this disease, you aren't paying attention."

"Of course she isn't." Nix strode to Kessandra, crossing her arms. "She's been trapped up here, guessing at what's going on below. Did you even know when those ballast tanks burst, they flooded the lower levels? Most of your passengers are dead, *Captain*."

"I'm aware of that." Navaan jabbed a finger at an indicator light, flashing red on the control panel. "Ramona called—"

"Ramona is dead too," Nix snapped, furiously. Her heart ached.

Captain Navaan paused, inhaled through her nose. It was clear this news hit her... and even clearer that she didn't have the wherewithal to care anymore. Nix watched her face rearrange into cold determination.

"Were all the bridge's crewmembers affected by dethalos, Navaan?" Suspicion drenched Hallie's voice as she redirected the conversation. The doctor pushed to her feet, leaving the corpse where it lay. "Or did you panic, like you did with that announcement?"

Now Navaan went rigid. "Don't you *dare* imply that I've made a mistake here. I'm the only force holding this ship together in the face of sabotage."

The *Luminosity* was nearing the huge wall of rock.

From this angle, the rails did indeed curve into a dark tunnel, and a heavy mechanism loomed to latch the *Luminosity* into place. They were running out of time to argue, and Nix really didn't want to crash into it. "You said you know how to dock the ship. Now's the time, Navaan."

Like it or not, the people of Fall only had one chance at escaping the city—and it relied on this ship. If anyone in Fall was still alive, they'd need to get this vessel safely docked. Everyone could agree on that, at least.

Navaan squinted at the tunnel, muttered to herself, and snapped at Jakart, "Pull that lever when I say so. Not a moment sooner, understand?"

Jakart glanced at Kessandra for guidance, and she waved a hand to allow it. He took position, and they delved into the tunnel, pitch black except for the occasional swirl of algae. None of the bioluminescent sea creatures swam here—and knowing they were entering the skull of Lumos itself, Nix couldn't blame them.

"Anchoring." Navaan twisted her head. "Now, Ensign!"

Jakart wrenched the lever down. Navaan flicked a few controls, twirled a knob, and the entire ship shuddered. A heavy *clang* echoed above them, then a second. Nix could barely see a conveyor belt of ichoron gears above them, attached to the railway. The ship jerked, then shifted into smooth motion as the belt pulled them forward.

The *Luminosity* started to rise.

And then—another explosion, deafening, but much closer.

Immediately, the lights went out, casting them in absolute darkness. No emergency lights now, no air filtering through the vents, nothing to indicate the ship was functioning anymore. Nix spun, squinting at the ceiling, the door, the shapes of everyone else.

"What just happened?" Hysteria tinged Navaan's voice. "Which one of you fucked with the emergency backup systems? Tell me, *now*."

"Navaan, we're here with you," Kessandra said, her voice calm.

"You're lying. This is a trap. You won't get to open this ship, not until I defer to Subarch Striadas. Not until we call the primarch." The sound of a gun's hammer clicking back. Nix tensed, unconsciously moving in front of Kessandra—but the subarch was already gone. Panic seized her chest.

Too late. A gunshot echoed.

Someone yelped. Hallie? Kessandra? What was happening?

Somewhere nearby, a body hit the floor.

Nix's mind flashed to Ramona, to the way her eyes dulled, to the soft smile on her lips as she died. She thought of Kessandra, collapsing against her in their bed as the sedative took control. She thought of Quian, his eyes milky, his mouth gaping.

In the distance, an otherworldly being chuckled, deep and malicious. Goosebumps prickled along Nix's arms.

And a pair of glowing red eyes illuminated the space, enough to show a woman dead on the floor.

"Kess. *Kess.*" Nix lunged.

A hand caught her arm—*Navaan*—and Nix spun to grab her.

Kessandra grunted in pain, going perfectly still as the ichoron blade pressed against her neck. "It's me. Dear, it's okay."

Nix relaxed, lowered her blade, but there was still a body on the floor. And those eyes above it. The Crypt Keeper, right here, *right now*. Nix could see it, and it could see her, and suddenly she felt like no one and nothing would be safe if she didn't attack.

Viciously, she sliced at the specter with her sarrant, her scream cutting the air.

A hollow laughter echoed, and the eyes vanished instantly.

Nix was left gasping for breath over a corpse, her sarrant trembling in the exact space the Crypt Keeper had occupied. Ichoron clearly didn't defeat ichoron here, since that *thing* still loomed like a horrible presence in the back of her brain.

"Nix—" Kessandra's fingers trailed along her arm. "What—did you see something?" Despite her gentle touch, her tone was sharp, dangerous.

Nix couldn't process everything fast enough. She sank to the ground, sheathing her sarrant, rolling over the body. Not Kessandra—and not Hallie. It was Captain Navaan. Which meant someone shot her with no warning. The wound was in the center of her throat, a place Kessandra wouldn't normally aim for... but it did the job.

"You killed her," Nix whispered. She was getting so fucking sick of people dying in this room.

On this ship.

In general.

Kessandra knelt beside her, swaying, but still managing to stay upright. "Dethalos isn't the only thing that can make a person lose their mind. Hallie, how did the chief engineer die?" She was referring to the body in the center of the room, the ill crewmember Nix couldn't save.

"Gunshot," Hallie replied grimly.

"Then Captain Navaan already proved she's willing to murder. We've anchored and will be in Fall very soon. But until then, we can't take the risk of her doing something dangerous."

It made sense. Nix still stared numbly at the corpse, feeling sick herself. Captain Navaan's face stared slack into nothingness. "I—"

"Nix."

Nix raised her eyes to meet Kessandra's. The blue flashes of algae were enough to see the concern in Kessandra's eye.

Kessandra pocketed her pistol and squeezed Nix's hand. "What did you see?" She spoke the words with weight, like she knew *exactly* what Nix had seen... and didn't want to believe it.

The Crypt Keeper didn't exist. It was all just Lumos,

fucking with their brains. But admitting it would be the same as telling Kessandra about the ichoron injection.

"N-Nothing." Nix cleared her throat. She had to get herself together. With a forced smile, she pulled Kessandra to her feet again. "It was dark. I thought she was attacking."

Kessandra's eye narrowed.

"Uh—we have another problem," Jakart said. "I think that last explosion started a fire."

Sure enough, smoke was curling through the vents now. Nix realized the bridge was brightening incrementally, and not from algae. No, this was the yellow light of incandescent bulbs from outside—which meant electricity. A glance at the windows confirmed her suspicions. The tunnel was illuminated above the waterline; they'd be lifted out of the water soon.

Fall awaited.

"If fire circulates on the ship, it'll eat up the little oxygen we have left," Hallie warned.

But that wouldn't happen very fast. So, what was the purpose of that final explosion? To truly kill everyone on the ship? It seemed redundant at this point. Nix's mind spun as she tried to determine Leon's logic, but it felt like there were gaping holes everywhere.

She needed to find him... and something told her he'd be on the upper levels by now. After all, every essential system was here, aside from the ballast tanks. If his goal was to turn this ship into a graveyard, this was the place to do it.

And they'd left the door wide open for him to follow.

No, *Nix* had left the door open. Fuck. She should have locked it after Ramona, but—well. Too late now.

The ship was nearly destroyed from the inside out. Most of the passengers were dead. Dethalos—or whatever the hell this was—might have been the trigger, but Leon, her own fucking ensign, her subordinate, her *friend*, had become more of a danger.

Time to fix her damned mistakes.

"Everyone, stay here." Nix eased Kessandra into a nearby chair. "I'll handle it."

Kessandra looked exhausted, but alarm filtered onto her face. She struggled to stand again. "You can't fight a fire right now. It's too dangerous."

Nix almost remarked that containing it might be possible from the bridge, and *Navaan* would have known exactly how. But Navaan was dead, and Nix couldn't even blame Kessandra's reasoning for shooting her. Instead, she gestured at the door.

"Everything up here seals. There has to be a way to close off the vents and trap the fire, right?" Nix waited, but no one argued against her. She grimly unsheathed her sarrant and spun the wheel of the door.

"I'll go, too," Jakart said.

"No. You stay with Hallie and Kessandra." Just in case.

"Absolutely not," Kessandra snapped. "You aren't going alone."

Nix rolled her eyes. "For someone who just agreed to follow my commands, you're doing a shit job, Subarch."

"I'm siding with Kessandra here." Hallie put a hand on Kessandra's shoulder, keeping her seated. "We'll barricade ourselves, but I'd rather not see you back on my table, Sergeant. Watch each other's backs."

Jakart crossed his arms. "Agreed."

Nix glowered at all of them. In truth, she wanted them bundled nice and safe—and another soldier would be helpful here if Leon doubled back—or Lumos was still lurking. But one of those was an incorporeal threat, and Nix couldn't voice it without drawing attention to a conversation she *really* didn't want to have right now.

She'd tell Kessandra about the ichoron coursing through her veins. Just… later. When they had a moment to breathe.

"Fine," Nix muttered. "Come on, Jakart."

He swept after her, and they sprinted out the door.

She didn't look at Kessandra again. She wasn't sure she could bear it.

30

THERE WAS A SECOND STAIRCASE, THANKFULLY ON THE opposite side of the corridor from Ramona's body. Nix stepped toward it, Jakart on her heels, and they emerged on the twenty-first floor: a cavernous space that stretched two stories high and housed hundreds of essential systems. Nix couldn't even begin to fathom everything here. A labyrinthine tangle of pipes, vents, and valves stretched across the space, connecting massive machinery. Somewhere deeper in the space, something hissed with steam.

Everything was dark. The only light came from tiny windows on either side, the tunnel's artificial light casting heavy shadows across the space—and a fire, ravenously chewing through what looked like coal from the furnaces. Black smoke billowed to the ceiling. Even from here, Nix could feel its heat.

Only a few machines were still operational. The

beating heart of the *Luminosity* was as deadened as the rest of it now.

Jakart pointed. "There's a control panel in that room—"

Nix elbowed him, pressing a finger to her lips. He cut off instantly, eyes widening, fingers tightening on his sarrant's spear-like hilt.

She doubted they were alone up here.

Together, they moved silently through the space, heading toward a staircase on the far left side. The operator's room was empty but bloodstained. Clearly a battle had already happened here, and there weren't any victors. Were the infected still roaming the space, or had Leon dispatched them all?

She wasn't keen to find out.

From here, she could see the fire spreading. On land, they might be able to fight it, but the only hope of extinguishing a blaze that size now was cutting off its oxygen. Desperation sliding down her spine, Nix studied the panel.

Jakart took position by the door. Long moments ticked by in silence, and then he whispered, "I can't believe Leon is a Triolan. He... well, nothing about him seemed suspicious. He was nice to me."

"He was nice to a lot of people," Nix muttered. Every thought of Leon in this context had her heart aching.

"Yeah." Jakart drew a trembling breath. "He handed me a drink, and introduced me to Riles. I was pretty homesick when we first boarded—it was good to have some company. I guess I didn't look too closely."

Ironic. Leon seemed to prey on those kinds of people; the ones just glad to have a companion, the ones in need of a friend. That almost made it worse. Nix clenched her eyes shut, ignoring the way her heart pounded. "I know."

She'd been staring at the control panel this whole time and realized—too late—that she had no idea which button to press for a lockdown. There was a red lever off to the left that might be an emergency shut-off.

Hmm. If Nix were an engineer, she'd definitely color a lockdown lever like that.

Kessandra would be rolling her eyes... ah, eye... at Nix right now.

Almost to spite Kessandra in spirit, Nix pulled the lever. She expected some kind of system to slam into place, but either this wasn't an important lever after all, or that explosion had damaged more than she cared to know.

Either way, things weren't going well. Nix ran through their options, brow furrowing. "Can we close the vents manually?" Her words were a bare whisper, and she glanced at Jakart.

Just in time to see a looming shape behind him.

"I am sorry about this," Leon said, quiet and grim.

Nix inhaled to shout, surging forward—but it was too late.

He buried a sarrant in Jakart's chest, wrenching it upward until the tip protruded through. The soldier stiffened, glanced down. "Wha—Leo?" In a panic, Jakart tried to wrench away, but the sarrant sliced further up, and his breath hitched all at once.

"Trust me," Leon said. "This is the *better* alternative."

Jakart went limp, eyes rolling into his skull.

His heart had been sliced.

"No," Nix snarled.

It was too late. Leon tugged his blade out with a sickening *schwick*, his expression pinched. "You should have left him in the bridge."

"You—" Nix unsheathed her sarrant in a swift motion, expression twisted in fury. "You *bastard*. He was your friend."

Leon glanced at the body at his feet. "I know. But I already made one mistake letting you live. I really thought you'd bleed out with Kessandra and that doctor, but apparently she worked some magic on you." Now Leon's gaze darkened. "How much ichoron did you take, Nix?"

Nix didn't reply. With a furious shout, she dove forward, her blade flashing in the dim light. It was oppressively hot in this room, but it wasn't sweat that dripped down her cheeks.

Leon met her blow for blow, grunting as she leapt over Jakart's corpse and furiously drove him backward. But Leon had trained with her for years, and was almost as skilled with a sarrant. Every strike was barely averted, the deadly sharp tip of Nix's sarrant glancing off his own blade. His army uniform was sliced in the process, and it drew Nix's attention.

He didn't deserve that uniform. Rage overtook Nix's entire body.

"You killed *everyone*. How could you?"

"Lumos feeds on fear," he snapped back. "I told you that."

Nix slashed at his chest. He hollowed his body and jumped back, but not fast enough to avoid a fresh rent in his shirt, or the thin red line that bubbled from his skin. He hissed, leapt over the banister, landing hard on his feet. Nix vaulted over the banister to follow—and was greeted with the barrel of a pistol, aimed between her eyes.

She froze.

"You're not listening to me." Leon's voice was tinged in anger, but he was clearly making a concentrated attempt to keep his tone level. "Lumos, your precious god, is supposed to be dead. Your people mined its veins for blood—and found ichoron. And through it, Lumos can absorb every negative emotion."

Behind him, the fire was growing in intensity. Sweat had already soaked through the back of Nix's shirt and threatened to drip into her eyes... eyes that were burning from the smoke. It was getting worse by the minute. She fought the urge to cough.

Leon cocked the pistol. "I killed them, yes. But their deaths cut off Lumos's food source. And when I shatter the dome, I can ensure its power never grows beyond this ocean. It will die here, yet again. I'll save everyone in Valkeshia and beyond. The sixty-first will survive. Your dad might, too."

It was the strain in his tone that scared her. The actual regret in his words, even as he committed these heinous acts. Nix wanted to grab his shoulders, shake him until he realized what he'd done. She wanted to kill him. She wanted to save him.

At what point was someone irredeemable?

Nix clenched her eyes shut. "It doesn't justify *this*, Leo."

"I'm not seeking atonement," Leon growled. "I'm putting an end to Lumos's reign well before it ever sees sunlight."

A deep laugh boomed in Nix's head, as painful as nails being driven into her brain.

Nix gasped. Her legs gave out, her sarrant clattered to the staircase as she grasped her head. Leon fired a shot at the sudden movement, but it glanced off the metal banister and pinged into the darkness. He ducked, craning towards the ricochet.

It was a blessed distraction. The pain in Nix's head vanished, gone so fast she almost wondered if she'd imagined it. Disoriented, she snatched her sarrant, careened around the staircase, and slammed her shoulder into him.

They both crashed to the floor. His pistol went flying, skittering under a nearby tankard. Her sarrant dropped to the floor, and she left it. Stabbing him wouldn't be as satisfying.

Instead, she slammed a fist into his face. Then another. A satisfying *crunch* echoed as she broke his nose. "You'll

never get to shatter the dome. I'm going to kill you here—
and then I'm going to take the sixty-first and hunt down
every fucking Triolan I find."

"Including the innocents?" He spat blood, his lips
crimson with it. "I thought you cared about justice."

"Shut the fuck up," Nix hissed, and raised her fist for
another hit.

He twisted her sarrant towards her, and she leapt back
to avoid the flashing ichoron blade. It nicked her arm, and
she gripped the wound, dancing away as Leon swept to
his feet. He tested the weight of her sarrant, gingerly
pressing one hand to his bloodied nose. "Shit, you pack a
punch. Even if you kill me, the explosives are set."

"You couldn't blow the hull underwater. What the hell
makes you think it'll work now?"

Leon laughed, the sound thick with cruel amusement.
"I was never trying to puncture the hull. I needed to reach
Fall, not die in the depths." He gestured above them, then
spat a glob of blood on the floor. "Ichoron glass is too
strong to shatter, but it's not immune to ichoron debris. A
well-placed explosion should cause enough damage to
crack the tunnel's ceiling. The pressure of the depths will
take care of the rest."

He was waiting for the *Luminosity* to reach Fall.
Everyone knew what the docks looked like: a curved
ceiling that bubbled into the proper dome. People were
funneled through their port of arrival, soldiers separated
from passengers, but it was all open to Fall. The buildings
wouldn't be much of a barrier.

If the tunnel's ceiling fractured, water would flood the tunnel first—and then wash into Fall proper.

No one would be able to stop it. There were no escape routes.

Nix's throat felt dry. She was unarmed, her mind buzzing with fear and an oppressive sense of dread. Leon twirled her sarrant, his expression grim. He didn't seem to be enjoying this... maybe she could play to that.

The fire was creeping closer. There wasn't much to burn, but years of coal dust and oil buildup kept the flames spreading amongst the metal machines. Its heat was burning now, and sweat had her feeling slick, her hair drenched against her neck.

"If you set off that charge, you're going to die too."

Leon sighed, glancing at the fire. "Nix, I'm not living through this. Even in Valkeshia, your warnings meant little to me." He clenched his jaw. "But I can't have you finding those charges. This is my life's work, and I intend to see it through."

He advanced, her sarrant a fatal weapon in his grasp.

Nix backed up, scrambling for options.

A gunshot pierced the air.

Leon jerked backwards, a wound on his shoulder blossoming with blood.

Kessandra stepped out of the shadows. She looked awful, her skin ashen, her gait unsteady, but she held the pistol with rigid confidence and fired two more shots.

Both went wide. Leon dropped the sarrant, pressed his hand into the wound, and ducked behind the machinery.

Without a word, he was gone. Nix growled, almost leaping after him—but couldn't bring herself to leave Kessandra in this state.

"You're losing your touch, Nines." She caught Kessandra seconds before the subarch crumpled to the ground. Kess seemed to be running a mild fever, but she didn't have any other wounds. Just overexertion, most likely.

Nix's heart still pounded.

Kessandra pressed a hand to her head. "Next time I'm saving your life, I'll take more time to aim."

Nix took the pistol from her, angling it where Leon had fled—but there was no sign of him. Dread crept over her, and she left Kessandra for a moment to sheath her sarrant. Leon's sarrant lay abandoned, and she would have given it to Kessandra if she trusted the subarch to keep ahold of it.

Unfortunately, Kessandra didn't seem capable of much right now.

"Jakart?" The word was a groan, and Kessandra grimaced as Nix took some of her weight.

"Dead." Nix's throat was thick. She wrote it off on the thickening smoke, but... well. That wasn't why. She craned into the darkness, coughing. "Where's Hallie?"

"The bridge," Kessandra kept her voice low, quiet. "Someone has to finish the docking procedures. The ship is essentially piloting itself now, but there are a few final buttons to be pressed."

"Maybe you shouldn't have killed our captain."

"We found a user manual." Kessandra scowled. "Navaan was too risky to be left alive."

Nix didn't have the energy to argue. The smoke was thickening, billowing into the space. "Your chess game is slipping." She wound her arm around Kessandra's waist, propping her upright, and glanced upward. "The fire's too big to extinguish now. But if I can find the explosives, we can disarm them." Somehow.

Kessandra, meanwhile, was staring at the orange flames on the far end of the room. She squinted at the tankards before them, then the machinery beyond, and her expression shifted into abject horror. "That's hardly our priority, Nix. We need to get Hallie and head to the lower levels—*now*."

"What?" Nix craned her neck to see what scared Kessandra so much.

All she saw was the dark shapes of machinery. Leon was gone.

Kessandra started towing her toward the staircase. She covered her mouth to stave off the acrid smoke, but it barely helped her rasping voice. "The carbon dioxide scrubbers. Those big tanks near the control deck. They're highly flammable."

"Shit." Nix flinched. "Then we *need* to stop the fire."

"Sergeant, save the people you're with, not the ones you're without." Kessandra's voice was sharp, almost scathing. "I will not let you die here—and if you insist on arguing, we'll both perish. Is that what you want?"

Nix wrestled out of her grasp, coughing. "You don't

understand, Kess. If that blows, it'll set off a round of explosives that will irreparably damage the ship's hull, *and* the tunnel above us. If we dock in Fall before that happens, everyone is fucked."

Kessandra's expression was grim. "Then it's already too late. We were docking when I came up here."

Nix hadn't realized it, but the ship wasn't moving.

They'd reached Fall.

"No. There has to be —"

Her words were cut off by a sudden blast. She barely had time to throw Kessandra into the stairwell before a rush of hot air washed over them, followed by the shockwave of a vicious explosions. All of Nix's senses were overwhelmed — and then darkness swept over her.

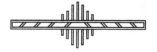

.

.

.

Not yet, little speck.

31

THE AIR WAS COLD AND WET. MIST STUCK TO HER SKIN, like the spray of water crashing against the dock in Valkeshia. The salty air stung her throat, burned her lungs. There was a roaring in her ears.

Nix groaned, prying open her eyes. Beneath her, the ground was solid... and wet. Everything ached. She wanted to sleep for a year, maybe an eternity, but something poked her mind. Half blind from the light, her fingers prodded for Kessandra—and found emptiness.

She blinked hard to clear her vision.

She'd been thrown from the *Luminosity*, clearly. The ship was a hulking behemoth resting against a long, concrete platform. The explosion had shredded the ship's upper levels, straight up to the clamp that secured it to the rail. The windows of the bridge were intact, but everything above it wasn't. The ripped remains of a metal staircase dangled twenty feet off the ground. Hissing air and creaking metal added to the cacophony in Nix's mind.

She rolled onto her hands and knees, coughing, gasping. But even as pain shredded her body—wounds were stitching themselves back together. In just a few seconds, she could breathe easier. In a minute of gasping, she had the strength to stagger to her feet.

Something wanted her alive.

Lumos.

Nix shuddered viciously, wiping blood off her face, scanning the platform for Kessandra. The dock was nearly destroyed, eerily empty of life; even the port authority building, a space normally teeming with soldiers and customs officials, loomed like an empty husk. Around her, huge chunks of debris had crashed onto the platform; Nix was lucky she hadn't been crushed.

Kessandra. Where was she?

"Kess—" Nix called, coughing. Her throat tasted like blood, her skin raw with quickly healing burns. Old scars remained. New ones—ones she earned after straight ichoron was injected into her heart—were gone.

Not good.

Nix staggered to her feet. "Kessandra! Where are you?" That roaring was far too loud. She had to shout over the noise, which meant it wasn't inside her head after all. Dread slid through her body as she squinted at the *Luminosity*... and saw the problem immediately.

A small hole had been punctured in the tunnel's roof.

Leon was right, that bastard. Ichoron metal *was*

enough to break the ichoron glass. Pressurized seawater spewed from the hole in a concentrated jet. The opening, no bigger than her fist, didn't seem to be growing any wider—a testament to the material's strength—but even that tiny puncture would be enough.

Fall was flooding.

Shit.

Maybe Fall's engineers could patch it. But the fact that no one had greeted the ship told Nix everything she needed to know about the state of the city—and its occupants. Help wasn't coming.

She started running, desperate now. "Kessandra! Nines, where are you?" The platform was huge, but massive chunks of the *Luminosity*'s carcass made it a warzone. She wove through the wreckage, flinching from the heat off the glowing chunks of steel, scouring scorch marks and massive grooves in the concrete platform for a glimpse of the crisp uniform Kess had donned like funeral attire last night, for a hint of her long, dark braids. Anything.

She had to be here. Because if she wasn't—

Tears pricked her eyes. "Kessandra!"

And then, she spun around another piece of debris and nearly tripped over a body. Kess. Relief warred with a fresh surge of panic, choking Nix as she crashed to her knees.

The woman was a mess. Patches of her skin had been burnt raw, and blood from a head wound dampened her dark braids. Her eye was still tightly wrapped, but her clothes were ripped, charred from the explosion. She wasn't moving.

She wasn't moving.

Nix scooped Kessandra into her arms, pressing a hand over the woman's mouth, feeling for air.

Agonizing seconds ticked past.

No.

"Stay with me. Come on." Nix pressed a shaking finger to the pulse point on Kess's neck, set another over her heart—but it was useless. She couldn't calm the tremor of her hands enough to feel for a heartbeat.

New method, then. Nix shook her, almost aggressively. "Wake up. *Wake up*, you asshole. You can't die here. Not like this." Now she pressed a fierce kiss to Kessandra's lips, dropped her forehead to Kess's chest.

"*Please*, Nines."

Had she really failed to accomplish the *one* goal she'd boarded this damned ship with? Had she let Kessandra die? Some fucking soldier she was. Some *knight*.

Her queen—

Nix choked on a sob.

Then... Kessandra shifted beneath her.

Hot tears spilled over Nix's cheeks. She pulled back, cupping Kessandra's face, kissing her forehead. Her words came as a tumble, almost a prayer—although to who, Nix didn't know anymore. "*Thank* you. Come on, Kess. You're okay. Open that eye for me."

Kessandra inhaled sharply, then groaned. "L-Lumos below." Her words were shaky, weak. "Nix?"

"I'm here. It's me." Nix swallowed a morose laugh, pulling back to assess Kessandra more clearly now. It was easy to slip back into a sergeant's mindset, taking command when Kessandra couldn't. She eased Kessandra back to the ground, hovering close. "Can you move?"

Kessandra's skin didn't patch itself back together, not like Nix's had, but the subarch could have been worse off. Nothing seemed broken, although pain was evident in every hitched, gasping breath.

Still, she was able to accept Nix's outstretched hand, pull herself into a sitting position with minimal help. It was amazing she hadn't been killed.

Miraculous, even.

A crimson gaze flashed in Nix's peripherals, and an ominous chuckle echoed in her head. *Miraculous*, it repeated, amused. The voice faded before Nix could stiffen, twist around. Her grip tightened around Kessandra protectively.

It didn't make sense. The ichoron eyeball was gone — Lumos shouldn't have any sway over what happened to Kessandra now. Not based on what they'd seen in the *Luminosity*.

Unless its power was growing.

Unless they didn't know everything this titan could do.

One thing at a time. Kessandra was orienting herself, assessing their location. She twisted — swallowing a gasp of pain — to see the city of Fall looming above the squat, concrete port authority office.

Nix had barely noticed the city before, but now her

eyes followed Kessandra's gaze. Fall was huge, as stunning as Valkeshia. Everything was alight, glowing from huge incandescent bulbs below, shining in the bioluminescence high above. Billboards were plastered on the sides of the buildings, which were all sharp edges and right angles compared to the sweeping curves of Valkeshia's architecture. It was a blend of familiar sights — towering spirescrapers, connected walkways, ichoron edging — but it left Nix feeling off-kilter.

"We're in Fall." Kessandra sounded grim.

"We're in Fall," Nix confirmed. "And Leon's explosion punctured the tunnel."

Kessandra craned to see the rushing water jettisoning toward the back of the *Luminosity*. The roaring of the small torrent of water hadn't grown any louder, but Kessandra winced nonetheless. The back half of the *Luminosity* dripped endless rivulets, and Nix imagined the water level in the tunnel was already starting to rise.

It wouldn't take long for the platform they were on to be submerged. A day, maybe two, before it began to leak into Fall proper.

"Well. This is not ideal," Kessandra said.

Understatement of the year. Nix tightened her grip around Kessandra's shoulders. "Sure isn't."

"Doctor Jesko — ?"

Guilt prickled Nix's chest; she hadn't even thought about the doctor in her haste. Now they both glanced at the *Luminosity*, at the smooth windows of the bridge. It was possible Hallie survived, but it was hard to rally even that flickering hope. The bridge looked undisturbed from the front, but that explosion had been extensive.

"I don't know," Nix said, numb.

Kessandra inhaled slowly. "We need to check." With great effort, she started struggling to her feet. She barely made it a few inches before crying out in pain, falling back into Nix's arms.

Shit.

"We're getting you somewhere safe first," Nix said, firmly. It was increasingly obvious that Kessandra was not okay. She needed medicine and hours of uninterrupted sleep—and it was obvious they were on their own in securing it.

"Hallie—"

"I'll find her, Kess. But I'm not losing you in the meantime."

"H-How kind," Kessandra said, but the fact that she didn't argue was telling.

Nix pushed to her feet, pulling Kessandra upright. She had to take most of Kess's weight, had to be careful where she gripped to avoid aggravating burns. Kessandra whimpered. It was rare that her calm, capable mask slipped, and it wrenched Nix's heart.

"Stay with me," Nix murmured. "Almost there."

Kessandra couldn't reply. Her energy was clearly focused on moving now, one step at a time. Silently, they picked through the wreckage, limping toward the port authority building.

Away from the *Luminosity*.

If Nix had her way, after finding Hallie, she would *never* go back on that ship. That was a death sentence, but it hardly mattered now anyway.

There were two separate doors of the port authority building: one for soldiers, funneled into the left, and a slightly more decorated side meant for normal citizens entering Fall proper. Nix chose familiar ground and veered toward the soldiers' half. The door, a looming metal monstrosity, opened under her touch. Inside was a huge processing room, coldly empty.

It was obvious there was a struggle here. Nix saw all the same signs as she had in the *Luminosity*: overturned furniture, smears of blood, pocks in the walls where bullets had buried. No bodies here, but that didn't mean much.

"Something tells me—" Kessandra cut off with a stifled groan, leaning heavier on Nix. "—Fall isn't faring better."

"What was your first clue?" Nix muttered, disgust and fear warring in her soul. She shoved both away; both emotions were a luxury she couldn't afford. "Come on. Up the stairs." There would most likely be private offices higher up, maybe even apartments for the staff. She didn't like the idea of staying in this huge room—not with doors on every wall.

Kessandra made it halfway up the staircase before gripping Nix too tightly, face ashen. "W-Wait. I need a breather."

Which was Kess-speak for: *In three seconds, I'll be unconscious.*

Heart in her throat, Nix eased Kessandra to the ground, crouching beside her as Kessandra shuddered with shallow breaths.

"Apologies," she finally managed to gasp. Her eye clenched shut, and for a moment, it didn't look like it'd reopen. "I'm just… not quite at my peak."

No shit. Nix didn't voice it, although it was a near thing.

They were only a few paces from the top of the staircase, and this building was silent as a tomb. It was a suitable risk, and she wouldn't be far—but it'd be better than getting ambushed when they stepped onto the second floor. Nix pushed to her feet, pressing her sarrant into Kessandra's hands. "Stay here. I'll find us somewhere safe."

Kessandra leaned her head against the concrete wall. Her braids cascaded over her shoulder, devoid of their usual rose-gold accouterments. She looked… bare. Vulnerable. Somehow, she still fit the nickname Nines, even looking like this.

"And you'll fight with—what? Your bare hands?" Even in this state, Kessandra's voice was wry.

"Something like that." Nix still had a knife tucked in her boot, and she plucked it out now, twirling it between deft fingers. "Shout if trouble finds you. I'm serious, Kess."

"Affirmative."

It would have to be enough. Nix jogged up the last flight of stairs and stepped into a long, utilitarian hallway.

The port authority building wasn't known for its glamor — it was just a processing center. The passenger side probably had nicer décor, but everything was designed to temper a new arrival's expectations… right until the moment they stepped into the city's grounds. Even the soldiers' side opened into an impressive garden that framed the ichoron city like a prize.

Nix swept through the nearby doors, hunting for anything empty and defensible. She found it behind the second door, a tiny office with a desk, a couch, and a single window overlooking the city. Wooden shades covered the window, casting the whole room in slatted darkness.

The door was sturdy enough, and once Kessandra was locked in here, Nix would sweep the building proper. She scoped the corners, but they still seemed alone.

That was even stranger. Where *was* everyone?

A vicious chuckle resonated in her head, and Nix ground her teeth.

Never mind.

Kessandra was still where she'd left her, although her physical state was less than ideal. Her head was listing to the side, the sarrant loose in her grip. Nix gently uncurled Kess's fingers from the weapon's hilt, then sheathed the sarrant and carefully scooped the subarch into her arms.

Even that motion jostled Kessandra too much. She moaned, burying her forehead into Nix's shoulder. "F-Fuck."

"Yep. Almost there, Nines." Nix pressed a kiss to her

forehead—it was hot with fever, which shot a fresh spike of worry through Nix's heart—and carried her into the empty office. She eased Kessandra on the couch, propped a simple pillow under her head, and smoothed the hair off her face. Her skin was still tacky with blood in places, but the head wound seemed to have stopped bleeding.

Nix left her there, scouring the drawers and cabinets for something useful. She found a blanket stuffed into the wardrobe closet beneath a military jacket, and tugged both out. The jacket became a blanket—the blanket became strips of cloth. Down the hall was a bathroom, and she used the sink to wet half the improvised bandages, then barricaded the door and got to work.

Kessandra grimaced as Nix began dabbing her face clean of blood. "T-This is hardly the time, Nix. You have to find Hallie." Her voice was weak, and it took concentration to open her eye. In the darkness, the smoky green color seemed almost black.

A doctor would be useful here.

Nix hated that *that* was her first thought—but it was.

"You are my priority." Nix spoke the words fiercely, daring her to protest. "I'm staying until I'm sure you're not going to die—or be ambushed while I'm gone."

A hoarse chuckle. "I'm not going to die." It'd have been more convincing if Kess didn't shift in evident pain. "But it's nice that you care."

"You're *all* I care about, Kess," Nix said quietly.

Their eyes met.

It was too much. Days of intense stress seemed like a

huge weight on Nix's shoulders, and her muscles trembled from the force of it. She wanted nothing more than to curl up beside Kess and sleep, but... well. Now wasn't the time.

She was beginning to wonder if that time would ever come.

Kessandra broke the mood, grimacing. "You have to find Hallie."

Clearly, she wasn't going to drop this—but she was probably right. Nix clenched her eyes shut, drew a steadying breath, and pushed to her feet. "Okay. I'm going to lock the door from the outside; only open it for me. Two knocks, a pause, three knocks, all right? Don't pass out before I get back."

"I'll do my best," Kessandra breathed, her eye already drifting shut.

Nix hated this. All of it. But she spun out the door, checked it was locked, and sprinted through the building to make sure no infected were lingering in the dark corners. The place was still creepily empty—even of corpses. Only the signs of a fight remained.

Everything about Fall was giving her the creeps.

Nix sprinted out of the building, toward the *Luminosity*. The time she was away from Kessandra blurred: dodging metal across the docking platform, finding a handhold on the twisted carcass of the huge submersible, hauling herself up the exterior hull as best she could. The *Luminosity* had fallen against the dock in a way that left the bridge windows relatively close to the ground. It didn't take long to climb level with it.

And there, hunched over the controls, was Hallie.

She wasn't moving. Blood dripped sluggishly from the control stand, pooling at her feet.

"Fuck. Hallie. *Hallie,*" Nix called, slamming her fists into the glass keeping them apart. But the windows of the bridge were intact, reinforced with ichoron, strong enough to withstand the pressures of the depths. There was no way to break it.

Nix swore she saw her chest rise — but when she squinted again, Hallie was still. A trick of the light... or raw hope? More likely, Hallie had been killed in the blast, and this was a fool's errand.

But she couldn't leave without checking.

Nix glanced upwards, but reaching the gnarled stairwell from which she and Kessandra had been forcibly vacated wouldn't be easy. Not that anything had been, lately.

She climbed it anyway, muscles straining with the effort. Soon, the route shifted from a gentle slope below the bridge to a dizzying, near-vertical ascent. The metal of every handhold twisted into dangerous edges that sliced Nix's hands, no matter how carefully she placed them.

Let's see how fast Lumos stitches me back together, she thought darkly.

The answer was, not very, and soon her blood-slicked hands began slipping, fingers numb from contact with metal cooled by the misty spray of an endless jet of pressurized seawater. She had one last handhold before the stairwell, one last point to push off and try to get inside. Arms straining with effort, Nix lunged—and the moment her fingers clasped around it, it splintered and crumbled.

She fell, slamming back onto the ledge beside the bridge. It shook the windows, stole the air from her lungs. For several moments, Nix just lay there, gasping, staring up at the rose-gold glass of Fall's dome.

Fuck.

Fuck.

She pulled herself up, swallowing a sob—of pain, of failure, she wasn't sure—and pressed against the glass of the bridge again.

After all that, Hallie still hadn't moved.

There was no other way inside, and the water deeper in the tunnel was rising, still shooting through that fist-sized hole. Nix slammed her fist against the glass one final time, but a truth settled deep in her bones.

She couldn't save everyone.

"I'm so sorry, Hallie," she whispered.

Slumped over the console, the doctor's corpse was still.

Silent and defeated, Nix climbed down the hull and trudged back to Kessandra.

32

They stayed the night inside the empty port authority building. The whole time, they never saw another soul.

Nix would never forget the hollow look in Kessandra's eyes after she whispered, "Hallie is gone."

"Oh," Kessandra replied, and sunk back onto the couch.

After that, they didn't talk much.

Kessandra woke in the early hours of the morning, groaning in pain. Nix had been sleeping fitfully on the thin carpet beside her, and she stared at the carved wooden base of the couch as Kessandra shifted this way and that, fingers feathering over the bandaged burns along her skin.

They didn't even have any painkillers. Nix had scoured the building earlier that night and found nothing of use—and didn't want to risk delving further into Fall with Kessandra in this state.

Feeling useless, consumed by self-loathing, Nix listened to Kessandra's stifled moans and the occasional hitching breath. She couldn't help, so she feigned sleep until Kess fell silent again.

Everything felt numb. Nix finally drifted off with tears pricking her eyes.

It was much later in the morning when Kessandra finally awoke in earnest. Nix was already up, squinting through the blinds at the city. The lights were apparently on a timer to simulate sunrise and sunset, but they'd been brightening in increments throughout the morning and now were at full blast.

Nix still didn't see any signs of life. It truly felt like they were utterly alone here.

"For a moment, I thought it was a bad dream," Kessandra murmured, staring at the low ceiling. Her eye was bloodshot, hazed with pain, but her voice sounded stronger.

Nix handed her a glass of water from the faucet down the hall. "I'm beginning to think our lives are just a nightmare, now. Feeling okay?"

"No," Kessandra said.

It was so abrupt that Nix snorted. "Sounds about right."

She helped Kessandra sit up, leaning her against the couch cushions, then dropped into the desk chair as the subarch nursed her glass of water. Long, quiet minutes ticked by, and Nix spun around in the chair so she was leaning over the back of it.

Kessandra noticed her staring. "What?"

"I'm waiting for your plan."

The subarch sighed. "My dear, if I had a plan, I'd have enacted it yesterday. Instead, I collapsed here and spent the night writhing in pain."

Nix quirked an eyebrow.

Kessandra pressed her lips together. "Fine. We haven't seen anyone nearby, which implies to me they moved further into the city. But considering they knew our arrival was imminent—and that the *Luminosity* is the only way out of Fall—I'm less inclined to think it was a voluntary migration."

"You think they were chased into the spirescrapers."

"I think we're far beyond rational behavior, and a firm militaristic hand might do more harm than good at this point."

Nix pinched the bridge of her nose. She'd wiped the first layer of grime off her skin last night with a few strips of that cloth blanket, but her fingers still felt gritty. "Okay. So, if the population is still alive, they're hiding—or being forced to stay somewhere else. Everyone on the *Luminosity* is dead, except us. My best friend is a traitor to Valkesh, and our god is trying to kill us. Answer me this."

Kessandra sipped the water, waiting.

"Who the *hell* is Aeris?"

She watched Kess closely, saw the spark of recognition flash across her face. Her eye dropped to the glass in her hands, her brow furrowed.

Nix set her jaw. "You know that name."

"I... don't know as much as I'd like." Kessandra grimaced, shifting position. "When I was young, I found a book in the primarch's suite. My parents were visiting, and I don't think he expected me to go digging through his drawers. The book was a handwritten account of ancient mythos, of two... ah, gods, or titans old enough to warrant the name... who went to war."

"Lumos and Aeris."

"I didn't believe it, even back then. As I aged, I wanted to less and less." Kessandra laughed darkly. "A disease can be countered. Cured. But a titan, asleep under the ocean, waiting to awaken? It sounded too ridiculous to be believed." Kessandra met Nix's gaze again, bags under her eye, tone weary. "How do we fight something like that?"

Nix had no fucking clue.

It was like Kessandra's perfect chess board had been toppled, the pieces scattered into an ichoron abyss. Like the entire game had been replaced with something new — something designed to destroy.

Nix pushed off the chair without thinking, stepped across the small space. When she dropped onto the couch beside Kessandra, the subarch wasted no time leaning carefully against her chest. Nix pulled her closer, minding Kess's wounds, resting her chin on Kess's head.

She needed to focus on what they still *had*, not what they had to do next. Right now, they were both alive. Relatively safe. Even with the rising water level, they could take a moment to breathe.

Not forever, but for now.

Maybe now was enough.

"I'm more interested to know how we'll get out of Fall alive," Nix said.

"I have a plan."

Nix snorted, the exhale jostling both of them. "That was fast."

Kessandra sniffed. "You know I rarely waste time. We find my cousin: Subarch Striadas. He commands Fall in the primarch's absence—he'll know the status of the city. And if he's dead... then we locate the university. They've been prioritizing scoping the ocean floor. I heard they're working on a small submersible that operates independently of a rail."

"An escape?" Hope swelled in Nix's chest. She hadn't thought about an independent submersible. Closer to the surface, the strong ocean currents were relentless—hence the *Luminosity*'s rail—but a smaller craft might be agile enough to navigate safely through.

"It's possible."

Neither of them acknowledged that anything that small wouldn't save many people.

One problem at a time.

"Okay," Nix said. "Whatever you need, Nines, I'll be there."

She didn't expect them to survive, but for now, they were together. Kessandra set her glass on the side table and wound their fingers together, tracing Nix's calloused thumb with her own.

Her voice held a hint of happiness—something that

warmed Nix's chest. Kessandra's voice was soft. "You always are, dear. At this point, I'm counting on it."

They sat in silence, contemplating the abyss.

And a dull headache pounded behind Nix's eyes.

The End... For Now

Nix and Kess will return in book 2
of the Gilded Abyss trilogy.

Acknowledgments

As always, lists paralyze me because I *just know* I'm going to forget someone. But I'll do my best.

To my family, who taught me to lean on reading, and my sister specifically, who opened the doors to writing all those decades ago. Thank you for giving me a lifelong passion.

To my friends—the ones who lift me up and cheer me on, who inspire me to be better every day. You guys are everything to me.

To my girlfriend, for being the best alpha reader and an even better friend. Your edits made this book what it is.

To the incredible professionals who made this book what it is. Carly Hayward, for all that plotting help. Idris Grey, for making sure Kessandra was as accurate and badass as possible. Kim Jakubowski, for scouring this book for sentence-level errors. Mariska Maas, for the gorgeous section dividers. Amphi, for her incredible cover typography, and that absolutely stunning blueprint of the Luminosity. And of course, Eilene Cherie, for absolutely *nailing* the cover illustration.

To my agent, Taryn Fagerness, for her incredible help with my writing career.

To the professors and staff at Emerson College, who coaxed me through this novel as my MFA thesis. It literally wouldn't exist without you and the Pop Fic program.

To the beta readers for their early feedback, and my ARC readers for their reviews—an indie author lives or dies by word of mouth. I can't thank you enough for taking the time.

And finally, to BookTok, for your unending support. I would be literally nowhere without the onslaught of writers, readers, and influencers who have shared my work with the world.

Thank you all!!

About the Author

Rebecca Thorne is an author of all things fantasy, sci-fi, and romantic... especially with badass lesbians. When she's not writing (or avoiding writing), Rebecca can be found traveling the country as a flight attendant, or doing her best impression of a granola-girl hermit with her two dogs.

She currently lives in Arizona, but is scheming to open a bookstore in a small, forested town.

Also by Rebecca Thorne

Adult Cozy Fantasies

(Perfect for anyone emotionally destroyed after this book.
You're guaranteed a happy ending with my cozies!)

Can't Spell Treason Without Tea

A Pirate's Life for Tea

—

Middle Grade

The Secrets of Star Whales

Printed in the USA
CPSIA information can be obtained
at www.ICGtesting.com
LVHW040810130324
774354LV00003B/127